MAJOR VIGOUREUX

MAJOR VIGOUREUX

A. T. QUILLER-COUCH

WILDSIDE PRESS

MAJOR VIGOUREUX

Published in 2007 by Wildside Press.
www.wildsidepress.com

CHAPTER I

IN THE GARRISON GARDEN

"Archelaus," said the Commandant, "where did you get those trousers?" Sergeant Archelaus, who, as he dug in the neglected garden, had been exposing a great quantity of back-view (for he was a long man), straightened himself up, faced about, and, grounding his long-handled spade as it were a musket, stood with palms crossed over the top of it.

"Off the Lord Proprietor," he answered.

The Commandant, seated on a bench under the veronica hedge, a few yards higher up the slope, laid down his book, took off his spectacles, wiped them, and replaced them very deliberately.

"The Lord Proprietor? I do not understand — " His face had reddened a little, as it usually did at mention of the Lord Proprietor.

"Made me a present of 'em," explained Sergeant Archelaus, curtly. "You don't mean to say you haven't noticed 'em till this minute?"

The Commandant put the question aside. "The Lord Proprietor has no right to be offering presents to my men — least of all, presents of clothes."

"If the Government won't send over stores, nor you write for any, I don't see how the man can help himself. 'Tisn't regulation pattern for the R'yal Artillery, I'll grant you: not the sort of things you'd wear on the right of the line. In fact, he told me 'tis an old pair he used to carry when he went deer-stalkin'."

"They are hideous, Archelaus; not to mention that they don't fit you in the least."

"They don't look so bad when I'm sitting down," said Archelaus, after a moment's thought, and with an air of forced cheerfulness.

"If that's all you can say in extenuation!—"

"Well, 'twas kindly meant, any way; for the old ones were a scandal — yes, be sure. What with sea-water and scrambling after gulls' eggs, they was becoming a byword all over the Islands."

The Commandant winced, not for the first time in this conversation.

"Treacher makes his clothes last," he objected.

"Sam Treacher's a married man, and gets his bad luck different."

"But — but couldn't you ask Mrs. Treacher to take your old ones in hand and put in a patch or two? That might carry you on for a few months, and if you grudge the expense, I don't mind sub-scribing a shilling or so."

Sergeant Archelaus shook his head. "What's the use?" he asked. "'Tis but puttin' off the evil day. If Her Majesty won't send us clothes, we must fall back on Providence. Besides which, I've taken the edge off these things, and don't want to begin over again. Last Wednesday I wore 'em over to the Off Islands, to practise 'em on the sea-birds; and last evening after dusk I walked through the town with 'em — yes, sir, right out past the church and back again, my blood being up, and came home and cut a square out of the old ones to wrap round the bung of the water-butt."

The Commandant eyed the sergeant's legs in silence, choking down half-a-dozen angry criticisms. No; he could not trust himself to speak; and, after a minute, cramming his clenched fists into the pockets of his frayed fatigue-jacket, he swung about on his heel and walked out of the garden with angry strides.

Was the Lord Proprietor making sport of him? — purposely making him and his garrison the laughing-stock of the Islands?

The Commandant walked up the road with a hot heart: past the Barracks and beyond them to the down, where a ruined windmill overlooked the sea. He wanted to be alone, and up here he could count upon solitude. He wanted to walk off his ill-humour. But the ascent was steep, and he, alas! no longer a young man; and at the windmill he was forced to stand still and draw breath.

At his feet lay the Islands, bathed in the light of a fast-reddening October sunset. Against such a sunset, if the air be very clear, you may see them from the cliffs of the mainland — a low, dark cloud out in the Atlantic; and in old days the Commandant had repined often enough at the few leagues which then had cut him off from the world, from active service, from promotion.

Gradually, as time went on, he had grown resigned, and with resignation he had learnt to be proud of his kingdom — for his kingdom *de facto* it was. The Islanders had used to speak of him sometimes as The Commandant, but oftener as The Governor. (They never called him The Governor nowadays.) His military establishment, to be sure — consisting of a master-gunner, four other gunners, and two or three aged sergeants — scarcely ac-corded with his rank of major; but by way of compensation he was, as President of the Council of Twelve, the chief civil magistrate of the Islands.

This requires a word or two of explanation. The Reigning Sov-ereign of England retained, as he yet retains, military authority over the Islands, and from him, through the Commander-in-chief, our friend held his appointment as military governor. But His Majesty

King William III and his successors, by a lease two or three times renewed, had granted "all those His Majesty's territories and rocks" — so the wording ran — to a great and unknown person of whom the Islanders spoke reverentially as The Duke, "together with all sounds, harbours, and sands within the circuit of the said Isles; and all lands, tenements, meadows, pastures, grounds, feedings, fishing places, mines of tin, lead, and coals, and all profits of the same, and full power to dig, work, and mine in the premises; and also all the marshes, void grounds, woods, under-woods, rents, reservoirs, services, and all other profits, rights, commodities, advantages, and emoluments within the said Isles; and a moiety of all shipwreck, the other moiety to be received by the Lord High Admiral; as also all His Majesty's Liberties, Franchises, Authorities, and Jurisdictions, as had before been used in the said Islands; with full power to hear, examine, and finally determine all plaints, suits, matters, actions, controversies, contentions, and demands whatever, moved and depending between party and party inhabiting the said Isle (all business, treason, matters touching life or member of man, or title of land; and also all controversies and causes touching ships, and other things belonging to the High Court of Admiralty always excepted)" — all this for an annual rent of Forty Pounds.

The Duke, in short, was by his lease made Lord Proprietor, with all civil jurisdiction. But, being far too great a man to reside in the Islands, or even to visit them, he entrusted his business to a resident Agent, and deputed his magistracy to an elective Council of Twelve, over which the Commandant for the time being invariably presided. But this custom (it should be explained) rested on courtesy and not upon right. Based upon compromise — for the boundaries between the civil and military jurisdictions were at some points not precisely determined — it had been found to work smoothly enough in practice, it had stood the test of a hundred and fifty years when, in the year after Sevastopol, Major Narcisse Vigoureux arrived in the Islands to take over the military command, and the Duke nominated him for the Presidency quite as a matter of course.

As President, he had power, with the assent of the Court, to inflict fines, whippings, and imprisonment — this last with the limitation that he could not commit to any prison on the mainland, but only to the Island lock-up; and also, if he chose, to prescribe the ducking-stool for refractory or scolding women. The office carried no salary; but as Governor under the Lord Proprietor he enjoyed a valuable perquisite in the harbour dues collected from the shipping. Every vessel visiting the port or hoisting the Queen's colours was liable, on coming to anchor or grounding, to pay the sum of two shillings and two pence. All foreigners paid double. And since, in addition to ships putting in from abroad, it sometimes happened that two hundred sail of coasters would be driven by easterly gales to shelter in St. Lide's Harbour, or roadstead, or in Cromwell's Sound, you may guess that this made a very pleasant addition to the Commandant's military pay.

In short, for a dozen years Major Narcisse Vigoureux had been, for an unmarried man, an exceedingly happy one. If you ask me how an officer bearing such a name happened in command of a British garrison, I answer that he was not a Frenchman, but a Channel Islander of good Jersey descent; and this again helped him to understand the folk over whom he ruled. The wrong-doers feared him; but they were few. By the rest of the population, including his soldiers, he was beloved, respected, not a little envied. For a bachelor he mingled with zest in the small social amusements of Garland Town, the capital of the Islands. He shone at picnics and water-parties. He played a fair hand at whist. His manner towards ladies was deferential; towards men, dignified without a trace of patronage or self-conceit. All voted him a good fellow. At first, indeed — for he practised small economies, and his linen, though clean, was frayed — they suspected him of stinginess, until by accident the Vicar discovered that a great part of his pay went to support his dead brother's family — a widow and two girls who lived at Notting Hill, London, in far from affluent circumstances.

In spite of this the Commandant's lot might fairly have been called enviable until the day which terminated the ninety-nine years' lease upon which the Duke held the Islands. Everyone took it for granted that he would apply, as his predecessors had twice applied, for a renewal. But, no; like a bolt from the blue came news that the Duke, an old man, had waived his application in favour of an unknown purchaser — unknown, that is to say, in the Islands — a London banker, recently created a baronet, by name Sir Cæsar Hutchins.

In general, all Garland Town relied for information about persons of rank and title upon Miss Elizabeth Gabriel, a well-to-do spinster lady, daughter of a former agent of the Duke's. But Miss Gabriel's copy of "The Peerage and Baronetage of Great Britain and Ireland" dated from 1845, and Sir Cæsar's title being of more recent — or, as she put it, of mushroom — creation, the curious had to wait until a newer volume arrived from the mainland. Meanwhile, at their whist parties twice a week, the gentry of Garland Town indulged in a hundred brisk surmises, but without alarm — "unconscious of their doom, the little victims played." It was agreed, of course, that the new Lord Proprietor would not take up his abode in the Islands. For where was a suitable residence? On the whole the Commandant had little doubt that things would go on as before, but he felt some uneasiness for Mr. Pope, the Duke's agent.

Within a fortnight, however, came two fresh announcements, of which the first — a letter from Sir Cæsar, continuing Mr. Pope in his office — gratified everyone. But the second was terrible indeed. The War Office had decided to disband the garrison and remove its guns!

Major Vigoureux' face had whitened as he read that letter, five years ago. It whitened yet at the remembrance of it. As for his hair, it had been whitening ever since.

For dreadful things had happened in those five years. To begin with, the new Lord Proprietor had upset prophecy by coming into residence, and had reared himself a handsome house on the near island of Inniscaw. . . . But here for a while let us forbear to retrace those five years with their humiliating memories. It is enough that the Commandant now walked with a stoop; that he wore not only his linen frayed but a frayed coat also; and that he who of old had so often wished that England would take note of his Islands against the western sun, now prayed rather that the fogs would cover them and cut them off from sight forever. He had practical reasons, too, for such a prayer; but of these he was not thinking as he turned there by the windmill, and spied Sergeant Treacher approaching along the ridge, and trundling a wheel-barrow full of manure. The level sun-rays, painting the turf to a green almost unnaturally vivid, and gilding the straw of the manure, passed on to flame upon Sergeant Treacher's breast as though beneath his unbuttoned tunic he wore a corslet of burnished brass. The Commandant blinked, again removed his glasses, and, having repolished, resumed them.

"Treacher, what are you wearing?"

"Meanin' the weskit, sir?" asked Treacher.

"Is it a waistcoat?"

"Well, sir, it used to be an antimacassar; but Miss Gabriel had it made up for me, all the shirts in store bein' used up, so to speak."

Too well the Commandant recognised it; an abomination of crochet work in stripes, four inches wide, of scarlet, green, orange-yellow, and violet. For years — in fact ever since he remembered Miss Gabriel's front parlour — it had decorated the back of Miss Gabriel's sofa.

"She said, sir, that with the autumn drawing on, and the winter coming, it would cut up nicely for a weskit," Treacher explained.

"Miss Gabriel," began the Commandant, "Miss Gabriel has no business—"

"No, sir?" suggested Treacher, after a pause.

"You will take it off. You will take it off this instant, and hand it to me."

"Yes, sir." Treacher obediently slipped off his tunic. "I don't like the thing myself; it's too noticeable, though warming. Miss Gabriel called it a Chesterfield."

"It's a conspiracy!" said the Commandant.

CHAPTER II

SERGEANT ARCHELAUS IS RE-FITTED

The Commandant, still with a hot heart, walked for a little way beside Sergeant Treacher. He carried the offending waistcoat slung across his arm, and once or twice hesitated on the verge of indignant speech; but by-and-by seemed to recollect himself, halted, turned, and, parting from Treacher without more words, marched off for his customary evening walk around the fortifications.

Let us follow him.

The garrison occupied the heights of a peninsula connected with St. Lide's by a low sandy isthmus, across which it looked towards the "country side" of the island, though this country side was in fact concealed by rising ground, for the most part uncultivated, where sheets of mesembryanthemum draped the outcropping ledges of granite. At the foot of the hill, around the pier and harbour to the north and east, clustered St. Hugh's town, and climbed by one devious street to the garrison gate. From where he stood the Commandant could almost look down its chimneys. Along the isthmus straggled a few houses in double line, known as New Town, and beyond, where the isthmus widened, lay the Old Town around its Parish Church. These three together made Garland Town, the capital of the Islands; and the population of St. Lide's — town, garrison, and country side — numbered a little over fourteen hundred. Garrison Hill, rising (as we have seen) with a pretty steep acclivity, attains the height of a hundred and ten feet above sea level. It measures about three-quarters of a mile in length and a quarter of a mile in breadth, and the lines of fortification extended around the whole hill (except upon the north-west side, which happened to be the most important); a circuit of one mile and a quarter.

*****

You entered them beneath a massive but ruinous gateway, surmounted by a bell, which Sergeant Treacher rang regularly at six, nine, and twelve o'clock in the morning, and at three, six, and nine p.m., and struck to announce the intervening hours: for the Islands had no public clock. To the left of this gateway the Commandant always began his round, starting from King George's Battery, to which in old days the Islanders had looked for warning of the enemy's approach. Then it had mounted seven long eighteen-pounders: now — The Commandant sighed and moved on; past the Duke's Battery (four eighteen-pounders), the Vixen (one eighteen and one nine-pounder), and along by a breastwork pierced with embrasures to the important battery on Day Point, at the extreme south-east. Here five thirty-two pounders — and, three hundred yards away to the west, in the great Windlass Battery, no fewer than eleven guns of the same calibre — had grinned defiance at the ships of France. Today the grass grew on their empty platforms, the nettles sprouted from their angles . . . and the Commandant — what was he doing here?

I fear the answer may provoke a smile. He was drawing his pay.

The guns, the garrison, were gone these five years; but by some oversight of the War Office neither the Commandant nor his two sergeants had been retired. Regularly, month by month, his pay-sheet had been accepted; regularly the full amount had been handed to him by Mr. Fossell, agent at Garland Town for Messrs. Curtis' Bank on the mainland. Clearly there was a mistake somewhere, and often enough his conscience smote him, urging that he ought, in honour, to call attention to it. He was defrauding the Government, and, through the Government, the taxpayer.

Yes; conscience put this plainly enough, and he felt it to be unanswerable. But if he obeyed conscience and published the mistake — good Heavens! what would happen to him? Already, three years ago, the Lord Proprietor had resumed the shipping dues which had made so welcome an addition to his income. On the strength of them he had made a too liberal allowance to his brother's widow; and now to maintain it he was driven to deny himself all but the barest necessary expenses. Yet how could he cut it down? The two girls were growing up. Their mother had sent them to a costly school. As it was, her letters burdened him with complaints of her poverty: for she was a peevish, grasping woman — poor soul!

Again, if he published the mistake, he impoverished not himself only but his two sergeants: and Treacher was a married man. He often drugged his conscience with this. But his conscience, being healthy, was soon awake and tormenting him.

It humiliated him, too. Government, which sent him his full pay, never sent him stores, ammunition, or clothing for his men. He wanted no ammunition; but his men needed clothing — and he dared not ask for it. Their uniforms were (as Miss Gabriel had more than once pointedly asserted in his hearing) a scandal to the Islands. Moreover, the price of hens' eggs ruling high in Garland Town, he had discovered that gulls' eggs made a tolerable substitute. It was in scrambling after gulls' eggs for his Commanding Officer that Sergeant Archelaus had ruined his small-clothes. . . . And now you know why in the course of his discussion with Sergeant Archelaus the Commandant had winced more than once.

Worst of all, the fatal secret tied his tongue under all the many slights (as he reckoned them) which the Lord Proprietor put on him. No; worst of all was the self-reproach he carried about in his own breast. But none the less the Commandant, as a sensitive man, chafed under the Lord Proprietor's tyranny, which was the harder to bear for being slightly contemptuous. He felt that all his old friends pitied him while they turned to worship the rising sun; while, as for Miss Gabriel (who had never been his friend), he feared her caustic tongue worse than the devil.

But to attack him thus through his men! Had Miss Gabriel and the Lord Proprietor conspired to inflict this indignity?

The Commandant was a sincere Christian: ever willing to believe the best of his kind, incapable of harbouring malice, or, except in the brief heat of temper, of imputing it to others. In the short three hundred yards between the Day Point and Windlass Batteries he repented his worst thoughts. He acquitted his enemies — if enemies they were — of conspiracy. The coincidence of the two gifts was fortuitous: they had been offered without guile, if also without sufficient care for his feelings. But this kind of thing must not happen again, and obviously the most tactful way to prevent it was, not to remonstrate with Miss Gabriel or with the Lord Proprietor, but to provide (somehow) his two sergeants with a refit.

The Commandant had arrived at this conclusion and at the Sand Pit Battery (five thirty-two pounders) almost simultaneously, when, across the breastwork, he was aware of Mr. Rogers, Lieutenant R. N., and Inspecting Commander of the Coast-guard, standing at the head of the slope just outside the fortifications, and conning the sea through a telescope.

"Hullo!" said Mr. Rogers — a short man with a jolly smile — lowering his glass and facing suddenly about at the sound of the Commandant's footfall. "Hullo! and good evening!"

"Good evening!" responded Major Vigoureux.

"Queer-looking sky out yonder."

"So it is, now you come to mention it." The Commandant, shaken out of his brown study, slowly concentrated his gaze on the western horizon.

"See that bank of fog? I don't know what to make of it. No wind at all; the glass steady as a rock; and a heavy swell rolling up from westward. Take hold of my glass and bring it to bear on the Monk" — this was the lighthouse guarding the westernmost reef of the Off Islands. "Every now and then a sea'll hide half the column."

"For my part," said the Commandant, "I've been out of all calculation with the weather for a week past. It's uncanny for the time of year."

"There's the devil of a rumpus going on somewhere, to account for the sea that's running," said Mr. Rogers, and checked himself in the act of handing the telescope across the breastwork, as he caught sight of Sergeant Treacher's waistcoat, which the Commandant was nervously shifting from his right arm to his left.

"Hullo!" said Mr. Rogers, again.

"It's — it's a sort of waistcoat," explained the Commandant.

"It may be," said Mr. Rogers. "But unless I'm a Dutchman, it used to be The Gabriel's antimacassar" — and with that Mr. Rogers winked, for he had (as the other knew to his cost) an artless, primitive sense of pleasantry. "A *gage d'amour*, I'll bet any man a sovereign. Come now!"

"I assure you—"

"And you two pretending before everyone that you're at daggers drawn! Trust an old one for slyness!"

(Once again this afternoon the Commandant winced.)

"Oh, but this is too rich!" Mr. Rogers continued, and the Commandant felt that only the intervening breastwork protected him from a nudge under the ribs. "I must take a rise out of the old lady tonight, when we meet at old Fossell's."

"I — I beg you will do nothing of the sort." The Commandant's voice shook with apprehension.

Mr. Rogers, mistaking the tremor in the appeal, recoiled suddenly from the extremely gay to the extremely grave. "My good fellow! Of course, if it's serious!—"

"'Serious!'" The Commandant stared at him for a moment. "Oh, damn the woman!" he broke out in sudden wrath, and went his way with long strides, while the Inspecting Commander looked after him with a broad grin.

The next battery, the Keg of Butter — so called from a barrel-shaped rock which it overlooked — was built of sods, and had mounted a single eighteen-pounder, on a traversing platform. Here, on the north-west side of the hill, the fortifications broke off, or were continued only by a low wall along the edge of the cliff; and here the path, or *via militaris*, turned off at a sharp angle and led back towards the Castle, under the walls of which the Commandant passed, as a rule, to complete his inspection by visiting the three batteries on the northern cliffs. But today he broke his custom, and returned to the Garrison Garden.

As he opened the gate, five o'clock sounded from the garrison bell, and at the first stroke of it he saw Sergeant Archelaus drive his spade into the soil, draw the back of his wrist across his forehead, and walk towards the veronica hedge for his tunic.

"Archelaus!"

"Sir!"

"I have been thinking over those trousers — " began the Commandant, picking his way between the briers that threatened to choke the path.

"And so have I," said Sergeant Archelaus; "and the upshot is, Do you spell 'em with a 'u' or a 'w'?"

"Now you mention it, I don't feel able to answer you off-hand; not without writing it down," said the Commandant. "But what on earth does it matter?"

"Nothin' — except that I was thinkin' to write him a letter, to thank him."

"For Heaven's sake — " the Commandant began, and checked himself. "I wouldn't do that, if I were you. In fact, I've been thinking the matter over, and it occurs to me that I have an old pair of dress trousers that might serve your turn; that is to say, if you could manage to unpick the red stripe off your old ones and get someone to sew it on. They are black, to be sure; but the difference between black and dark blue is not so very noticeable. And the cut of them inclines to the peg-top, that being the fashionable shape when I bought them — let me see — in fifty-seven, I think it was."

"I know 'em," said Sergeant Archelaus. "They were sound enough two months back, when I sprinkled 'em over with camphor, against the moth."

"I think they will do excellently."

"They'll do, fast enough," Sergeant Archelaus asserted; "though it seems like deprivin' you."

"Not at all, Archelaus; not in the least. Why, I haven't put on evening dress half a dozen times since I came to the Islands."

"And that's a long time, to be sure, sir. But one never knows. The Lord Proprietor might take it into his head, one o' these days, to invite you to dinner."

"Few things are less likely. And even if he did, and the worst came to the worst, I might borrow Mr. Rogers', you know," added the Commandant — and with a smile; for he stood six feet, and Mr. Rogers a bare five feet five, in their respective socks.

"He might ask you both together. 'Twould be just of a piece with his damned thoughtlessness."

"Hush, Archelaus!" his master commanded sternly, and reproached himself afterwards for having felt not altogether ill-pleased.

"Well, sir, I thank you kindly; and I won't deny 'twill be a comfort to go about with the lower half of me looking a bit less like a pen-wiper. But what be I to do with the pesky things? Return 'em?"

"On no account. You might even thank him — by word of mouth — if you have not already done so."

"I haven't. To tell the truth, the pattern took me so aback at first going off. . . . But when you came in by the gate, there, I was turning it over in my mind that the garrison oughtn't to be beholden to a civilian—"

"Quite right, Archelaus."

"And, that bein' so, it might be dignified-like to return gift for gift. Now, the Lord Proprietor's terrible fond of bulbs; 'tis a new craze with him; and in spading over the border here I'd a-turned up a dozen or so of those queer-looking Lent-lilies you set such store by— " Sergeant Archelaus pointed towards a little heap of daffodil bulbs carelessly strewn on the up-turned soil.

These bulbs had a history.

Close on thirty years before, a certain Dutch skipper — his name is forgotten — happened to be sailing for Bordeaux with a general cargo, which included some thousands of tulips, and a few almost priceless ones, for a rich purchaser who wished to introduce tulip-culture into the Gironde. The Dutchman's vessel was a flat-bottomed galliot, fitted with lee-boards, but liable to fall away from the wind; and, encountering a strong southerly gale as he attempted to round Ushant, he was blown northward into the fogs, and, through the fogs, upon the Islands.

Against what followed, the chances were at least a thousand to one. His vessel, blind as to her whereabouts, and helpless among the tide-races, missed rock after rock, blundered her way past every sunken peril — to be sure, she was flat-bottomed, but the soundings varied so from moment to moment that the crew, after running a dozen times to the boats in the certainty of striking, fully believed themselves bewitched; until, in St. Lide's Pool, as they made seven fathoms and hoped for open water, the fog lifted suddenly, and they saw Garrison Hill right above them.

This befell them a short hour before sunset. The skipper rounded up to the wind, dropped anchor, got out a boat, and groped his way shoreward — for the fog had descended again, even more speedily than it had lifted.

Groping his way, and still attended by his amazing good luck, the Dutchman, where he had expected rocks, came plump on a pier of hewn masonry. At the pier-head, which loomed high above them, a man struck a light and displayed a lantern; and, looking up, the crew were aware of many people standing there and chattering in the dusk — chattering in the low soft tone peculiar to the Islanders. The skipper hailed them in Dutch, and again in French, these being the only languages he spoke. The Islanders, helping him ashore, made signs that they could not answer, but took him and his men up the hill to the Garrison, then commanded by a Colonel Bartlemy.

Colonel Bartlemy could speak French after a fashion, and so could his excellent wife. Between them they entertained the wanderers hospitably for the space of five days, at the end of which the Dutchman went his way before a clear north wind, and in charge of an Island pilot. But before departing he presented his hosts — it was all that either he could give or they would permit themselves to accept — with a quantity of remarkably fine bulbs from his cargo.

Now, possibly, being a Dutchman, he took it for granted that anyone could recognise these bulbs for what they were. But Mrs. Bartlemy did not; for she had spent the most of her life in various garrisons, which afford few opportunities for gardening. None the less, she was, for a soldier's wife, a first-rate housekeeper; and, supposing these bulbs to be onions of peculiar rarity, she forthwith issued invitations to the *elite* of the Island, and ordered over a leg of Welsh mutton from the mainland. I will not attempt to tell of the dinner that ensued: for Miss Gabriel made the story her own, and everyone who heard her relate it after one of Garland Town's *petits soupers* — as she frequently did by special request — declared it to be inimitable. Suffice it to say that the tulips were boiled, but not eaten.

A few bulbs, of smaller size, escaped the pot, and Mrs. Bartlemy, in her mortification, ordered the cook to throw them away, or (in the language of the Islands) to "heave them to cliff." The cook cast them out upon a bed of rubbish in a corner of the garrison garden, where by-and-by they were covered with fresh rubbish, under which they sprouted; and, next spring, lo! the midden heap had become a mound of glorious trumpet daffodils!

So they were left to blossom, refreshing the eyes of successive Commandants year after year as March came round and the March nor'-westers set their yellow bells waving against the blue sea. Major Vigoureux delighted in them — were they not his name-flower? But no one took pains to cultivate them, as no one suspected their great destiny. They bloomed year by year, and waited. Their hour was not yet.

"By all means, Archelaus, let us do it tactfully," agreed the Commandant. "We must suppress those trousers of his at all costs. Yet I would avoid anything in the nature of a rebuff, and if you think the Lord Proprietor would be gratified, you are welcome to take him as many of the bulbs as you please. Only leave me a few; for God knows our garden has few ornaments to spare."

"I'll take 'em over to Inniscaw and thank him by word o' mouth," said Sergeant Archelaus, hopefully. "It'll save me the trouble of spelling trousers,' anyway."

"It would be easier, as well as more accurate," said the Commandant, pensively regarding the Sergeant's legs, "to call them trews. Not," he went on inconsequently, "that I have anything to say against the Highland Regiments. I was brigaded once for three months with the Forth-Second, and capital fellows I found them."

With a mind relieved, the Commandant walked off towards the Barracks, pausing on his way to pick up Miss Gabriel's antimacassar-waistcoat, which he had taken the precaution to leave outside the gate.

Three-quarters of an hour later he emerged in clean shirt and threadbare, but well-brushed, uniform, arrayed for Mr. and Mrs. Fossell's whist-party. As he passed the Garrison gate, Mrs. Treacher, who sometimes acted deputy for her husband, began to ring the six o'clock bell. He halted and waited for her to finish.

"Mrs. Treacher," he said, "can you tell me the price of flannel?"

"Flannel," answered Mrs. Treacher, "is all prices, according to quality."

"But I am talking of good ordinary flannel, fit to make up into a man's shirt."

"Then you couldn't say less than one-three-farthings, or one-and-a-ha'penny at the lowest."

"And how much would be required?"

"Good Lord!" said Mrs. Treacher. "As if that didn't all depend on the man!"

"I was thinking, Mrs. Treacher, to present your husband with one: that is to say, with the material, if you will not mind making it up."

Mrs. Treacher curtsied. "And I thank you kindly, sir, for 'tis not before he needs one, which, being under average size and the width just a yard, as you may reckon, he oughtn't to take more than three-and-a-half yards at the outside."

"Three-and-a-half at one-three-farthings — that makes — Oh, confound these fractions!" said the Commandant. "We'll make it four shillings, and you had best step down to Tregaskis' shop tomorrow and choose the stuff yourself." He counted out the money into Mrs. Treacher's hand, and left her curtseying. As he went, he jingled the few coins remaining in his breeches pocket. They amounted to two-and-seven-pence in all — and almost a week stood between him and pay-day.

CHAPTER III

THE COMMANDANT FINESSES A KNAVE

"I remember the Bartlemys perfectly," said Miss Gabriel, addressing the company as they sat around Mr. and Mrs. Fossell's dining-table and trifled with a light collation of cordial waters and ratafia biscuits — prelude to serious whist. "I carry them both in my mind's eye, though I must have been but a tiny child when he succumbed to apoplexy, and she left the Islands to reside with a married sister at Scarborough. Very poorly-off he left her. Somehow, our Commanding Officers have never contrived to save money — even in the old days, when the post was worth having."

Miss Gabriel said it lightly but pointedly, with a glance at the Commandant. The company stared at their plates and glasses. It was well-known that (as Mr. Rogers put it) Miss Gabriel "had her knife into" the patient man, and there were tongues that attributed her spitefulness to disappointment. Fifteen years ago, when Major Narcisse Vigoureux — no longer in his first youth, but still a man of handsome presence — had first arrived in the Islands to take over his command, Miss Gabriel was a not uncomely woman of thirty. *Partis* in the Islands are few, as you may suppose. He was a bachelor, she a spinster; she had money, and he position. What wonder, then, if the Islanders expected them to make a match of it?

For some reason, the match had never come off, and although she might convince herself that the simplest reason — incompatibility — was the true one, Miss Gabriel could hardly have been unaware that the women looked upon her as one who had missed her chance, and even blamed her a little — as women always will in such cases — in a conspiracy of sex acknowledging its weakness. Perhaps this made her defiant.

She was handling the Commandant truculently tonight.

"Of course," she continued, "even in those days the post — don't they say the same in England of a Deanery? — was looked upon as finishing a man's career. I don't know, for my part, the principle upon which the Horse Guards — it used to be the Horse Guards — sent Colonel Bartlemy down to us."

"By selection, ma'am," said the Commandant, still patiently, as she paused; "by selection among a number of applicants."

"I didn't want to be told that," snapped Miss Gabriel. "What I meant was, the Commander-in-Chief probably knew something of the man — had informed himself of something in his record — before sending him down to this exile."

"And a jolly good exile, too!" put in Mr. Rogers, heartily.

"It used to be," said Miss Gabriel. "This Colonel Bartlemy, for instance, was a coward. I've heard it told of him that once, during his command, a sort of mutiny broke out in the Barracks. It happened at a time when the newspapers were full of nonsense about France invading us by a sudden descent; and the noise, reaching him in the quarters where he lodged with his wife and one general maid-servant, put him in a terrible fright. He had fenced off these quarters of his for privacy, because Mrs. Bartlemy thought it would be a good deal better for the maid-servant; and they communicated with the Barracks by a staircase with a door of which he kept the key. On the first alarm he ran to this door and called through the key-hole for his orderly; but the orderly, who himself was taking part in the disturbance, did not hear. So the Colonel called up his wife and the servant, and joined them at the head of the stairs after he had slipped on his belt and sword. By this time the noise below was deafening. The Colonel, putting a brave face on it, managed to get the key into the lock and turn it. Then, as he flung the door open, he turned with a bow to his wife and said very politely, in French — for they were in the habit of talking French before the girl — 'Passez devant, madame!'"

"How did it end?" asked Mr. Rogers, after a guffaw.

"Oh, it turned out to be just a barrack brawl. The soldiers were always the worst-behaved lot in the Islands, and perpetually grumbling — though in those days," added Miss Gabriel, "I always understood that they were fed and clothed sufficiently."

The Commandant whitened. Mrs. Fossell, a nervous body in a cap with lilac ribbon, rose in some little fluster, and opined that it was almost time to cut for partners.

A few minutes later the Commandant found himself seated opposite Mr. Fossell, with Miss Gabriel and Mr. Rogers for opponents — Miss Gabriel on his left. He prepared to enjoy himself, for whist meant silence, and he could have chosen no better partner than Mr. Fossell, who played a sound game, and with a perfectly inscrutable face.

"Dear me!" said Miss Gabriel, in the act of picking up her cards, "it seems as if this had happened a great many times before! What do you say, Mr. Fossell, to staking half-a-crown on the rubber, just to enliven the game? You don't object on principle, I know, to playing for money."

"No, indeed, ma'am," answered Mr. Fossell. "I am content if the others are willing — not that for me the pleasure of playing against you needs any such — er — adventitious stimulus."

Miss Gabriel appealed to Mr. Rogers.

Mr. Rogers thought it would be great fun. "Come along, Vigoureux," he almost shouted, "you can't refuse a lady's challenge!"

What could the poor Commandant do? Almost before he knew he had nodded, though with a set face, and by the nod committed himself. He felt his few coins burning in his breeches' pocket against his thigh, as if they warned him.

But, after all, Fossell was an excellent player. With the smallest luck, he and Fossell ought to be more than a match for a pair of whom, if one (Miss Gabriel) was wily, the other played a game not usually distinguishable from bumble-puppy.

They won the first game easily.

They had almost won the second when a devastating seven trumps in Mr. Rogers's hand (which he played atrociously) saw their opponents almost level — the score eight-seven. In the next hand, Miss Gabriel — for this was old-fashioned long whist — held all four honours, and took the game.

The Commandant looked at Mr. Fossell. But a financier is not disturbed by the risk of half-a-crown.

Only half-a-crown! — but for the Commandant a week between this half-a-crown and another.

He wondered what Fossell would say — Fossell, sitting there, so imperturbable, with his shiny bald head — if he knew.

"Game *and*!" announced Mr. Rogers.

By this time the players at the second table, aware of the half-a-crown at stake, were listening in a state of suppressed excitement — suppressed because the Vicar, being deaf, had not overheard Miss Gabriel's challenge, and the others feared that he might disapprove of playing for money.

The Vicar, who played against Mr. and Mrs. Pope, with Mrs. Fossell for partner, had a habit of soliloquising over his hand on any subject that occurred to him. The rest of the table deferred to this habit, out of respect or because by experience they knew it to be incurable, since only by conscious effort could he hear any voice but his own.

By such an effort, holding his hand to his ear, he had listened to Miss Gabriel's anecdote about Colonel Bartlemy; smiling the while because he had heard it many times before and knew it to be a good one; innocently unaware that it covered any caustic subintention. It had started him on a train of reminiscence which he pursued at the card-table (good man) for twenty-five minutes, recalling himself to the cards with a faint shock of surprise whenever it became his turn to play, as one who would protest — "What, again? And so soon?"

"Yes, indeed," the Vicar's voice struck in across the strained silence, "there is an old story that Oliver Cromwell left behind him, in garrison here, a company of the Bedfordshire Regiment, and that in time they were completely forgotten. (Let me see. Spades are trumps, I believe. . . . 'Clubs'? Your pardon Mrs. Fossell, but I remember it was a black suit.) Yes, and seeing no prospect of recall they married in time with our Island women, and that" — here the Vicar gathered up a trick which belonged to his opponents — "is, by some, alleged to be the reason why the Islanders use a purer English than is spoken on the mainland. Ah, quite so; yes, I played the ten — then it was your ace, Mrs. Pope? I congratulate you, ma'am."

The Commandant, overhearing, could not forbear a glance at Miss Gabriel. It conveyed no resentment, scarcely even a reproach; it turned rather, as by dumb instinct, upon the author of the wound, and asked perplexedly: — "What have I done to you, that you treat me thus?" I have no doubt that Miss Gabriel caught the glance. She did not answer it; but her grey eyes glinted beneath their lids as she bent them upon the cards Mr. Fossell was dealing in his usual deliberate way — glinted as though with a spark of flint struck out by steel.

"The story may be apocryphal," pursued the Vicar, addressing deaf ears around the other table; "though, for my part, I incline to think there may be a substratum—"

Mr. Fossell turned up the queen of hearts. The Commandant held ace, ten, and two small trumps, with a strong hand in diamonds, which Mr. Rogers, by a blundering lead, enabled him to establish early. Actual honours were "easy"; but by exhausting trumps at the first opportunity, he scored three by tricks. The next hand gave their opponents three points — two by honours, and the trick. Three all.

The Vicar was heard to observe that, on the whole, intermarriage among the Islanders had not produced the disastrous effects usually predicted of it; and that, therefore, an infusion of fresh blood, at some date more or less remote, might reasonably be conjectured, even though incapable of proof.

The Vicar, as he said this, looked across at Mrs. Fossell interrogatively. He was really expecting her to lead trumps, but she mistook him to be asking her assent to his theory. To keep the ball rolling, she opined that what had happened once need not necessarily happen again, especially in these days when locomotion was making such strides. She hazarded this in the lowest key; but it happened in just that momentary hush upon which the faintest remark falls resonantly. The Commandant heard it across the room as he waited for Mr. Rogers to cut the cards; and the Vicar, by a freak of hearing, picked it up at once.

"My dear lady," he demanded, "are you talking of progenitiveness!"

"N-no," stammered Mrs. Fossell, in confusion. "Nothing of the sort. I was referring to the garrison here being left out of mind — like the regiment you spoke of—"

Miss Gabriel tapped the table impatiently. "Mr. Rogers," she said, "I think we had better attend to the game. Major Vigoureux is waiting for you to cut." She said it with her eyes upon the Commandant's hand, which was trembling. He wondered, as he dealt, if she had observed that it was trembling. If so, had she guessed the true reason?

The score mounted to nine-eight. The Commandant lifted a hand to his brow as Mr. Fossell, whose turn it was, took up the cards and began to deal methodically, without a trace of discomposure.

"Half a crown! and if he lost, one penny left to last him to next pay day!" A terrible thought seized him. "And what if, when he presented himself at Mr. Fossell's bank on pay-day, the money was not forthcoming?" Nonsense! He was unhinged. . . . The money had always arrived punctually . . . but the whole world seemed to be in conspiracy against him tonight, and his luck along with it.

Mr. Rogers, who had a trick of sorting out his suits between his fingers, hesitated for a few moments, put his cards together, and with an air of fierce determination, led a small heart.

Again the Commandant's right hand went up to his brow. The room was very close and still. But the Vicar remained unaware of the general excitement, and across the silence the Vicar was heard to say confidentially: —

"Between you and me there was a time when I hoped our friend the Commandant might make a match of it."

The poor Commandant! . . . With his gaze fixed on the cards, he felt that every ear was listening, every eye turned upon him. He must do something desperate to break the horrible spell, to turn the luck. . . . He held ace, king, knave of hearts, and knew well enough that, in sound whist he ought to play the king. But why had Mr. Rogers led hearts? Mr. Rogers did not often lead even from a strong suit unless it contained at least one honour.

The Commandant risked it and finessed his knave. Miss Gabriel had been waiting, watching him intently. Her mouth shut almost with a snap of triumph as she put down the queen.

It was, as it happened, the one heart in her hand. She closed her triumph, a few rounds later, by trumping the Commandant's ace and king. Mr. Fossell looked at his partner, in sorrow rather than in anger. Mr. Rogers laughed uproariously as he counted up the tricks.

"Double or quits, I suppose?" he suggested.

But the Commandant rose. "Your pardon, Miss Gabriel," he said, laying his half-crown on the table, "if I play no more for money tonight. Indeed, I was going to ask Mrs. Fossell to forgive me if I spoil one of her quartettes by withdrawing. To tell the truth, I am not myself — a slight dizziness—"

"A glass of hot brandy-and-water?" suggested Mr. Fossell. "Nay, then, a thimbleful — I insist!"

The Commandant made his excuses as politely as he could, and found himself in the street. The night was pitch-dark and the road full of sea-fog — a fog so thick that it completely shut off the rays of the many lighthouses twinkling around the Islands, and obscured the few street lamps that illuminated Garland Town. A slight breeze blew up from the west and damped his brow; for his dizziness had been something more than a pretence, and he walked with his hat in his hand.

On such a night a stranger might well have lost his way; but the Commandant steered for Garrison Hill without a mistake, and up the hill towards the Barracks. Garland Town is early a-bed. He passed no one in the streets. But in St. Hugh's, as he went by the closed door of a cottage, halfway up the ascent, he recalled the night, years ago, of his first arrival in the Islands. He had come a week before the garrison expected him, and there had been no one to meet him on the quay when he arrived in the dusk of an October evening. Darkness had descended on the Islands before he started from the quay to climb to his new home; and here — just here, at this doorway — he had paused to ask his way. The door had stood open then, with a panel of warm firelight lying across the roadway, and as he halted and peered into the room — it was a kitchen, and the light from the open hearth glinted on rows of china plates ranged along the dresser — he saw two girls beside the fire; the one seated and reading from a book in her lap, the other on the hearth-mat half reclined against her sister's knee, over which she had flung an arm to prop her chin as she listened.... He remembered the sand strewn on the slate floor, the fresh sea-smell in this room so confidingly open to the night — the scene so intimate, so homely, that the traveller standing in the doorway with the sea-spray on his cloak could scarcely believe in the tide-races across which he had been voyaging for hours. He stood, the hum of them in his ears, a doubtful intruder; and while he stood, the girl in the chair had risen and bade him good evening in purest English.

"You have come by the boat? You will be from the mainland?" she said, and he wondered a little, not being used as yet to hear his country spoken of as the mainland. "And I am going to England tomorrow," she added. "The boat which brought you will take me over on its return journey."

"You know England well, I expect?" He found himself saying this for lack of anything better.

"She has never been outside the Islands," said her sister, who also had risen. "And it is the same with me. But tomorrow she is going — " the girl paused here, not it (seemed) in pain, but wistfully, as in a kind of solemn awe at the prospect. "We left the door open for father. He has a fancy to see the light across the road as he comes up the hill. But he is late tonight at the fishing."

The Commandant, glancing around the room, divined — he could not tell why — that these girls were motherless. His eyes fell on the open book which the elder sister laid on the chair as she rose. The firelight enabled him to read its page-heading, printed in thick, blunt type — "King Lear"! These girls, the one of them about to visit unknown England, were reading Shakespeare together.

"*Urbem quam dicunt Romam*" — he felt a wild inclination to question them, to ask what they expected to learn of England from Shakespeare, and from that play of all others. But being a shy man, then as ever, he forbore, and contented himself with asking the way to the Barracks.

They went with him to the door to direct him; and so, wishing them good-night, he had gone up the hill. That was all. He had never seen the elder sister again; did not know to this day what business had taken her away to the mainland, not to return. The younger had married a pilot, and was now the mother of a growing family in Saaron Island, which lies next to Brefar, which faces Inniscaw. Her farmstead there (the solitary one on the island), stood a short way above the landing quay; and once or twice, catching sight of her in her doorway and lifting his hat as he went by (for the Commandant was ever polite), he had found it in his mind to stop and inquire after her sister.

He had never translated this resolve into action. The Commandant — as everyone knew on the Islands — was "desperate shy," or "that shy you'd never believe." But the scene had bitten itself upon his memory, and he recalled it almost as often as he passed the door. He recalled it tonight, as he stumbled by it in the fog and uphill to his cheerless lodgings.

What a blind thing was life! blind even as this fog — and his home in it these cheerless Barracks; to which nevertheless he must cling, in spite of his honour, an old man, good for nothing, afraid to be found out! He groped his way to the front door, opened it with his latchkey, lit the candle which Sergeant Archelaus had considerately placed at the foot of the stairs, and, climbing them to his bedroom, flung himself on his knees by the bed.

Now the architect of the Barracks had designed them upon a singular plan, of which the peculiar inconvenience was that almost every room led to some other; which saved corridor space, but was fatal to privacy.

Beyond the Commandant's bedroom, which opened upon the first floor landing of the main staircase, lay a room in which he kept his fishing clothes, and in which Sergeant Archelaus sometimes lit a fire to dry them by.

It was a small room, well shielded from the draughts which raged through the building in winter; and here Sergeant Archelaus had lit a fire tonight and sat before it, sewing an artilleryman's stripe upon the Commandant's cast dress trousers.

Hearing a noise in the outer room, and not expecting his master's return for at least a couple of hours, he hurried out in some perturbation, with the trousers flung across his arm — to find the Commandant kneeling at his devotions.

"I beg your pardon, sir!"

"It's of no consequence," said the Commandant, looking up (but he was desperately confused). "I — I always say my prayers, you know."

"What? Before undressing?" said Sergeant Archelaus.

CHAPTER IV

THE GUN IN THE GREAT FOG

Politely though he had contrived his departure, the Commandant left Mrs. Fossell's whist-party to something like dismay. A passing indisposition — no excuse could be more reasonable. Still, nothing of the kind had ever interrupted these gatherings within Mrs. Fossell's recollection, and she could not help taking a serious view of it.

"A passing indisposition," was Mr. Fossell's phrase, and he kept repeating it — with an occasional "Nonsense, my dear" — in answer to his wife's gloomy forebodings.

"But I shall send round, the first thing in the morning, to inquire," she insisted.

"Do so, my dear."

"It can't be serious, ma'am," Mr. Rogers assured her jollily. "You heard him decline my arm when I offered to see him home."

"In my opinion," said Miss Gabriel, "the man is breaking up." She touched her forehead lightly with the tip of her forefinger.

"Breaking up?" echoed her host and Mrs. Pope, incredulous. "My dear Elizabeth!" began Mrs. Fossell.

"Breaking up," Miss Gabriel repeated with a very positive nod of her head. "He has not been the same man since the Lord Proprietor took over the presidency of the Court and he refused, upon pique, to be elected an ordinary member. Say what you like, a man cannot be virtual Governor of the Islands one day and the next a mere nobody without its preying upon him."

"He made light of it at the time," observed Mr. Fossell, who (it goes without saying) was councillor; "although I ventured to remonstrate with him."

"And I," said Mr. Pope, who (it also goes without saying) was another. "In the friendliest possible way you understand. I pointed out that the Lord Proprietor was, after all, the Lord Proprietor, and, as such, did not understand being thwarted. Very naturally, as you will all admit."

"It's human nature, when you come to think of it," put in the Steward's wife (she preferred the title of Steward to that of agent, and was gradually accustoming society to the sound, even as in earlier years, when a young married woman, she had taught it to substitute "agent" for "factor"). If, during the interval when her husband's dismissal seemed inevitable, she had lost no opportunity of prophesying evil of the new Lord Proprietor, she made up for it now by justifying his every action.

"If that's the ground you're going on," spoke up Mr. Rogers, who, with all his faults was nothing of a snob, "it's human nature for Vigoureux to feel sore. As for the magistracy, he's not the man to value it one pin. It's the neglect; and to meet the old fellow mooning around his batteries as I did this very afternoon — I tell you it makes a man sorry."

If this speech did Mr. Rogers credit he cancelled it presently by his atrocious behaviour at cards. The symmetry of the party being broken, Miss Gabriel announced that she had enjoyed enough whist for the evening, and that nothing in the world would give her greater pleasure than half-an-hour's quiet talk, with the Vicar — that was, if Mrs. Fossell and he would not mind cutting out and surrendering their seats to Mr. Fossell and Mr. Rogers. In saying this she outrageously flattered the Vicar, with whom it was impossible to hold conversation in any tone below that of shouting. She meant that she was prepared to listen; and she knew that no flattery was too outrageous for him to swallow. She knew also that Mrs. Fossell in her heart of hearts abhorred cards, and would be only too grateful for release, to look after the preparations for supper and scold the parlour-maid outside. So the Vicar and Mrs. Fossell cut out, and Mr. Fossell and Mr. Rogers replaced them as partners against Mr. and Mrs. Pope.

Mr. and Mrs. Pope always played together. No one knew why, but it had come to be an understood thing. Of "calls" and "echoes" the play of Mr. and Mrs. Pope was innocent; but when Mrs. Pope, being second hand, hesitated whether to trump her opponent's card or pass it, Mr. Pope had an unconscious habit of saying, "Now dearest," when he desired her to trump; and another unconscious habit, when Mrs. Pope had the lead and he wanted trumps, of murmuring, "Your turn, darling." These two habits Mr. Rogers had noted; and being in merry pin tonight over winning his half-crown, at a moment when Mr. Fossell, having the lead, appeared to hesitate (but the hesitation was only a part of Mr. Fossell's deliberate play), he leaned over and playfully suggested, "Your turn, darling!"

Mr. Fossell stared in the act of putting down a trump. For a moment he appeared to think that Mr. Rogers had gone mad; then, in spite of himself, the lines of his mouth relaxed.

"I do not think," said Mr. Pope, heavily — and the lines of Mr. Fossell's mouth at once grew rigid again — "I do not think you two ought to signal for trumps in that fashion."

His partner looked up innocently. In the slow pause Mr. Rogers was growing purple in the face, when again the Vicar's voice broke across the silence. "The Lord Proprietor's power in former days — I speak only of former days — may well have warranted the Government in stationing a military officer here to keep some check on him. For instance, he shared all ordinary wrecks with the Lord High Admiral, but a wreck became his sole property by law, if none of the crew remained alive; a dangerous reservation, ma'am, in times when justice travelled slowly, and much might happen in the Islands and never a word of it reach London."

Miss Gabriel put up both hands — they were encased in mittens, and the mittens decorated with steel beads — as if to close her ears.

"We must be thankful, indeed," she began, and paused in dismay as the floor of Mrs. Fossell's drawing-room trembled under her, and at the same moment the window sashes rattled violently throughout the house.

"Good Heavens!"

"What was that?"

The players dropped their cards. All listened.

"Upon my word," suggested the Vicar, who had heard nothing, but felt the concussion, "if it weren't positively known to be empty one would say the powder magazine at the Garrison—"

"Oh, Richard! Richard!" — here Mrs. Fossell came running in from the dining-room with a dish of trifle in her hands — "Is it an earthquake?"

"I — I rather think not, my dear!"

"At any rate it can't be the end of the world?" She turned and appealed to the Vicar, and from the Vicar again to her husband. "And if it is not, I wish you would come to Selina, for she has dropped the cold shape all over the floor and is having hysterics in the better of the two armchairs!"

Indeed, Selina's hysterics could be heard.

"Earthquake? Fiddlesticks, ma'am!" said Mr. Rogers, buttoning his pea-jacket and turning up its collar. "What you heard was a gun. There is a vessel in distress somewhere, and we shall have my men here in a moment with news of her."

"But there was no sound," objected Mrs. Pope.

"Fog, ma'am — fog; sound don't travel in a fog, and ships oughtn't to. There has been a nasty bank of it to the south'ard ever since morning, and you may bet that's the mischief."

He went into the hall for his lantern, brought it back, lit it, and carried it out to the front door.

"Whe — ew!" he whistled, as he opened the door and stood, with lantern lifted high, staring into the night.

The guests behind him wondered; for all was quiet outside — too quiet, to ears accustomed to the wind which forever sings across the islands, even on summer days, mingling its whispers and soft murmurings with the hum of the distant tide-races. But while they wondered, Mr. Rogers's figure grew vague and amorphous in a cloud of fog that drifted past him into the passage. The light in his lantern had turned to a weak flame of yellow, and seemed on the point of dying out.

"Ahoy, there! Is that Mr. Rogers?" called a thin voice out of the night.

"Ahoy! Mr. Rogers, it is. What's wrong?"

"Thank God I've found you!" The voice sounded suddenly quite close at hand, and a man blundered against the doorstep.

"Eh?" — the others saw Mr. Rogers give back in astonishment — "The Lord Proprietor?"

"Safe and sound, too, by Heaven's mercy," said the Lord Proprietor, plucking off his peaked cap and shaking the water from it. He carried a lantern, and his jacket and loose trousers of yellow oilskin shone with the wet like a suit of mail. "All the way from Inniscaw I've come, in the gig. Peter Hicks and old Abe pulled me, and the Lord knows where we made land or what has become of them. Man, there's a vessel ashore — a liner, they say! Didn't you hear the gun a minute since?"

"Yes, yes; but where is she?"

"That's more than I know. Somewhere among the Off Islands; on the Terrier, maybe, or the Hell-meadows. All I can tell you is that old Abe brought the news to the Priory, almost three hours ago: his son-in-law, young Ashbran, had seen her in a lift of the fog — a powerful steamship with two funnels and a broad white band upon each. She hadn't struck when he saw her; but she was nosing into an infernal mess of rocks, and the light closing down fast. I didn't see Ashbran himself; Abe believed he had put across to warn your men. But as the old man couldn't swear to it I told him to get out the gig and fetch Peter Hicks, and so we started."

"I'm wondering why those men of mine haven't brought me warning. Ashbran can't have reached them."

"He started late, belike, and lost his way in the fog; or it's even possible — though you won't believe it — that your men started to find you and have lost themselves. My good sir, you never knew such a fog!"

"Yet I left word with the chief boatman," mused Mr. Rogers. "He knows perfectly well where I am."

"Does he?" said the Lord Proprietor. "Then it's more than I do. What house is this?"

"Why, Fossell's. Good Lord! didn't you know?"

"My dear Sir Cæsar — " Mr. Fossel stepped forward solicitously.

"Eh? So it is. . . . Good evening, Mr. Fossell! That picture of the Waterloo Banquet seemed familiar, somehow." The Lord Proprietor nodded towards a framed engraving on the wall. "Yes, to be sure — and Landseer's 'Twa Dogs.' But this is worse than the Arabian Nights! We must have missed the harbour by miles!"

"You came ashore at Cam Point, most probably," Mr. Fossell suggested. "The tide sets that way, and from Cam Point it is but a step."

"A step, is it? Man, I've been wandering in blank darkness for a full hour. Twice I've found myself on the edge of a cliff. I've followed walls only to be led into open fields. I've struck across open fields, only to tumble against troughs, midden heaps, pig-styes. I walked straight up against this house, supposing myself somewhere near the batteries on Garrison Hill — though how I had managed to miss the town was more than I could explain."

"The wonder is you ever fetched across from Inniscaw."

"It's my belief we had never done it, but for the tide. The night was black as your hat when we started, but fairly clear. We kept sight of the lamp on the pier-head until halfway across. Then the fog came down; and then— !"

"Well, it's good hard causeway between this and St. Hugh's," said Mr. Rogers. "We can't miss it. Afterwards. . . . However, you'll step along with me to the Guard-house, Sir Cæsar, and as soon as the weather lifts at all one of my men shall put you back to Inniscaw."

"On the contrary, my good sir, I go with you."

Mr. Rogers looked at him, as he buttoned up his pea-jacket.

"We won't argue it here," he said. "You don't guess what it means, though, searching for a wreck among the Off Islands on a night like this. Not to mention that there's a sea running. . . ."

And yet, apart from the fog, there was nothing in the weather to suggest shipwreck and horrors. For a fortnight the Islands had lain steeped in the sunshine of Indian summer; a fortnight of still starry nights and days almost without a cloud. As a rule, such weather breaks up in a gale, of which the glass gives timely warning. But the mercury in Mr. Fossell's barometer indicated no depression — or the merest trifle. The drenched night air was warm: to Miss Gabriel, inhaling it in the passage by the drawing-room door, it seemed to be laden with the scents of summer, and Miss Gabriel had not lived all her life in Garland Town without learning the subtle aromas of the wind, to distinguish those that were harmless or beneficent from those that warned, those that threatened, those that were morose, savage, malignant, those that piped a note of madness and meant a hurricane. Nor did the fog in itself appear to her very formidable. To be sure, she had never known a thicker one; but the Lord Proprietor (saving his presence) had probably exaggerated its terror. He was — let this excuse be made for him — a landsman, comparatively new to the Islands.

Probably Mr. Fossell and Mr. Pope and the Vicar took the same view. The news of the wreck had excited them, and they were offering to accompany Sir Cæsar and Mr. Rogers to St. Hugh's Town, on the chance of some information.

"And we had best go with them, my dear," suggested Miss Gabriel to Mrs. Pope. (Their houses stood side by side and contiguous, on a gentle rise at the foot of Garrison Hill, where the peninsular of New Town broadens out and New Town itself melts into St. Hugh's.)

Mrs. Fossel begged them to wait and keep her company until the gentlemen returned. "It is impossible," she urged as an inducement, "that Selina can go on making this noise forever."

But Miss Gabriel had taken her decision, and from a decision Miss Gabriel was not easily turned.

"My dear," said she, reaching for her cloak, "the gentlemen may not return until goodness knows when, and I have a prejudice against late hours."

They started in a body. The fog, to be sure, was a deal worse than ever Miss Gabriel could have credited. Still, the gentlemen using their lanterns and tapping to right and left with their sticks, they found the hard causeway, and blundered along it towards St. Hugh's, the ladies with their shawls drawn over their heads and their heads held down against the drifting wall of moisture.

They had made their way thus for about four hundred yards — that is to say, about a third of the length of the causeway — when suddenly the fog ahead of them became luminous, and they perceived torches waving.

"Mr. Rogers! Is that Mr. Rogers?" called a voice.

"Ay, ay, men!" Mr. Rogers hailed in answer, recognising his coastguard. "I am coming — fast as I can," he added, having at that moment run into a wall.

"A wreck, sir!"

"Ay! Where is it?"

"Somewhere beyond St. Ann's, sir, as we make it — out towards the Monk. There was a gun fired, and Dick, here, thinks as he saw the lighthouse send up a signal; but lights there's none that the rest of us can make out—"

"Hark!"

Again the fog shook with the concussion of a gun.

"Due west, as I make it out," said Mr. Rogers. "Are the boats ready?"

"Aye, sir; the jolly-boat manned and off, and the gig launched and lying by the slip."

"Then run, men!"

"Why, they've left us!" gasped Mrs. Pope, as the glare of the torches melted into the fog.

"It doesn't matter," Miss Gabriel assured her bravely. "We have only to keep straight on."

CHAPTER V

THE S.S. MILO

Major Vigoureux fell asleep almost as soon as his head touched the pillow. He owed this habit originally to a clear conscience, and although (as the reader knows) his conscience was no longer quite clear, the habit had not forsaken him.

He dreamed that he was presenting himself at Mr. Fossell's bank, and giving Mr. Fossell across the counter a number of plausible reasons why his pay should be handed to him as usual. He knew all the while that his arguments were sophistical and radically unsound; but he trusted that he was making them cogent. (Why is it that in dreams we feel no remorse for our sins, but only a terror lest we be found out? I cannot tell; but the best men and women of my acquaintance agree that it is so.) Mr. Fossell preserved an impassive, inscrutable face; but every time the Commandant ventured a new argument Mr. Fossell's high, bald head twinkled and suddenly changed colour like a chameleon. It was green, it was violet, it was bathed in a soft roseate glow like an Alpine peak at sunset; and still while he argued the Commandant was forced to dodge his body about lest Mr. Fossell should catch sight of a mirror fixed in the opposite wall, and perceive how strangely his scalp was behaving. Finally, Mr. Fossell turned as if convinced, walked away to an inner room, and came back bearing a bag of money, round and distended — so tightly distended, indeed, that the Commandant called out to him to be careful of the contents. But the cry came a moment too late; for the bag, as it touched the counter, exploded with a dull report, collapsed, and flattened itself out into a playing-card — the queen of hearts!

At this point the Commandant excusably found himself awake, and sat up blinking at Sergeant Archelaus, who stood in a haze of fog by his bedside with a lighted candle.

"You heard it?" asked Sergeant Archelaus.

"Heard it?" echoed the Commandant, trembling, not yet in full possession of his senses. "Of course, I heard it. The Bank — ." Here he checked himself and rubbed his eyes.

"You're dreaming; that's what's the matter with you," said Sergeant Archelaus, using the familiarity of an old servant. "There's a ship on the rocks."

"A ship? Where?"

The Sergeant, candle in hand, stepped to the casement, which the Commandant, following his custom, had opened a little way before getting into bed.

"Lord knows where she be by this time, if St. Ann's pilots ha'n't found her. The gun sounded from west'ard, down by the Monk."

"Fog, is it?" asked the Commandant, staring about him and remembering.

"Fog it is," answered Sergeant Archelaus, and added, "Poor souls!"

"Thick?" By this time the Commandant had flung back the bed-clothes and was thrusting his feet into his worn slippers.

"I never seen a thicker in my born days."

"If we had a gun—"

"Ah — if," agreed Sergeant Archelaus, curtly, and turning, let his voice rise in a sudden passion. "Why did I wake ye? Set it down to habit. I've known the time when the sound of a gun would have fetched forty men out of the Barracks to save life or to take it; and a gun within thirty seconds to alarm all the Islands. But we! What's the use of us?"

"Get on your coat," said the Commandant, sharply, putting on his trousers. "Get on your coat and run to the bell — that is, if Treacher—"

But at this moment the muffled note of a bell began to sound through the fog, vindicating Treacher's vigilance. Treacher, however, was not the ringer. The Commandant had scarcely slipped on his fatigue jacket, and begun to search in the wardrobe for his overcoat, when Treacher's voice sounded up the staircase, demanding to know if the garrison was awake.

"Awake?" called back Archelaus. "Of course we be, and coming before you can sound th' alarm. Reach down the bugle, man — from the rock behind th' door, there — and sound it."

Treacher sounded. He was out of breath, and the two high notes quavered broken-windedly; but the Commandant's chest swelled with something of old pride. The alarm would reach the town, and the town would know that the garrison had not been caught napping. He snatched at the candle from the candlestick in Sergeant Archelaus' hand and rammed it into the socket of a horn lantern he had unhooked from the cupboard.

"Come along, men! Keep sounding, Treacher — keep sounding!"

Even so he had called once — a many years ago — in the trenches under the Redan. Treacher sounded obediently, and down the hill all three staggered — past the garrison gates, with a call to Mrs. Treacher to pull for all she was worth — and still forward among the ruts and loose stones, all so familiar that relying on tread alone (as in fact they did) they could not miss their way. Below them, along the quay, and on the causeway at the head of it — voices were calling and lights moving; but the fog reduced the shouts to a twitter, as of birds, and the torches and lantern to mere glow-worm sparks. The coastguards were embarking and the Lord Proprietor, just arrived upon the scene, was running about — as Sergeant Archelaus put it afterwards, "like a paper man in a cyclone" — calling out the names of volunteers for the lifeboat.

If Sergeant Archelaus ever afterwards spoke disparagingly of the Lord Proprietor's activities that night, something may be forgiven him; as something may be forgiven the Lord Proprietor — for on such occasions men blurt out what rises to their lips.

The fog had found its way into Treacher's bugle before our three heroes reached the quay; but he continued to blow his best; and there, at the end of the causeway, Sir Cæsar ran into them — ran straight into the Commandant, almost knocking out his breath — calling, as he ran, for someone to take bow oar in the lifeboat.

"Will I do?" asked Sergeant Archelaus, coolly, as became a soldier.

"You?" The Lord Proprietor thrust his torch close. "Oh, get out of my way — this is work tonight, work for men! And you" — catching sight of the Commandant — "how much do you think you are helping us with this tom-fool noise?"

The Commandant drew himself erect, but before he could answer, the Lord Proprietor had gone his way, waving his torch and still shouting for someone to man the bow thwart.

There was a slow pause.

"Can you get to our boat, Archelaus?" asked the Commandant. The two sergeants heard his voice drag on the question. They could not see his face.

"She's afloat, sir," answered Sergeant Archelaus.

"Find the frap then, and pull her in."

"Is it our boat you're meaning, sir?" asked Archelaus, hesitating.

"Certainly."

"There's a certain amount of sea running, sir, out beyond the point."

"I observed as much this evening."

"Very good, sir." Something in the Commandant's voice forbade further argument.

They were afloat almost as soon as the coastguard, and a full five minutes before the life-boat. Sergeant Archelaus pulled stroke, and Sergeant Treacher bow. The Commandant steered, his lantern and pocket compass beside him in the stern sheets.

The boat — she had once been a yacht's cutter — measured sixteen feet over all. She was fitted with a small centre-plate, and carried a lug sail (but this they left behind; it was in store, and would have been worse than useless). They pulled out into a fog so thick that only by intervals could the Commandant catch sight of Sergeant Treacher's face, and Sergeant Treacher's eyebrows and sandy moustache glistering with beads of mist.

They had left the pier but a short two hundred strokes behind them when the little tug belonging to the Islands came panting out of the harbour with the lifeboat in tow, and passed on, blowing her whistle, to overtake and pick up the coastguard galley. So unexpectedly her lights sprang upon them, and so close astern that Treacher, with a sharp cry of warning — for the Commandant's gaze was fastened forward — had barely time to jerk the boat's head round and avoid being cut down. Then, dropping his paddle, he made a grab at the painter and flung it, calling out to the lifeboat's crew to catch and make fast. But either he was a moment too late in flinging, or the lifeboatmen, themselves bawling instructions to the tug's crew, were preoccupied and did not hear. The rope struck against something — the lifeboat's gunwale doubtless — but no one caught it, and next moment the tug had slipped away into darkness and into a silence which swallowed up the shouts and the throb of her engines as though she had dropped into a pit.

"Darn your skin, Sam Treacher!" swore Sergeant Archelaus. "There goes a couple of hours' pulling you might have saved us!"

"Then why couldn't you have given warning?" retorted Treacher. "Pretty pair of eyes you keep in that old head of yours!"

"Be quiet, you two!" the Commandant ordered. "They'd have caught the painter if they wanted us."

He fell silent, bending his head to study the compass in the lantern's ray. "Not wanted" — "not wanted" — the paddles took up the burden and beat it into a sort of tune to the creak of the thole-pins. As a young officer he had started with high notions of duty; nor, looking back on the wasted years could he tax himself that he had ever declined its call; only the call which in youth had always carried a promise with it, definitely clear and shining, of enterprise and reward, of adventure, achievement, fame, had sunk by degrees to a dull repetition calling him from sleep to perform the spiritless daily round. He did not sigh that the definite vision had faded; it happened so, may be, to most men, though not to all. To most men, it might be, their fate played the crimp; they followed the marsh-fires out into just such a blind waste as this through which he and his men were groping — darkness above and below; darkness before, behind, to right, to left; darkness of birth, of death, and only the palpable fog between. He did not sigh for this. What irked him was the thought that while he had followed the mill-round of duty, strength had been ebbing away and had left him useless.

Yes, there lay the sting. Twenty years ago how like a schoolboy he would have dashed into this fog, careless of consequence, eager only to find where men needed his help! He might have found, or missed; but twenty years ago men would have hailed his will to help. Now he was useless, negligible. In an ordinary way these neighbours of his might disguise their knowledge, through politeness or pity; but at a crisis like this the truth came out. The Lord Proprietor had treated him as a pantaloon, and these lifeboatmen — so little they valued him — could not be at the pains of catching a rope.

He steered, as nearly as he could calculate, west-by-south, allowing at a guess for the set of the tide. The wall of fog, which let pass no true sound, itself seemed full of voices — hissing of spent waves, sucking of water under weed-covered ledges, little puffs and moanings of the wind. He had reckoned that he was bending around shore to the south of the roadstead, heading gradually for St. Lide's Sound and giving the rocks on his port hand a wide berth; when of a sudden Archelaus called out, and he spied a grey line of breaking water — luckily the sea was full of briming tonight — at the base of the fog, quite close at hand. It scared them so that they headed off almost at right angles. This adventure not only proved his reckoning to be wrong, but complicated it hopelessly.

They were in open water again, still making — or at any rate the boat so pointed — west-by-south. The short scare had shaken him out of his brooding thoughts. He saw now, minute after minute, but the sea beyond the edge of the boat's gunwale, heaving up and sliding astern as it caught the shine of the lantern. The lantern shone also against the knees of Archelaus, and lit up the checkboard pattern of the eleemosynary trousers. It was a provocative pattern, but the Commandant heeded it not. . . .

He looked up from Sergeant Archelaus' knees to Sergeant Archelaus' face, and past it to the face of Sergeant Treacher, now a little more distinct. The two men had been pulling for an hour, and the Commandant saw that they were tired — tired and very old. He recognised it at first with a touch of anger. He felt an instant's impulse to curse and bid them row harder. But on the instant came gentle understanding, and restrained him.

"Archelaus," he said, "you are the older; take the tiller here and give me the oar for a spell."

Archelaus was not unwilling. Besides, was it not his commanding officer who gave the order? He relinquished his paddle with a grunt of exhaustion, and the Commandant stood up to take it, laying both hands on it while Archelaus stumbled past to the stern-sheets. . . . And at that moment a miracle befell.

The fog must have been thinning. The Commandant, standing with both hands on the paddle and his face to the bows, saw or felt it part suddenly, and through the parting lights shone and voices sounded, with the heavy throb of a vessel's screw.

Clank! clank! and it was on them, almost before Sergeant Archelaus could let out a cry — the stem, the grey-painted bows of a vast steamship, ghostly, towering up into night. A bell rang. High on the bridge — but the bridge soared into heaven — a pilot's voice called out in the Island tongue. As the great bows glided by, missing the boat by a few yards, the three men stared aloft until they had almost cricked their necks; and aloft there, as Archelaus raised his lantern, the Commandant read the vessel's name — "Milo" — glimmering in tall gilt letters.

Faces looked down from her rail, faces from the shadow of the hurricane' deck; a line of faces and all looking down upon the little Island tug that had fallen alongside and drifted close under the liner's flank, a short way abaft her red port-light. A murmur of talk went with the faces, as it were a stream rippling by, and mingled with the splash of water pouring over-side from the pumps. It sounded cheerfully, and from the voices on board the tug and in the lifeboat and galley towing astern our Commandant gathered that the danger was over. Again Sergeant Treacher hailed and flung a rope; this time the lifeboat's crew caught it and made fast.

"Reub Hicks is aboard," said a voice, naming one of the St. Ann's pilots. "He picked her up not twenty furlongs from Helldeeps after she had missed the Little Meadows by the skin of her teeth."

"How in the name of good Providence she got near enough to miss it, being where she was, is the marvel to me," said another.

"She did, anyway," said the coxswain; "for Reub himself called down the news to me in so many words."

The Commandant gazed up at the gray shadow reaching aloft into darkness. He knew those outer reefs of which the men spoke. A touch of them would have split the plates of this tall fabric like a house of cards. He and Archelaus had witnessed one such wreck, eight years ago; had waited in broad daylight, helpless, resting on their oars, unable to approach within a cable's length of the rocks, upon which in ten minutes a steel-built five-master, of 1,200 tons, had melted to nothing before their eyes — "the rivets," as Archelaus put it, "flying out of her like shirt buttons." But that had happened on one of the outermost reefs, beyond the Off Islands, far down by the Monk Light. How the *Milo*, no matter from what quarter approaching, had threaded her way by the Hell-deeps was to him a mystery of mysteries. She was groping it yet, her engines working dead slow; but the fog during the past hour had sensibly lightened and Reub Hicks held open water between him and the Roads, though he still kept the lead going. At the entrance of the Roads he sent the tug forward to help the steerage, and so brought her in and rounded her up as accurately as though she had been a little schooner of two hundred tons.

As the great anchor dropped, and amid the deafening rattle of its chain in the hawse-pipe, the crew astern cast off and drew their boats alongside, eager to swarm aboard and hear news of the miracle. From his galley Mr. Rogers shouted up to the captain to lower his ladder. He and his chief boatman mounted first, with a little man named Pengelly, a custom's official, who happened to make one of the lifeboat's crew — for the *Milo* had come from foreign, and thus a show was made of complying with the Queen's regulations. But the whole crowd trooped up close at their heels, and with the crowd clambered Sergeant Archelaus and Sergeant Treacher.

The Commandant had given them permission. He would remain below, he said, and look after the boat, awaiting their report.

The crowd passed up and dispersed itself about the deck, congratulating all comers, and excitedly plying them with questions. The Islanders are a child-like race, and from his post at the foot of the deserted accommodation ladder the Commandant could hear them laughing, exclaiming, chattering with the passengers in high-pitched voices.

He stood with his boat-hook, holding on by the grating of the ladder's lowest step, and stared at the gray wall-sides of the liner. Yes, the ship was solid, and yet he could not believe but that she belonged to a dream; so mysteriously, against all chances, was she here, out of the deep and the night.

Someone had lashed a lantern at the head of the ladder. Lifting his eyes to it in the foggy darkness, the Commandant saw a solitary figure standing there in the gangway and looking down on him — a woman.

She lifted a hand as if to enjoin silence, and came swiftly down a step or two in the shadow of the vessel's side.

"You are Major Vigoureux?" she asked in a quick whisper, leaning forward over him.

"At your service, madam," he stammered, taken fairly aback.

"Ah! I am glad of that!" She ran down the remaining steps and set her foot lightly on the boat's gunwale. "You will row me ashore?"

"If you wish it, madam." He was more puzzled than ever. He saw that she wore a dark cloak of fur and was bare-headed. She spoke in a sort of musical whisper. Her face he could not see. "In a minute or two my men—"

"We will not wait for your men," she said, quietly, seating herself in the stern sheets. "They can easily be put ashore — can they not? — in one of the other boats."

From under her fur cloak she reached out an arm — a bare arm with two jewelled bracelets — and took the tiller. "I can steer you to the quay," she said, and leaning forward in the light of Sergeant Archelaus' lantern, she lifted her eyes to the Commandant.

The Commandant pushed off, shipped the paddles into the thole pins, and began to row, as in a dream.

CHAPTER VI

HOW VASHTI CAME TO THE ISLANDS

"You do not remember me, Major Vigoureux?"

The Commandant looked at her, across the lantern's ray. Something in her voice, vibrating like the rich, full note of a bell, touched his memory . . . but only to elude it.

The face that challenged him was not girlish; the face, rather, of a beautiful woman of thirty; its shape a short oval, with a slight squareness at the point of the jaw to balance the broad forehead over which her hair (damp now, but rippled with a natural wave, defying the fog) lay parted in two heavy bands — the brow of a goddess. Her eyes, too, would have become a goddess, though just now they condescended to be merry.

Tall she was, for certain, and commanding. Her cloak hid the lines of her body, whether they were thin or ample; but, where the collar opened, her throat showed like a pillar, carrying her chin upon a truly noble poise. It was inconceivable (the Commandant said to himself) that he had met this woman before and forgotten her.

He came back to her eyes. They challenged him fearlessly. He could not have described their colour; but he saw amusement lurking deep in their glooms while she waited.

"I am sorry. It is unpardonable in me, of course—"

"And I, on the contrary, am glad," she interrupted, with a laugh that reminded him of the liquid chuckle in a thrush's song, or of water swirling down a deep pool; "for it tells me I have grown out of recognition, and that is just what I wanted."

This puzzled him, and he frowned a little.

"You know the Islands?" he asked. "This is not your first visit?"

"You shall judge if in this darkness I steer you straight for St. Lide's Quay; and I take you to witness — look over your shoulder — there is no lamp on the quay-head to guide me, or at least none visible." She laughed again, but on the instant grew serious. "Yes," she added, "I can find my way among the Islands, I thank God." And this puzzled him yet more.

"You know the Islands; you are glad to return to them?"

She nodded.

"Yet you do not wish to be recognised?"

She nodded again. "I came, you see, sooner than I intended. The *Milo* was clean out of her course."

"That goes without saying," said he, gravely.

"She was bound for Plymouth. So, you see, this little misadventure has shortened my journey by days." She paused. "No; I ought not to speak of it flippantly. I shall be very thankful in my prayers tonight . . . all those women and children. . . ."

Again she paused.

"Is my hand trembling?" she asked, lifting it and laying it again on the tiller, where it rested firm as a rock. Only the jewels quivered on her rings and bracelets, and their beauty, arresting the Commandant's gaze, held him silent.

"To be frank with you," she went on, "I left the ship in a hurry, because I was afraid of being thanked. I don't like publicity — much; and just now it would have spoiled everything." This explanation enlightened the Commandant not at all. "Besides," she added with a practical air, "I left a note with my maid, to be given to the captain; so he won't imagine that I've tumbled overboard; and she can send my boxes ashore tomorrow, if you will be kind enough to fetch them before the *Milo* weighs."

"But, meanwhile?" he hazarded.

"Oh, meanwhile, I must manage somehow for the night. I slipped a few things into my hand-bag here." She drew her fur cloak a little aside, and displayed it — a small satchel hanging from her waist by a silver chain. The Commandant had a glimpse at the same moment of a skirt of rose-coloured silk, brocaded in a pattern of silver.

"And when we land," he asked, "where am I to take you?"

"I am in your hands."

He stared at her, dismayed. "But you have friends?"

"None who would remember me; not a soul, at least, in St. Lide's."

"There is the Plume of Feathers Inn, to be sure—"

"If you recommend it," she said, demurely, as he hesitated.

He almost lost his temper. "Recommend it? Of course I don't."

"Well, from what I remember of the Plume of Feathers — unless it has altered—"

"Wouldn't it be wiser to turn back?" he suggested, desperately, staring into the fog, in which the lights of the *Milo* had long since disappeared.

"What? When we have this moment opened the quay-light? There! . . . didn't I promise you that I knew my way among the Islands?"

In the basin of the harbour the fog lay thicker than in the roads, and they had scarcely made sure that this was indeed the quay-light before their boat grated against the landing-steps of the quay itself. The Commandant, after he had shipped his oars and checked the way on her, pressing both hands against the dripping wall, put up one of them and passed the back of it slowly across his forehead. He was considering; and, while he considered, his companion stepped lightly ashore. "Forgive me," he pleaded, recollecting himself. "At least, I should have offered you my hand."

"Thank you, I did not need it."

"But listen, please," he protested, scrambling out upon the steps, painter in hand, and groping for a ring-bolt. "You cannot possibly stay the night at the Plume of Feathers—"

He heard her laugh, as he stooped, having found the ring, to make fast the rope.

"Commandant, have you ever travelled across Wyoming — in winter, in a waggon? Very well, then; I have."

"Surely not in the clothes you are wearing?" The Commandant, as any one in the Council of Twelve could tell you, was no debater; yet sometimes he had been known to triumph even in debate, by sheer simplicity. "The only course that I can see," he continued, "is to seek some private house, and throw ourselves upon the — er —"

"Front door?" she suggested, mischievously.

" — hospitality — upon the hospitality of the inmates. To them, of course, I can explain the situation—"

"Can you?"

The Commandant stood for a moment peering at her, and rubbing the back of his head — a trick of his in perplexity. "Upon my word, now you come to mention it," he confessed, "I don't know that I can."

"Whom shall we try first? Miss Gabriel?" ("Now, how in the world," wondered the Commandant, "does she know anything of Miss Gabriel?") "Very well; we go together to Alma Cottage — she still lives at Alma Cottage? — and knock. The hour is two in the morning, or thereabouts. Miss Gabriel, overcoming her first fear of robbery or murder, will parley with us from her bedroom window. To her you introduce me, by the light of your lantern; a strange female in an evening frock; a female grossly overladen with jewels (that, I think, would be Miss Gabriel's way of putting it), but without a portmanteau."

"We might try the Popes, next door," suggested the Commandant flinching. "Mr. Pope is a man of the world."

"Is he?" she asked, after a pause, in which he felt that she struggled with some inward mirth. "But we cannot so describe Mrs. Pope, can we? Also we cannot knock up Mr. and Mrs. Pope without disturbing Miss Gabriel next door."

"Nor, for that matter, can we knock up Miss Gabriel without disturbing Mr. and Mrs. Pope."

"Quite so; we may reckon that all three will be listening. Therefore, when Mr. Pope or Miss Gabriel (as the case may be) begins by demanding my name — which, by an oversight, you have forgotten to ask—"

"Pardon me," said the Commandant, simply, "I did not forget. I waited, supposing that if you wished me to know it, you would tell me."

"Ah!" she drew close to him, with a happy exclamation. "Then I was not mistaken: You are the man I have counted to find. . . . And you are a brave man, too. But we will not push bravery too far and disturb Miss Gabriel."

"If you can suggest a better plan—"

"A far better plan. I suggest that you offer me a room tonight at the garrison."

"My dear madam!" the Commandant gasped.

"It will be far better in every way," she went on composedly; "that is, if you are willing. To begin with, you have rooms and to spare. Next, there will be no bother in introducing me, except to Mrs. Treacher."

"Ah, to be sure, there is Mrs. Treacher!" the Commandant murmured. "But, madam, all the rooms in the Castle are unfurnished, ruinous, and have been ruinous for fifty years. The Treachers occupy the only two in which it were possible to swing a cat."

"Then we must borrow Mrs. Treacher and take her along to the Barracks for chaperon. You may leave it to me to persuade her."

Without waiting for his answer she ran lightly up the steps, the heels of her rose-coloured satin shoes twinkling in the light of the Commandant's lantern as he blundered after her.

The pavement of the quay had not been laid for satin shoes. Much traffic had worn the surface into depressions, and these depressions were fast collecting water from the drenched air. But although the fog lay almost as thick here as at the foot of the steps, she picked her way among these pitfalls, avoiding them as though by instinct. Beyond the quay came a cobbled causeway; and beyond the causeway a narrow street wound up towards the garrison gate. Past rains, pouring down the hill, had worn a deep rut along this street, ploughing it here and there to the native rock, zig-zagging from centre to side of the roadway and back again obedient to the trend of the slope. But over the causeway, and up the channelled street she found her footing with the same confidence, steering far more cleverly than the Commandant, who followed as in a dream, amazed, oppressed with forebodings. It was all very well for her to talk lightly of persuading Mrs. Treacher. If she could, why then she must be possessed of a secret as yet unrevealed to Mrs. Treacher's husband after thirty-odd years of married life. The Commandant, too, knew something of Mrs. Treacher . . . an obstinate woman, not to say pig-headed.

Was she a witch — this stranger in silk and jewels who walked in darkness so confidently up the tortuous unpaved street? — this apparition who, coming out of the seas and the dumb fog, talked of the Islands and the Islanders as though she had known them all her life?

As if to prove she was a witch, she paused before the very cottage which once already tonight had given pause to his steps and to his thoughts. The fog had been thinning little by little as they mounted the hill, and at a few paces' distance he recognized the closed door, daubed over with that same staring paint which your true Islander uses for choice upon his boat.

"You remember this door?" she asked, pointing to it as he overtook her.

Witch she might be, but why should he give away to her this innocent small secret?

"Of course I remember it," he answered; "passing it as I do, half-a-dozen times a day."

"Yes," she said, almost as if speaking to herself; but her voice, for the first time since their meeting, seemed to be touched with a faint shade of dejection. "Naturally you would not remember it for any other reason."

He was silent.

"Yet," she went on, "you really ought to remember that door, Major Vigoureux, if only for old sake's sake; for it was, I believe, the first you entered when you came to the Islands. That was in the year—"

"Never mind the year," interrupted the Commandant, hastily. "I remember it well. I almost never pass the door without remembering it."

"Ah!" she cried, putting her jewelled hands together, and the Commandant took it for an exclamation of triumph at her cleverness. "But other tenants have the house. The man who was master of it is dead."

"You know everything, it seems to me. Yes; he was a widower, and late that evening at the fishing. It was an evening when he should not have been late; for the door stood open for him, and his daughters — he had two daughters — sat expecting him. It was the open door that drew me to ask my way." Here he paused.

"Go on, please."

"One of the girls was to leave the Islands next morning for the mainland, which she had never seen. She told me this. And she sat reading aloud to her sister, there by the fire."

"Go on."

"That is all. Yes, that is all — except that the book was Shakespeare, and the girl — " He paused again, staring at her between sudden enlightenment and stark incredulity. "You — you don't mean to tell me *you* were that girl!"

She nodded; and as, forgetting politeness, he held the lantern close to her face, he saw two large tears brim up, tremble, and hang for a second before they fell.

"You?" he murmured.

She nodded again. "I am Vashti — Vazzy Cara, they called me, Philip Cara's daughter. I daresay, though, you never heard my name? No, there is no reason why you should. And my sister, Ruth—"

"She is married and lives on Saaron Island. But you know this, of course? You who seem to know everything about us."

"My sister writes me all the news. . . . So now," she added smiling, "it is all explained, and there is no mystery about me after all. Are you so very much disappointed?"

But the Commandant continued to stare. No mystery? That the fisherman's daughter with the Island lilt in her voice — well he recalled it! — should have turned into this apparition of furs and jewels? . . . And yet the metamorphosis lay not in the furs and jewels, but in her careless air of command, of reliance upon her power, beauty, charm — whatever her woman's secret might be; an air of one accustomed to move in courts, maybe, or to control great audiences, or to live habitually with lofty thoughts; an air of one, above all, sure of herself. The poor Commandant had lived the better part of his life in exile, but by instinct of breeding he recognised this air at once. Vashti, however, seemed to mistake his astonishment, for she frowned.

"Well?" she asked, a trifle impatiently.

"Your sister never told us," he stammered. "At least — that is to say—"

"Do you suppose she was ashamed of me?"

"Ashamed?" he echoed, for indeed no such thought had occurred to him. If ever a man could have taken *honi soit qui mal y pense* for his motto, it was our Commandant.

"Ah, to be sure!" she said slowly, but less in indignation (it seemed) than in disappointment with him. "Naturally that would be the explanation to occur to you, living so long in such a place."

She turned on her heel, half contemptuously, and resumed her way, walking with a yet quicker step than before. The Commandant, aware that he had offended, but not in the least understanding how, toiled after her up the steep incline to the garrison gate.

They reached the door of the Barracks. To his surprise it was standing open, and from behind the ragged blind of his sitting-room — to the left of the entrance hall — a light shone feebly out upon the fog. He could not remember that he had lit the lamp there, nor that he had left the front door open.

Vashti paused upon the doorstep and turned to him:

"My good sir," she said curtly, "run and fetch Mrs. Treacher to me, for goodness' sake."

He hesitated, on the point of stepping past her to open the door of the lighted room. Her manner forbade him, and he stood still, there by the doorstep, gazing after her a moment as she disappeared into the dark hall. Then, as he heard the door latch rattle gently, he turned to hurry in search of Mrs. Treacher.

He had taken but a dozen steps, however, when her light foot-fall sounded again close behind him. She, too, had turned and was following him almost at a run.

"Why didn't you tell me?" she gasped.

He swung up his lantern. Her eyes were wide with a kind of horror; and yet she seemed to be laughing, or ready to laugh.

"Tell you?" he echoed.

"Oh, but it was unkind!"

"But — but, excuse me — what on earth—"

"Why, that you were entertaining ladies!"

"Ladies!"

She nodded, still round-eyed, reproachful. "Two of them — sitting on your sofa! And, I think — I rather think — one of them is Miss Gabriel!"

CHAPTER VII

TRIBULATIONS OF MRS. POPE AND MISS GABRIEL

"We have only to keep straight on," said Miss Gabriel.

"Ye-es," said Mrs. Pope, less hardily. "I really think the gentlemen might have waited for us."

"For aught they know," said Miss Gabriel, "it's a matter of life and death. And we cannot be more than two hundred yards from our own gates."

"In my opinion," persisted Mrs. Pope, who was apt to turn peevish when frightened, "a man's first duty is to look after his own."

"Is it?" snapped Miss Gabriel, herself no coward. "Well, you must argue that out with Mr. Pope, if you haven't made up your minds about it by this time. For my part, I never wanted a man to look after me, I thank the Lord."

"It would have been more gallant, and that you must allow." Mrs. Pope stuck to her point (which is a capital thing to do in a fog), but only to let it go abruptly a moment later. "Besides," she added, "my new cap is no better than a pulp already. I can feel it. Sopping isn't the word."

"Fiddlestick!" said Miss Gabriel. "You and your cap!" She, herself, was not frightened, only a little nervous. "If you ask me, it's better you were thinking of those poor souls out on the rocks yonder. Little enough they'll be thinking, just now, of such things as caps!"

"Of course," hazarded Mrs. Pope, after they had groped their way forward for twenty paces or so, "if you are quite certain where we are—"

"We are among the Islands," said Miss Gabriel, tartly, feeling the roadway with the edge of her shoe, for her sole had just encountered turf; "and this is one. My dear Charlotte, if you could refrain from bumping into me at the precise moment when I am standing on one leg—"

"How can I help it, in this darkness?" whimpered Mrs. Pope. "Besides" — with sudden spirit — "if you want to stand on one leg, I shouldn't have thought this the time or the place."

"T'cht!" said Miss Gabriel, striding forward with gathering confidence; but at the seventh stride or so a sharp exclamation escaped her, as she stood groping with both hands into the night.

"What's the matter?"

"It's a wall, I think. . . . I had almost run against it. . . . Yes, this must be the wall of Buttershall's garden."

"Are you sure?"

"Certain. We have been bearing away to the right; people always do in a fog."

"Then if this really is Buttershall's garden — and I only hope and trust you are not mistaken — we can bear away from it to the left, on purpose, and then as likely as not we shall find ourselves going straight," reasoned Mrs. Pope, lucidly.

"My dear Charlotte" — Miss Gabriel was within an ace of calling her a fool — "if this is Buttershall's garden—"

"But a moment ago you were sure of it!"

"And so I am. Very well then; since this is Buttershall's garden, we have only to hold on by the wall and go forward, and that will take us—"

But here the wall ended, and the sentence with it.

"Ai-ee!"

"Are you hurt? . . . I said," asserted Mrs. Pope, desperately, and with conviction, "that one of us would break a limb before we finished."

"It seems to be — yes, it certainly is — a pump." Miss Gabriel's voice had begun to shake by this time, but she steadied it. "For the moment I — I half thought it might be a man."

"I would to heaven it were!" said Mrs. Pope, fervently.

"My dear Charlotte!"

"My dear Elizabeth, I mean it. And, what's more, I wouldn't care who he was. A pump? What earthly use is a pump? It must be Mumford's then, if it is a pump."

"It can't be."

"Why not?"

"For the simple reason that Mumford's is on the other side of the road."

"Then we *are* on the other side of the road, as I have been maintaining all along."

"Would you mind walking round it? . . . Yes, you are right. It is Mumford's pump, for I have just bruised my wrist against the handle. Can you find the trough?"

"The astonishing thing to me," announced Mrs. Pope, groping her way with trepidation, "is that nobody shows a light. I don't like to call people unfeeling; but really, with folks in distress out at sea, and the guns firing, I wouldn't have believed such callousness."

They made the circuit of Mumford's pump, and assured themselves — for what the knowledge was worth — that it really was a pump, and Mumford's. But this cost them dear, for at the end of the circuit, or rather of a circuit and a half, they had lost all sense of their compass bearings.

"And after all," Mrs. Pope began afresh, her mind working sympathetically in a circle, "I don't understand what Mumford's pump is doing on the wrong side of the road."

"Don't be a ninny, Charlotte! Of course, it's not on the wrong side of the road."

"But you said it was." (Pause.) "You really did say so, Elizabeth, for I remember it distinctly." (Another pause, and a sigh.) "For my part, I never pretended to have what they call the bump of locality."

The poor lady prattled on, more and more querulously, and to the increasing exasperation of Miss Gabriel, who on the whole believed that they were making for home, yet could not shake off a haunting suspicion that they were moving in a direction precisely opposite. Moreover, the behaviour of Mumford's pump troubled her more than she cared to confess, even to herself. It stood on the right of the road as you went towards St. Hugh's; but they had encountered it upon the left. Therefore, either they had been walking off the road, though in the right direction, or — terrible thought! — somewhere or somehow they had turned right about-face, and were walking away from St. Hugh's. . . .

As a matter of fact, they were bending away from the road in a line which would lead them past the rear of their own back gardens. Their feet no longer trod the causeway. They were on turf, and, so far as they could feel it in the darkness, the turf seemed to be mounting in a fairly stiff slope. Miss Gabriel stooped to feel the grass with the palm of her hand, and just at that moment her ears caught the faint note of a bell, some way ahead.

She stood erect, with a little cry of dismay.

"That settles it. We have turned round!"

"Why, what makes you think so?"

"Listen to that bell! Can't you hear it?"

"Of course, I hear it?" Mrs. Pope apparently was nettled by the question. "But I don't see—"

"The church bell — we are walking straight towards Old Town."

"It don't sound to me like the church bell."

"That's because of the fog. Nothing sounds natural in a fog. . . . The Vicar is having it rung to alarm the people in Old Town. I heard him say this very night that it used to be the custom when a wreck went ashore. . . . Besides, what other bell could it be? There is no other bell."

Mrs. Pope was silent, though unconvinced. She did not suggest the garrison bell, for even to her scattered intelligence it was a thing incredible that they should at this moment be rounding the slope of Garrison Hill, at the back of St. Hugh's.

"Anything might happen in a fog like this; and if I don't wake up to find myself over the cliffs, it's no thanks" — bitterly — "to them we might have relied on. But I don't believe it's the church bell, not if you went on your bended knees."

"Then, what do you say to this?" announced Miss Gabriel, triumphantly.

Mrs. Pope would reserve her opinion until she saw what Miss Gabriel had hold of.

"Railings," said Miss Gabriel. "We are at the corner of Church Lane, and here's the railing close alongside of us. Now we have only to keep by the railing and feel our way — if you'll follow me — and we must find the churchyard gate. The man ringing the bell will certainly have a lantern, and will take us home."

"I don't fancy churchyards at this time of night," said Mrs. Pope; "and what's more, I never did."

"You must make up your mind to one, then; that is, unless you prefer to wait here till morning."

They advanced, feeling their way by the rails, Mrs. Pope close behind Miss Gabriel's heels. The bell continued tolling, not far away; yet somehow after three minute's progress they appeared to be no nearer to it.

"Church Lane was never so long as all this," asserted Mrs. Pope, coming to a desperate halt; "and you needn't try to persuade me."

"It does seem a long way," Miss Gabriel conceded; "but no doubt the fog magnifies things."

"You had the same tale just now, about the church bell. For my part, I don't believe in your church bell, and — listen!"

"Eh?"

"It has stopped ringing!"

So it had. It was too much, perhaps, to say that Miss Gabriel's blood ran cold, there in the darkness, as Mrs. Pope clutched and clung to her; but certainly her heart sunk.

"All the better," she said, bravely, clenching her jaw that her teeth might not be heard to chatter. "Whoever was ringing the bell will be returning this way presently, and we can ask his help."

But here inspiration came to Mrs. Pope.

"It's my belief," she said, "we are not in Church Lane at all, but in the churchyard; and these rails don't belong to Church Lane, but to old Bonaday's grave."

"My dear Charlotte! When we've been following them for at least two hundred yards!"

"My dear Elizabeth, that's just it. We've been following round and round them, and at this rate there's no reason why ever we should stop, in this world."

"You don't say. . . . But, after all, there's an easy way of proving if you are right. You walk to the left, feeling round them, and I'll walk to the right, and then, if it really is Bonaday's grave, we shall meet."

"Oh, but I couldn't! Elizabeth, if you leave me — if once I lose hold of you — I shall die next moment."

"Then there's only one thing to be done. We must stay here and cry out at the top of our voices, and both together."

"Yes, yes. . . . Why didn't we think of it before?"

"For," argued Miss Gabriel, "a bell doesn't ring of itself; and if we can hear the bell, very likely the man who was ringing it can hear us."

"Will you begin, Elizabeth? I declare to you my whole cage of teeth is loose—"

"Help!" called Miss Gabriel. Her voice, despite herself, quavered a little at first. "Help! Help!"

"Help — help — help!" chirupped Mrs. Pope, much as an extremely nervous person seeks to attract the attention of a waiter.

"Louder . . . much louder. He-lp!"

"Help — help — he-lp! Oh, Elizabeth, and in a churchyard, too!"

"Louder still. . . . He-el-lp!"

"Help! . . . It's like waking the dead. . . ."

"He-el-lp!"

"Hi, there! Who is it, and whatever on earth's the matter?" answered a voice from somewhere on their right.

"Oh, listen, Elizabeth! Heaven be praised! . . ."

"Who is it?" sounded the voice again, and a dot of light shone through the wall of fog.

"Answer him, Elizabeth!"

"Him? It isn't a man's voice, but a woman's . . . unless the fog. . . . Hi, there! Help! Here are two ladies. . . . Why, it's — it's Mrs. Treacher!"

For the fog had parted suddenly, and through it, as through a breach in a wall, stepped Mrs. Treacher with a lantern, which she held up close to their faces.

"Eh? Mrs. Pope and Miss Gabriel? Well, I declare!"

"Bless you, Mrs. Treacher! But, however came you here?"

"Why not?" asked Mrs. Treacher, after a pause.

"Here, in the churchyard! . . . You don't tell me you've lost your way, too?"

"No, I don't," answered Mrs. Treacher, shortly, lifting her lantern. "Churchyard? What churchyard?"

"We thought. . . . We were under the impression. . . ." Miss Gabriel's voice rocked a little before she recovered her self-command. "Would you mind telling us where we are, and what railings are these?"

"You're on Garrison Hill," said Mrs. Treacher, who disliked Miss Gabriel. "And you have hold of the rails round the old powder magazine. But what you're tryin' to do with 'em, and at this hour of night, I'll leave you to explain."

But here, for the first time since their troubles began, Mrs. Pope came to her companion's help. She did so by leaning back limply against the railings and declaring that she, for her part, was going to faint.

Mrs. Treacher caught her as she dropped, and with Miss Gabriel's help supported her up the slope to the Barracks, less than fifty yards above.

"The Barracks?" exclaimed Miss Gabriel, halting as Mrs. Treacher's lantern revealed to her through the fast-thinning fog a portion of the whitewashed façade. "Oh, but I couldn't — on any account whatever!"

"You'll have to," answered Mrs. Treacher, shortly, "that is, unless you'd rather have her laid outside on the bare road, and in a dead faint, too."

Indeed, Mrs. Pope was in a state of collapse that silenced all scruples. Mrs. Treacher — a powerfully-built woman — caught up the all but inanimate lady in both arms, and bore her into the passage, nodding to Miss Gabriel to unhitch from its nail a lamp which hung, backed by a tin reflector, just within the doorway.

"Unhasp the door to the left, please. We'll rest her down in the Commandant's parlour. There's a sofa — though he do mostly use to keep his books and papers upon it." She laid down her burden. "Oh, you needn't fear to look about you! The men folk be all off to the wreck, and won't be back till Lord knows when."

Miss Gabriel, however, was not looking about her. Her gaze, following the ray of the lamp as she held it aloft, travelled across the stooping shoulders of Mrs. Treacher and fastened itself upon a garment of gaudily-striped woolwork — her antimacassar — lying across the arm of the sofa where the Commandant had tossed it impatiently.

"Terribly messy a man always is when left to himself," said Mrs. Treacher, rising and stepping to a corner cupboard. "If he keeps such a thing as a drop of brandy on the premises, it'll be here, I reckon."

But the cupboard was empty. For the sternest of reasons the Commandant had, for two or three years past, denied himself the taste of strong waters.

Mrs. Treacher passed the back of her hand across the bridge of her nose. "I'll step over to the Castle," she announced, "for a drop of gin I keep against Treacher's attacks." (Let not Mrs. Treacher's idiom frighten the reader. She meant only that her husband suffered from an internal trouble which need not be specified, and that she kept the gin by her as a precaution.)

"And there's a quill pen of the Commandant's on the writing-table," she added; "if you'll burn the feather of it under her nose."

She bustled off. Miss Gabriel stepped to the table, picked up the quill, and held it over the lamp's flame; but her eyes still questioned the antimacassar. She was bending close to it when Mrs. Pope emitted a fluttering sigh and lifted her eyelids feebly.

"You are feeling better, dear?" asked Miss Gabriel, solicitously.

At this moment the latch of the door rattled gently. She looked up in surprise, for Mrs. Treacher could scarcely have gone and returned in so short a while.

The door opened. On the threshold stood a vision — a woman clad in furs — a woman with diamonds flashing on her white throat where the furs parted.

Miss Gabriel gasped.

The apparition stood for a moment, looked her in the eyes, and was gone, closing the door softly.

Miss Gabriel tottered, and sank back against the sofa's edge.

CHAPTER VIII

A BRIEF REVENGE

"Ladies?" ejaculated the Commandant. "In my quarters?"

Vashti nodded demurely. "I think you might have told me," she said in a tone of mild reproach.

"But — my dear young lady—"

"Thank you —"

"Hey?"

" — for calling me young." She reached out a hand, and, taking the lantern from him, held it high so that the beams fell on her face. "It is many years since our first meeting, and unhappily we have the date of it fixed. Give me credit that I reminded you; for I don't mind confessing that, though it hasn't come to a quarrel yet, my looking-glass and I are not the friends we were."

Here, had the Commandant been a readier man, he might have answered with a compliment, and a truthful one. For indeed it was a very beautiful face that the lantern showed him, and — here was the strange part of the business — it had been growing younger since she stepped off the ship, and somehow it must have contrived, in spite of the darkness, to convey a hint of its rejuvenescence, for the word "young" had slipped from him quite involuntarily.

But, after all, there is nothing so subtle as simplicity, and, after all, the Commandant managed to imply that she must be a witch.

"Then, my dear young lady," he replied, "since you have spirited these females into my quarters, I can only ask you to go and spirit them away again."

She shook her head.

"What! You won't? . . . Very well, then, I must deal with them, while you go off with the lantern and search for Mrs. Treacher."

"You are a brave man," said she; "and — and I think — by the look of them — you are going to have great fun."

The Commandant stood for a moment rubbing his chin and staring after the lantern, as it vanished in the fog. With a shake of the shoulders he pulled himself together, marched into the Barracks, and boldly opened the door.

"Miss Gabriel!"

"Major Vigoureux!"

"Certainly, ma'am — these being my own quarters, unless — "
He paused and gazed around, as if to make sure that his eyes were not deceiving him.

"Yes, yes — and at this time of night. As I was just saying to

Charlotte here, 'Think what a terrible construction one might put on it!'"

The Commandant lifted his eyebrows. ("I behaved like a brute," he confessed afterwards, "but the woman, a few hours before, had shown no mercy to me.") "Indeed, ma'am?" said he. "A construction? Then you must invent one for me, please, since I can think of none."

"We have had the most terrible experience, sir — the most terrible fright! You have seen Mrs. Treacher?"

"Has anything happened to Mrs. Treacher?"

"No — but it all came about through the fog—"

" — and my husband deserting me," put in Mrs. Pope.

The Commandant passed a hand across his brow. The gesture seemed to express perplexity; in truth it covered amusement and a kind of fearful joy in his newly-found talent for dissimulation.

"My dear Mrs. Pope," he answered, his voice faltering a little, "You don't mean to tell me that your excellent husband—"

"Of course she doesn't," snapped Miss Gabriel. "She means to say that the gentlemen were escorting us home, but, meeting the coastguard with the news of this terrible wreck—"

"A wreck, ma'am?"

"Why, God bless the man! Don't you know? Haven't you heard the guns going? . . . But of course you have. Mrs. Treacher told me you were down helping with the boats — you and her husband and Archelaus, though what help you three supposed yourselves capable of giving," wound up Miss Gabriel, reverting for a moment to her customary manner, "I don't pretend to guess."

"As for that," the Commandant answered gravely, "I am happy to tell you there has been no wreck. True, a vessel in distress — a large liner — had found herself among the Hell-deeps, of all abominably awkward places. But by the mercy of Heaven she managed to extricate herself, and has dropped anchor, not half an hour ago, in the Roads."

Miss Gabriel stared. "The Hell-deeps . . . and at anchor in the Roads?" she repeated stupidly. "Oh, will someone kindly tell me whether I am standing on my head or my heels! A large liner? — the thing's impossible! And in a fog that thick you couldn't see your hand before your face!"

"Are you quite sure, ladies," asked the Commandant, still gravely, "that you are not exaggerating the thickness of the fog, somewhat?"

"What?" Miss Gabriel took him up, like an echo. "When we started for home and found we were halfway up Garrison Hill, and all the time convinced we were at Old Town, in the churchyard!"

The Commandant shook his head; and it must be conceded that he had some excuse.

"But why in the churchyard?" he asked, gently.

"Because of the bell. If it comes to that" — Miss Gabriel threw herself desperately on the offensive — "how do you account for the woman we saw here, just now?"

"I beg your pardon? A — a woman, did you say?" (Oh, Major Vigoureux!)

"Yes, sir — a woman; a bedizened woman."

"My dear Elizabeth," pleaded Mrs. Pope feebly, "are we quite sure that we saw her? — that it wasn't a — a sort of mistake? It certainly seemed — for a moment — But really, you know, there is no one in the Islands—"

"My dear Charlotte, didn't we see her with our own eyes?"

Mrs. Pope sighed. "It seems to me I have seen such a number of things — of incredible things — tonight."

"You are sure it wasn't Mrs. Treacher?" suggested the Commandant, wickedly.

"Mrs. Treacher! Mrs. Trea — Does Mrs. Treacher go about in silks and furs and low bodices with a thousand pounds' worth of diamonds on her abandoned neck?"

"Certainly not to my knowledge. But," said the Commandant, turning, as the door opened, "you had better ask her for yourself."

Now, it may be that Mrs. Treacher had also allowed Vashti to bewitch her. At any rate, she cordially hated Miss Gabriel, and she took, then and there, what she herself called afterwards, a strong line.

"What are they wanting to know now?" she demanded, addressing the Commandant.

"Miss Gabriel wants to know" — he answered, in a husky voice, while he pretended to trim the lamp — "if you go about in silks and furs."

"No, I don't," replied Mrs. Treacher, setting down the bottle of gin. "And what's more, I don't go a-sheevoing it around Garrison Hill in the small hours, and a-holding on to railings, and a-clammering for strong drink."

"That will do, Mrs. Treacher," interposed her master, suddenly reduced to contrition at the sight of Miss Gabriel, who stood speechless, opening and shutting her mouth like a fish. "The ladies have lost their way in the fog, and were, on the whole, extremely fortunate to reach here without accident. They will agree, I daresay, that the sooner I escort them home the better. Fetch me a lantern, if you please."

"It — it is extremely good of you," stammered Miss Gabriel.

"My dear madam!" he protested, with a good-natured smile.

Miss Gabriel did not respond to it. But, though bitterly angry, for the moment she was cowed, and she made no further reference to the mysterious lady.

She declined the Commandant's arm. Mrs. Pope, however, took it almost eagerly, and on the way down the hill he obtained from her a voluble if somewhat incoherent account of the night's adventures. He did his best now to make light of them. Accidents even more extraordinary had happened in fogs before now. He related how two companies of the Naval Brigade, under Sevastopol, had come within an ace of firing on each other. . . . He told of the *Milo*, and her wonderful escape, but said nothing of Vashti. In the midst of his narrative he found himself wondering what answer he could make if they questioned him again upon the apparition.

But neither Mrs. Pope nor Miss Gabriel made further allusion to it. Their silence, for which at first he was merely thankful, began to puzzle him after a while.

Could it be possible that he, too, had been cheated by an apparition?

He took leave of the ladies at their respective gates, retiring delicately as soon as, waiting in the road, he had assured himself that they were within doors. Miss Gabriel admitted herself with a latch-key. Mrs. Pope's timid knock was answered by her astonished husband, who, having just returned from the harbour, and assuming his spouse to be long since in bed and asleep, had lit a candle to explore the dining-room cellaret.

The front door was shut on their reciprocal surprise, and the Commandant withdrew. He had sighed, before now, as he had shut Mr. and Mrs. Pope's front gate after an evening's whist. Doubtless they were a stupid couple.

*****

A light shone from the Barracks — from the office window to the right of the door. Within the office Vashti had dragged the sofa across the room and sat, with her fur cloak thrown back, toasting her shoes before a warm fire. In the dancing flame of it her diamonds sparkled as she turned to him.

"Mrs. Treacher is upstairs," she said, "hunting out sheets to air for me. Now fill your pipe, please, and sit down and tell me all about it."

Major Vigoureux found an old pipe on the mantel-shelf, dived in the tobacco jar for a few dry crumbs, filled, and lit and stamped out a spark that had dropped on the hearth-rug.

"It isn't a creditable story," said he, puffing slowly, and blinking at the flash of jewels below her white throat. "In fact, I behaved like a brute."

"Tell me about it," she repeated.

So he told her; and found himself smoking and watching her, while she laughed softly, leaning forward to the fire, and gazing into the heart of it.

CHAPTER IX

THE SALVING OF S.S. MILO

Major Vigoreux awoke at daybreak with a vague sense that something important had happened or was going to happen — a feeling he had not known for years. It was so strange that he sat up wondering, rubbing the back of his head.

Then he remembered, and called out to Sergeant Archelaus.

Sergeant Archelaus appeared, a moment later, ready dressed, and on more than usually good terms with himself. He had indued his master's trousers, and, save for an unfashionable bagginess at the hips, they fitted him surprisingly well.

"Good morning, Archelaus. Did you happen to hear, last night, at what time the *Milo* weighs anchor?"

"I heard the captain, sir, tell the pilots to be aboard at half-after-seven. But with a vessel of her size you may count on their waiting till high-water or thereabouts."

"In any case" — the Commandant consulted his watch — "we have not too much time. Where is Treacher?"

"Downstairs, sir, along with his missus, stoking the kitchen fire, with mattresses built up before it like a sandbag battery. Seems to me the woman's been spending half the night airing one thing and another. She says the place is like a vault. Not," added Archelaus, magnanimously, "that I mind her talk."

"Quite right, Archelaus. I particularly hope you won't quarrel with Mrs. Treacher while she is here waiting on Miss — er — on the lady."

"If," said Archelaus, darkly, "as how I wanted to quarrel with a female, I should have taken and married one long ago. As 'tis, when the woman's tongue becomes afflicting, I turns round and pities Treacher. There's more ways of doing that than in so many words, and you'd be astonished how they both dislikes it."

"At any rate," said the Commandant, mildly, "they have saved you the trouble of being late with the fire this morning. So you may fetch me my shaving-water at once, please."

He sprang out of bed and reached for his dressing-gown, astonished at his own good spirits. "It does make a difference," said he aloud, though the remark was addressed to himself.

"It do," said Archelaus, turning in the doorway.

"I — I beg your pardon?" The Commandant turned about, a trifle confused.

"It may seem a little thing; but it gives a man self-respect, and

I'm glad you noticed 'em." Archelaus looked down at his legs, complacently. "Always supposin'," he added, "they don't take me for a Frenchman, owing to the fulness hereabouts."

Yes, certainly, it made a difference — to rise in the morning with a sense of something waiting to be done. So the Commandant put it to himself while he shaved, standing at his dressing-table under the barrack window. The window was set high in the wall: too high to afford him a view of the Islands, even though he stood on tip-toe. But through it and above the open pane he caught a glimpse of blue sky and lilac-coloured cloud, touched with gold by the risen sun. He could guess the rest. A perfect morning! — clean and crisp, with the sea a translucent blue, and sunlight glittering on the Island beaches; the air still, yet bracing, and withal ineffably pure — a morning mysterious with the sense of autumn, but of autumn rarified by its passage over the salt strait, deodorised, made pure of marsh fog and the rotting leaf.

The Commandant hummed to himself in the intervals of his shaving, which nevertheless he performed meticulously by force of habit. It was his custom to shave, and very carefully, before taking his bath. For years he had made a ritual of his morning toilet: so many passes of his razor across the strop (to be precise, one hundred and fifty, neither more nor less), so many douches with the sponge, so many petitions afterwards on his knees. Yes, it is to be feared that his prayers, no less than his shaving, had become a drill, though one may plead for him that he always went through it conscientiously. A stroke too few across the strop — a petition to the Almighty missed — either would have worried him with a feeling that the day had been begun amiss. He was poor, but with the never-failing well on Garrison Hill he could come clean as the richest to his prayers. Even Miss Gabriel had to admit that the poor man (as she put it) knew how to take care of his person.

"We shall be in good time, Archelaus," said the Commandant, with a side glance at his watch; "that is, if you'll step down the hill and get the boat ready."

Archelaus, whose hearing had not improved of late, checked himself in the act of filling his master's tub.

"I didn't clearly catch what you said, for the splashing. . . . Boat? If you want the boat, I put her off to the moorings last night. Found her tied up and bumping against the quay steps, quite as if money was no object to any of us."

"Thank you. Yes, I relied on your finding and mooring her properly. Well, now, when you are ready I want you to unmoor her again. We are going off to the liner to fetch Miss — that is to say — the lady's boxes."

Sergeant Archelaus faced about slowly, cap in hand.

"Oh — oh!" said he slowly. "Relative of yours, sir? — making so bold."

"Dear me, no; nothing of the sort."

"Paying lodger, perhaps. . . . Or else we've come into a fortune all of a sudden, an' that accounts for Treacher's playing ad lib. with the coals — begging your pardon again."

The Commandant winced, and came within an ace of gashing himself severely. He had forgotten the penny in his pocket, the gulf between this and pay-day . . . and Vashti, no doubt, was used to fare daintily, luxuriously!

"I really think" — he turned on Archelaus in sudden anger — "you might know better than to stare into the glass when I am shaving. Moreover, you forget your place, and inexcusably, even for an old servant."

Archelaus resumed his filling of the bath, and, having filled it, withdrew without another word.

Yes; but while the manner of Archelaus' speech had deserved rebuke, in the matter of it Archelaus was right. The matter of it was urgent, too, and not to be played with. In an hour or so Vashti would be awake. . . . She must delay dressing until her boxes arrived; but, once dressed, she would expect breakfast. The larder, to his knowledge, contained but the rusty end of a flitch of green bacon — that, and perhaps a couple of rusty eggs, a loaf, and some salt butter. Fool that he was! And a minute ago he had greeted the day so light-heartedly!

What was to be done? In the pauses of sponging and towelling himself, the Commandant asked the question again and again. Could he go to Mrs. Treacher and borrow back the four shillings he had given her last night? Fish, new-laid eggs, fresh butter, marmalade, the best tea procurable in the Islands. . . . Yes, undoubtedly four shillings would go a long way towards providing breakfast. But after breakfast would come luncheon, and after luncheon —

There was Mr. Tregaskis, of the Shop. Mr. Tregaskis sold almost everything "advantageous to life" — as Shakespeare's exiles said upon another island: everything from bacon and pickles to boots, iron-mongery, and sun-bonnets. For twelve years the Commandant had dealt with Mr. Tregaskis, paying whatever Mr. Tregaskis charged him, and always in ready money. He knew, moreover, that Mr. Tregaskis gave credit: and yet, after twelve years of ready-money dealing, he winced as he saw himself entering the shop and proposing to open an account. He foresaw himself inexorably driven to it. But he foresaw himself also stammering out the suggestion with every sign of conscious rascality. And, after all, was it honest to enter a shop and open an account with one penny in pocket? Suppose that, next pay-day, no pay were forthcoming!

He must approach Mr. Tregaskis: there was no help for it. Yet the prospect pleased him so little that, as he walked down the hill to the quay, he decided to put off the interview, and was almost running past the shop (which had just been unshuttered) when Mr. Tregaskis himself appeared, framed of a sudden in the upper and open half of his shop doorway.

"Eh? Is it you, sir? Good morning!" he called.

"Good morning! And a fine morning, too, Mr. Tregaskis."

"After a night of marvels. You've heard about the liner, sir, out in the Roads? . . . 'Tis all a mystery to me how she ever found her way in."

"I am putting off to learn the particulars. And, by the way, Mr. Tregaskis" — the Commandant paused — "I intended to call in upon you on my way back."

"Anything I can do for you, sir, and at any time," responded Mr. Tregaskis. "I suppose, now," he added, "you'd take it as a liberty if I was to ask for a seat in your boat?"

"Not in the least. There she is, waiting off the quay steps: so if you have business on board, put on your hat, come along with me, and welcome!"

"Thanking you kindly, sir. Which I was reckoning that — she being from foreign parts and the Islands the first place she've touched at, I might pick up a bravish order in the way of fresh milk and eggs, not to mention that Job Clemow sold me half-a-hundred-weight of plaice, with a cod or two, that he took on the spiller yesterday."

"Come along, by all means," repeated the Commandant, moving off towards the quay steps; and Tregaskis, having tucked his shop-apron around his waist and run into the back passage for his billy-cock hat, hurried in his wake.

Reuben Tregaskis — known throughout the Islands as The Bester — was a genial ruffian of familiar accost, red-faced, round in the stomach, utterly unscrupulous at a bargain. The Commandant did not like him, and particularly disliked the prospect of asking him a favour. Most of all he regretted, as they pushed off, that chance this morning had forced him to put such a man under a small obligation. He feared that, when it came to asking leave to open an account, he might seem to be using this advantage. (Such a fear, it scarcely needs saying, was groundless. In his business dealings, The Bester was superior alike to gratitude and rancour, and would bargain with his own mother as with his worst enemy.)

The Commandant, oppressed with his own thoughts, bent his

attention upon the steering, and punctuated with monosyllables only the exuberant flow of Mr. Tregaskis' conversation, which, bye-and-bye, as they neared the roadstead, resolved itself into offers of wagers on the length, tonnage, and actual carrying capacity of the liner.

She lay very nearly in the middle of the roadstead, broadside-on to the morning sunshine, and the more the Commandant studied her the more he wondered at last night's miracle. She had not yet begun to weigh, though he discerned a couple of St. Ann's pilots talking with an officer on the bridge. Presently the officer left them, and descended to the deck, where he stood in the gangway awaiting the boat.

"Major Vigoureux?" he asked, lifting the peak of his cap, as she fell alongside.

The Commandant, not a little astonished, returned the salutation. "That is my name, sir."

"I have been expecting you," said the officer. "I am Captain Whitaker, at your service — the skipper of this vessel, in fact, and thankful enough, I can tell you, to be alive this morning and in command of her. Madame's boxes are on deck here, if you do me the favour to climb on board. . . . Ah, and here is Madame's maid, to give account of them!"

The Commandant, drawing breath at the head of the ladder, and glancing down the *Milo's* majestic length of deck, was aware of four large trunks, and beside them a neat, foreign-looking woman, who curtsied in foreign fashion as she came forward.

"M'sieur will take my duty to Madame, and tell her that I have done my best to pack to her orders. The rest I am to report from Plymouth, when we arrive."

"And I daresay," put in Captain Whitaker, with an amused turn of the eye towards the trunks, then back at the Commandant, "Madame would call these 'just a few necessaries.' Though I say to you, sir," he went on gravely, "that all the *Milo's* hold — and the *Milo* will carry close on four thousand tons — hasn't room enough to stow what Madame deserves, be it in clothes or jewels."

"I — I beg your pardon?"

"She hasn't told you? No; I bet she wouldn't," said Captain Whitaker. "Come down to my cabin, sir, and let me offer you a brandy-and-soda? No? Then, perhaps, you'll do me the honour to join me at breakfast — which must be ready at this moment," he added, as eight strokes sounded on the ship's bell forward. "Never mind the size of the trunks, sir; one of my men shall help you ashore with 'em."

In the Captain's cabin, which had a floor of parquet and panels of teak set in mahogany, stood a table with a white cloth upon it, and a breakfast array of blue-and-white china. A steward, in a blue suit with brass buttons, brought the meats in dishes of polished electroplate, and on a small sideboard stood other dishes with small spirit lamps burning beneath. The Commandant seated himself; ate, drank, and marvelled.

"You know Madame?" asked Captain Whitaker, helping himself to a dish of kidneys and bacon. He nodded, intercepting the Commandant's gaze. "We keep them in ice, if you're not above trying our fare. You'll find they are not bad. My other meals I take with the passengers, but I breakfast alone, as a rule."

The Commandant's mind ran on the breakfast yet to be extracted from Mr. Tregaskis' shop.

"You know her?" asked Captain Whitaker.

"I once had the pleasure — years ago—"

"If that's so" — Captain Whitaker nodded — "we'll take her praises for granted. She's great; you can sum it up at that. By the way, did she happen to tell you why she is leaving the ship here?"

"Yes; she went ashore in a hurry, she said, to avoid being thanked—"

"Then I guessed right."

" — though," confessed the Commandant, "I haven't a notion what she meant."

Captain Whitaker set down his breakfast-cup and buttered himself a piece of toast, gazing the while long and earnestly at his companion.

"No? Then I'll tell you. The passengers don't know it as yet, though I've caught a guess or two flying around; but the truth is sure to come out, sooner or later. Man, it was she that saved the *Milo* last night, in that ghastly twenty minutes before we picked up the pilot. . . . Oh, I see by your face you don't believe me! — but you must take it or leave it. Shall I go on?"

"Go on," said the Commandant.

"We were due out of New York on the 27th, but missed our tide in clearing and didn't pass the bar till early next morning. We carried fifty-nine saloon passengers, seventy-five second, and a hundred and twenty-five steerage, with a crew of a hundred exactly. Besides these we had the mails — two hundred and twenty bags — and a fair amount of dollars in specie (I needn't tell how much.) The weather was thick from the first with a heavy sea running on the other side. We met it full just outside Sandy Hook, and for three days I pitied the passengers. The third night out the mischief happened. I had left the bridge soon after four bells and was just turning in for my beauty-sleep when I heard an unholy racket below in the engine-room, and felt the ship slow down of a sudden. One of the rods had kicked loose from its gib and started to flail around death and destruction. Thanks to Crosbie, our first engineer, she was brought up before kicking our insides out, and we hove to; but the repairs cost us close on eighteen hours. By daybreak the weather was thickening worse than ever, though with no great amount of wind, and we started again in a fog so thick that from the bridge you could see her bows, and only just. Well, that's how it was with us, all the way across. We seemed to carry the fog; and though it lifted a bit, off and on, it never looked like giving us a chance of an observation. All yesterday afternoon I was worried by the thought that we'd overrun our reckoning and must be somewhere near the Islands, and about two o'clock — though the soundings were good — I ordered the engines to be reduced below the half-speed at which she was running.

"To ease the passengers' minds I had arranged for a concert in the saloon after dinner, and Madame — she had booked with us under a name that wasn't her own to dodge the New York newspaper men, but the passengers recognized her — had promised me to sing to them. (You have heard her, eh? — it makes you cry, and not mind, either, who sees you.) I remember now that she looked at me pretty straight when she gave the promise, but seeing me not minded to speak, she asked no questions.

"Well, the concert came off. At any other time I'd have given pounds to be sitting there and listening; but the worry on my mind kept me to the bridge, and from there I heard her, the notes lifting up through the saloon sky-light as if heaven and earth had somehow got capsized or else an angel had come aboard to sing us clear of the fog. There were three of us on the bridge — myself, and the third officer, Mr. Francillon, and a seaman called Petersen; and when the song ended — it was a little Italian something-or-other, very bright and gay — and the clapping began and the calls for an encore, I couldn't stand it any longer, and I was afraid she'd be starting on 'Home, Sweet Home,' or something of that sort, and I didn't want Mr. Francillon to see my face. So I made up an excuse and sent him off to the chart-house for a pair of dividers (which I didn't want), and away he went.

"When he was gone I stood by the wheel for a bit listening as the clapping died down. It stopped at last, and I braced myself up and waited to have my feelings wrung, when just behind me I heard a step on the ladder. Of course, I took it for Mr. Francillon returning, and I wheeled about, short-tempered like, to tell him he needn't be tip-toeing — we weren't on the bridge to listen to grand opera — when what do I see but Madame! 'You needn't look so cross, Captain,' she says; 'for I know well enough I'm breaking all rules, and I'll go away quietly and sing to them again. But we're somewhere near the Islands, and the call came on me to warn you!' 'Why, truly, ma'am,' I answered, 'I believe we're not far off them.' 'We're close to them,' she answered me, nodding her head. 'I'm Island-born, Captain, and I feel 'em in my blood.' I put this down to craziness — hysterics — or whatever you choose to call it; but just to soothe her mind and get her down quietly off the bridge I sang out to the leadsman to know if he had found soundings. I was bending over the rail when I felt a touch on my arm, and heard her cry out 'Starboard! Hard a-starboard — hard!' — just like that." Captain Whitaker dropped his voice to a low, fierce whisper as he imitated her. "It took the helmsman sharp and sudden, so that he had begun to put the wheel down before he realised that the order didn't come from me; and the next moment Madame had flung herself upon it and was helping with both hands. 'Hullo!' says I, stepping after her smartly, and as good as asking if she or I commanded the *Milo*. The passengers below had started to sing 'D'ye ken John Peel?' and were yelling out a lot of silly hunting-cries with the chorus. I could hear nothing above the racket. But, sure enough, looking to port over my shoulder as I laid hand on the wheel to check it, I saw a whitish smear that meant breakers; and the smear no sooner showed than above it a great black cliff stood out as if 'twere a moving thing and meant to carve into us right amidships — a great cliff with a rock on it like the Duke of Wellington's nose. A man from the top of it could have jumped onto our bulwarks, and I shut my eyes as it overhung, waiting for the crash; but it slid by and was gone like a slide you pass through a magic lantern.

"'Port now! Port for your life!' she called out; and I saw first of all her hand go out to push Petersen off, and then the little sparks flickering on her rings as she gripped the spokes, and checking 'em, dragged the wheel back hand over hand. A man's strength she must have had. 'Help me,' was all she said, in a kind of panting voice, and as I caught hold to help it over, 'That was the Head! Hard up, now! and ring down for full speed!' 'Full speed!' I grunted, yet pressing on the wheel all the time — 'It's stop her you mean, and anchor.' 'What, here? with Hell-deeps on your starboard bow and a five-knot tide running! Full speed ahead — there's no room to swing — no, nor half.' She stopped my hand on the bell and rang down herself, 'full speed ahead'; and the passengers whooping away at 'John Peel!' all the while.

"Then, as the engines began to run, she looked at me, still holding on by the wheel. 'They may do it,' she said, 'they may do it. At half speed she'd never point off, against a five-knot tide.' 'God have mercy on us!' was all I could say. 'If you know — ?' 'Know?' she caught me up. 'I was brought up to know. But she'll never do it if she don't pick up way. . . . Ah, that's better!' she said with a kind of sigh staring over the starboard bow into the fog. 'Now!' — and we held our breath, all of us; for Mr. Francillon was back on the bridge standing close behind her and wondering what the devil was up. She let thirty seconds pass, and then turned to him as if he'd been there all the while and she knew it.

"'Look astern,' she said, 'and maybe, if you're clever, you can see the Monk.'

"'The Monk!' We cried this out together; for that we had passed the Monk without sighting her or catching sound of her fog-horns was a thing incredible.

"'But so it is,' said she. 'We have passed the Monk; passed it close. Don't I know the Pope's Head on Lesser Teague? Now hard-a-port still — for we've the Gunnel Dogs somewhere there to lee-ward, and they're worse almost than Hell-deeps.'

"We were racing by this time. There was nothing in the world to see — only the fog, which had turned, within the last minute, to dusk; and nothing to feel except that we were racing down between the walls of it like a stick caught in a mill heat. Worse it was; we were driving down full tilt with a five-knot tide under us. If we struck there was one consolation; the end would come soon. As 'John Peel' ended we could hear the tide race take up the tune and hum it on the wind of our passage; and above it I heard the third officer call out that he had glimpsed a light astern.

"'The Monk!' said Madame, nodding her head to me to help her in easing off the wheel.

"And I don't know, sir, if you have ever been through a gale at sea; a really tight gale, I mean; with a while in it — maybe an hour only, maybe twenty-four — when the odds are slowly turning against you. Then there comes a point when, with nothing to show for it, you feel that you are holding your own; and another point when you feel that, bar accidents, the worst is over. The sea seems to break just as savage as ever, and you can't swear that the wind has lessened. You have nothing to point to, but, all the same, you know, and can thank the Lord.

"That's how it was with the *Milo*. I couldn't say when the danger ceased; but I found myself looking at Madame across the binnacle lamp and she was looking at me. My hand went out and I rang down for half-speed, then for dead slow. We stood there and listened while the engines changed their beat from one to the other. In the saloon they had started a comic song with a chorus. Said she, after a bit, 'You can bring up now and wait for morning. North of the Gunnel here there's an eddy slack where the tides meet, and you may count on thirty fathoms.'

"I called down to know what the lead reported. I felt my voice shaking and the leadsman's voice shook a bit too as he called back that he had found the bottom with the red seventeen fathom mark. Half a minute later he sang out that his line had lost it. I was just about calling to let go anchor when away on our starboard bow we heard the pilots hailing. We sent up a flare, and at sight of it the lighthousemen, away on the Monk, began banging, and small blame to them!"

CHAPTER X

THE ADVENTURES OF FOUR SHILLINGS

As he finished his story Captain Whitaker stood up and reached out a hand to open a glass-fronted cupboard in which he kept his books and papers. The Commandant, mistaking his movement, rose also.

"No, no, sir," the Captain corrected him. "Sit down and finish your breakfast. The fact is, when her maid, last night, handed me the letter telling me she had gone ashore, I sat down and wrote an answer. Here it is, and I was going to ask you to deliver it for me."

The Commandant took it, and placed it carefully in his breast pocket. "I thank you," he answered, "but I have breakfasted. If you don't mind — it occurs to me that, if I delay, some of your passengers will soon be about the decks, and will see the luggage going overside, and ask questions."

"And that's well thought of," interrupted Captain Whitaker, "though I expect the luggage is all in your boat before this. How far lies your house from the quay, by the way?"

The Commandant answered that his house — the Barracks — stood at the very top of the hill.

"Why, then," said the Captain, leading the way up the companionway, "the least I can do is to send a couple of my men along with you to help. Your fellows — you'll excuse me — don't look equal to it. Pensioners, eh?"

The Commandant winced. "One of them," he answered stiffly, "is on the active list. His strength would surprise you, sir."

"H'm!" said the Captain, with a glance at Sergeant Archelaus.

"The other — but where is Tregaskis?"

"Gone off, sir, to do business with the steward," explained Archelaus, saluting.

"The other is a Mr. Tregaskis, a respectable man, and our principal tradesman in Garland Town. He has a design, I believe, to sell you whatever you may want in the way of fresh provisions."

"Certainly. The steward can go ashore, too, and do business with him, and his boat will bring the others back. Here — Hoskings! Arnott!" Captain Whitaker called to a couple of seamen, and sent a third off to summon the steward.

Five minutes later the Commandant found himself back in his boat, seated besides the *Milo's* steward, and confronting a tall pile of luggage. The two seamen had already put off with Mr. Tregaskis in the steward's boat.

"And you will present my duty to Madame?" said Madame's maid, looking down from the ship's side. "And tell her that I charge myself to see the rest of her luggage safe to the hotel, where I will report myself and wait for Madame's orders."

Captain Whitaker waved good-bye. Archelaus pushed off and fell to the oars. The Commandant took the tiller. As the boat pointed for shore the garrison bell on the hill rang out nine o'clock.

Nine o'clock! The notes of the bell struck apprehension upon the Commandant's heart. His guest would certainly be awake by this time, and as certainly hungry. To be sure, she could not attire herself until her boxes arrived — at any rate, would not appear. And yet, with such a strong-willed person, he could not be certain. A lady capable of landing on a foggy night in an evening gown and diamonds, and of walking up the street of St. Hugh's in shoes of rose-coloured satin, might well be capable of descending to breakfast in those garments.

To breakfast! — and as yet that breakfast had to be bought, and on credit!

He wished now that he had offered to convey Mr. Tregaskis back in his own boat. He might (he told himself) have broached his proposition on the way.

The *Milo's* steward, affably inclined, let fall a remark or two upon the Islands. He opined that they were quaint. The poor man meant well, but was a person slightly above his station, and clipped his words. This gave him a patronising tone, which the Commandant, in his impatience, found offensive. He answered in curt monosyllables, which in turn caused the steward to mistake him for a stand-offish gentleman.

The steward was a very resplendent figure indeed. The morning sunlight, which drew sparkles from the brass-buttoned suit and brass-bound cap beside him, exposed pitilessly the threadbare woof of the Commandant's uniform coat. There had been nothing amiss with the coat, yesterday; nothing to observe, at least — - And, "Confound the fellow!" thought the Commandant, "how am I to get rid of him and have a word with Tregaskis?"

For desperate ills, desperate remedies. Drawing alongside the quay, where Mr. Tregaskis and the two seamen had landed and stood waiting, the Commandant called upon his best service voice, concealing the shake in it:

"Mr. Tregaskis!"

"Sir?"

"I desire a word with you."

"Yes, sir."

"And in private," went on the Commandant, stepping ashore

and marching straight up the steps.

"Certainly, sir." After all, and not so long ago, Major Vigoureux had been Governor and Chief Magistrate of the Islands, with power to inflict fine and imprisonment. Mr. Tregaskis (conscious, perhaps, of some close dealings in the not remote past) turned obediently and led the way to his shop door at the corner of the hill, thence through the shop, and thence to the threshold of a dark parlour behind it, into which he was passing when the Commandant's voice brought him to a stand.

"We will talk here, if you please," said the Commandant.

"Certainly, sir," Mr. Tregaskis turned about.

"I want," said the Commandant, "half a pound of your best tea, half a dozen new laid eggs, an amount of bacon which I leave to you, and a pot of marmalade."

"With pleasure, sir. Anything I can do—"

"And on credit."

"As I said sir — to be sure — and hoping that I have given satisfaction hitherto — " Mr. Tregaskis, still a trifle flurried, fell to rubbing his hands together, thus producing an appearance of haste before he actually collected himself and hurried to execute the order.

"Good God!" thought the Commandant to himself. "Am I browbeating this man?"

He watched as Mr. Tregaskis cut and weighed out the butter and bacon and tied them up into parcels, with the help of a small boy summoned from the back premises; or rather, the small boy (Melk by name, which was short for Melchisedek) did the weighing and tying while Mr. Tregaskis stood over him and exhorted him to look sharp, or he'd never make a grocer. The steward watched from the doorway, puffing a cigarette, and expressed a hope that he was not excluding the light. The Commandant wished him a thousand miles away. Sergeant Archelaus had borrowed a light trolley from the quay; the two seamen had loaded it; and already Madame's luggage was halfway up the hill, and must infallibly reach the Barracks before Madame's breakfast could overtake it.

"And when would you like it sent, sir?" asked Mr. Tregaskis, nodding at the piles on the counter.

"Sent?" echoed the Commandant. "I beg your pardon," he went on hastily. "I had meant to ask you for the loan of a basket. I will carry the things myself."

"Indeed, sir?" Mr. Tregaskis hesitated. "You are welcome to a basket, of course, if you think it wise."

"I am not ashamed to be seen carrying a basket, Mr. Tregaskis."

"No, indeed, sir! But the hill being steep — and a little exercise would do Melk, here, all the good in the world."

"I prefer to carry the goods myself, I thank you." (Was everybody in a conspiracy to take the Commandant for a very old man?)

He waited impatiently until the basket was filled, slung it on his arm, and hurried out of the shop with such impetuosity that the steward, still lounging in the doorway, had scarcely time to skip into the roadway and give passage.

"They must be going in for some kind of feast, up to Barracks," said the boy Melk meditatively, after a pause.

"Why?" asked Mr. Tregaskis, looking up from the counter.

"Because," said the boy, "Old Mother Treacher was here, not ten minutes ago, and the way she spent her money was a caution. There's the best part of four shillin' in the till, if only you'll look."

"What did she buy?"

"Eggs mostly — and bacon — and marmalade."

Mr. Tregaskis walked to his shop door, and stared up the hill after the Commandant.

"Must be going off their heads," he decided, and shook his own doubtfully. "It can't be a merry-makin' either; for, when you come to think of it, folks don't feast off such things as streaky bacon."

"Not off this sort, any'ow," airily agreed the steward, who had been examining a piece on the counter.

*****

The Commandant had started fiercely enough to climb the hill, but by the time he reached the bend of the hill where stood the cottage which had been Vashti's home he was drawing difficult breath. Indeed, he was on the point of setting down his load and resting when, as he turned the corner, he came full upon Mrs. Banfield, the good wife of the present occupier, in conversation with Mrs. Medlin, her neighbour across the road. The two women were staring up the hill, each from her doorway, but at the sound of the Commandant's footsteps they turned and stared at him instead: whereat he blushed and hung on his heel for a moment before charging through the cross-fire of gossip.

"Good morning, ladies!"

"Aw, good morning to you, sir," answered Mrs. Banfield, with a curtsey, and gazed hard at his basket. "Nothing wrong up to the garrison, I hope?"

"So far as I know, ma'am, nothing at all."

"Seein' that great stack of luggage go up the hill," explained Mrs. Medlin, "why naturally it made a person anxious. And when you put a civil question, as I did to Sergeant Archelaus, and he turns round and as good as snaps your head off, why a person can't help putting two and two together."

"Indeed, ma'am, and what did you make the result?" asked the Commandant, politely.

"Why, sir, Mrs. Banfield here was reckoning that the Government had sent stores for you at last, and says I, 'You may be right, Sarah, and glad enough we shall a-be to hear of it, for it do make my heart bleed to remember old days and see what the garrison is reduced to in vittles and small-clothes. But,' says I, 'the luggage comes from the great steamship, and the great steamship comes from America, and that Government would be sending stores from America, even in these days of tinned meats, is what, beggin' your pardon, no person could believe that wasn't born a fool.'"

"Which I answered to Mrs. Medlin," said Mrs. Banfield, "'Granted, ma'am,' I said, 'but, food or no food, I'd sooner swallow it than believe what you were tellin' just now.'"

"And what was that?" asked the Commandant, turning on Mrs. Medlin.

"Why, sir, knowing the Lord Proprietor to be no friend of yours—"

"Hush, Mrs. Medlin — hush, if you please!"

"Of course, sir, if you don't want to hear—"

"I certainly cannot listen to any talk against Sir Cæsar. It would be exceedingly improper."

"I warn' going to say anything improper," Mrs. Medlin protested stoutly. "And I wonder, sir, at your thinking it, after the years you've given good-day to me."

"Why, bless the woman!" interjected Mrs. Banfield, "you might talk as improper as you pleased and the Governor wouldn't understand your drift — he's that innocent-minded. But what she meant, sir, was that the Lord Proprietor had turned you out, belike — as everyone knows he has a mind to — and that a new Governor might be coming in your place."

The Commandant flushed. "My dear Mrs. Banfield, the Lord Proprietor has nothing to do with the military command here, either to appoint or to dismiss. I cannot forbid your gossiping; but it may help you to know that every soldier on the Islands holds his post directly under the Crown."

Mrs. Banfield gazed at the basket with the air of one who, seeming to yield, yet abides by her convictions. "The Crown's a long way off, seemin' to me," she objected; "and contrariwise I do know that when the Lord Proprietor wants his way on the Islands he gets it. Though it were ten times a week, he'd get it, and no one nowadays strong enough to stand up to him."

"My dear Mrs. Banfield!"

But Mrs. Banfield was not to be checked. "He's a tyrant," she declared, her voice rising shrilly; "and I'd say it a hundred times, though I went to the lock-up for it. He's a tyrant: and you, sir, are too simple-minded to cope with 'em. Yes, yes — 'a Christian gentleman' — everyone grants it of you, and — saving your presence — everyone is sorry enough for it. You wouldn't hurt a fly, for your part. Man, woman, or child, you'd have every soul in the Islands to live neighbourly and go their ways in peace. No doubt 'tis good Gospel teaching, too, and well enough it worked till this rumping little tyrant came along and pushed you aside. Goodness comes easy to you, sir, I reckon; but it bears hard upon us poor folk that want someone to stand up for us against injustice."

"The Lord Proprietor, Mrs. Banfield, has a strong will of his own; but I certainly never heard that he was unjust."

"Then you haven't heard, sir, what's happening over on Saaron?"

"On Saaron, ma'am?"

"On Saaron, sir. . . . Eh? No, to be sure. . . . Folks may suffer on the Islands in these days, but what use to tell the Governor? He was good to us in his time, but now he has cut himself off from us with his own troubles. . . . Did anyone tell you, sir, the text that old Seth Hicks preached from, over to St. Ann's, at the last service before the Lord Proprietor closed the Meeting House? 'I will lift up mine eyes,' said he, 'to the hills, from whence cometh my help,' and then, having given it out, the old fellow turned solemn-like t'ards the window that looks across here to Garrison Hill. 'Amen,' said some person in the congregation; 'but 'tis no use, brother Seth, your seeking in that quarter.'"

The Commandant, who had set down his basket, lifted it again wearily. "Mrs. Banfield," said he, "won't you at least put it down to my credit that, having (as you say) my own troubles, I don't bother my neighbours with 'em?"

"Why, bless your heart, sir — that ever I should say it — that's what hurts us sorest! We can fit and fend along somehow, never you mind; but when for years you shared our little tribylations and taught us, forrigner, tho' you were, to be open with 'ee as daylight, it do seem cruel that you can't enjoy a bit of trouble on your own account but you must take it away and hide it."

The Commandant's eyes moistened suddenly. "Is that how the Islanders look at it, Mrs. Banfield?"

"It is, sir."

"Well, well," said the Major. "I never guessed. . . . I am a blind old fool, it seems. But" — and here, blinking away the moisture, he smiled at Mrs. Banfield almost gaily — "I can begin at once to make amends. The luggage that went up the hill, just now, belongs to — to a friend of mine — a visitor who will be my guest for a short while at the Barracks. And this" — he tapped the basket — "is for my friend's breakfast. In exchange for this information you shall tell me now what is the matter over at Saaron."

"The matter is, the Lord Proprietor has given the Tregarthens notice."

The Commandant's eyes grew round in his head as he stared at Mrs. Banfield, who answered by nodding her head briskly, as though each nod was the tap of a hammer driving home a nail.

"What? Eli Tregarthen — that married Cara's younger daughter — that used to live — " The Commandant recited this much in the fashion of a child repeating "The House that Jack Built." His gaze wandered past Mrs. Banfield to the blue-painted doorway behind her.

"It don't matter, that I can see, where the woman used to live," said Mrs. Banfield; "but it do matter to my mind that a Tregarthen has farmed Saaron for six generations, and now 'tis pack-and-go for 'em."

"But why?"

"Why?" echoed Mrs. Banfield, fiercely. "Because, as you was tellin' just now, sir, my lord has a strong will. Because my lord wants Saaron for his own. Because he wants to shoot rabbits. Because rabbits be of more account to him than men — and I don't blame him for it, seein' that all the men on the Islands be turned to mice in these days. Oh, 'tis an old tale! But there! You never heard of it. You never heard — not you — that the man was even unjust!"

"But, my dear Mrs. Banfield—"

"Go'st thy ways, good Governor. You was the poor man's friend — one time; but now there's too much Christianity in you. . . . And no more will I answer until you tells me who your guest is, that eats two breakfasts in one morning."

The Commandant gazed at her in mild surprise. Doubtless he would have asked the meaning of this cryptic utterance; but at this moment the two seamen from the *Milo* issued forth from the gateway up the road; and, descending a few paces, turned to call back farewell to Mrs. Treacher, who, having escorted them so far, halted under the arch and stood, with hands on hips, to watch them out of sight.

"Wish 'ee well, I'm sure!" said Mrs. Treacher. "You understand we be poor people in these parts."

"Don't mention that, ma'am," said one of the seamen, politely.

"There's no talk of favours, as between us and Madame," called out the other.

They passed the Commandant and saluted. On a sudden it

struck him that these men would expect a small monetary acknowledgment for their trouble; and hastily nodding good-morning to Mrs. Banfield and Mrs. Medlin, he ran staggering up the slope to the gateway.

"Mrs. Treacher!" he panted, dumping down his burden, "I — er — it so happens that I have no small change about me."

"Me either," said Mrs. Treacher, idiomatically, and bent over the basket. "What's this?"

"You will forgive my mentioning it, Mrs. Treacher; but these good fellows very likely expected a sixpence or so for their trouble. If you wouldn't mind lending me back — for a short time only, a couple of shillings out of the four that — that I—"

"Very sorry, sir," said Mrs. Treacher, "but I spent 'em."

"What! Already?"

"Which I didn't like," pursued Mrs. Treacher, stonily, "to insult the lady's stomach with the kind of eatables I found in the larder. So while you was away, sir, I took the liberty to slip down to Tregaskisses and lay out three shillings. Which, finding no one in charge but that half-baked boy of his, I got good value for the money; and a sight better bacon than this, I don't mind saying — for all you have been so lavish."

She peered into the basket and looked up sharply. It was a cross-examining look, and seemed to ask where he had found the money for all this extravagance. The Commandant, evading it, turned and stared down the road, where already the two seamen had passed out of sight.

"You needn't mind them, sir," said Mrs. Treacher, reassuringly. "It's light come and light go with sailors."

Nevertheless, when the Commandant turned to accept the assurance, half eagerly and yet less than half convinced, she would not meet his eye; but picked up the basket and staggered along with it to the Barrack door. "There's a saying," said Mrs. Treacher, eagerly, halting there, "that sufficient for the day is the evil thereof. I've found it comforting before now. But it don't seem to allow for three meals per diem; and how to make bacon and eggs for dinner look different from bacon and eggs for breakfast is a question that'll take thought. You didn't happen to think upon cheese, now?"

"I did," said the Commandant, triumphantly. "There's half a pound of cheese — the very best Cheddar — or, so Tregaskis assured me."

"Tregaskis!" Mrs. Treacher put down her nose and sniffed the basket. "Tregaskis never sold better than third-class American in all his life."

"She comes from America," the Commandant hazarded.

"I shouldn't advise you to build on that," said Mrs. Treacher, dubiously; "but we'll hope for the best; and with beer in the place of tea it mayn't look altogether like breakfast over again."

He was stepping into the passage when she touched his sleeve in sudden contrition.

"I didn't mention it before, sir; but hearing as the sailors had brought up her boxes, she outs with this and asks me to give it to them for their trouble."

Mrs. Treacher held out a golden sovereign. The Commandant stared at it.

"You kept it back?" he gasped.

"I had to, sir. A couple of ignorant seamen — that didn't want it, either!"

"Give it to me!"

"There's one blessing — you can't possibly overtake 'em," said Mrs. Treacher, as the Commandant snatched the coin.

He gazed down the hill, and decided that to this extent she was right. With one hand gripping the sovereign, and the other lifted to his distraught brow, the Commandant strode to the room where Vashti sat at breakfast. She looked up and welcomed him with a gay smile.

CHAPTER XI

PLAN OF CAMPAIGN

Vashti sat on the low stone wall beyond the Keg of Butter Battery and gazed out over the twinkling Sound and the Islands. The wall ran along the edge of the cliff and moreover was ruinous, as the Commandant had cautioned her when she chose her perch.

For a while she did not appear to have heard him, but sat with lips half-parted as though they drank in their native air, and with eyes half-closed — but whether in mere delight or because through the present they were looking into the past, the Commandant could not determine. She had invited him after breakfast to conduct her round the old fortifications, and he had done so in some dread of her questions and comments. But she had asked scarcely a question and made no comment at all. She was thinking less of the change in his batteries and defences than of the change in him, as with a deeper knowledge of women he might have divined. In the inanimate work of man's hands woman takes no real interest, whatever she may feign, but of man himself she is insatiably curious and critical. So while the Commandant, moving with her from one battery to another, had halted and stared down on the grass-grown platforms, ashamed and half-afraid lest by lifting his eyes he should challenge her pity, he missed to perceive and missed altogether to guess that hers were occupied in taking note of him, of his threadbare coat, of the stoop of his shoulders, of the whitened hair brushed back from his temples.

They had made the round of the batteries in almost complete silence; and coming to the wall above the Keg of Butter she had perched herself there and bent her eyes seaward.

She may or may not have been aware that this gave him opportunity to take stock of her in his turn, and that he was using it very deliberately, letting his gaze travel over her profile, or so much of it as she presented to him, and so from point to point of her attire down to her well-made walking shoes — all with a kind of grave wonder. Once only he glanced up and to the northward, where low on the horizon a faint line of smoke lingered in the wake of the *Milo*, already hull-down on her way; and his glance seemed to ask for assurance that he was not dreaming, that the steamship had really come and gone and left him this unaccountable guest.

It was just at this moment that she answered him.

"Yes, I can easily understand that you feel it," she said in a musing tone.

"Eh?" The Commandant had almost forgotten his warning about the ruinous state of the wall. His eyes had wandered back from the horizon to the close coils of hair above her neck and to the lobe of her small ear which (as he found himself noting) had never been pierced to admit an earring. She turned, and as she caught his gaze he blushed in no little confusion.

With the point of her sunshade she indicated the deserted battery on his left.

"Though I suppose," she went on, still musing, "all these fortifications were really out of date for years before Government dismantled them."

"If that were true," he replied, "it would date my uselessness further back than ever."

"Your uselessness?" she echoed, and now it was her eyes that expressed a grave wonder. "But you were Governor of the Islands; and you are Governor still, are you not?"

"These batteries," he went on hastily, "though antiquated, were never out of date, never useless; and there will be reason enough to regret them if ever an enemy's squadron makes a pounce on the Islands."

"Poor little Islands!" Vashti looked across the Sound with a smile. "It seems almost comic somehow that anyone should dream of attacking them!"

"Ah!" said he, almost bitterly, "you have been living in great cities and enlarging your mind."

"And in great cities, you imply, it is easy to despise, to forget?" She laughed softly. "Brefar — Saaron — Inniscaw!" she murmured, addressing the Islands by name, "here is one who tells me I forget you! Sir, we will take a boat this very day, and I will sail you out to the Off Islands and prove to you if I forget."

"There is no need, Miss Vashti" — he hesitated over the "Miss," but she did not correct him, and he went on more boldly. "I had a talk this morning with Captain Whitaker, of the *Milo.*"

Vashti looked up with a quick smile. "He told you? . . . I am so glad! Yes, yes: I did not in the least want to have all those passengers crowding around me and paying me ridiculous compliments. But false modesty is another thing altogether, and I don't mind telling you I am quite inordinately proud of myself."

"You have a right to be."

" — as I don't mind confessing that I was horribly afraid at the time. But I am glad again, that Captain Whitaker told you. It was pretty good — eh? — after fifteen years."

She asked it frankly; not archly at all, but with a sudden earnest look that seemed to hold some sadness; and before the Commandant could reply this sadness grew and became so real that he wondered at his having doubted it at first glance.

"Fifteen years!" she went on. "We all have a quarrel against time, we men and women, but on grounds so different that a man scarcely understands a woman's grievance nor a woman a man's. With you it all rests in your work. Fifteen years knock holes in your fortifications, tumble your guns into the sea, send along a new generation of men to pull down what you have built, to rebuild in a flurry of haste, and see their work in its turn criticised and condemned by yet a new company of builders. At this we women only look on and marvel. Why all this fuss, we ask, over what you do? Why all this hopeful, hopeless craving to leave something permanent? The Islands, here, will outlast anything you can build. I come back after fifteen years, and they are unchanged; they would be unchanged were I to come back after a hundred. The same rocks, the same bracken, the same hum of the tides; the same flowers; the same blue here, below us, the same outline of a spear-head there, beyond St. Ann's, where the tide forces through the slack water; the same streak of yellow yonder on the south cliffs of Saaron. . . . Our grievance is more personal, more real . . . and so should yours be, if you could only see it. It is to ourselves — to you and me, to any man and woman — that time makes the difference. You worry over your fortifications. Why? It is in ourselves that the tragedy lies. To lose our looks, our voice — to grow old and mumble — " She broke off with a shiver.

The Commandant smiled sadly. He had too much sense to pay an idle compliment. "If that be the tragedy, Miss Vashti," said he, "then we are wise in our folly, which bids us rest our hopes in our work though its permanence be all an illusion. We cannot cheat ourselves with a tale that we shall not grow old, but we are able to believe, however vainly, that our work will live."

"Yes," she admitted, "you are wise in your vanity — or would be, were it wisdom to shut one's eyes to fate. Let us grant that men are happier than women — than childless women at any rate. You do not know what it is to be a singer, for instance; to wake up each morning to a fear 'Has my voice gone? One of these days it will certainly go, but — Lord, not yet!' We must build on what we have. We must cling to our youth, knowing that after our youth comes darkness. No, sir, I do not blame men for setting up their rest upon what they do rather than upon ourselves; but for setting it upon that part of their work which, being the more visible, the more visibly decays."

The Commandant pondered while his eyes studied the grass-grown platform. He shook his head. "You puzzle me, Miss Vashti," he confessed.

"Why, sir, you have been mooning around these fortifications quite as though they had made up your life and their ruins stood for your broken purposes; whereas for fifteen years you have been Governor of the Islands and my sister tells me you are a good man. Surely, then, your real life has lain in the justice you have done, the wrongs you have righted, the trust you have built up in the people's hearts, and not in these decaying walls which no enemy ever threatened in your time nor for a hundred years before you came."

But again the Commandant shook his head.

"I say nothing of the first few years," he answered slowly. "I liked the people and I tried to do justice. But all that has passed out of my control. The Lord Proprietor takes everything into his own hands."

"Still on the Council — " she urged.

"I am no longer a member of the Council."

"You resigned? Why?"

"Because I saw that Sir Cæsar was bent on humiliating me; and he had the power."

Vashti prised at a loose stone from the wall with the point of her sunshade.

"I have read somewhere," she said, after a pause, "that no wise man should avoid being a magistrate, because it is wrong to refuse help to those who need it, and equally wrong to stand aside and let worse men govern ill."

"The Lord Proprietor does not govern ill. He likes his own way; but he is a just man — " The Commandant hesitated and paused.

"A just man until you happen to thwart him. Is that what you were going to say?"

"No," he answered, smiling. "I was about to say that once or twice I have found him something less than fair to me. To others — " But here he paused again, remembering that morning's conversation on the hill.

"I do not much believe," persisted Vashti, "in men who act justly so long as they are not thwarted. . . . But you would remind me no doubt that, if questions are to be asked and answered this morning, it is I who should be giving an account of myself. Well, then, I have come to the Islands with a little plan of campaign in my mind, and last night it occurred to me suddenly that you were the very person to help. I am — you will excuse my telling you this, but it is necessary — a passably rich woman; that is to say, I have more money than I want to spend on myself, after putting by enough for a rainy day; and I can earn more again if I want more. I have no 'encumbrances,' as foolish people put it; no relatives in the world but my sister Ruth and her children. No two sisters ever loved one another better than did Ruth and I. We lost our mother early, when Ruth was just three years old, and from then until she was a grown woman I had the mothering of her, being by five years the elder. You have seen something like it, I dare say, in other poor families where the mother has been taken; but I tell you again that never were pair more absolutely wrapped up in one another than were Ruth and I. We shared each other's thoughts by day, we slept together and shared each other's dreams. Oh!" — Vashti clasped her hands and looked up with brimming eyes — "I can see now how beautiful it all was."

The Commandant bowed his head gravely. "I can believe it," he said; and as if he had stepped back fifteen years he found himself standing again on the hill and looking in upon the fire-lit room — only now the picture and the two figures in it shone with divine meaning.

"I know what you would ask," she went on. "Why, then, you would ask, did I ever leave the Islands? . . . But this had always been understood between us. I cannot tell you how. For years we never talked about it, yet we always talked as if, some day, it must happen. The fate was on us to be separated; and the strange part of it was," continued Vashti, throwing out her hands involuntarily, and with this action changing as it were from a confident woman back to a child helpless before its destiny, "we understood from the first that I, who loved the Islands, must be the one to go, while Ruth would find a husband here and settle down, nor perhaps ever wish to cross over to the mainland. You see, of the two I was the reader; and sometimes when I read Shakespeare to her — for we possessed but a few books, and some of these, like 'The Pilgrim's Progress,' had no real scenery in them to take hold of — sometimes when I read Shakespeare, or 'The Arabian Nights,' or 'Mungo Park's Travels,' and the real world would open to me, with cities like London, or Venice, or Bagdad, and with woods like the Forest of Arden, and ports with shipping and great empty deserts, then Ruth would catch hold and cling to me, as if I was slipping away and leaving her before the time. . . . Yet we both knew that the time must come, in the end. Do you understand at all?" she broke off to ask.

"Yes," he answered. "I cannot tell how, but as you put it I seem to see it all."

She glanced at him with a quick, grateful smile. "Well, that is just how it happened, and if I were to explain and explain I couldn't make it any clearer. You understand, too, there was never any question of my leaving Ruth until she was grown a woman and could see with a woman's eyes. Then I knew she was safe. She had more common-sense even than I. She was born to marry — I never doubted that; but when I saw also that she was a woman to choose for herself and choose wisely — why, then I saw also, and all of a sudden, that the time had come and I was better out of the way; better, because a teacher has to know when to stop and trust the teaching to prove itself. Else by lingering on, he may easily do dreadful mischief, and all with the best will in the world. Do you understand this, too?"

Again the Commandant bent his head; for again, without knowing how or why, he understood.

"Well, I left the Islands, and there is no need to trouble you with my own story — though some day I will tell it if you care to hear. It contains a great deal of hard work, much good fortune, some suffering, too; and on the whole I am a very grateful woman, as I ought to be. . . . But we were talking of Ruth. She married, as she was born to marry, and her husband is a good man. She has children, and her letters are full of their sayings and doings, as a happy mother's should be. So, you see, our instinct was wise, and I did well to depart."

The Commandant considered this for a moment before answering: for her tone conveyed a question, almost a challenge.

"You were wise, perhaps, to go. But why in all these years have you never come back?"

She looked at him earnestly, and nodded. "Yes," she said, "I was afraid you would ask that; and yet I am glad, for it forces me to make confession, and I shall feel better to get it over. . . . Ruth loves me still, you see; but, of course, her husband comes first, and after her husband — if not sometimes before him — her children. That is as it should be, of course."

"Of course," the Commandant echoed.

"And of course I foresaw it. Remember, please, that I foresaw it before ever there was a question of young Tregarthen; so that my jealousy, if you are going to laugh at it, had nothing to do—"

"I am not in the least inclined to laugh."

"Thank you. We were not as ordinary sisters, you see, and . . . and there is another thing I must tell you," she went on with a brisk change of tone. "Though Ruth and I have always written regularly, there is one thing I have always kept hidden from her — I mean my success, as you will call it. At first this wasn't deliberate at all. . . . A great chance came to me, a chance so good that I could hardly believe — yes, so incredible even to me, that I dared not talk of it, but walked humbly, and taught myself to think of it as a dream from which I must awake, and awake to find people laughing at my hopes. I hid it even from Ruth. . . . Afterwards, when the dream had become a certainty, it seemed yet harder to tell her. I had concealed so much, and to tell her now seemed like triumphing over her — so full her letters were of simple things and of her happiness in them. I was afraid my news would overawe her, would change her in some way; that she would think me some grand person, and not the sister to whom she had told all her mind — not, you must understand, that Ruth could be envious if she tried. But have you never seen how, when a man grows rich or powerful suddenly, his old friends, the best of them, draw away from him, not in envy at all, but just because they feel he has been taken from them?"

"Yes," said the Commandant, "I have seen such cases."

"And I wanted still to be Vazzy to her — even though I must come after husband and children."

"She knows, then, as little about your — your success — or almost as little, as I do?" asked the Commandant, quaintly.

Vashti broke into a gay little laugh. "But I am going to tell her now," she answered, rising — "and that is where I want you to help me. She has no idea at all that I am here, and I want — that is my little plan — to look in upon her before I make myself known. I want to see Ruth — my own Ruth — moving about her house; to feed my eyes on her good face, and learn if it has changed as I have tried to picture it changing; to know her as she has been during these years, not as she will be when we have kissed and I have told her. . . . I would steal upon her children, too, and watch them. . . . It is wonderful to think of Ruth's children!"

She sprang on to the crumbling wall, and stood erect there, shading her eyes, gazing towards Saaron Island, where the forenoon sun flashed upon the beaches and upon the roof of one small farm, half hidden in a fold of the hills. The Commandant put out a hand to steady her, for her perch was rickety and almost overhung the sea.

"Ruth is there! . . . To think of her so happy there — to see her, almost! Oh, sir — but if you could understand that the nearer I have travelled back, the more foolish my jealousy has seemed to grow, with every fear, every doubt!"

"Miss Vashti" — the Commandant spoke seriously, still with his arm stretched out ready to grip her by the skirt if she should overbalance herself or the treacherous wall give way — "I am glad, for your sister's sake, you have come; but I must warn you that all is not right on Saaron Island."

She turned slowly, and looked down upon him there from her altitude.

"What is not right?" she asked; and, while he hesitated, "You are not telling me that her letters have hidden anything?"

"No."

"Is it illness, then? Has anything happened to the children?"

"No," he answered again, and without more ado he told her the news he had heard from Mrs. Banfield.

"But" — she still looked down on him wondering — "but you told me just now that the Lord Proprietor was a just man?"

"I have not looked at the rights and wrongs of the case," he said hastily, conscious that he was incurring her scorn. "The Lord Proprietor may have much to say on his side."

"You have not inquired, then?"

"The news came to me only this morning, quite by chance."

"By chance?" she caught him up, and, springing off the wall, stood on the firm turf facing him. "But you are, or were, Governor of the Islands."

Again he bent his head. "I have told you that I no longer serve the Council even. The Lord Proprietor does not consult me."

Vashti gazed around her, on the broken roof of the ammunition shed, the dismantled platform, the unkempt glacis below it. "For what work, then, do they pay you?" she asked, bitterly.

"For none," he answered, but without resentment. "And — excuse me — " he went on, fumbling in his pocket, and producing a sovereign, which he tendered to her, "but your mention of pay reminds me to return you this, which Mrs. Treacher has handed to me. It appears — I must apologize for her — that she received it from you to give to the men who carried up your box from the steamer; but that, being a little frightened at the amount, she withheld it, thinking that possibly you had made a mistake."

Vashti took the coin. Her face was yet flushed a little — as he read it, with anger.

"It is true," said she pensively, "that I am fifteen years a stranger here."

His face brightened. "Ah," said he, "if you will make allowance for that, we may yet put everything right!"

CHAPTER XII

SAARON ISLAND

Saaron Island lies about due north of Brefar, which looks eastward upon Inniscaw across the narrow gut of Cromwell's Sound. There was a time (the tale goes) when these three Islands made one. At low-water springs you may cross afoot between Saaron and Brefar, and from either of them, with a little more danger, to Inniscaw, picking your way between the pools and along the sandy flats that curve about the southern end of the Sound and divide it from the great roadstead. Also there are legends of stone walls and foundations of houses laid bare as the waters have sunk after a gale, and by the next tides covered again with sand.

But of the past history of Saaron next to nothing could be told, even by Ruth's husband, young Farmer Tregarthen, who rented the Island and the one habitable house upon it. He could not even have explained how so bleak a spot as Saaron had come to possess this farmhouse, which was one of the roomiest on the Islands. He only knew that it had been built for one of his forefathers, and that this forgotten Tregarthen, or the Lord Proprietor who had chosen him for tenant, must have held ambitious views of the amount of farming possible on Saaron. So much might be guessed from the size and extent of the out-buildings. The "chall" or byre, for instance, had stalls for no less than twelve cows, whereas today all the Island's hundred-and-twenty acres barely afforded pasturage for two. Considering this, he was divided between two opinions; the first, that his ancestors had pastured their cattle upon Brefar, driving them to and fro across the flats at low water; the second, that in the old days the soil had been fertile, and that either the sand, which drove across it in the prevailing westerly winds, devastating every green herb, had started its invasion within the last hundred years or so, or that his forerunners had possessed and lost some art of coping with it. He had trenched the sand in many places on the southern and easterly slopes of the two hills into which the Island was divided, and along the valley between them, and everywhere, at the depth of two feet or less, the spade found a fine, strong clay, capable of carrying any crop.

Young Farmer Tregarthen in his slow way pondered a deal over this and similar problems. Indeed, you might say that in one sense the Island was never out of his thoughts. He had been born on it. At the age of sixteen he had succeeded to the farm (though it was nominally leased to his mother), and to the fight which his father had begun — the warfare which his enemy, the sand, never allowed him to relax. He could almost remember his father resuming it and repairing the stone hedges which enclosed the old fields. In those days Saaron had supported, or failed to support, five families; but of these all but Tregarthen had lost their clutch on the barren rock and drifted away to other islands. He could remember their going. He passed their roofless cottages half a dozen times a day.

They had subsisted mainly by kelp-making and piloting, helped out (it is to be feared) by more than a little smuggling. There were conclusions to be drawn from the cellars in the farmhouse, too ample for the needs of a small farmer. Tregarthen had a shrewd notion that most of the guineas which his mother had hoarded in a stocking had come at one time or another from the contraband trade; also he had a notion that his father's renewed activities in digging and hedging must have coincided pretty accurately with the building of the coastguard station upon St. Lide's and the arrival of a Divisional Officer. But if smuggling flourished once, it had fallen on evil days, and its secrets had been hidden from his childhood. Also about that time the pilotage had decayed in competition with the licensed pilots on St. Ann's, and but a few hovelling jobs in and about Cromwell's Sound fell to the share of the men of Saaron. (He could recall discussions and injurious words, half-understood at the time, faint echoes of that old quarrel between the two islands.)

But the kelp-making had been in full swing; and the business had a plenty of mystery and picturesqueness to bite it upon a child's memory. All the summer through, day after day, at low water, the Islanders would be out upon the beaches cutting the ore-weed and dragging it in sledges up the foreshore, where they strewed it above high-water mark, to dry in the sun. On sunny days they scattered and turned it, on wet days they banked it into heaps almost as tall as arrish-mows. From morning until evening they laboured, and towards midsummer, as the near beaches became denuded, would tail away, in twos and threes, and whole families, to camp among the Off Islands and raid them; until, when August came and the kelping season drew to an end, boat after boat would arrive at high-water and discharge its burden.

These operations filled the summer days; but it was towards nightfall that the real fun began. For then the men, women, and children would gather and build the kilns — pits scooped in the sand, measuring about seven feet across and three feet deep in the centre. While the men finished lining the sides of the kiln with stones, the women and girls would leap into it with armfuls of furze; which they lighted and so, strewing the dried ore-weed upon it, built little by little into a blazing pile. The great sea-lights which ring the Islands now make a brave show; but (say the older inhabitants) it will not compare with the illuminations of bygone summer nights, when as many as forty kilns would be burning together, and island signalling to island with bonfire-lights that flickered across the roadsteads and danced on the wild tide-races. From four to five hours the kilns would be kept burning, and the critical moment came when the mass of kelp began to liquefy, and word was given to "strike." Then a dozen or fourteen men would leap down with pitchforks and heave the red molten mass from side to side of the kiln, toiling like madmen, while the sweat ran shining down their half-naked bodies; and sometimes — and always on Midsummer Eve, which is Baal-fire night — while they laboured the women and girls would join hands and dance round the pit. In ten minutes or so all this excitement would die out, the dancers unlock their hands the men climb out of the pit and throw themselves panting on the sand, leaving the kelp to settle, cool, and vitrify. But while it lasted the boy knew of no excitement comparable with it. Little wonder that he remembered those fiery pits with the dark figures dancing around their brims! But yet more unforgettable was the smell of the burning kelp had been more than enough — that acrid, all-permeating, unforgettable odour. His mother had never been able to endure it. When the wind drove the smoke from the beach, she would shut every door and window, and build up every crevice with a barricade of sandbags; all in vain. It crept into the house, choking the besieged, causing their eyes to smart and their heads to ache, and scenting clothes, linen, furniture. Even the food tasted of it.

The kelp-making, however, was but a memory now, though a pungent one. A night's work at the kiln produced from two to three hundred-weight, and the price in the good seasons ranged from £4 to £5 a ton; so many shared the labour that a family had much ado to earn £10 in a whole season. Under such conditions, too, the work was roughly done. Too often the sides of the kiln would fall in and the sand — always the curse of Saaron — would mingle with the kelp and spoil it. And when some wiser folk in Scotland learned to prepare it under cover, in ovens with paved floors, the Islanders lost their market, almost in a single season.

Tregarthen could recall the kelp-making, but neither the circumstances of the collapse nor the sufferings that followed it. Children observe the toil, but are usually quite blind to the troubles of their elders. He only knew that the poorer families almost of a sudden drifted away from Saaron, that he and his father and mother were left alone on the island, that his father had begun to busy himself with farming and required his help, and that in consequence he was released from lessons. His mother, a farmer's daughter from

Holy Vale in St. Lide's — the one nook in the Islands where you lost sight and almost sound of the sea, and could look out of window upon green trees — was a better-most person and something of a scholar. (The Tregarthens had always gone to the main island for their wives.) She taught the boy to read, to write a little, and even to cipher up sums in addition and subtraction. Also she took him over to Brefar to church on every fine Sunday and taught him his catechism, on the chance (often rumoured) that the Bishop would come across from the mainland to hold a Confirmation. But the Bishop of those days had a weak stomach, and, on the advice of his doctor, kept postponing the voyage.

Thus the boy grew up into a strong, slow man, gentle of manners, shy of the sound of his own voice, but tenacious of purpose and stubborn when his will was crossed. Except for the few months when he went wooing after Ruth Cara — in the year after his mother's death — his life, hopes, purposes, dreams and waking thoughts concentrated themselves upon Saaron, and from the day he brought his bride home to it the island became more than ever his sufficing world. He knew a thousand small things concerning it — secrets of the soil, of the tides, of the sand drift — voices of the wind, varying colours of the sea, and what weather they foretold — where this moss grew, that bird nested — in what week the wild duck arrived, on what wind the geese might be looked for, and what feeling in the spring air announced that the guillemots were due. He had learnt these things unconsciously, and was quite unaware of his knowledge, having never an occasion to review it or put it into words. Moreover, it was strangely limited. To his ancestors, to the folk who had lived here before him, he never gave a thought, except to wonder what their tillage had been or why they had rounded off a hedge at such and such a corner. Of the history of his own farmhouse he could tell you next to nothing, and nothing at all of the small ruined church he passed at least twice a day — though this testified that Saaron had been populous once on a time. How long had the Tregarthens lived on the Island? How far back beyond the five or six generations attested by the signatures on old leases hidden away in his strong-box? One might as well ask how long the sandpipers and oyster-catchers had bred on their separate grounds under the north slope of the cliffs towards Brefar. On the summit of the hill stood eleven mounds, and in each mound (so tradition said) lay the burnt bones of royalty. Was he, perhaps, descended from these Island kings? Tregarthen would not have given sixpence to discover. They were dead, and less than names: the place of their burial belonged to him, and he had to wring a livelihood from it to support his wife and family. Sometimes, when he thought of his three youngsters — of the boy especially — the man felt a vague longing which puzzled him as well by its foolishness as by its strength; a longing to pass, when his time came, into these barren acres and watch (though helplessly) while his heir improved what he had painfully won. It was absurd, of course, to desire any such perpetuity; wicked, perhaps. It could not be reconciled with heaven and the future life promised by the Bible. Yet it haunted him, though at rare intervals, and not importunately. To the past he gave never a thought.

Ruth Tregarthen, his wife, was one of those women who find their happiness within their own doors. The farm-house stood some way up the slope of the southern hill, facing eastward over the valley which curved a little at its feet and spread into a line of small flat meadows around the East Bay, where the farmer kept his two boats; and the site had been chosen here to avoid the seas which, with a gale falling on top of the equinoctial springs, are driven up the valley from east and west, and meet to form an isthmus, cutting the Island in two.

The state-rooms of the farm-house — parlour, hall, and best bedrooms — looked eastward upon Cromwell's Sound; but the waters of the Sound were hidden from the lower windows by a stout hedge of tamarisk. The kitchen window at the back — by far the largest in the house, as the kitchen itself, where the family took its meals on every day but Christmas Day and Good Friday, was the true focus of the household — looked across the town-place, or farm-yard, upon another tall hedge of tamarisk, above which climbed the hill, steep, strewn with small white stones, shutting out the Atlantic.

The kitchen table stood close beside this window, just beyond the edge of the bacon-rack; and directly opposite, across the wide paved floor, was a wide open hearth, fitted with crooks and brandises, where all the day long something or other would be cooking, and where the night through the logs smouldered and fell in soft grey ash, to be fed and stirred to flame again in the early morning. Yes, and as though this was not enough, the hearth had beside it an iron door which, being opened, disclosed to the children a long narrow hole filled with fire; vision to them of a passage leading straight to hell, though their own mother (and she so gentle) stoked it with bunches of furze, and drew from it loaves and saffron cakes, hot and detectable.

To the children it seemed that their parents seldom or never talked, and never by any chance took a rest.

Their names were Annet, Linnet and Matthew Henry, and this was the order of their ages — Annet nine, Linnet seven, and Matthew Henry rising five. On fine days they attended school at Inniscaw, being rowed to and fro across the Sound by John Nanjulian (Old Jan), the hind, or Stevy, the farm-boy. These, with Melia Mundy, the house-girl, whose parents lived on Brefar, made up Farmer Tregarthen's employ, and took their meals at table with the family.

The school which Annet, Linnet, and Matthew Henry attended had been built by the Lord Proprietor on Inniscaw shore, to serve the three islands of Inniscaw, Brefar, and Saaron. The children brought their school-pence weekly, on Friday mornings; but, of course, their pence did not pay — scarcely even began to pay — for the cost. Also there were days, and sometimes many days together, when no boat could be put across; and, considering this, the Lord Proprietor (who was a philanthropist in his way, but his way happened to be a despotic one) had commanded his architect to prepare plans for a smaller school on Brefar. This, to be sure, would not help the three children on Saaron; but it gave him yet another reason to feel indignant with that fellow Tregarthen for clinging so obstinately to his solitude and barren acres.

The children themselves did not regret living so far from school; for they were ordinary healthy youngsters though brighter-witted than most, and felt as other youngsters feel towards that wise and elderly beneficence which boxes them up in a room for instruction. To be sure they missed the games in the play-ground before and after school; but this was no such loss as the reader, remembering his own childhood, might be disposed to think. For, sad to tell, only a few of the hundreds of thousands of children attending schools really understand games, or can be said to have learnt to play, and the Island children were in this respect some way behind their brothers and sisters on the mainland. If at whiles the small trio looked back wistfully as old Jan rowed them homeward, or if the shouts that followed across the water from the playground now and again reproached them, on the whole they would not have changed places with their school-fellows even at a price. After all, no island in the world could compare with Saaron. Their father had never said this, but they were sure that he thought it; and their father knew everything. As he walked along he would say suddenly, "Go there" — but without lifting his eyes, just waving his hand towards the spot — "and there you will find a bunting's nest, or a stone-chat's"; nor once in a dozen times would he be mistaken.

There were compensations, too, in living on an island where on any morning you might wake and find a gale of wind blowing, forbidding you to go to school. But even in fine weather one could always look forward to Saturday and Sunday, each a whole holiday.

It was Saturday. The three had opened their eyes soon after day-break and lay in their cots "chirruping," as their mother called it — talking, planning out a campaign of adventures for the long two days before them. The sun shone through their nursery window, which faced the East. They had curled themselves to sleep before the great fog came up and covered the Islands, and the sound of guns had neither awakened them nor reached their dreams. They awoke to a clear morning sky, and while they chatted, waiting the order to tumble out and dress, their father looked in at the nursery door and astonished and excited them with news of a great steamer which had entered the Roads in the night and was already lifting anchor to pursue her voyage.

From the hill above the farmhouse they watched her, after breakfast, as she steamed past the southern point of the island, nosed her way slowly through Chough Sound, between Inniscaw and St. Lide's, and so headed away to the northward until her smoke lay in a low trail on the horizon. They had never before seen a steamer of her size.

Thus strangely began a day which the three had still stranger cause to remember. They had planned to take their dinner wrapped in their handkerchiefs and climb to the old tombs on the hill over-looking Brefar, then to play at being Aztecs, from hints which Annet had dug out of an old History of Mexico on her mother's bookshelf, and at hiding treasure from the Spaniards, whose ships were to come sailing through the Off Islands. Having concealed their hoard, they were either to descend upon the Western Bay, which they called The Porth, and there offer a bloody resistance to the invaders, or (this was Annet's notion, which for the present she kept to herself) to wait until the north channel dried and make a desperate escape across the sands to Brefar. The trouble was, she could not be sure of low water being early enough to let them dash across and back before dusk again. She was a brave girl — a great deal braver, at least in these adventures, than her sister Linnet; but she had to bear in mind that Matthew Henry was but five years old and easily tired, and also that if they arrived home after dusk her mother would be anxious and her father angry. So she nursed the project in her own heart, and when the three had taken seizin of the northern hill, eaten their manchets of saffron cake, and shared their canful of milk, she took up a post from which, while the others scanned the offing for Spaniards, she could watch and time the ebb of the tide on the flats.

The afternoon was sunny; the flat rock on which they were perched lay out of the wind's reach; and to beguile the interval of waiting Annet drew out a book which she had brought with her — a much-worn copy of Hans Andersen which had arrived at Christmas, three years ago, as a gift from that mysterious Aunt Vazzy of whom their mother talked so often. Linnet stoutly maintained that this aunt of theirs, whom they had never set eyes on, must be a fairy herself — neither more nor less; and Annet had her doubts on this point. But the book, at any rate, was real, with a real inscription on the fly-leaf; and the children (though some of the stories puzzled them) believed it to be the most beautiful book in the world.

Each child had a favourite story. Matthew Henry's was "The Tinder-Box," and he would wake in the night from dreams, deliciously terrible, of the three dogs "with eyes as big as coach wheels." Linnet, who had a practical mind, preferred such as dealt with rolling-pins, flat-irons, and shirt-collars, because these were familiar objects, and their histories usually ended cheerfully — (she liked "The Ugly Duckling" because he was a duckling, but objected to much of the tale as being too sad). Annet declared for "The Little Mermaid," which is perhaps the saddest of all; and this was the one she chose today, though half-penitently, because she felt pretty certain that it would make Linnet cry.

But today Linnet no sooner recognized the opening of the story than she set her face defiantly; and when Annet reached that most pathetic passage where the little mermaid glances down sorrowfully at her fish's tail, and "Let us be merry," says the grandmother, "let us dance and play for the three hundred years we have to live," Linnet lifted her chin, stared hard at the horizon and said resolutely — albeit in a voice that trembled a little —

"I don't believe there are any such things as mermaids!"

Young Matthew Henry opened his mouth and stared, round-eyed at such dreadful scepticism.

Annet, too, gazed up from her book.

"But the story says there are," she answered, simply and gravely.

"Who ever saw one?" persisted doubting Linnet.

"Hundreds of people — " Annet began, and with that, as a shadow fell on the rock, she lifted her eyes and uttered a little cry.

Just above, on the flat tombstone that jutted over the ridge, stood a beautiful lady, and looked down on them.

CHAPTER XIII

THE LADY FROM THE SEA

How it happened the children never precisely knew. When they came to compare notes that evening their recollections varied on several important particulars. But this was certain, that before they could rise and run — and Matthew Henry protested that, for his part, he had never an idea of running — the apparition had stepped down from her pedestal and seated herself among them in the friendliest way.

"Good day!" she nodded. "Now let me see ... this is Annet, and this is Linnet, and that is Matthew Henry, and I hope you're all uncommonly well."

Annet gasped that they were quite well, thank you. Who and what could she be, this lady out of nowhere? ... Not a witch, for no witch could smile with such a beautiful face or wear such beautiful clothes. On the other hand, Annet had not supposed that fairies were ever so tall. Yet something of the sort she must be, for she knew their names. ...

"You want to know where I come from? But that is easy." The stranger reached out a white hand with a diamond upon it, and Annet yielded the book to her without resisting. "I come from here" — and she tapped the pages mysteriously.

"But how can that be?" demanded Linnet, who was always the matter-of-fact one. "Out of a book! Such things do not happen."

Vashti laughed merrily. "I assure you," she answered, with a glance at the fly-leaf, "I have been in the book all the while you were reading; and," she added, her eyes softening as they rested on the child, "of you three it is Linnet who is most like her mother."

They had not thought of this before, but she had no sooner said it than they knew it to be the truth; and the discovery made her more marvellous than ever.

"Yes," she went on, "I have lived inside this book; and, what is more, I know the man who wrote it."

She looked around on the three faces; and — so strange are children — for the first time in his life Matthew Henry at once asserted himself as a person entirely different from his sisters. For Annet and Linnet merely looked puzzled; to them the book was a book, just as the hill upon which they sat was a hill, and they had never troubled their heads about such a thing as an author. But Matthew Henry opened his infantine eyes still wider.

"Tell us about him," he demanded.

Vashti eyed the child curiously for a moment before answering. "He lives in the north," she said, "in a city where the sea is sometimes frozen for weeks in the winter, and where night after night you may see the Northern Lights over the roofs. That is why he writes so much of snow and fir-trees and cold winters."

Annet nodded. "I have seen the Northern Lights — once — from Saaron here," she announced proudly. "Father took me out of my bed and held me up to the window to look at them; Linnet, too — but she was too young to remember, and Matthew Henry was not even born at the time."

"But tell us," persisted Matthew Henry, "about the man who wrote the book."

"Well, the Northern Lights were shining in the streets on the night when I met him. I drove to his house in a sleigh from the theatre — if you know what a theatre is?" Vashti paused dubiously; but Annet nodded and assured her —

"That's all right. We don't know about these things, but they are all in the book."

"And so," said Vashti, "is the man himself, or most of him. He was a queer, shy old man, with oddly-shaped hands and feet, but oh, such timid eyes! And he lived in a fine house all by himself, for he had no wife. In the days when he wanted a wife he had been an Ugly Duckling, and now, when he had turned into a swan, it was too late to marry. He was very old indeed; but this was his birthday, and he had lit up all his rooms for us and made a great feast, and at the feast he made me sit on his right hand. . . . There were princesses to do him honour, but he chose me out because I had sung to him; and the princesses were not angry because he was an old man. Out in the streets the people were letting off fireworks, and while he talked to me I could hear the whole sky banging with rockets and crackers. It put me in mind of his story of 'The Flying Trunk.' But he talked of Italy and the South, because I had come from there; and of the Mediterranean and of beautiful inland lakes which he had known, but would never see again; for he was over seventy. And he told me that, in spite of the snow and frost outside, he could feel the spring coming northward again with the storks. It was the last time (he said) that he should ever see it, but he filled his glass and drank to me because, as he put it, I had sung the South back to him for this last time. So now you know why I was proud to come to you out of his book."

"But," said Linnet, gravely, "we were reading about mermaids; and you can't be one of *them*, because there aren't any."

Matthew Henry would by no means allow this. "But Jan's father caught one," he objected, "in a pool just inside Piper's Hole, where she was left by the tide. He has told us about her, dozens of times. And besides," he added, getting in a home-thrust, "if there isn't any such thing, why were you crying over the story, just now?"

"I wasn't," contended Linnet, very red in the face. But she shifted her ground. "Why," pointing to Vashti's skirts — "her clothes aren't even wet, to say nothing of a tail!"

Vashti laughed. "My dears, you are both right and both wrong. As for the mermaids, Linnet, they were friends of mine before I reached your age, and you must let me introduce you to one by-and-by, to cure you of disbelieving. But you are right about me. I am not a mermaid; and yet I have come from the sea . . . like the Queen Zenobia."

"Who was she?" asked Annet, speaking for the others.

"She was a Queen in Carthage, more than two thousand years ago. She came to the Islands in a ship, to visit the tin-mines which used to lie between them and the mainland before the sea covered them, and from which she drew her great wealth. Her ship arrived in the middle of the Great Storm; and before she came to land, here on Saaron, the waters were rolling over the richest part of all her dependencies. Little she cared; for in the first place she had never seen it, and could not realise her loss, and moreover her ship had been tossing for three days and nights, past all hope, so that she was glad enough to reach a shore, however barren. She reached it, holding on to the shoulders of a brown man, a Moor, who swam for land as the ship began to break up; and the story goes that when his feet touched the sand he fell forward and died, for the swimming had burst his heart. But have you never heard the song about it?" Vashti sank her voice and began to chant, and low though the strain was, and monotonous, the children had never heard such wonderful singing —

> It was the Queen Zenobia
> With her gold crown,
> That sailed away from Africa
> With a down-derry-down!
>
> — To westward and to northward
> From Carthage town,
> Beyond the strait of Cadiz
> The sky began to frown.
>
> "Well-a-mercy!" cried her ladies,
> All of high renown;
> "I think the sea is troublesome
> And we shall all drown."

The seas came white aboard
And wetted her gown;
"Would I were back in Carthage
A-walking up and down!

That I were back in Carthage
Which is dry ground,
I would give my jewels
And a thousand pound."

Then round went the good ship,
And thrice she went round,
The third time she brast herself
With a down-derry-down!

Some cried misericordia,
And others did swoun;
But up there stood a guardsman
A naked man and brown —

"You are the Queen of Carthage
And gey young to drown;
But hold you to my girdle
That goes me around;

And swim with me to Saaron,
As I will be bound."
"Your girdle it is breaking
That goeth you around."

"Nay, hold you to the girdle
That is strong yet and sound;
My heart you felt a-breaking,
But here is dry ground."

With white sand and shingle
The shore did abound;
With white sand she covered him
And built him a mound.

With flotsam and with wreckage
The shore was all strown;
She built of it a cottage,
And there she sat down.

"Though this be not Africa,
Nor yet Carthage town,
Deo-gracey," said Zenobia,
"That I did not drown!"

"That's where the tune changes," interrupted Matthew Henry,

clapping his small sunburnt hands together.

"You know the song then?" asked Vashti, looking from one to the other.

All three nodded. "We know a verse or two," Annet answered. "Mother was always singing it when she rocked Matthew Henry to sleep, and sometimes we get her to sing as much as she can remember for a treat."

"But she can only remember five or six verses," said Linnet; "and her voice is not beautiful like yours."

Annet and Matthew Henry protested. Their mother's was a beautiful voice; one of the most beautiful in the world.

"But not beautiful like hers," Linnet persisted. "I mean that it's quite different."

They admitted this — so much their loyalty allowed them. "And I like the end of the song best," Linnet went on, "because it's cheerfuller. It goes on 'At daybreak she dressed her. . . .'"

But for a moment or two, though she felt the children's eyes fastened on her expectantly, Vashti did not resume the song. Those same expectant eyes were open windows through which she looked into the past, as into a house tenanted by ghosts. Through Annet's, through Linnet's, she saw familiarly, recognising the dim children that played within and beyond the shadow of the blinds. But the child Matthew Henry's frightened her. She and Ruth had lost a brother once. He had died in infancy, a scrap of childhood, almost forgotten. . . . Yes, Matthew Henry's eyes too had a playroom behind them; and there too a shadowy child played at hide and seek.

Her voice shook a little as she picked up the old song —

> At daybreak she dressed her,
> Her wet hair she wound,
> When she saw a lithe shepherd,
> Stood under the mound.
>
> He stood among the wreckage
> With crook and with hound,
> Alone in the morning,
> That most did astound.
>
> "O tell to me, lithe shepherd,
> What king owns this ground?"
> "No king, ma'am, but Zenobia,
> A Queen of renown."
>
> "Lithe lad, she is shipwrecked;
> Myself saw her drown."
> "Then 'tis you are Queen of Saaron

If you will step down.

"I have sheep, goat, and cattle
And a clear three pound,
If you'll mate with me and settle
In goods we will abound."

"Well-a-way!" sighed Zenobia,
"I have lost Carthage town,
But I like this lithe shepherd
So handsome and brown.

"If I marry you," said Zenobia,
"Farewell to renown!
If I marry you," said Zenobia,
"I mate with a clown.
But I'll marry you for all that,
With a down-derry-down!"

"And," said Linnet, as the song concluded, "they married and had twelve children — six boys and six girls. Mother told me about it."

But Matthew Henry turned to the singer gravely. "Is it true?" he asked. "And are you really Queen Zenobia?"

"Come and see," said Vashti, rising. "The sands are bare between us and Brefar, and if Linnet is brave enough we will take a boat and she shall be shown the cave where Jan's father caught the mermaid."

"But we must get back again," objected Annet.

"I will see that you get back again."

"The sands may not be safe."

"When you told us yourself that they were quite safe!" protested Matthew Henry. "And you said you would lead us over and back without any danger at all."

"The fact is," said Vashti, quietly, "Annet feels herself responsible for you, and thinks that very likely I am a witch."

The child faced her bravely, biting her lip upon the inward struggle.

"You are not a witch," she said. "Your eyes are too good. And, besides, there are people in Brefar who will take care of us if we miss our way back."

Vashti smiled, and again half sadly, for out of her own past this child confronted her. "That is brave, Annet; brave enough for the moment, though by and by we shall have to be braver. See how the sands shine below us! Shall we race for them and see who wins?"

She took Matthew Henry's small, unresisting hand, and the four pelted down the slope. Something in Vashti's eyes — it could not have been in the words of her last answer, for they were mysterious enough — had apparently reassured Annet, who cast away care and called back in triumph as she won the race down to the golden sands.

They were damp yet in patches, and these patches shone like metal reflecting the greenish-blue spaces that showed between the clouds in the heart of the gathering sunset. But along the fairway the sand lay firm to the tread, yet soft to the look as a stretch of amber-coloured velvet laid for their feet. Beyond rose Brefar, with its lower cliffs in twilight, its rounded upper slopes one shining green. Vashti had kilted her gown higher and helped the two girls to pin up their short skirts. All had taken off their shoes and stockings, for here and there a shallow channel must be waded.

They crossed without mishap, and, having shod themselves again, mounted the turfy slope where the larks flew up from their hiding-places among the stones. Vashti's talk was of the birds, for in all Brefar the spot best worth visiting is Merriman's Head, where the birds congregate in their thousands — cormorants, curlews, whimbrels, gulls and kittiwakes, oyster-catchers, sandpipers — these all the year round — and in early summer the razorbills and sea parrots. Zenobia, it appeared, knew not only Merriman's Head, but every rock, down to the smallest and farthest in the Off Islands, where these creatures nested. She spoke to them of the island from which Annet took her name — a low-lying ridge to the west of St. Ann's, curved like a snake, in nesting-time sheeted with pink thrift. There the sea-parrots breed, and so thickly that you can scarcely set foot ashore without plunging into their houses; but there is a mound near the western end where no sea-parrot may come, for the herring-gulls and the black-backs claim it for their own. She spoke of Great Rose, still further westward, where the gulls encamp among the ruined huts once used by the builders of the Monk Lighthouse; of Little Rose, where the great cormorant is at home; of Melligan and Carregan, the one favoured by shags, the other by razor-bills and guillemots. And so talking, while they wondered, she brought them across the hill to the great headland.

Merriman's Head, in truth, is itself an islet, being cut off from Brefar by a channel, scarcely eight feet wide, through which the seas rush darkly with horrible gurglings. The cleft goes down sheer, and was cut, they say, with one stroke of a giant's sword. Beyond it the headland rises grim and stark — a very Gibraltar of the birds, that roost in regiments on its giddy ledges.

As the children came down to the brink a flock of white gulls seemed to drop from the rock, hung in the air for a moment, and began wheeling overhead in wide circles, uttering their strange cries. A score of little oyster-catchers, too, tucked up their scarlet legs and skimmed off in flight. But the majority kept their posts and looked down almost disdainfully.

"They know we can't get to them," said Matthew Henry. "But wait till I am grown up! Then I'll come over to Brefar and build a bridge."

"You will not need a bridge when you are grown up," said Vashti. "See!" She stepped back a pace or two, and the children, before they guessed her purpose, saw her flash past them and leap. She cleared the chasm, easily alighted, and stood smiling back at them, while the birds poured out from their ledges, cloud upon cloud of them. Their wings darkened the air. Their uproar beat from cliff to cliff, and back again in broken echoes, like waves caught in a narrow cave and rebounding. Vashti looked up and laughed. Like a witch she stood, waving her arms to them.

"It is easy," she called back to the children; "easy enough, if you don't let the water frighten you. Why, Annet could jump it if she dared. Annet . . . but no, child! go back!"

But Annet, with a quick glance at her, and another at the water swirling below, had set her teeth and stepped back half-a-dozen paces. She would follow this woman, witch or no witch.

Linnet cried, too, and Matthew Henry. Vashti, stretching out both hands to wave back the child, opened them suddenly to catch her — and not too soon, for Annet alighted on a rock that sloped back towards the gulf, and had measured her powers against the leap so narrowly that her heels overhung the water and her body was bending backward when Vashti gripped, and, dragging her up to firm ground, took her in both arms.

"But why? Why, Annet?"

"I don't know," Annet answered, almost stupidly. The danger past, she felt faint of a sudden and dazed; nor could she understand what the strange lady meant by embracing her again, almost with a sob, and murmuring:

"The little water, and so hard to cross! But we had the courage, Annet — you and I!"

She turned and lifted her voice in a long, full-throated cry, that sent the birds flying in fresh circles from the eyries over which they were poising; and before its echoes died between the cliffs a boat came round the point — a boat with one man in it, and that man Major Vigoureux.

At another time they might have wondered how a boat came here, and why the Governor himself — whom they had seldom seen, but regarded from afar with awe — should be in charge of it. But the afternoon had fed them full with marvels. Here the great man was, and in a boat, and the strange lady stood apparently in no awe of his greatness.

"The little ones are tired," said Vashti. "We will sail them home and land them on Saaron."

The Commandant backed his boat skilfully into the passage between the walls of rock, lifted the two younger ones on board, and then stretched out a hand to the other shore to help Vashti and Annet. When all were stowed, he pushed out for an offing, and hoisted his small lug-sail, while Vashti took the tiller.

The breeze blew off the shore. The little boat heeled, flinging the spray merrily from her bows. Beyond and under the slack of the sail a golden sea stretched away to the dying sunset.

It was an enchanted hour, and it held the children silent. In silence they were landed on the beach of West Porth, and climbed over the hill to their house. From its summit they looked down upon a small sail dancing through the sunken reefs towards the Roads, away into the twilight where the sea lights already shone from the South Islands.

CHAPTER XIV

AFTER SERVICE

"They are good children," said Vashti, as she and the Commandant sat at breakfast together next morning, which was Sunday.

The Commandant did not answer for a moment. He was stirring his tea, in a brown study, nor did he note that Vashti's eyes were resting on him with an amused smile. She supposed these fits of abstraction to be habitual with him, due to living and taking his meals alone; but in fact his thoughts were wrestling with two or three very urgent problems. To begin with, he had plunged yet deeper in debt to Mr. Tregaskis. The total, to be sure, amounted to something under twenty-five shillings; but to a man with just one penny in his pocket this left no choice but between recklessness and panic, and the Commandant's spirits swung from one to the other like a pendulum. Panic asserted itself in the small hours, when he awoke in his bed and wondered what would happen when pay-day came, should it bring no pay with it . . . and to a man lying sleepless in the small hours, the worst seems not only possible but likely. Then, as daylight waxed and he awoke again from a short doze, to his surprise he found himself absolutely reckless. As well be hanged for a sheep as for a lamb! The ordeal lay three days off, and in three days anything might happen; but meanwhile this was certainly happening — a woman accomplished and beautiful had stepped into his life and was changing all the colour of it. He guessed the danger, put purposely averted his thoughts from it and from the certainty of scandal. Archelaus, Treacher, Mrs. Treacher — all three had been sworn to secrecy, and all three could be trusted. These folks read no harm, nothing beyond an amusing mystery, in Vashti's sojourn, and in particular she had made Mrs. Treacher her obedient slave. Yet the secret must come out, and in spite of Archelaus, who had brought his master's boat round and moored her cunningly under the lee of the rocks overhung by the Keg of Butter Battery. There, while the weather held, the Commandant and his guest could slip away without fear of prying eyes and sail off among the islands — as they had sailed off yesterday, Vashti sitting low and covering herself with a spare-sail, until beyond sight of St. Lide's quay and the houses on the slope. To be sure they had to reckon with Mr. Rogers' telescope, or rather to leave it out of account. If Mr. Rogers' telescope should prove indiscreet, Mr. Rogers must be let into the secret, and might be relied on to join the conspiracy.

The Commandant, however, was in no hurry to share his happiness. Since his youth he had made few friends, and in all his life had never known comradeship with a woman. Suddenly, and as a well-spring in the desert, Vashti had come into the dull round of his duty — his purposeless, monotonous duty — to refresh it; nor perhaps were the waters less sweet for the feeling that they were stolen. So he lived in the day, and put off thinking of the inevitable end.

One thing only troubled his happiness. He foresaw that the end, when it came, would mean for him something more serious than parting. He could not have told why, but from the moment when Vashti had turned on him and asked, "For what work do they pay you?" he had known that henceforward his conscience would not sleep until he had made a clean breast to the War Office and resigned his commission. It was not that her question told him anything new; only that he saw himself judged in her eyes, and in their light discovered that his conscience had been tolerating what was really intolerable. Her departure, then, would mean the end of all things; for on the very next day he would send in his papers and face the world alone — the very next day, and not until then. So much respite he gave himself; and this respite, and not the prospect of parting, cast the only shade upon his happiness. For he felt that he held her friendship on a false pretence; that if she knew the truth, she would despise him. That is why the Commandant sat in a brown study.

"They are good children," repeated Vashti, "but like all other children they know nothing of their elders' troubles. I remember that I was nine or ten before ever it occurred to me that my father could have any troubles. . . . Now from the top of the hill where those three youngsters sat talking their fairy-tales, I looked over Cromwell's Sound and saw their father, Eli Tregarthen, pulling across from Inniscaw. By the very stoop of his shoulders over the paddles I seemed to read that the world had gone wrong with the man, and when he beached his boat and walked up the hill towards Saaron Farm, I felt sure of it. Of course you may laugh and set it down to fancy, for the man was a good three-quarters of a mile away."

The Commandant, however, did not laugh. "I think, very likely, you are right," said he; "and the man had been over to Inniscaw to make a last appeal to the Lord Proprietor."

"I wonder," mused Vashti, "if he is the sort of man to tell his wife?"

The Commandant pondered this and shook his head, meaning that he found it hard to answer. "I know very little of Tregarthen. In manner, though polite enough, he always struck me as reserved to the last degree."

"Men of that manner are often the frankest with their wives," said Vashti; "though again, if you ask me how I know it, I must answer that I can't tell you." She sat for a moment, her brows puckered with thought; then, leaning forward, rested her elbows on the table, while with eyes fixed seriously upon him she checked off the pros and cons on her fingers. "On the one hand Eli Tregarthen, being a reserved man, and brought up on Saaron, probably loves the island after a fashion that Ruth understands very dimly if at all. I love my sister—"

The Commandant nodded.

" — But all the same I know where she is weak as well as where she is strong. She never had that feeling for the Islands which helps me to guess how her husband feels about Saaron. I can't explain it" — here Vashti opened her palms and lowered them till her arms from the elbows rested flat upon the table. "Perhaps I can't make you, who were not born here, understand why it would be grief to me to think of being buried in any other earth. But I expect that Eli Tregarthen feels it, and feels that, if they uproot him from Saaron, his life will from that moment become a different thing, in which he has not learnt — perhaps never will learn — to take much interest. It's queer that, with just this difference between us, Ruth should have been the one to stay behind and I the one to go. But fate is queer. . . . Ruth is like her namesake in the Bible; home for her is the roof covering those she loves, and would be though she changed the Islands for the other end of the world. Therefore," said Vashti, sagely, "if she feels for her husband's trouble at all, it would be not as for a trouble that afflicted them both equally; she would be sorry for him as she would be if he were hurt or diseased. And you know that silent men, like Tregarthen, when they are struck by disease, will sometimes hide it from their wives to the last possible moment — will tell no one, but least of all their wives."

"Yes, that is true," the Commandant agreed.

"On the other hand" — here Vashti resumed her checking — "Ruth has a wonderful gift of coaxing people to confide in her even those things they very much doubt her understanding. She used to get me to tell my woes for the mere consolation of feeling her cheek against mine. She had a wonderful knack, too, of obliging me to be open with her, without ever asking it; and unless those children's faces and talk misled me quite, they were formed in a house where the parents keep no secrets from one another. . . . You can always tell."

This was news to the Commandant; and he admitted that, as an old bachelor, he had never observed it.

"Always!" insisted Vashti, nodding. "They spoke of their father quite as if he were one of themselves; which is not only rare, and not only proves that Eli Tregarthen is a good man, but persuades me that, being in trouble, he has told his wife."

"You are reasoning beyond my depths," said the Commandant. "But it all sounds admirably wise, and I grant it. What next?"

"Why, if Eli has told her, she will be in trouble today and I must go to her."

"To Saaron? This morning?"

"To Saaron, certainly; but not this morning, if you are engaged."

"To tell the truth I had meant to go to church; that is, if you can spare me."

Simple man that he was, he had meant — having a load to lift presently off his conscience — to receive and be confirmed by the Sacrament. "Ye that do truly and earnestly repent" — the words had been in his ears at the moment when he took his resolve. Hopeless though the prospect might be, he steadfastly intended to lead a new life.

"My friend," said Vashti. "I am contrite enough already for the amount of your time I have wasted. We will put off our voyage until the evening."

He smiled wryly, remembering how she had asked, "For what work do they pay you?"

But Vashti having decided upon an evening expedition, would not listen to his offer to sacrifice his church-going; and so to church he went, and confirmed himself, and remained to take the Sacrament on his new resolution.

Now whether or not he would have remained could he have divined what was happening on Garrison Hill I have no wish — as it would be indecent — to inquire.

But let us go back to Miss Gabriel.

*****

Miss Gabriel, all the previous day, had been suffering from a sense of defeat, and at the hands of an enemy she had fallen into the habit of despising. A woman (or a man, for that matter) of Miss Gabriel's temper sees the world peopled with antagonists, and (perhaps fortunately for her *amour propre*) cannot see that her occasional victor is not only quite indifferent to his victory but has very possibly succeeded on the mere strength of not caring two pins about it, or even on the mere strength of not knowing that there was any fight going on. Such insouciance would have galled Miss Gabriel past endurance had it not, mercifully, lain outside her range of apprehension. As it was, she felt that the Commandant had taken her easily, at a disadvantage, and routed her — horse, foot, artillery, baggage.

And at the moment she had collapsed without a struggle. There lay the sting. She had meekly thrown up her hand, though it held one exceedingly strong trump. That woman in furs and diamonds. . . . Why had she not insisted on the existence of her own eyes and held her ground, demanding whence that woman came and what she did on Garrison Hill at such an hour?

The longer Miss Gabriel thought of it — and she thought of it all the next day — the more firmly she refused to believe herself the victim of an hallucination. She lived frugally; her nerves and digestion were alike in excellent order; in all her life she had never suffered from faintness, and but once or twice from a headache. The keenness of her eyesight was notorious, and she had a healthy contempt for anyone who believed in ghosts. . . . Moreover, Charlotte Pope, though inclined now to hedge about it, had undoubtedly seen the apparition.

"I wish, Elizabeth, you could find something else to talk about," pleaded Mrs. Pope, with a shiver. "You and I know everyone on the Islands and there's no one in the least like — like what we saw; while as for her jewels, they must have cost hundreds, if they were real."

"Ha!" exclaimed Miss Gabriel, with a decided sniff.

"I don't mean 'real' in that sense, Elizabeth; and I put it to you, Where could she have come from?"

Miss Gabriel could not answer this, nor did she try. "Then you *did* see her?" she was content to say.

"I — I thought I did."

"And I, Charlotte, am positive you did. Have you told your husband about it?"

"Not yet."

"Don't, then. Between ourselves, my dear Charlotte, an idea has occurred to me, and I fancy that if Major Vigoureux thinks he can delude me with his painted hussies he will find himself mistaken!"

More, for the moment, Miss Gabriel would not disclose. But it is to be feared that her design occupied her thoughts in church next morning to the detriment of her spiritual benefit. The good folk of Garland Town had — and still have — a pleasant custom of lingering outside the church porch for a few minutes after service to exchange greetings and a little mild gossip with their neighbours; and to Mr. and Mrs. Pope, thus lingering, Miss Gabriel attached herself with an air that meant business.

"Fine morning," said Miss Gabriel.

"The weather," assented Mr. Pope, clearing his throat, "is quite remarkable for the time of year. As I was observing to Mrs. Fossell, a moment ago, we might be in August month. Whether we attribute it or not to the influence of the Gulf Stream, in the matter of temperature we are wonderfully favoured."

"Quite so," said Miss Gabriel; "and I was about to propose our taking advantage of it for a short stroll on Garrison Hill, to whet our appetite." She heard Mrs. Pope gasp and went on hardily, "You and I, Mr. Pope, can remember the time when all the rank and fashion of Garland Town trooped up regularly after divine service to Garrison Hill. 'Church parade,' we used to call it."

"Indeed yes, Miss Gabriel — and with the Garrison band playing before us. Those were brave old days; and now I daresay that except for a stray pair of lovers no one promenades on Garrison Hill from year's end to year's end."

"It shocked me, the other night, to discover how completely I had forgotten it."

"You had indeed, ha-ha!" laughed Mr. Pope, with a roguish glance at his wife.

Miss Gabriel, too, glanced at her, and even more expressively. "Admire my boldness," it seemed to say, "and oblige me by imitating it as well as you can." Mrs. Pope began to tremble in her shoes.

"Oh, it was ridiculous! And I have a fancy to go over the ground again and prove to you, and to ourselves, how ridiculous it was. Shall we?"

"With pleasure." Mr. Pope bowed and offered his arm. In Garland Town, if you walked with two ladies it was *de rigueur* to offer an arm to each.

The stars in their courses seemed to be helping Miss Gabriel's design. Her one anticipated difficulty — for she sought an interview with Mrs. Treacher, to pump her in the presence and hearing of the Lord Proprietor's agent — had been a possible interruption by the Commandant. To her glee she had noted that the Commandant kept his seat after service. For another thirty minutes at least the coast would be clear.

She had never a doubt of bribing Mrs. Treacher — or, to put it more delicately, of inducing her to talk. Mrs. Treacher's manner had been brusque the night before last; but Miss Gabriel's own manner was brusque, whether to friend or to foe, and nice shades of address escaped her. Mrs. Treacher was certainly poor, and with a poverty to which a shilling meant a great deal. And Miss Gabriel had a shilling ready in her pocket, as well as half-a-crown as a heroic resource in case of unlooked-for obstinacy. But the shilling would almost certainly suffice. Had not the donative antimacassar already established a claim upon the Treachers' gratitude?

Again, the stars in their courses seemed to be fighting for Miss Gabriel's design. For as the two ladies climbed the hill on Mr.

Pope's arm, and when they were almost abreast of the barrack door, who should appear at the garden gate, on the opposite side of the road, but Mrs. Treacher herself? Catching sight of the visitors she halted in startled fashion, with her hand on the hasp of the gate.

"So few ever walk this way in these times," said Miss Gabriel, "I declare we have frightened the poor woman. Mrs. Treacher!" — she lifted her voice as she advanced.

"Ma'am."

"Mrs. Pope and I have been feeling not a little ashamed of ourselves that at the time we did not — er — recognise your — your kindness to us the other evening."

"Night, to be accyrate," said Mrs. Treacher, still interposing her ample body between them and the entrance to the garden. "Didn't you?"

"You put yourself to some inconvenience on our account," pursued Miss Gabriel; "and — and if you won't mind accepting — " Miss Gabriel held out the smaller coin by way of finishing the sentence.

"What's that for?" asked Mrs. Treacher.

"The circumstances were so unusual, and in a way — ha, ha! — so amusing—"

"Oh!" Mrs. Treacher interrupted. "Unusual, was they? I'm glad to hear it."

"Why, of course, they were unusual," Miss Gabriel persisted, albeit a trifle dashed; "and indeed so incredibly absurd that we have brought Mr. Pope to hear your account of them; for, I assure you, he'll hardly believe us."

Mrs. Treacher looked at Mr. Pope solemnly for the space of about ten seconds, and then as solemnly at the ladies.

"*What* won't he believe?"

"Why" — Miss Gabriel plucked up her courage — "there was so much that afterwards, when we came to compare notes, neither of us could explain — as, for instance, who was the strange lady that walked into the room and was evidently surprised to see us, as we were naturally surprised to see her— -"

Mrs. Treacher turned slowly again to Mr. Pope, whose face (since this was the first he had heard of any strange lady) expressed no small astonishment.

"Poor man!" she murmured, sympathetically, "did they really go so far as all that?"

"I assure you — " began Mrs. Pope stammering.

"Oh, go your ways and take 'em home!" cut in Mrs. Treacher. "I'm a friend to my sex in most matters; but to come askin' me to back up such a tale as that, and for a shillin'!" She turned her palm over and let the coin drop on the soil at her feet.

But here unhappily, at the height of Mrs. Treacher's indignation, a sneeze sounded from a bush across the patch of garden; and the eyes of her visitors, attracted by the sound, rested on an object which Mrs. Treacher, by interposition of her shoulders, had been doing her best to hide — a scarecrow standing unashamed in the midst of the garrison potato patch — a scarecrow in a flaunting waistcoat of scarlet, green, and yellow!

"My antimacassar!" gasped Miss Gabriel.

"The Lord Pro — " Mr. Pope checked the exclamation midway. "You will excuse me, ma'am. I was referring to the lower part of the figure."

"Was ever such ingratitude?"

"It is worse, ma'am — ten times worse. You may call it sacrilege."

CHAPTER XV

BREFAR CHURCH

"It was all my fault," confessed Vashti.

"I was thinking so," said the Commandant, drily. "It had not occurred to me that Archelaus and the Treachers were acting on their own initiative."

Vashti laughed, and her laugh rippled over the waves to meet the sunset gold. They had taken boat beneath the Keg of Butter Battery, and were sailing for Saaron with a light breeze on their quarter. Evening and Sabbath calm held the sky from its pale yellow verges up to the zenith across which a few stray gulls were homing. From Garland Town, from St. Ann's, from Brefar ahead of them, came wafted the sound of bells, far and faint, ringing to church, and the murmuring water in the boat's wake seemed to take up Vashti's laugh and echo it reproachfully, as she checked herself with a glance at her companion's face, which also was reproachful and sternly set, but with a slight twitch at the corners of the mouth to betray it.

"Forgive me!" she pleaded, but her voice, too, betrayed her.

"You are not penitent in the least."

"As you are only pretending to be angry. Remember that I belong to the 'profession,' and no amateur acting can impose on me."

"You will admit that you have behaved abominably." The Commandant conceded a smile.

"Oh, abominably!"

"And perhaps you will be good enough to indicate how I am to restore my credit with — with those people. When I met them coming down the hill and pulled up to salute, Miss Gabriel froze me with a stare, Mrs. Pope looked the other way, and her husband could only muster up a furtive sort of grin. 'Excuse me,' it seemed to say; 'things may right themselves by and by, but for the present I cannot know you.' The three between them knocked me all of a heap. Of course I could not guess what had happened, but I made sure they had seen you."

"It was the closest miss that they did not. When they hove in sight I was actually standing in front of our masterpiece, with my back to the road; calling orders to Archelaus and Treacher, who were at work stuffing *them* (so to speak) with straw. I fancy they have forgotten, on Garrison Hill, to guard against surprises. At any rate, we should have been taken in a highly unsoldier-like fashion if Mrs. Treacher hadn't kept her eye lifting. She gave the alarm, and we scuttled into the bushes like rabbits, and watched while she held the gate. What is more, I believe she would have fended off the danger if Sergeant Archelaus hadn't sneezed; and then — oh, then! — " Vashti paused, her eyes brimful of laughter.

"He broke cover?"

"I snatched at the tail of his tunic — hastily, I will admit — but until he had stepped past me I had no idea he meant to be so foolish. It came away in my hand. They heard the noise it made in ripping."

"But they did not see you?"

"No; for seeing that the mischief was done Sergeant Treacher stepped out too. You should have heard them explaining to Miss Gabriel! But they were quite brave and determined. They told me afterwards that rather than allow one of the visitors to enter and catch sight of me they would have picked up all three and carried them outside the garrison gate."

"The Lord Proprietor will certainly hear of this," said the Commandant, musing.

Vashti, who had bent to pin the sheet closer, lifted her head and regarded him with a puzzled frown; then, averting her eyes, let them travel under the foot of the sail towards the sunset.

"Decidedly the Lord Proprietor will hear of it," she said, after an interval during which he almost forgot that he had spoken. "Indeed, if it will help to get you, or Archelaus, or anyone out of a scrape, I propose to call on him tomorrow and confess all. Do you think he will be lenient?"

There was a shade of contempt in the question, and it called a flush to the Commandant's cheek. He was about to answer, but checked himself and sat silent, looking down at the foam that ran by the boat's gunwale.

"He must be worth visiting, too; that is, if one may reconstruct him from — from them."

The Commandant smiled. "My dear lady, you have already made one attempt to reconstruct him from them."

Vashti pondered awhile, her chin resting on her hand and her eyes yet fixed upon the sunset.

"I give you fair warning that I am here on a holiday," she murmured.

"I don't know what you consider a fair warning; but I had guessed so much."

"The first for fifteen years," she pursued; "and I won't promise that I shall not behave worse — considerably worse. Are you very angry with me?"

"My dear," answered the Commandant ("My dear," it should be explained, is the commonest form of address in the Islands, and one that even a prisoner will use to the magistrate trying him), "if you really wish to know, I am enjoying myself recklessly; and it would be idle to call my garrison to put you under restraint, since you have already suborned them. I started, you see, with the imprudence of showing you my defences, and now you have us all at your mercy."

"You have been more than good to me," said Vashti, after a pause; "but the fortress is already vacated." She nodded towards a valise which rested under the thwart by the foot of the mast. "Mrs. Treacher packed it for me," she explained, "and her husband carried it down to the boat. If Ruth needs me — as she almost certainly does — and if her husband will tolerate me, I shall sleep on Saaron tonight."

"But you will come back?" he asked, dismayed.

"Certainly not, unless the Lord Proprietor drives me to seek refuge."

The Commandant did not answer. He had known that this happy time must be short; he had known it from the first, and that the end would come unexpectedly.

The wind had fallen slightly, and the boat crept up to the entrance of Cromwell's Sound with sail that alternately tautened its sheet and let it fall slack. The single bell of Brefar Church yet rung to service; but the sun had sunk beneath the horizon, and the sea-lights were flashing around the horizon before Saaron loomed close on the port hand; and as they crept towards the East Porth under the loom of the Island, a row-boat shot out from the beach there, and headed up the Sound towards Brefar.

"Hush!" commanded Vashti, and peered forward.

But a boat putting out from Saaron at this hour could only belong to Saaron's only inhabitants, and could be bound but on one errand. And Ruth was in her, for, presently, as the children's voices travelled back across the still water, Vashti heard Matthew Henry's pitched to a shrill interrogative and calling his mother by name.

"They are rowing to church, the whole family," said Vashti. "We can follow as slowly as we choose."

She listened a moment, but the oars in the boat ahead continued their regular plash. It may be that Tregarthen had failed to discern the small sail astern of him in the gloom of the land. She lowered it quietly, stowed it, found and inserted the thole-pins, and shipped the paddles. Yet it seemed that she was in no hurry to row. She but dipped a blade twice to check the boat from swinging broadside-on to the tide, and so rested silent for minute after minute, gazing through the gloom towards the bright sea-lights.

And it seemed to the Commandant, seated and watching her,

that he could read some of the thoughts behind her gaze. His own went back again to the night of his first coming to the Islands, when, as at sunset he supposed himself to have discovered them, all of a sudden they discovered him — reef after reef opening a great shining eye upon him; and some of the eyes were steady, but most of them intermittent, and all sent long gleaming rays along the floor of the sea; a dozen sea-lights and eleven of them yellow, but the twelfth (that upon North Island) a deep glowing crimson. Since then and for fifteen years they had been his friends. Nightly he watched them for minutes from his window before undressing for bed; and in fanciful moments they seemed to draw a circle of witchcraft around the Islands.

If they meant so much to him what must they mean to her who had left home, dear ones, and all memories of youth? — and who, returned from exile, stood with her hand upon the latch of the old cupboard!

"Ruth will have changed," said Vashti, speaking aloud, but to herself. "It is impossible that she has not changed."

She dipped her paddles and began to pull, gently at first and almost languidly; but by and by strength came into her arms and the boat began to move at a pace that astonished the Commandant.

*****

Brefar Church stands on a green knoll close by the water's edge and only a few yards above a shingly beach where the Islanders bring their boats to shore. Its bell had ceased ringing long before its windows came into view with the warm lamp light shining within; and the beach lay dark under the shadow of the tamarisks topping the graveyard wall. Vashti, not in the least distressed by her exertions, sprang ashore and sought about for a good mooring-stone. She had found one almost before the Commandant, following, could offer to help her in her search. Together they hauled the boat a few yards up from the water.

"Are we to go inside?" the Commandant asked, looking up at the lighted building.

Before Vashti could answer a reedy harmonium sounded within and the congregation broke into the "Old Hundredth" hymn —

"All people that on earth do dwell,
Sing to the Lord with cheerful voice—"

The incongruity of it, sung by a handful of fisherfolk here on an islet of the Atlantic — the real congruity (if indeed the Church be, as the Bidding Prayer defines it, "the whole body of Christian people dispersed throughout the world") — was probably less perceptible to the Commandant after fifteen years' sojourn on the Islands than to Vashti, newly returned from great continents and crowded cities. But if she smiled the darkness did not betray her. The Commandant saw her lift a hand beckoning him to follow, and followed her up the knoll to a whitewashed gate glimmering between the dark masses of the tamarisks.

She opened it and disappeared into the churchyard. He followed, stumbling along the narrow path, and overtook her at the angle of the south porch. She was in the act of mounting upon a flat tombstone which lay close in the wall's shadow. A panel of light streamed from the window directly above, and fell on Vashti's face as she drew herself erect upon the slab and leaned forward, her fingers resting on the granite mullions; but a light not derived from this shone in her eyes a moment later. With a little sob of joy she pressed her forehead close against the leaded panes.

The Commandant heard the sound, and guessed the cause of it. The light in her eyes he could not see. He stood among the dark nettles, looking up at her, waiting for the hymn to conclude.

The "Amen" came at last. He heard the shuffling of feet as the congregation knelt to pray . . . and, with that, Vashti turned and bent to whisper to him.

"She is there — almost abreast of us, standing by the pillar. She is kneeling now — my own Ruth — and her face is hidden."

He supposed that she bent to step down from the slab, and he put up a hand to help her. A tear fell on the back of his fingers, as it were a single raindrop out of the night. . . . But she turned impulsively, and pressed her face again to the glass.

"She is praying. She will not look up again. . . . She would not turn her eyes just now, though her own sister stood so close! They were lifted to the lights in the chancel and to the dark window." Then, as it seemed, with sudden inconsequence, she added: "Forgive me, sir! You have been kind to me, and it is so many years — so many years—"

"My dear," said the Commandant, gravely, as he handed her down, "you honour me more than I can tell. All my life I shall remember that you have so honoured me."

But it did not appear that she heard him. Letting go his hand, she seated herself on the edge of the tombstone, and looked up at him with eyes that, barely touched by the light from the window, seemed to him strangely, almost pitifully childish — eyes of a child that had lost its mother young.

"Her face was not changed, or a very little; far less than I feared. She is beautiful, my own Ruth — beautiful as she is good."

"And happy?" he found himself asking.

"Happy and unhappy. Happy in her good man, in her children? — oh, yes. But unhappy, just now, because they are unhappy and in trouble. There was a gloom upon Eli Tregarthen's face, a look of pain—"

"Of anger, too, and of wonder mixed with it, I daresay. He has been hit by a blow he does not understand."

"But we will help them."

The Commandant stared into the darkness. There was gloom, too, on his face, had there been light enough to reveal it.

"The Lord Proprietor is a very obstinate man."

"Yes, yes; but I mean that we will help them tonight. I cannot bear to think of Ruth carrying her trouble home and lying awake with it."

"Perhaps she will not." The Commandant remembered how he himself had carried a burden to church that morning and left it there.

"Ah!" exclaimed Vashti, swiftly, guessing his thought, though not the occasion of it. "That may do for you and me. For my part, I am not a religious woman — I mean, not religious as I ought to be. Yet I understand. Often and often when worried or out of temper I go to church and sit there alone until peace of mind comes back to me. But I have no husband, and you no wife; whereas with Ruth all her soul's comfort is bound up in those she loves. While Eli Tregarthen wears that look on his face, she can never go home happy."

"But have we power to lift it?"

"We will try, and tonight."

She stood up, cast one look behind her at the lighted window, and led the way back along the path, through the gate, and down the knoll to the beach. While she cast off the rope from its mooring-stone he eased the boat off and launched her.

"Shall I take the paddles?" he asked.

No; Vashti would pull back as she had come; and as she pulled she talked of Ruth, out of her full heart. He listened, between joy and pain — joy to be sitting here, honoured with her confidences, though he had none but a listener's share in them — here, in the still, scented evening, caressed by her marvellous voice; and pain, not because her talk charged life full of new meanings, every one of which he felt to be vitally true and as certainly missed by his own starved experience, but because it took him for granted as a kindly stranger, an outsider admitted to these mysteries, and warned him that his time on this holy ground was short; nay, that it was drawing swiftly to a close. And how could he go back to the old monotony, the old routine?

He remembered that, to whatever he went back, it would not be to these — at any rate, not for long. The future might hold degradation, poverty of the sharpest, hard work for a pittance of daily bread; but at least his dismissal would send him back to a life in which lay somewhere these meanings that trembled like visions of light in the heart of Vashti's talk. They gave him glimpses of the heaven which, by their remembered rays, he must seek for himself. How many years had he wasted — how many years!

They moored the boat close under the cliff's shadow, and, climbing the rocks, between the cove and the East Porth, sat down to wait. Vashti sat in reverie, plucking and smelling at small tufts of the thyme; then, rousing herself with a happy laugh, she challenged the Commandant to name her all the islets, rock by rock, lying out yonder in the darkness. He tried, and she corrected omission after omission, mocking him. What did he care? It was enough to be seated here, close with her in the starry, odorous night.

Presently she tired of the contest, and clasping her knees began, without warning given, to croon a little song —

> *"Over the rim of the moor,*
> *And under a starry sky,*
> *Two men came to my door*
> *And rested them wearily.*
>
> *Beneath the bough and the star*
> *In a whispering foreign tongue,*
> *They talked of a land afar,*
> *And the merry days so young."*

She sang it as though to herself, or as though answering the murmur of the tide on the rocks at their feet; but at the third verse her voice lifted:

> *"Beneath the dawn and the bough*
> *I heard them arise and go —*
> *But my heart, it is aching — aching now,*
> *For the more it will never know."*

The song died away in a low wistful minor, as though it breathed its last upon a question. "The merry days — the merry days, so young," she echoed, after a pause, and lifted her head suddenly.

"Hark!"

The sound — it was the plash of oar — grew upon the darkness. A light shot out beyond the last point of Brefar, and its ray fell waving on the black water. It came from a lantern in the bows of the Tregarthen's boat, and as it drew nearer the two listeners could distinguish the children's voices.

They shrank back there in the shadow above the ledge, as the boat took ground and Eli Tregarthen, stepping ashore in his sea-boots, set the lantern on the stones of the beach, lifted out the children, and lent a hand to Ruth. The little ones scampered up the path; but Ruth waited by her husband while he heaved the boat high and dry with his easy, careless strength, and saw to her moorings. When all was done, and as he stooped to pick up the lantern, she came to him, and put a hand on his arm. So, and without speech, they went up the path together.

The rays of the lantern danced on the furze-bushes to right and left of the path. . . . Vashti leapt to her feet; her hands went up to her lips and hollowed themselves to a low call.

"Lul — lul — loo — ee!"

From the brake above came a little cry, a little gasping cry; and gruffly upon it Eli Tregarthen's voice challenged —

"Who goes there?"

"Caa-ra! caa-ra! . . . Oh, Ruth — my sister!"

The Commandant saw Tregarthen's lantern lifted above the gorse, and by the light of it Ruth came down to the narrow pathway — came with the face of a ghost, as Vashti sprang up the slope towards her.

"Vassy! Not Vassy!— -"

But Vashti's arms were about her for proof. The Commandant, standing below in the shadow of the brake, heard the younger sister's sobs.

"Vassy! And tonight!"

"Tonight, and for many nights— -"

"Thank God! Thank God!"

The Commandant, by the light of the lantern which Eli Tregarthen held stupidly, saw them go up the path, their arms holding each other's waist. They disappeared, but their questions and eager, broken answers, as they climbed towards Saaron, came down to him where he stood alone, forgotten.

He stood there for half an hour almost. Then, as he felt the chill of the night he recalled himself to action with a shiver, and shouldered Vashti's valise. Slowly he climbed the hill with it, to Saaron Farm, and rapped on the door.

Tregarthen opened to him, staring.

"I have brought your sister-in-law's luggage."

"Is it the Governor? . . . But won't you step inside, sir?"

"I thank you; no. It is late," answered the Commandant, curtly, and turned on his heel.

As he went by the window he saw — he could not help seeing —

Ruth in her chair, with Vashti on the hearth beside her, clasping her knees. The children looked on in a wondering semi-circle.

He stumbled down the hill, and as he went he heard the door softly close behind him.

CHAPTER XVI

THE LORD PROPRIETOR'S AUDIENCE

Sir Cæsar Hutchins, Lord Proprietor, paced the terrace of his great house at Inniscaw, and paused ever and anon to survey the prospect with a lordly proprietary eye. He had breakfasted, and at breakfast (to use his own words) he always did himself justice. Indeed, throughout a strenuous business career he had never failed to take very good care of himself, and was now able to enjoy a clear conscience with an easy digestion.

The reader may ask with some surprise how such a man, accustomed all his life to the bustle and traffic of Finsbury Pavement, E. C., could choose, in his middle age, to turn his back on these and purchase an exile out in the Atlantic, where no one bought or sold shares, and where only Mr. Fossell, perhaps — and he from a week-old newspaper — caught an echo of the world's markets, whether they rose or fell. But, in truth, Sir Cæsar had chosen carefully, deliberately. He had always intended to enjoy in later life the wealth for which he had worked hard in his prime; and as soon as his fortune was assured, he had made several cautious but determined experiments to discover where enjoyment might abide. He had, for instance, rented a grouse-moor, and invited a large company to help him, by shooting the birds, to feel that he was getting a return for his money. But somehow his guests, though very good fellows in London, did not harmonize (to his mind) with the highland wastes. He was glad when they departed; the scenery improved at once — at any rate, he took more pleasure in it. He tried a deer forest and found this tolerable, but he soon made the further discovery that shooting bored him, that is to say, all shooting of higher rank that the potting of rabbits. He was one of those enviable persons who "know what they like." If he made trial of these expensive recreations, it was simply because he saw men ambitious for them, and supposed they would certainly yield some gratification to explain it; but, having made trial for himself and missed the gratification, he abandoned them without a sigh. Hence his wardrobe had come to include a pair of deer-stalking breeches, very little the worse for wear. (He had never anticipated any satisfaction in wearing a kilt).

At another time he had owned a steam yacht; and this had taught him that he liked the sea and suffered no inconvenience from its motion. But from the yacht itself he derived small satisfaction after he had shown it to his friends, and been envied by poorer men for possessing such a toy. It might have been amusing to carry these admirers about with him in extended cruises; but they, being poor, were busy and could not afford the time, while his rich acquaintances owned steam yachts of their own. Moreover, though unaccustomed to sport, he had always taken a fair amount of exercise; his liver required it; and at yachting — that is to say, sitting on deck in a comfortable chair — he put on flesh at an alarming rate. Therefore, from this pastime also he retired.

Though these experiments were in themselves uniformly unsuccessful, he had not made them in vain; but, keeping his wits about him, had arrived by a process of exhaustion at some of the essentials of pleasure; and this, after all, was not so bad for a man who had started with no knowledge concerning it and with a deal of false information. He knew now that he required exercise, that he could be happy in solitude, and that his landscape would be all the better if it neighboured on the sea. (Of his immunity from seasickness he was honestly prouder than of anything his money had been able, as yet, to purchase.) He had scarcely made these discoveries when the lease of the Islands came into the market.

Then, as he read the advertisement in the *Times* newspaper, in a flash he had divined his opportunity, had seen a happy future unrolled before him. His error hitherto had lain, not in exchanging Finsbury Pavement for scenes where the free elements had play, but in seeking to change himself and do violence to his own habits of mind and body. In the Islands he could practice, as a benevolent despot, that mastery of men which had given him power in the city; he could devote uncontradicted to the cause of philanthropy — or with only so much contradiction as lent a spice to triumph — those faculties which he had been sharpening all his life in quest of money. They remained sharp as ever, though the old appetite had been dulled.

He was a widower. He had no ambition but his own to consult; he alone would suffer if he made a mistake — and he felt sure he was not making a mistake. Though not given to day-dreams (Finsbury Pavement discouraged him), he had an ounce of imagination distributed about his brain (few, even among money-making men, succeed with less), and it had once or twice occurred to him that a king's must be, in spite of drawbacks, a highly enviable lot — at any rate in countries west of Russia. Well, here was his chance.

He took it boldly; and today, had you asked him, he would have acknowledged with a smile that he did not repent. All kings, to be sure, have their worries. The army had not shown itself too well affected towards the new reign. But when an army consists of three soldiers. . . .

The Lord Proprietor, gazing down from his terrace upon the

twinkling waters of the roadstead, caught sight of a row-boat coming across from St. Lide's, and as it drew near, recognised its sole occupant for Sergeant Archelaus.

He felt for his cigar case, chose and lit a cigar, and rested his elbows on the balustrade of the terrace, watching, while the old man brought his boat to the landing-quay, landed leisurely, and crossed the meadow to the foot of the gardens, where, at the pace he was keeping, one might allow him a couple of minutes at least before he re-emerged into view at the foot of the steps leading up to the terrace. But, as it happened, a bare fifty seconds elapsed before he came darting out of the boscage and scrambled up the stairway in a sweating hurry, two steps at a time.

"You shouldn't, Sergeant; you really shouldn't — at your time of life," expostulated the Lord Proprietor, kindly, withdrawing the cigar from his mouth.

"Then you shouldn't keep ostriches," retorted Sergeant Archelaus, as he gained the topmost step and, after a fearful glance behind him, sank against a pilaster and mopped his brow.

"Take care of that urn!" cried the Lord Proprietor, in a warning voice. "It contains a *Phormium tenax* that I wouldn't lose on any account."

"A what?"

"A New Zealand Flax. . . . The ostriches chased you, did they?"

"They did — the pair of 'em. It goes against a man's stomach, too, being chased by a bird."

"To me," said the Lord Proprietor, "it is gratifying evidence that they are recovering their spirits, which were hipped after the long voyage from Cape Town. But here, in the Gulf Stream, my theory is that we can acclimatise almost anything, animal or vegetable. Already they begin to feel its invigorating influence."

"Talking of vegetables, sir" — Archelaus shifted a canvas bag from his shoulders to the ground and began to untie the string which bound its neck.

"Pray take breath," suggested the Lord Proprietor. "At your age — and with the little exercise you get on Garrison Hill—"

"We don't keep ostriches," said Archelaus, curtly. "But, talking of vegetables, the Governor sends his compliments to you, sir, and begs your acceptance of a few choice plants in return for the small clothes you lent me."

"'Lent' you, Archelaus? 'Gave,' you mean."

"Oh, sir, but — excuse me — I couldn't — there was them ostriches to be considered."

"It has occurred to me," went on the Lord Proprietor, who was in the best of moods this morning, "that those — er — breeches might be a trifle conspicuous — a shade too highly pronounced in pattern — to be worn with uniform."

"As for that, sir," answered Archelaus, tactfully, "life on the Islands isn't like active service, where a man has to be careful about exposing himself to marksmanship."

"In Inverness a pattern like that would excite no comment."

"I've never been there," said Archelaus.

"It — er — harmonises, as it were, with the natural surroundings: with the loch, the glen, the strath. So with those curious tartans to which the Scottish highlanders are — er — addicted. Seen by themselves, and to a sensitive, artistic eye, they appear crude and almost violent in their contrast of colours; but seen in conjunction with the expanse of native moorland, the undulating stretches of the heather—"

"'Tis but niggling scenery we have in these parts, to be sure," agreed Archelaus.

"I have sometimes thought that *mutatis mutandis* the same may be true of the bagpipes, the strains of which — 'skirl,' I believe, is the proper expression — are not altogether discordant with the moaning of the wind over those desolate moors or the cries uttered by their wilder denizens; though, speaking personally, I never could endure the instrument."

"Me either," agreed Archelaus again, shuffling a little on his feet, as the dreadful truth began to dawn on him, that the Lord Proprietor meant to present him with yet another pair of trousers.

Sir Cæsar, however, chose to play for a minute with his benevolent design.

"There is no more delicate study," he went on, "than that of acclimatisation. None which requires a nicer union of artistic daring with artistic judgment, patience, with decision. . . . I propose to go in for it pretty extensively on Inniscaw."

"Yes, sir?"

"The ostriches have been a great encouragement."

"I suppose, now, when you get accustomed to 'em—"

"Though I have yet to prove that they will breed here. Yet, why not? The Gulf Stream, I am assured, has a stimulating influence upon all forms of organic life, animal as well as vegetable. It may be compared with that inward volcanic heat which, in and around the Bay of Naples, clothes the shore with verdure, and is not without responsibility for the passions of the inhabitants. . . . But, as I was saying, a man must use judgment. A plant may thrive when transferred across a thousand miles of ocean, may propagate itself even more freely than in its native habitat, and yet, to the artistic eye, be never truly at home. Its colour, of flower or foliage, refuses to blend with our landscape, to adapt itself to our Atlantic skies. It is my hobby, Sergeant, to discover not only what imported plants will flourish with our soil and climate, but what particular one is worthiest of cultivation; and, having discovered that, I propose to bend all my best energies upon it. . . . Eh? But where did you get those remarkably fine bulbs?"

Archelaus held out three in the palm of his hand.

"From the garrison garden, sir; with the Governor's compliments, and understanding you to take an interest in bulbs."

"Daffodils? Some species of narcissus, at any rate."

The Lord Proprietor took one of the bulbs and examined it, turning it over. "I had no idea that Major Vigoureux — er — went in for this sort of thing, or I'd have done myself the pleasure of visiting his garden."

"You wouldn't find much in it, sir," said Archelaus, hastily, remembering yesterday's adventure. "At least not much to interest you. To tell the truth, the Governor sets very little store by these, though they look pretty enough in March month. But wanting to show his feelings in the matter of those trousers—"

"You shall have another pair!"

"Oh!" said Archelaus, in spite of himself, and though he had miserably foreseen the offer for ten minutes past.

"And you may take back my thanks to the Commandant, and tell him that I hope, within the next few days, to pay him a call."

Archelaus touched his forelock, bringing up his palm at the right military salute — in those days a complicated operation. To himself he breathed a thanksgiving that the Fair Lady (as he and the Treachers called Vashti) had taken her departure from Garrison Hill overnight. Ever since breakfast he had been feeling sadly dejected about it and so (if appearances might be trusted) had his master. There is a fearful joy, after all, in living on a volcano.

But, alas, for Sergeant Archelaus! He was at this moment standing on the crust of a volcano, and that crust was momentarily wearing thinner.

The shore beneath the great house of Inniscaw has two landing quays, of which the eastern (Archelaus had used the western) lies hidden from view of the terrace, and can be approached by a boat keeping close under St. Lide's shore. Engrossed in his lecture upon acclimatisation, the Lord Proprietor had missed to perceive a boat making for this eastern quay; and so had Archelaus, for the simpler reason that he stood with his back to the view.

"Step into the house with me, and you shall make your choice between half-a-dozen pairs," the Lord Proprietor invited him.

"If you are sure it's not troubling you," said Archelaus.

"My good man — " began the Lord Proprietor, leading the way; and with that he turned about, surprised that Archelaus was not following. "Eh? What's the matter?"

But Archelaus, speechless, was staring along the terrace to its eastern end, where, at the head of a flight of steps leading down among the shrubberies, a head had suddenly uprisen into view — a head in a gray bonnet with trimmings of subdued violet — the head of Miss Gabriel.

"H'm!" said Miss Gabriel, and turned to Mr. and Mrs. Pope, who were mounting the stairway at her heels.

CHAPTER XVII

THE LORD PROPRIETOR RECEIVES A DOUBLE SHOCK

"H'm!" said Miss Gabriel again, as she once more surveyed the shrinking Archelaus. "So you allowed you'd steal a march on me?"

"I had no such thought, ma'am," stammered Archelaus.

"You'll get no good out of it, anyway; and of that I warn you. Good morning, sir!" — this with a curtsey to the Lord Proprietor.

"Good morning, ma'am! How d'ye do, Pope? — and your good lady is well, I hope? But to what do I owe this unexpected — er — honour?"

"Him," said Miss Gabriel, nodding, and with scarcely a change of tone.

"To Sergeant Archelaus, ma'am? Why, what has he been doing?"

"You might better ask — " Miss Gabriel answered slowly, emphatically, with her eye on the culprit — "what he has not."

"Whichever you please, ma'am. Come!"

"I find a difficulty in putting a name to it," pursued Miss Gabriel, still in the same level tone. "But Mr. Pope will bear me out. If he doesn't, I shall still allow no false delicacy to stand between me and my duty."

"Miss Gabriel means, sir," explained Mr. Pope, "that the articles in question—"

"What articles, man?" asked the Lord Proprietor, as Mr. Pope, in his turn, hesitated.

"Trousers," said Miss Gabriel, setting her face. "No, Charlotte" — she turned upon Mrs. Pope — "this is no time for mincing language. They were on a scarecrow, sir, in the very middle of the garrison garden, along with my waistcoat—"

"Your waistcoat, ma'am!"

"That is to say, with my antimacassar, which I had converted into a waistcoat and presented, in the innocence of my heart, to Treacher; the clothing of these men being nothing short of a scandal. But for scandal, sir, their clothes won't compare with their doings. Not to mention—"

"My dear lady, I implore you, let us take one thing at a time! You wish to make some statement about a scarecrow — in the garrison garden — adorned (am I right?) with a waistcoat you were once kind enough to present to Sergeant Treacher, and (I gather) with a pair of trousers about which you are less explicit." The Lord Proprietor paused. His eyes grew round with sudden, terrible suspicion. "You don't mean to tell me — " he asked slowly.

Miss Gabriel nodded, and wagged an accusing forefinger at Archelaus.

"That's just what I *do* mean. And if you want a picture of guilt, look at that man!"

The Lord Proprietor turned and stared at him, gasping.

"My trousers? *Mine?*" But here speech failed him, and he stood opening and shutting his mouth like a newly-landed fish.

Archelaus flung a wild glance about him, vainly seeking escape.

"You're looking at it in the wrong light, all of you," he mumbled, feebly.

"And on the Sabbath, too!" put in Mrs. Pope.

"This man" — the Lord Proprietor held up a hand as though calling Heaven to witness — "On what pretence do you suppose that he came here this morning? Why, to thank me! To thank me for those very — er — articles of which you tell me he makes a public mock! Look at the bag in his hand — what do you suppose that it contains?"

"Adders," suggested Mrs. Pope. "I shouldn't be surprised."

"You may well say so, ma'am. It might well be adders. Indeed, I'm not sure it isn't worse."

"Oh!" Mrs. Pope, already backing before the horrors of her own imagination, caught at the balustrade for support.

"Daffodils, ma'am! A present of daffodil bulbs, with the Commandant's compliments, and in acknowledgment of my gift! Could hypocrisy go farther?"

"Major Vigoureux," said Miss Gabriel, "was never a friend of mine. Let those who thought better of him defend him now, when he shows himself in his true colours."

But here Archelaus pulled himself together.

"The Governor," he answered sullenly, "had nothing to do with it. The Governor was in church at the time, as is well known to all of you."

"Yes, yes," interposed Mrs. Pope. "Let us be just. The Commandant was certainly in church at the time. On our homeward way we met him returning from church; and I would add, sir — if you will forgive me — that he is a gentleman quite incapable of suggesting or conniving at so vulgar a trick."

"H'm!" The Lord Proprietor accepted this with a snort, for he could not help being aware of its truth. But his wrath still needed a vent, and he turned upon Archelaus again.

"The Governor?" he echoed. "Are you ignorant that Major Vigoureux is not Governor of these Islands, nor has he been for three years? — even if he had ever a right to the title."

"He's *my* Governor, anyway," answered Archelaus, turning more and more dogged; "and he's Treacher's; and I reckon you'll find, if you try any games, that he's Treacher's missus' Governor, too."

"Insolent!" — This from Miss Gabriel.

"I ain't denyin' it, ma'am. Insolent I be, and a little freedom o' speech about it is no more than your rights. Insolent I've behaved, and if you'll take and ask the Governor to punish me for it, 'tisn't more than I deserve. He'll do it, be sure. As Mister Pope told you just now, the Governor's a gentleman; he wouldn't play such a trick, not if you was to offer him the world and the kingdoms thereof; and he'll be teasy as fire when he hears about it. But I warn you, ladies and gentlemen, all, don't you take the law into your own hands over this distressin' case, but go to him meek-like an' say you want Arch'laus punished. That's all. Leastways, that's all, unless you ask my honest opinion on the breeches in question, which is, that I wouldn't put 'em astride a clothes-horse and call him a son o' mine."

The Lord Proprietor stepped back, purple in the face.

But Miss Gabriel flew at game higher than Archelaus.

"That is all very well," she interposed, in her coldest, most incisive tone. "But to whom does the credit of this insult belong if not to Major Vigoureux? You may talk till doomsday, my man, before I'll believe that you and Treacher thought of it." She stood for a second or two, eyeing him. "A-ah!" she said, a little above her breath. "I thought as much! . . . There *was* a woman, Charlotte, and that woman is at the bottom of the whole business. I ask you, if you doubt it, to look at his face."

"She'd nothin' to do with it," affirmed Archelaus, stolidly, drawing the back of his hand across his brow.

"She?" mocked Miss Gabriel. "And pray who is 'she'?"

Archelaus made a bold effort to recover himself. "Why, Treacher's missus . . . unless you mean the Ghost."

"That Treacher's missus (as you call her) bore her hand in the sport I have the evidence of my own eyes; and if by 'the Ghost' you allude to a painted hussy that Mrs. Pope and I surprised, the other night, in your master's quarters, I advise you to keep that for the Marines. Sir," — Miss Gabriel turned to the Lord Proprietor — "this petty insult of the scarecrow is the smallest part of our complaint against Major Vigoureux. We have reason to believe — we have ocular proof — that the Major is at this moment and by stealth entertaining a most undesirable guest at the Barracks."

"My dear Elizabeth, we cannot be altogether sure!" objected

Mrs. Pope.

"Speak for yourself, Charlotte." Miss Gabriel folded her hands and bent on Archelaus a gaze under which he felt himself withering. "I am quite sure."

"Undesirable, ma'am?" asked the Lord Proprietor, thoroughly mystified. "In what sense undesirable?"

" — Unless," answered Miss Gabriel, tapping her foot, and with the air of one who curbs a virtuous impatience, "unless you can suggest a term more appropriate to a Jezebel; in which case I shall stand corrected."

"Jezebel? Jezebel? But, my dear Miss Gabriel, consider before you bring such a charge: here especially in the presence of Major Vigoureux's servant, who will doubtless report it to his master. Reflect how serious it is. Reflect—"

"Why, bless the man!" Miss Gabriel cut him short disdainfully. "As if I hadn't been reflecting for three days on end! Let him sue me for slander if he dare. I'll stick to my guns, if I kiss the book upon it; and what's more, so will Charlotte Pope."

"I never said so, Elizabeth," pleaded Mrs. Pope.

"And very wisely, ma'am." Sir Cæsar nodded approval. "For, as I was about to say, reflect upon the extreme improbability — nay, the utter impossibility — that — er — such a person could visit the Islands unnoticed and actually spend three days on Garrison Hill undetected by any save yourself. Nay, if we grant the miracle of her arrival, who is to assure us that she has not by this time as mysteriously vanished? In that case, what have we to show for our suspicions? How, setting aside the Major's indignation, shall we find ourselves less than a laughing stock for the whole population of the Islands?"

"And sarve ye right!" added Archelaus, who began to perceive that this thundercloud had its silver lining. But if he counted on daunting Miss Gabriel, he was mistaken.

"Turn you round, my man," snapped that indomitable lady. "Turn you round, and give me a look at those coat-tails of yours. Ha!" she exclaimed, as Archelaus, by habit obedient to the word of command, faced about towards the balustrade. "There was a coat-tail missing yesterday, if I remember, when you crept out from the bushes like a whipped urchin, and now there's two: and you'll be telling me that these fine stitches were put in by Jane Treacher, who is like most soldier's wives, and sews like a cow!"

"The Lord have mercy upon us!" said Archelaus, in a hushed voice.

It took them two or three seconds to understand that the words were not an answer to Miss Gabriel; that he had spoken them to himself, staring — as he still stared — down the steps, down the green alley leading to the terrace.

Then, perceiving that something was amiss with the man, they too stepped to the balustrade and looked down — as up the leafy path came the very woman of their speculations — Vashti, faultlessly arrayed, trailing a neat parasol and humming a song as she drew near.

"The same!" gasped Miss Gabriel. "I call you to witness, Charlotte!"

"But, you'll excuse me," Mr. Pope objected, "she don't appear to answer precisely to a Jezebel."

"You men think of nothing but outward show," snapped Miss Gabriel.

"Well, and that's something," Archelaus put in with affability, his spirits rising as the danger drew nearer. "Talk about Garrison Hill! She seems to be pretty well at home on Inniscaw, too." For Vashti, halting in the chequered sunlight beneath a trellised arch, had reached up the hooked handle of her sunshade to draw down the spray of a late autumnal rose, and stood for a moment inhaling its odour.

It may be that just then she caught sight of the watchers upon the terrace. If so, not a movement betrayed her. As though reluctantly, she released the branch and, as it sprang upward, resumed her way up the path, disappearing for a moment under a massed canopy of Virgin's Bower. A few seconds, and she would emerge into view again, almost at the foot of the terrace stairs.

They waited.

"But whatever has become of the woman?" asked Miss Gabriel.

"It's confoundedly odd!" growled the Lord Proprietor.

"She may have turned down a by-path."

"There's no by-path within fifty yards of her. More likely she's stopping to take a smell of the clematis. . . . We might step down and see." The Lord Proprietor suited the action to the words and led the way.

"In my opinion, if you want it," said Archelaus, "you won't find her there. Because why? She's a ghost."

"A ghost?" quavered Mrs. Pope.

"Nonsense, my dear!" Her husband offered his arm to assist her down the steps. "Such a beautiful young person!"

"The first time I saw her she didn't frighten me at all," agreed Mrs. Pope; "but if she's going to bob in and out of sight in this way, I shan't sleep in my bed tonight."

A cry from the Lord Proprietor startled them. He had plunged down the path beneath the overarching clematis. They ran to overtake him, and found him staring at vacancy. Vashti had vanished, apparently into thin air.

"Oh, but this is midsummer moonshine!" declared Sir Cæsar. "The woman must be hiding somewhere near. Miss Gabriel, if you will kindly attend to Mrs. Pope, her husband and I will search the thickets hereabouts."

They searched in the thickets and along the garden paths, but without recovering a trace of the unknown. Not so much as a glimpse of her skirt rewarded them.

Sergeant Archelaus abandoned the search early, dodged into the plantations on the left, and went his way chuckling, back to his boat.

"A terrible trying morning," he allowed, as he cast loose; "but the end was worth it."

CHAPTER XVIII

VASHTI PLEADS FOR SAARON

For twenty minutes Sir Cæsar and Mr. Pope beat the shrub-beries, and even carried their search down to the great walled garden which was one of the wonders of Inniscaw. Tradition said that the old monks had built it, of bricks baked upon the mainland; and that it had been their favourite pleasance, because its walls shut out all view of the sea. Certainly if the old monks had built this garden, they had built it well. The Priory itself, of Caen stone, had lain in ruins for at least two hundred years before the Lord Propri-etor came to clear the site and build his new great house on the old foundations; but these brick walls defied the tooth of time.

Magnificent walls they were, four feet in thickness, heavily but-tressed; the bricks set in mortar tougher than themselves. They enclosed two acres of rich black soil at the mouth of Inniscaw's one valley, where it widens into a marsh beside the shore. Between them and the water's edge stood the Lord Proprietor's new schoolhouse, above a small landing quay; and within the schoolhouse a class was singing as Sir Cæsar and Mr. Pope entered the old garden. The chil-dren's voices came floating prettily over the old wall — so prettily that Abe Jenkins, the septuagenarian gardener, ceased working to comment upon it, leaning on his hoe and addressing Eli Tregarthen, who lounged by the gateway leading to the shore.

"Always fond of children, I was," said Abe Jenkins, "though I never picked up courage to marry. 'Twas the women that always daunted me. And now I've a-come to a time o' life that I'm glad of it. A married man throws his roots too deep, an' when Death come along, 'tis always too soon. He wants to bide and see his youngest da'rter's child, or he wants to linger and mend a thatch on the linhay — his married son can't be brought to see the importance o't. . . . What with one thing and another, I never knowed a married man yet was fit to die; whereas your cheerful bachelor comes up clean as a carrot. What brings you across from Saaron today, Tregarthen? I'll wage 'tis to fetch your children back from school."

"Partly," assented Eli.

"Iss; partly, that, an' to listen here to their voices soundin' so pretty across the wall. And partly, I reckon, 'tis on the chance to get speech with the Lord Proprietor and persuade 'em to let you bide on Saaron. But that you'll never do. Mind, I'm not sayin' a word against th' old curmudgeon. He's my employer, to start with, besides being what God made 'em. But, reason? You might as well try reason on the hind leg of a jackass. Go thy ways home, Tregarthen: go thy ways home an' teach yourself that all this world and the kingdoms thereof be but what the mind o' man makes 'em, and Saaron itself but a warren for rabbits."

Tregarthen shook his head.

"A barren rock. . . . Come now, bring your mind to it!" Abe suggested, coaxing.

"'Tis no good, Abe."

"A cottage in a vineyard — what says holy Isaiah? A lodge in a garden of cucumbers — a besieged city—"

"Abe Jenkins!" — It was the Lord Proprietor's voice calling from the upper gate.

"Y'r honour!" Abe snatched his hoe and wheeled about sharply as the great man came down the path with Mr. Pope at his heels.

"How long have you been working here?" demanded Sir Cæsar. "Perhaps I had better have said 'idling,'" he added, with a frown and a curt nod at Tregarthen in the gateway. Sir Cæsar's gray eyebrows had a trick of bristling up, like a cat's, at the first hint of unpleasantness, even at sight of anyone who crossed his will; and they bristled now.

"'Been workin' here the best part of the morning," answered Abe, with an old man's freedom of tone and a complacent look backward at the patch of turned soil. "And 'might have been workin' yet but the children singin' their hymn yonder" — with a jerk of his thumb towards the wall that hid the school building — "warned me 'twas time to knock off for dinner."

Now, the Lord Proprietor had meant his question for preface to another. "Had Abe, while at work, caught sight of a strange lady anywhere in the garden?" The question, if put just then, and in Tregarthen's hearing, might have changed the whole current of this small history; for Tregarthen was a poor hand at dissimulation — or, rather, was incapable of it. But the sight of his back, as he turned away, caused Sir Cæsar's eyebrows to bristle up yet more pugnaciously.

"Hi, sir?"

Tregarthen turned slowly.

"You are waiting here to fetch your children from school, I suppose?"

"Yes," said Tregarthen.

"And isn't that an instance, man, of what I tried to make you understand two days ago? Cannot you see what time and trouble you'll be saving yourself — let alone the children — when you're comfortably settled on Brefar and within half-a-mile of a handy school?"

"Yes," said Tregarthen again. His eyes met the Lord Proprietor's without servility as without disrespect, but with a kind of patient wonder.

"Well, then" — Sir Cæsar turned to Mr. Pope for confirmation — "here is a man who — to give him his due, eh? — works as hard as any on the Islands; harder, I daresay, than his own hired labourer—"

Mr. Pope nodded.

" — A man," continued Sir Cæsar, "who never gives himself a holiday; a man whose nature it is to grudge every hour of the day that isn't employed in wringing money out of a desert. Come now!" — warmed by his own eloquence to a geniality equally hearty and false, Sir Cæsar swung around again upon Mr. Pope — "I daresay we may call him, to his face, about the best of my farmers!"

Mr. Pope inclined, with the half of an embarrassed smile. As an agent, he felt any such appreciation of a tenant to be, if not dangerous, at least uncalled for, liable to be misinterpreted. He contented himself with answering — in a murmur — that Mr. Tregarthen had given the estate in the past every satisfaction; that it would surprise him indeed if (at this time of day) Mr. Tregarthen were (of all men) to raise trouble.

But the Lord Proprietor, as a master of men, brushed this hesitancy aside, and with jovial tact. "A first-rate fellow," he insisted. "One of our best! Only pig-headed, as the best always are. And so, when I offer him a choice of two farms, each better than his present one, he must needs take it into his head that I'm doing him an injury. Such a man" — here Sir Cæsar wagged a forefinger at the accused — "needs to be protected against himself. Such a man needs to be told — and pretty straight — that he is injuring others besides himself, and that, as I have authority in these Islands, so I owe it to my conscience to forbid his letting his children grow into little savages."

Eli Tregarthen looked up as though a stone had struck him. The colour on his face darkened. Hitherto (though suffering from it) he had not argued, even in his own mind, against Sir Cæsar's evicting him from Saaron. He had resented it, as one resents mere brute force; but he had not argued with that which had never presented itself as resting upon argument. . . . Though he knew himself to be a slow-witted man, Eli had a clear sense of his wife's wisdom, and that wisdom irradiated for him any argument which came — as this accusation of neglecting the children surely came — within range of Ruth.

"If you dare to say that again," said Eli, "I'll knock your head off."

All three of them heard it — the Lord Proprietor, Mr. Pope, and old Abe — though neither could believe his ears. For Eli had spoken quite quietly and distinctly. Mr. Pope was the first to recover; but before he could get in a word, Eli was following up the attack — still not hastily, still with a slow pause on every word.

"You? What do you know of children, that never had a child? And what do you know of Saaron or any other island, that never took your life here nor made your living? You fill your pockets in a London shop; you go off to an auction, and there you bid for these Islands, that you've never seen. But what did you buy, you little man, over and above the power to make yourself a nuisance in your day? Was it understanding of the Islands? Or a birthright in 'em? Or a child to leave it to? . . . There, I do wrong to be angered with 'ee — you've got so little by your bargain! But you put a strain upon a man, you do — talkin' of children in that way. Children?" The man paused with something like a groan. An instant before it had been in his mind to tell Sir Cæsar passionately that, so far from grudging the time spent in fetching Annet, Linnet and Matthew Henry from school, he looked forward to it as the one bright break in a day that began before sunrise and lasted till after sunset. It had been on the tip of his tongue, too, to say, with equal passion, that any man who spoke of them as savages insulted his wife's care of them. But eloquence had come to him, now for the first time in his life, as an inspiration. At the first check he stammered, and broke down; and so, with a hunch of his shoulders, turned his back on his audience and walked off heavily down the lane.

Mr. Pope, with great tact, laid a hand lightly on the Lord Proprietor's arm and conducted him back to the gate by which they had entered. There, yet gasping for speech, the great man lifted his eyes, and was aware of Mrs. Pope and Miss Gabriel distractedly advancing along the path.

With a gulp he pulled himself together, and walked forward to inform them that the chase had been unsuccessful; that not a glimpse of the fugitive had been discovered. Resuming a hold upon his gallantry, he hoped that his visitors would remain for luncheon. "After which," he added, with a creditable smile, "we may, if we will, resume the search in more philosophical mood."

But here again Mr. Pope was tactful. He divined that his patron was suffering; that the wound needed, for the moment, solitude and silence to ease its smart. He was sorry to deprive the ladies of such a pleasure; but, for his part, business called him back to Garland Town. He had, he regretted to say, an engagement at two o'clock sharp. To be sure, if the ladies chose to stay, he could send back the boat for them. . . . But this he said knowing that his wife was thoroughly frightened, and that (as she herself put it later) wild horses would not induce her to remain, lacking his protection.

The Lord Proprietor escorted his visitors down to the landing quay and there helped the ladies to embark. The search for the fair fugitive (he promised them) should be vigorously prosecuted. She was not likely to elude it for long, and he would at once report success. The leave-takings over, he stood by the shore until the small boat had made her offing, and so, with a farewell lift of the hat, turned and walked moodily towards the house.

He was relieved to be alone after the morning's very painful experiences. Twice since breakfast he had been wounded in his dignity, and nowhere does a man of his nature suffer more acutely. Nor could the wounds be covered over and hidden, for he had taken them openly, almost publicly. His anger swung helplessly forward and back between the two outrages, both to him inexplicable. To be sure he had not reckoned on any gratitude for the gift of the breeches. But what had he done that they should be flaunted on a scarecrow? . . . Oh, it was monstrous!

As little could he understand Tregarthen or Tregarthen's language. Some gadfly must have stung the man. A few acres of the barrenest land in the whole archipelago — and the fellow talked as though he were being dispossessed of an Eden! Yes, and as though that were not enough, he had used the flattest disrespect. The Lord Proprietor was not accustomed to disrespect. From the first his Islanders had treated him with the deference due to a king. Save and except the Commandant, no man had ever crossed his will or disputed his authority.

His rage swung back again upon the Commandant. It was all very well to plead that the Commandant had been in church at the time; but, after all, an officer must be held responsible for his men's doings. Let Major Vigoureux beware! More than once the Lord Proprietor had been minded to memorialise the War Office and inquire why the taxpayers' money should be wasted to maintain three superannuated soldiers at full pay in a deserted barracks.

"Upon my word," said the Lord Proprietor to himself, "I've a mind to run over to Garrison Hill and ask Vigoureux what the devil he means by it. Either he knows of this, or he doesn't: I'll soon learn which. In either case I'll have an apology; and, what's more, I'll teach him who's master here, once for all."

He had reached the terrace, and paused there for a moment to draw breath after his climb, at the same time throwing a glance across the blue waters of the roadstead towards Garrison Hill and the white buildings upon it slumbrous in the autumn haze. The glance threatened mischief to that unconscious fortress and a sharp nod of the head confirmed the threat.

"Yes, yes, this very afternoon! The sooner the better!"

He swung about and stepped across the terrace to a French window that stood open to the air and sunshine. It was the window of the morning room, where he usually took his luncheon, and he passed in briskly, meaning to ring the bell and give orders to have the meal served at once. But, as he stepped across the low sill somebody rose in the room's cool shadow and confronted him, and he fell back catching at the jamb for support and staring.

It was the stranger herself: the woman for whom they had all been vainly searching!

"Good morning!" said Vashti, with a self-possessed little bow. "Oh, but I fear I have startled you?"

"Ah — er — " the Lord Proprietor pulled himself together with an effort — "Well, to tell the truth? you did take me by surprise; the more so that—"

"It was dreadfully uncivil of me — not to say impudent — to walk in here unannounced. But the fact is I could find no door along the terrace; nothing but windows. Forgive me."

"Certainly, madam, certainly. . . . The front door is, so to speak, at the rear of the building. . . . But I was going to say that you took me the more by surprise because, as a matter of fact, I had just given up hunting for you."

Vashti laughed. She looked adorably cool and provoking; and still, as he stared at her, the Lord Proprietor wondered more and more whence in the world she came. He knew little of female beauty (the late Lady Hutchins had been plain-featured) and less of clothes; but three or four times in his life, at public functions, he had mixed with the great ones of the land, and here patently was one of them. Her speech, dress, bearing, all proclaimed it; her easy self-possession, too, and air of authority. Out of what Olympus had she descended upon these remote Atlantic isles?

"I saw that you had company," she answered, "and I ran away. To tell you the truth I was a little afraid of them — that is to say, of some of them. But what was Archelaus doing here?"

The Lord Proprietor frowned.

"Did he come to apologise? Oh, but that is just one of the reasons that brought me here! You must not be angry with Archelaus; no, really, it was not his fault, at all, but mine."

"I think, ma'am," said the Lord Proprietor, "we are talking at cross-purposes."

"No, no, we are not," she corrected him briskly with a little laugh. "We are talking about that unhappy scarecrow." She paused, as though checked by irrepressible mirth, and he flushed hotly.

"And no, again!" she went on, perceiving this; "I was laughing at Archelaus — poor fellow! — overtaken here by his accusers. Did they make it very painful for him?"

"Even supposing him capable of shame — which I doubt — I certainly do not think he suffered more than he deserved."

"You are very much annoyed?" asked Vashti, suddenly serious. "Well, then, I am sorry. It was all my suggestion — though it never entered my head that anyone would be walking that way and catch sight of — of the thing. I meant it to be a little surprise for the Commandant when he came home from church; though when he returned and heard what had happened, he scolded me terribly."

"You will excuse me" — the Lord Proprietor drew himself up stiffly — "if I fail to see either where the humour comes in, or why you — a stranger, unknown to me even by name—"

"Ah, to be sure! My name is Cara."

"Then, as I was saying, Miss Cara, I fail to see—"

"And you are quite right of course," Vashti made haste to agree. "I ought not to have done it. But weren't you, too, a little bit to blame? It wasn't very nice of you, you know."

"I beg your pardon? What wasn't very nice of me?"

"Why, to hurt their feelings; and especially the Commandant's. He is a poor man; poor, and sensitive, and easily hurt."

"You are talking to me in riddles, Miss Cara. I have done nothing at all to hurt the Commandant's feelings."

"Not intentionally, of course. I told him — and I told the sergeant too — that I was sure you never meant to wound them. It would have been too cruel."

"But," protested the Lord Proprietor, "I have done nothing, I tell you; nothing beyond presenting Sergeant Archelaus with — with an article of attire of which he stood badly in need. Miss Gabriel, some weeks ago, drew my attention to the state of the poor fellow's — er — wardrobe, and suggested that something might be done."

"I thought so," Vashti nodded. "I dare say now," she went on, after seeming to muse for a moment, "you are one of those strong-minded men who find it hard to understand how sensible people can worry over what they put on their backs!"

"That happens to be a constant source of wonder with me," he confessed; "though for the life of me I can't tell how you came to guess it."

"Never mind how I guessed it," said Vashti, smiling. "The point is, that you take this lofty and very scornful view of clothes, and yet you must have noticed that many men of your acquaintance — men otherwise sensible — take quite another; that in the city, for instance, a hard felt hat is not usually worn with a frock coat."

"Granted," said the Lord Proprietor; "though I could never understand why."

"And you have noticed that soldiers are even more particular; and the reason with them is perhaps a little more easily grasped. Their uniform is a symbol, so to speak. It stands for the service to which a good soldier should be devoted."

"If you had seen that man's small-clothes!"

"Yes, I grant that Archelaus neglects his regimentals. But to neglect them, and to be willing to mix them up with civilian clothes, are two very different things. Perhaps you did not think of this?"

"Really, now," answered Sir Cæsar, "I should not have supposed that it mattered what these men wore, in such an out-of-the-world spot."

Vashti's eyes rested on him for a second or two, in a kind of wondering despair at his obtuseness. But she controlled herself to reply quite patiently:

"At any rate, it was wrong of me to encourage the men's resentment, and I came here this morning to beg your pardon."

He acknowledged this with a bow, but stood silent for a moment, eyeing her.

"You are a relative of Major Vigoureux?" he asked, after a pause.

"No."

"You are staying with him, I understand?"

"No." Vashti shook her head, with a smile. "But I very much want you to forgive me," she went on; "for I have another favour to ask you."

Again he bowed slightly. "You give my curiosity no rest, Miss Cara, and I perceive you mean to satisfy it only in your own way. As for the — er — incident we have been discussing, pray consider that — so far as you are concerned — I dismiss it." He did so with a slight wave of the hand. "You wish to ask me a favour?"

"I do. I came to plead with you; to say a word on behalf of Eli Tregarthen, your tenant on Saaron Island."

The Lord Proprietor started. "Are you at the bottom of that also?" he asked, angrily.

Vashti's eyes opened wide in astonishment.

"I beg your pardon?" she murmured. "I do not understand."

"It seems to me," he caught her up, "that for a total stranger, you are losing remarkably little time."

"In what, sir?" she demanded, facing him fairly, with a lift of her handsome chin.

"In subverting my authority, ma'am; or, rather, in prompting others to subvert it. . . . Though, to be sure," he went on, in sarcastic wrath, "it may again be an accident that I happened on Eli Tregarthen less than an hour ago, and that he used very insolent language to me in the presence of my agent."

"It was not only an accident," said Vashti, slowly, and with patent sincerity; "it was one that, since I came here to urge his suit, I would have given a great deal to prevent." She paused, and for a moment seemed to be musing. "Must I understand, then, that you refuse to hear a word in his favour?"

"The man is a fool!" Sir Cæsar clasped his hands behind him under his coat-tails, and paced the room. "His insolence to me apart, he is a complete fool! I offer him the choice of two farms — either one of them acre for acre, worth twice the rental of Saaron. . . . I simply cannot understand!"

"No," said Vashti, with a little sigh, "you cannot understand."

He had reached the fireplace, and wheeled round on her, his back to the hearth and his legs a-straddle.

"What can I not understand?" he demanded.

"Many things." Vashti met his eyes for a moment, then turned her own to the window and the blue waterways beyond the terrace, beyond the massed tree-tops of the pleasure grounds. "Many things, and the Islands in particular. You did not understand just now that a soldier, though condemned to stand sentry in a forgotten outpost, can still be sensitive for the honour of his service, because the root of his life lies there. You cannot understand that the root of Eli Tregarthen's life goes down into the soil he has tilled from childhood as his parents tilled it. To you Garrison Hill is a tumble-down fort, and Saaron Island a barren rock; yet you call them yours, because you have purchased them. And, nevertheless — to do you justice — you are not one who rates everything by its price in money. If you were, I could beg you to take a higher rent for Saaron and leave Eli Tregarthen undisturbed."

He shook his head. "The man pays me a fair rent; as much as I can conscientiously ask. I have a conscience, Miss Cara, and a sense of responsibility. It is not good that Tregarthen lets his children run wild there, so far from school."

"And if, sir," she went on, "you are doing this for the children's sake, I could promise you that there are means to educate them better than any children on the Islands. But the difficulty does not lie with the children. It lies in your sense of possession, which makes Saaron Farm there" — she waved a hand — "an eyesore in the view from this window, and simply because Eli Tregarthen has crossed your will. You defend an instinct of selfishness that takes about five minutes to pass into a principle with any man who buys land. You maintain the landlord's right to ordain the lives on your estate, and command them to be as you think best; nor does it seem to you to affect your claim for power that we understood and drew our nature from the Islands for years before ever you came to hear of them."

"Radicalism, ma'am!"

"Yes, sir. It is for the roots I plead, against your claim that the surface gives all."

He thrust his hands under his coat-tails again, and took a turn up and down the room.

"I do not affect to agree with you, Miss Cara," said he, not looking towards her when she stood by the French window, but stretching out his hand to the bell. "Yet, as owner of these Islands, I desire to be just. I desire also to understand these Islanders, of whom, it appears, you know so much more than I. And if you do me the honour to take luncheon with me — " Here he broke off, to ring at the bell-pull. "But I warn you I am tenacious as well as curious, and shall demand to know a little more of my lecturer."

He turned and stood blinking. Vashti had disappeared. The room was empty.

He took a step to the open window, sprang out upon the terrace, and glanced to right and left.

The terrace, too, was empty. He hurried to the stairway leading down through the shrubberies. Not so much as the glimpse of a flying skirt rewarded him.

CHAPTER XIX

THE COMMANDANT'S CONSCIENCE

"The Lord Proprietor to see you, sir!"

Archelaus, presenting himself at the door of the Commandant's office, with a slightly flushed but inscrutable face, drew aside and flattened himself against the door-jamb to let Sir Cæsar enter.

The Commandant closed the book in which he had been adding up accounts which never came right, and stood up in something of a flurry. He was dressed with more than ordinary care. The lapels and collar of his uniform-coat had been treated to a vigorous brushing. In fact, he was arrayed for action: to step down the hill in an hour's time, to call upon Mr. Fossell at the Bank and draw his pay, if any should be forthcoming.

"Good morning, Major!"

"Good morning, Sir Cæsar." The Commandant nodded towards a chair.

"I thank you." Sir Cæsar set down his hat upon the edge of the writing-table, drew off his gloves, tossed them into his hat, and seated himself. "I — er — called in the first place to speak about an unfortunate — er — incident that happened on Garrison Hill here last Sunday."

"Ah," said the Commandant, "so you have heard about it? I am sorry."

"Sorry for what, sir?"

"Sorry that anyone should have thought it worth while to carry tales to you; but also sorry for the incident itself."

"It appears to me, Major Vigoureux, that the incident demands some apology."

"I have made it."

Sir Cæsar crossed his legs and coughed to clear his throat. "I think, my dear sir," said he, in a tone at once slightly pompous and slightly nervous, "I really think it's time that you and I came to an understanding; that we — er — recognised, so to speak, the situation, and played with the cards on the table. Do you agree with me?"

"I might," answered the Commandant, guardedly; "that is to say, if I understood."

"I acquit you, of course, of any active share in the incident, and I am assured that Archelaus and Treacher were no worse than accomplices. It appears that the real culprit was a totally different person, and," he went on, after a glance at the Commandant's face, which betrayed nothing, "it may save time if I tell you that she has confessed to me."

"Excuse me, I was not proposing to make any remark."

"But who in the world is the young person?"

The Commandant's eyebrows arched themselves slightly. "She is a lady," he answered, in a dry voice. "If she omitted to tell you her name, the omission was no doubt intentional, and she has carried her confession just so far as she intended it to go."

"She called herself Cara; but the name tells me nothing. Who is she? I agree with you as to her address and appearance: she is in every respect — er — presentable. A relative, may I inquire?"

"No."

"A friend, then? You will pardon me? A delicate question to put, of course."

Again the Commandant's eyebrows went up slightly. "She was my guest for a day or two," he answered.

"*Was?* Then where in the world is she staying now?"

"If she did not tell you — " began the Commandant, but Sir Cæsar interrupted him impatiently.

"Tell me? Devil a bit of it, and that's partly why I'm here. Vanished like a witch, begad, while I was turning to ring the bell! And where she went or where she came from are mysteries alike to me."

"Why, then," the Commandant pursued, in a steady musing voice, "it seems to follow that, even if I knew, I have not her permission to tell."

The Lord Proprietor uncrossed and recrossed his legs irritably. "Come, come, Vigoureux, this will hardly do. Will it, now? I put it to you as a man of the world. No doubt it's all innocent enough, but folks will talk. And, after all, I'm responsible for any — er — scandal affecting the Islands. Hey?"

The Commandant rose with a sudden flush on his face.

"Scandal, Sir Cæsar? Oh, to be sure, I cannot understand you."

"Tut-tut!" The Lord Proprietor smiled. "Of course, we know there's nothing in it. A young lady — youngish, at least — and you old enough to be her father. But, all the same, tongues will wag."

"And they have been wagging?" The Commandant, after a short turn across the room and back, stood over him, his hands crossed under his coat tails. "But yours, sir, is the only one that has dared to wag in my presence."

"Sir!" The Lord Proprietor jumped to his feet.

"You have put many humiliations upon me, Sir Cæsar; and because they affected me only, I have endured them. But in this you go too far."

The Lord Proprietor, on the verge of an angry retort, checked himself, with a short laugh.

"I refuse to lose my temper with you," said he. "You are unreasonable. You misconceive me as imputing scandal when, as a matter of fact, I was trying to assure you that I rejected the imputation. For me, the disparity in age alone—"

The Commandant, with a wave of his hand to the door, turned away wearily.

"I merely thought it right to warn you," pursued Sir Cæsar, taking heart of grace as his opponent appeared to weaken, "that others may be less charitable. And they look to me. I think — I really think — you might consider the delicacy of my position; that I am — er — ultimately responsible for the good name of these Islands."

But here he paused with a start; for the Commandant had wheeled about suddenly, and stood over him, and the Commandant's eyes were dangerous.

"Sir Cæsar" — the Commandant controlled his voice with an effort, for it shook a little — "in the last few minutes some things have been made plain to me which were hitherto obscure. I have wondered sometimes, here in these forsaken barracks, at actions of yours which seemed deliberately calculated to annoy one who — Heaven knows — started with every wish to be friendly. Saving my own small personal dignity, of which from indolence I have been too careless, I have reserved nothing of my old importance in these Islands which, before you purchased them, I had governed. Men, even the least assuming, do not forfeit all power, all consideration, without a wrench; and I am but human. I relinquished them, and without the help of a single kind word from you, by which the sacrifice might at least have been mitigated. I wondered. Later, when you heaped one small humiliation upon another, I concluded that I must have had the misfortune to incur your personal dislike, and told myself, after searching for the cause and finding none, that personal dislikes are usually inexplicable. But now I see that I have been doing you an injustice; that your affronts were not considered; that you have all along, likely enough, been entirely unconscious of offence; that, in short, you are as Heaven made you, and I cannot hold a quarrel with any man's mere defects, whether congenital or of breeding. I shall not waste time by inquiring to which of the two classes your obtuseness should justly be assigned. It is enough that I recognise the mistake and apologise for it. I see now that you are obtuse — that and nothing more. But since your obtuseness wounds more than you can possibly divine; and since in this instance it injures a lady, I shall ask you to pay my poor quarters the last respect you owe them, and quit them without further discussion."

He stepped to his writing-table and struck on a small hand-bell. Promptly on the summons Sergeant Archelaus appeared in the doorway; so promptly, indeed, that he might have found it hard, under cross-examination, to rebut the charge of having stood listening outside.

The Lord Proprietor, however, was in no condition to put a searching question. He arose, gasping, his eyes rolling from the Commandant to Archelaus and back. He felt for his hat like a man groping in the dark, clutched it, and set it on his head with an experimental air, as though it would not have entirely surprised him to find his feet in the place of his head.

"I suppose," he stammered, "it has occurred to you that you may pay for this?"

"It occurred to me," answered the Commandant, coolly and amiably, "that you might threaten it."

"You shall, by God!"

The Commandant bowed.

"You shall certainly repent this, sir." The Lord Proprietor crammed his hat on his head.

"May I ask you to observe that my servant is standing in the doorway?"

Sir Cæsar turned, shot a glance at Archelaus, and for an instant appeared to be on the point of including master and man in one denunciation. But either he thought better of it or his rage choked him. With a final tap on the crown of his hat, to settle it firmly on his brows, he strode past the rigid figure by the threshold and out into the open air.

He had never been so outraged! For fifty or a hundred yards, as he descended the hill, his fury almost blinded him. His face was congested; the back of his neck swollen and purple, as though apoplexy threatened. His ears showed red as a turkey's wattles. He stumbled on the ill-paved path. What! To be lectured thus by a man whose continued residence on the Islands was a public scandal — a fellow who, past all usefulness, lived on in lazy desuetude, content to take the taxpayers' money while doing nothing in return! And the worst — the gall, the wormwood of it — was that this despised foe had silenced him — nay, had silenced him almost contemptuously. "But wait a bit, my fine fellow!" swore the Lord Proprietor, blundering down the hill. "Wait until we hear what the War Office has to say about your precious garrison; or until, failing satisfaction there, I get a question asked in Parliament about you!"

Could the Lord Proprietor have looked back at this moment into the room where sat the victorious enemy, he might have been in some measure consoled.

The Commandant, having dismissed Archelaus with a wave of the hand, waited while the door closed, and dropping into the chair before his writing-table, bowed his head upon his hands. . . . Oh, it is easy to talk lightly of riches, and of the power that riches give! But in this world it is not so easy for a man with just one penny in his pocket to stand up against an enemy solidly backed by a banking account. He feels that though his cause be right and his conscience clear, his position is precarious: that the world, if it knew the truth, would regard him almost as an imposter. The feeling may be unreasonable, the fear cowardly; but there it is, and it had cost the Commandant all his pluck to face the encounter out. Moreover, his conscience was not clear.

Sir Cæsar, too, had (all unwittingly) planted an arrow and left it to rankle. "Old enough to be her father!" The Commandant shut his lips hard upon the pain. He could not expel it: he knew it would awake again in the watches of the night: but for the present he must ignore it. He had a second ordeal to face.

As he sat there for a minute or two, his face resting on his hands, his spirit abandoned to weakness, he heard the steady ticking of the clock on the chimney-piece behind him. He counted the strokes, and all of a sudden they recalled him to the present. He pulled himself together, stood up, and, reaching down a clothes-brush from its hook beside the door, walked over to the chimney-piece and to a small mirror that stood behind the clock.

"Old enough to be her father." Again, as he caught sight of his face in the glass the smart revived; but again he expressed it, and fell to brushing his worn tunic with extreme care. It had always been his practice to dress punctiliously before going into action, even on dark nights in front of Sevastopol, where all niceties of dress were lost at once in the slush of the trenches. His forage-cap received almost as careful a brushing as his tunic: and from his cap he turned his attention to the knees of his trousers and to his boots, one of which was cracked, albeit not noticeably. He had half a mind to black its edges over with pen and ink, but refrained. Somehow it suggested imposture, and today he winced sensitively away from the first hint of imposture. He must walk down-hill delicately, like Agag. Tomorrow Harvey, the Garland Town cobbler, would repair the damage with a couple of stitches, at the cost of one penny: and the Commandant reflected with a melancholy smile that he possessed precisely that sum.

His toilet complete, he took a last look in the mirror to assure himself that his face betrayed none of the anxiety eating at his heart. It was paler than ordinary, but calm. He drew a long breath, and walked out to the front door. At his feet the chimneys of the small town sent up their mid-day smoke; beyond, the Atlantic twinkled with its innumerable smile. The hour was come. As he stepped out upon the road he cast a glance to right and left along his deserted batteries, and answered the smile of Ocean whimsically, ruefully. If only, as an artilleryman, he could have summoned Mr. Fossell's Bank by a dropping shot! This business of hand-to-hand assault belonged by rights to another branch of the service.

Mr. Fossell stood behind the counter in conference with a junior clerk, and the sunshine pouring through the windows — the only plate-glass windows in Garland Town — gilded the dome of Mr. Fossell's bald head. As the Commandant entered, Mr. Fossell looked up and nodded pleasantly, in a neighbourly way, albeit with a touch of ironical interrogation. He had heard gossip from his friend Pope of the doings on Garrison Hill, and, so far as he allowed himself to be jocose, he meant his glance to be interpreted. "Well, you are a pretty fellow! And pray what account are you going to give of yourself?" But very different thoughts preoccupied the Commandant, and his fears took alarm.

"Good morning," said the Commandant, and forced a smile. "You have been expecting me, I hope?"

"Dear, dear!" Mr. Fossell affected surprise. "You don't tell me that pay-day has come round again already?" This again, was a form of pleasantry which he repeated month after month; but today he slightly over-acted it.

"The — the money is here?" stammered the Commandant.

"My dear Major, I hope so — I sincerely hope so," Mr. Fossell answered, with a humorous look around him. "I do most sincerely trust we may be able to meet your demand for — let me see, fifteen-eighteen-six, is it not? — without being forced to put up the shutters." Mr. Fossell chuckled quietly.

The Commandant drew a long breath.

"Always supposing," resumed Mr. Fossell, "that the draft is in order, as usual; on which point, to tell you the truth, I have been too busy to satisfy myself. But the paper arrived two days ago, and is in my office — if you will excuse me for a moment."

He stepped towards a door at the back, panelled with frosted glass, opened it, and disappeared into his office. The Commandant waited. Three minutes passed.

"Very fine weather, sir, for the time of the year," said the clerk, blotting an entry and looking up from his ledger.

"Eh? Oh, certainly . . . yes, very fine indeed." The Commandant recalled himself with a painful effort.

"And the glass steady as a rock." The clerk closed a smaller book at his elbow and replaced it in a line of similar volumes on a shelf above the desk behind him. "I saw you out, sir, in your boat, the day before yesterday, to the west of Saaron — fishing for bass, or so I took the liberty of guessing."

"For bass? . . . Yes, oh, most decidedly."

"Knowing fish, the bass!" hazarded the young man, combing his side-locks with his pen and carefully bestowing it behind his ear. "You found the water a bit too clear, sir, I expect?"

"So far as I remember — " began the Commandant, and paused. (What on earth was delaying Fossell?)

"You will excuse me, sir, but might I ask what bait you employ as a rule?"

The Commandant answered that for preference he used sand-eels. The clerk replied that sand-eels took some getting; and that, if the remark wouldn't be taken amiss, it was all very well to talk of sand-eels when you were in a position to employ a couple of men to spend half a day in netting them for you; but that for a young chap in his position, sand-eels were out of the question.

"There's the bank-hours, to begin with," he wound up, lucidly; "and, besides, when you've caught 'em they're the most perishable bait going."

The Commandant incoherently promised to reserve a portion of his next catch, and to send Archelaus with a creelful; all this with his eyes wandering in desperation to the glass door. The young man was profuse in thanks.

"You will excuse my discussing sport with you, sir? Sport, they say, puts all men on a level — though, of course, I should not dream of claiming—"

But at this point the glass door opened, and Mr. Fossell emerged, briskly, holding what appeared to be a fair-sized stone.

"How will you take it?" he asked, depositing this upon the counter.

"I beg your pardon?" the Commandant stammered, his eyes riveted on the stone.

"Notes or gold?" Mr. Fossel picked the specimen up, and rubbed it gently with his sleeve. "Now, that's a queer thing, eh? My brother-in-law sent it to me last week, and I've been using it for a paper-weight, not being a scientific man. But just you look into it. He tells me there are hundreds lying about where he lives — Ogwell, the place is, in Devonshire, just behind Newton Abbot — and that they're called madrepores. He's a humorous fellow, too, is my brother-in-law. You see the joke, of course?"

"I can't say that I do, exactly," the Commandant confessed.

"Good gracious! Fossil — Fossell: this is a fossil, you see, and I'm called Fossell: and so he sends it to me. He has made a good deal of fun out of my name before now, in his humorous way. Not that I mind, of course."

"I dare say not. Did you say that the papers were all right?"

"The papers?... Yes, of course, the papers are all right. Will you take it in notes or gold?" "In gold, if you please." The Commandant caught at the edge of the counter, while his heart leapt, and the bank premises seemed to whirl around him.

"Fifteen-eighteen-six... be so good as to verify it, if you please," said Mr. Fossell, counting out the coins — the blessed coins! "But I want you just to take a look into the thing. Looks like a piece of coral, eh? See the delicate lines of it? And my brother-in-law tells me it was once alive — a kind of fish — and got itself embedded in this piece of limestone because it was too lazy to move. A lesson in that" — Mr. Fossell wagged his head sagely — "if we choose to take it! To be sure, it happened thousands of years ago; but there it is — and here are we. For my part, I don't look at things humorously like my brother-in-law. I like to find a serious moral where I can."

The Commandant counted the coins and dropped them into his pocket. Their weight seemed to make a man of him again. He bent and affected to examine the madrepore.

Mr. Fossell bent also. He was on the point of asking — in a low voice, that the clerk might not overhear — for an explanation of Miss Gabriel's gossip. But at this juncture a client entered, and the Commandant escaped. He went up the hill with a new centre of gravity: so different is a load in the pocket from a load on the heart.

CHAPTER XX

THE GUITAR AND THE CASEMENT

"A parcel for you, sir!"

Sergeant Archelaus had spied the Commandant coming up the hill, and met him on the barrack doorstep with the news.

"A parcel?" The Commandant had walked straight from the bank to Mr. Tregaskis' shop, and there paid his account; but he had made no purchases. "There must be some mistake, Archelaus; I have ordered nothing in the town."

"From the mainland, sir."

"God bless my soul!"

"Yes, sir, and marked 'Fragile'; a good-sized box, but uncommon light to handle. The steamer brought it across this morning, and I've carried it into the office and placed hammer and chisel handy."

"Now what in the world can this mean?" asked the Commandant, a minute later, after studying the box and its label. He turned to Archelaus, who had followed him into the office in a state of suppressed excitement. "It is certainly addressed to me; and yet — It must be half-a-dozen years, Archelaus, since anyone sent me a parcel from the mainland."

"There's but one way to discover," said Archelaus, picking up the chisel. "Shall I open it, sir?"

"No; give it to me." The Commandant took the tools from him and easily pried open the lid, for the scantling was light, almost flimsy. Within lay an object in an oilskin case, by the shape of it, apparently a violin; and yet somewhat larger than a violin.

Yes, certainly it was a musical instrument; and the Commandant had no sooner made sure of this than with his hand on the string that tied the wrapper, he paused.

"It is evident, Archelaus" — his tone betrayed some disappointment — "that this parcel belongs to Miss Cara. Having no address of her own that could be given with safety, she has ordered it to be sent to me."

"Ben't you even going to open and take a look at it?" asked Archelaus, as his master slowly replaced it in the box.

"I think not. . . . Miss Cara will call for it, no doubt, since no doubt she has been watching for the steamer's arrival."

Archelaus withdrew, reluctantly, not without a sense of expectation cheated. Nor, as it proved, was his grievance altogether groundless. The Commandant stood for a minute or so in a brown study, eyeing the box. Then, his curiosity overmastering him, he reached out and drew the parcel forth again; turned it over in his hands, and very slowly undid the strings, which were of green ribbon.

The wrapper fell apart, disclosing a guitar.

The instrument was clearly an old one, and, as clearly of considerable value, being inlaid with tortoise-shell and mother-of-pearl in delicate arabesques that must have cost its unknown maker many months, if not whole years, of patient labour. Its varnish, smooth and transparent as finest glass, belonged to the same date, and had been laid on, if not by the same hand, by one no less careful. Something more than a craftsman's pride had surely inspired the exquisite workmanship, the deft and joyous pattern that chased itself in and out as though smiling at its own intricacy. A gift for the artist's mistress, perhaps? Or a toy for some dead and gone princess? . . . Yet it had been played upon, and recently. One or two of its relaxed strings showed evidences of fraying; and the sender had tied a small packet of new strings around the neck.

The Commandant, after peering into its pattern for a while, held the guitar out at arm's length; and, holding it so, broke into a short laugh — at the thought that this thing had been sent to him.

Yet, here it was. Undoubtedly it belonged to Vashti, and his heart leapt at the thought that she would be coming to fetch it. For three days he had been missing her. It seemed that she had chosen to pass out of his life as suddenly, as waywardly, as she had invaded it; that, crossing the threshold of Saaron Farm, she had closed its door upon him and upon a brief episode to be remembered by him henceforth as a dream only — a too happy dream.

> *"Ah, had we never met — or, having met,*
> *Had I been wiser or thy heart less wild!"*

He had pulled home that Sunday night, to brood alone over a half-dead fire; and, brooding there, had surmised what the morrow made certain — that she had taken with her yet more than she had even brought; that even what colour, what small interest, had formerly cheered the daily round on Garrison Hill and made it tolerable, was now gone out of it forever.

Well, for good or ill, this, at all events, would need to be endured but a little while longer. His discharge was in sight. He had posted his letter.

He did not tell himself that but for Vashti it had never been written. Or, if this crossed his mind, it suggested no more than gratitude. Quite unwittingly she had helped him play the man. He had done the right thing, let follow what might.

He could not force his mind upon possible consequences, to face them or to fret over them. Between this present hour and then, one thought, like a bright angel, stood in the way. Vashti was coming!

Ah, but when? Would she come openly, by day, as she had invaded Inniscaw? . . . He spent the afternoon in his office, sorting out useless correspondence, clearing desks, drawers, pigeon-holes of the accumulations of years, unconsciously preparing for the day of his discharge. It kept his thoughts employed, and he worked hard — reading through the dusty papers, tearing them up, consigning some to the waste-paper basket others to the fire, which by-and-by grew sullen under its task. Twilight fell. . . . She would come, then, after dusk, and secretly — mooring her boat in the hiding-place under the Keg of Butter Battery, away from inquisitive eyes. At half-past five Archelaus brought him his tea. At six, having washed and refreshed himself, the Commandant fell to work again more doggedly. Only now and again he broke off for a few moments to listen. But Vashti did not come.

He worked until half-past nine. He heard the clock strike the half-hour from the chimney-piece, and looked up almost in dismay. It was certain now that she would not come. Of a sudden, as though to hide from him the full measure of his disappointment, as he had been hiding from himself the full eagerness of his hopes, a loathing took him — a savage scorn of his useless labour. He stared at his grimed hands with a shiver of disgust, and, rising impatiently, swept together the fragments of paper strewn about the floor, tossed them upon the dying fire, and went off to his room for another wash.

She would not come; and there remained yet an hour between him and his usual bed-time. Returning to his office, he met Archelaus on the stairs.

"Going to bed, eh?" asked the Commandant.

"Ay, sir," Archelaus answered, and paused for that remark on the weather which, in the Islands, always goes with "Good morning" or "Good night." "Glass don't vary very much, and wind don't vary, though seemin' to me it's risin' a little. Still in the nor'west it is; and here ends another day."

The Commandant looked at him sharply, but passed down-stairs with no more than a "Good night." So Archelaus, too, was feeling life to be empty? . . . Archelaus had bewailed the past before now, and the vanished glories of the garrison, but never the tedium of his present lot.

The Commandant, on re-entering his office, did a very unusual thing. It has been said that he could no longer afford himself tobacco. But an old briar pipe lay on the chimney-piece among a litter of notes and memoranda that had escaped the afternoon's holocaust. He took it up wistfully, and, searching in a jar, at the end of the shelf, found a few crumbs of tobacco. Scraped together with care, they all but filled the bowl. He lit the dry stuff from a spill — the last scrap of paper to be sacrificed — and sank, puffing, into his worn armchair.

It was in his mind to map out his domestic expenditure for the coming month; for the settlement with Mr. Tregaskis had made a desperate inroad upon his funds in hand, and he gravely doubted that even with the severest pinching he would be able to remit the usual allowance to his sister-in-law. The question had to be faced . . . he was not afraid of it . . . and yet his thoughts shirked it and wandered away, despite all effort to rally them. "Old enough to be her father. . . ." He had foreseen that these words would awake to torment him; but he was not prepared for the insistency with which the pain stirred, now when long toil should have deadened it — now when, as the clock told him that his hopes for today were vain, he realised how fondly all the while he had been building on them.

"Old enough to be her father." — For distraction from the maddening refrain he rose up, drew the guitar again from its box, unwrapped it, and took it back to his chair for another examination. He noticed the wrapper as he laid it aside. It was new; the material new, the stitching new. She had sent for the instrument with a purpose, and the oilskin case had been made with a purpose. . . . How went the old song? —

> "Were I but young for thee, as I haz been,
>   We should have been gallopin' down in your green.
> And linkin' it owre the lily-white lea;
>   And ah, gin I were but young for thee!"

Of a sudden he sat up stiffly, at the sound of a tap-tap on the window-pane behind him.

Yes, decidedly the sound came from the window. The wind — as Archelaus had said — was rising; but this was no wind. Someone stood outside there in the darkness. He sprang up, stepped to the casement and threw it open. For a moment his eyes distinguished nothing. He peered again and drew back a little as a figure stepped close to the sill, out of the night.

"You!"

"Who else?" answered Vashti, with a little laugh. "Give me your hand, please." He stretched it out obediently, and she took it and clambered in over the sill.

"It is cold outside," she announced, looking around her with something between a shiver and a deliberate shake of her cloak. It was the same furred cloak in which she had come ashore from the *Milo*. Spray clung to it; and there was spray, too, on her hair. It shone in the lamplight.

"The wind has been getting up ever since sundown," she announced. "I have had a pretty stiff crossing; but the boat is all right, under the Keg of Butter." Then, as he still stared at her, "You don't keep too warm a fire, my friend."

"I had given you up, and was getting ready for bed."

"Then you expected me? The guitar has come?"

Before he could answer she had caught sight of it, and picking it up from the armchair where the Commandant had dropped it, settled herself and laid the instrument across her lap.

"Also," she went on, throwing back her cloak, while she examined and tightened the strings, "I will confess that your guest is hungry." She looked up with a laugh. "In fact I came not only to fetch my guitar, but to sup with you and tell you of my doings."

The Commandant turned to the door. His face had suddenly grown gray and desperate.

"Ah, yes — supper, to be sure!" he said, and strode from the room.

As the latch fell behind him, Vashti glanced over her shoulder, put the guitar aside, and arose to stir the fire. The poker plunged into a heap of flaked ashes. "Paper? But the whole grate is choked with it. And, what is more, the whole room smells of burnt paper."

She turned about, and, with her back to the hearth, surveyed the room suspiciously. Her gaze fell upon the waste-paper basket, heaped high and brimming over with torn documents. This puzzled her again, and her brow contracted in a frown. But just then she caught the sound of the Commandant's footsteps returning along the flagged passage, and bent anew over the fire.

The Commandant appeared in the doorway with a plate of ship's biscuit in his hand, and on his face a flush of extreme embarrassment.

"Do you know, I really am ashamed of myself," he began with a stammer, holding out the plate. "But Archelaus has gone to bed, and — and this is all I can find."

"Capital!" she answered gaily. "Let us break into the back premises and forage. After my burglarious entry that will just suit my mood."

"I'm afraid — " he began, and hesitated. "I am very much afraid — " There was unmistakable trouble in his voice, and again he came to a halt.

Vashti straightened herself up. Her eyes were on him as he set the plate down on the table, but he avoided them, attempting a small forced laugh. The laugh was a dead failure. Silence followed it, and in the silence he felt horribly aware that she was grasping the truth — the humiliating truth; that moment by moment the scales were falling from her eyes that still persistently sought his.

The silence was broken by the noise of a poker falling against the fender. He started, met her gaze for a moment, and again averted his.

"You don't mean to say—"

Her voice trailed off, in pitiful surmise. Silence again; and in the silence he heard her sink back into the arm chair — and knew no more until, at the sound of one strangling sob, terrible to hear, he found himself standing at the arm of her chair and bending over her.

"My dear!" He used the familiar Island speech. "My dear, you must not — please!"

"And I have been living on you, ruining you!"

"My dear . . . it is all paid for. It was paid for today. If ever a man was glad of his guest, I am he."

But she bent her head over the arm of the chair, sobbing silently. He saw the heave of her shoulders, and it afflicted him beyond words. But, though he longed, he dared not put out a hand to comfort her.

"You mistake — yes, you mistake. . . . It has been nothing. . . . I was only too glad," he kept stammering weakly.

She pulled herself together and sat upright. A moment her tear-stained eyes met his, then turned to the fire, which had begun to dance again on its small heap of coals.

"Now I see," said she, resting an elbow on the arm of the chair and so supporting her chin, while she stared resolutely into the blaze. She had resumed command of her voice. "Ah, pardon me, now I understand many things that puzzled me at first. . . . I — I am not a fool in money matters." She hesitated.

"I know you are not," he assured her gently. "And that, if you will understand, increased the small difficulty."

"Yes, I understand. But somehow — it was a long time since I had been acquainted with — with—"

"Want," he suggested. "Since you know the worst, do not hurt me more than you are obliged."

"God knows," she said, after an interval of musing, "I would hurt you last of all living men. Will you be kind to me, and trust me?"

"On conditions."

"Yes?" She glanced up with a strange eagerness in her eyes. "What conditions?"

"That you do not pity me at all; that you believe I have suffered nothing, or only such pain as has edged the joy of serving you."

She looked away and into the fire. "You make me very proud," she said. "Yes. I can easily grant your conditions. I could not pity a man who practised so noble a courtesy."

The Commandant shook his head with a whimsical smile. "My dear," he answered, "it's undeniably pleasant to stand well in your opinion, but I am not used to compliments, and you run some risk of making me a vain fellow. You asked me to trust you. With what?"

"With the reason why you are poor."

"That," said he, "can be very simply told," and, briefly, in the simplest possible style, he told her of his brother's death, and how his sister-in-law and her family had been left in destitution. "You see," he wound up, "it's just an ordinary sad little tale. Cases of that kind happen daily, all the world over. One must be thankful when they happen within reach of help."

"Is your sister-in-law thankful?" asked Vashti, sharply. "But there!" she added, as he stared at her obviously at a loss to find the question relevant. "You are quite right. It really does not matter two pins whether she is thankful or not." She turned her eyes to the fire again and sat musing. "But I am glad to have heard the story," she went on after a while. "It explains — oh, many things! I have been blind, inconsiderate; but I am seeing light at last. Do you know, my friend, that at first I found a great change in you?"

"Why — bless me! — you had only seen me once before in your life, and then for two minutes!"

"Listen, please, and don't interrupt. I found a great change in you, and the reason of it seemed to lie all on the surface. You had brought ambitions to the Islands, but you had forgotten them. You kept your kindness, your good nature, but you had forgotten all purpose in life. In all, except a few personal habits, you were neglecting yourself; and this neglect came of your being content to live purposeless in this forgotten hole, and draw your pay without asking questions. Forgive me, but I seemed to see all this, and it drove me half wild."

He bowed his head. "I know it did," he answered very slowly, "and that is how you came to save me."

"Is — is this another story?" she asked, after eyeing him a moment or two in bewilderment.

"If you will listen to it." He drew his writing chair over to the fireside, and then, facing her across the hearth he told her the second story as simply as he had told the first, but more nervously, leaning forward with his elbows on his knees, now and again spreading out his hands to the fire on which he kept his eyes bent during most of the recital. Vashti, too, leaned forward, intent on his face. One hand gripped the arm of her chair — so tightly that its pressure drove the blood from the finger tips, while the wonder in her eyes changed to something like awe. "And so," the commandant concluded, "the letter has gone. I posted it today."

"What will happen?"

"I really cannot tell." Without lifting his gaze from the fire he shook his head dubiously. "But at the worst, the girls are grown into women now. They have been excellently well educated — their mother saw to that and made a great point of it from the first — and by this time they should be able to help, if not support her entirely."

"Man! Man! Will you drive me mad?"

Vashti sprang from the chair.

"I have been unjust. I have been worse than a fool!" She flung back her cloak, and, clasping her hands behind her, man-fashion, fell to pacing the room to and fro. The Commandant stood and stared. Something in her voice puzzled him completely. In its tone, though she accused herself, there vibrated a low note of triumph. She was genuinely remorseful — why, he could not guess. Yet, when she halted before him, he saw that her eyes were glad as well as dim. She held out a hand.

"Forgive me, my friend!"

"Do you know," stammered the Commandant, as he took it, "I should esteem it a favour to be told whether I am standing on my head or my heels!"

How long he held her hand he was never afterwards able to tell; for at its electric touch the room began to swim around him. But this could not have lasted for long; because, as he looked into her eyes, still seeking an explanation, she broke off the half-hysterical laugh that answered him, and pulled her hand away sharply at a sound behind them.

Someone was throwing gravel against the window.

"Commandant!" a voice hailed from the darkness without.

For an instant the two stood as if petrified. Then with a second glance at the window, to make sure that the curtain was drawn, Vashti tip-toed swiftly to the door, catching up the guitar on her way.

"Hi! Commandant! Are you waking or sleeping in there?"

The Commandant stepped to the curtain. Vashti opened the door and slipped out into the passage. The door closed upon her as he pulled the curtain aside for a second time that night and opened the casement.

"Who's there?"

"So you *are* awake?" answered the voice of Mr. Rogers. "May I come in?" And, silence being apparently taken for consent, a foot and leg followed the voice across the window-sill.

CHAPTER XXI

SUSPICIONS

The foot and leg were followed by Mr. Rogers' entire person, and Mr. Rogers, having thus made good his entrance, stood blinking, with an apologetic laugh. "You'll excuse me — but I took it for granted the door was barred, and seeing a glimmer of light in the window here—"

"Anything wrong?" asked the Commandant.

"Nothing's wrong, I hope" — Mr. Rogers stepped over to the warm fire. "But something's queer." He fished out a pipe from the pocket of his thick pilot coat, filled it, lit up, and sank puffing into the armchair from which, a minute ago, Vashti had snatched up her guitar. "Hullo!" he exclaimed, as his eyes fell upon the empty packing-case. "You don't mean to tell me that you've been smuggling?"

The Commandant shook his head and laughed, albeit with some confusion. "The steamer brought it this morning. I assure you it held nothing contraband. . . . But I hope that little game is not starting afresh in the Islands? It gave us a deal of trouble in the old days; and there was quite an outbreak of it, as I remember, some three or four years before you came to us. Old Penkivel" — this was Mr. Rogers' predecessor — "used to declare that it turned his hair gray."

"He told me something beside, on the morning he sailed for the mainland; which was that but for the help you gave him as Governor he could never have grappled with it. Maybe this was sticking in my head just now when I started to walk up here and consult you."

"Well, and what is the matter?"

"Oh, a trifle. . . . Do you happen to know Tregarthen, the fellow that farms Saaron Island?"

The Commandant started.

"Eli Tregarthen? Yes, certainly . . . that is to say, as I know pretty well everybody in the Islands."

"What sort of a fellow?"

"Quiet; steady; works on his farm like a horse, week in and week out; never speaks out of his turn, and says little enough when his turn comes."

"That sort is often the deepest," observed Mr. Rogers sententiously, and puffed. "And Saaron Island there, close by the Roads, lies very handy for a little illicit work."

"You are right, so far," the Commandant admitted; "and history bears you out. In the old kelp-making days, when half-a-dozen families lived on it, Saaron gave more trouble than any two islands of its size."

"It's none the less handy for being deserted." Mr. Rogers drew out a penknife and meditatively loosened the tobacco in his pipe.

"Handier. But you are wrong in suspecting Tregarthen; that is, unless you have good tangible evidence."

"I don't say that it amounts to much, but it's tangible. In fact, his boat is lying here, just now, close under the Keg of Butter."

The Commandant turned on his heel and took a pace or two towards the window, to hide his perturbation and give himself time to consider. . . . Vashti's boat! And Vashti on the premises at this moment! What was to be done? How on earth could he get her away?

"You discovered this yourself?" he found himself asking.

"No; I happened to be in the Watch House with the chief boatman checking the store-sheets, when Beesley, whose watch it is, came in and reported. I see what you're driving at. Your own boat is lying under the Keg of Butter, as everybody knows, and you suggest that I am duffer enough to mistake her in the darkness for a boat at least two-foot longer."

Mr. Rogers laughed good-naturedly.

"But the answer is," he went on, "that Beesley found two boats lying there; and Beesley, who knows every craft in the Islands, swears that the one belongs to you no more certainly than the other to Farmer Tregarthen. Moreover, she was moored on a shore line, and we pulled her in and examined her. Sure enough we found name and owner's name cut on her transom — 'Two Sisters: E. Tregarthen.' Now, what d'you make of it?"

"Very little," answered the Commandant, recovering himself; "and that little in all likelihood quite innocent. Someone, we'll say, wishes to cross over from Saaron to St. Lide's this evening — on any simple errand, say to fetch a parcel from the steamer. Why shouldn't that someone, knowing the Keg of Butter to be good shelter with plenty of water at all tides, have landed and left the boat there?"

Mr. Rogers shook his head. "Why there, and not at the pier? The pier lies almost a mile nearer, and there's a fair wind — or almost a fair one — for returning; while from the Keg of Butter no one can fetch Saaron under a couple of tacks. That's my first point. Secondly, if Eli Tregarthen has honest business here, whether with the steamer to fetch a parcel (parcels must be running in your head tonight), or in the town to fetch a doctor, the pier is obviously his landing-place. Why, there isn't a house in the Island, barring these Barracks, that doesn't stand half-a-mile nearer the pier; not to mention that landing at the Keg of Butter involves a perfectly unnecessary climb up one side of Garrison Hill and down the other. Lastly, my dear sir, look at the time! Close on eleven o'clock, and all Garland Town in their beds. Again, I ask what honest business can Eli Tregarthen have here at such an hour?"

The Commandant felt himself cornered. An insane hope crossed his mind that, while the Lieutenant sat talking, Vashti had contrived to slip out of the house and down to the shore. It was followed by a saner one, that she had done nothing of the sort; for, to a certainty, the boat would be guarded.

"You have taken precautions?" he asked, and felt himself flushing at the dishonesty of the question.

"I have posted Beesley in charge, and sent the chief boatman off to the pier-head to keep a close watch on the steamer. She sails at seven-thirty tomorrow, and though I never heard a hint against her skipper, it's only right to be careful. I've amused myself before now, planning imaginary frauds on the revenue; and if anyone cares to risk opening up that game afresh, the Islands still give him a-plenty of openings."

"Yes, yes," agreed the Commandant, and checked a groan. He had thought of warning Vashti to slip down to the quay and borrow a boat there without asking leave. Some explanation might be trumped up on the morrow — as that the wind was foul for returning from the Keg of Butter. No one would accuse Eli Tregarthen of borrowing a boat with intent to steal: his taking it would be no more than a neighbourly liberty.

But, with the chief boatman watching the pier-head, she would be discovered to a certainty.

The Commandant's last hope was gone.

Just as he realised this, to his utter astonishment, he heard the voice of Archelaus grumbling outside in the passage. And Archelaus had gone to rest an hour ago!

"Pretty time of night this, to come breaking a man's rest!" growled the voice of Archelaus, audibly, and not without viciousness, as though he meant it to be heard.

"Good Lord!" exclaimed Mr. Rogers. "You don't tell me we've roused the old fellow out of bed? And I reckoned I was making no more noise than a mouse!"

"He may have heard you throw that gravel against the pane." The Commandant took a step towards the door, but halted irresolutely.

"Then he's a light sleeper," commented Mr. Rogers, "and an

even more dilatory dresser. Why, good heavens!" — the Lieutenant started up from his chair — "he's undoing the bolts! Somebody's at the front door: one of my men to report, I'll bet a fiver!"

He would have rushed out into the passage, but the Commandant caught him by the arm.

"No need to hurry, my friend! Whoever it is, Archelaus will bring word."

Many hasty surmises whirled together in the Commandant's brain — the first, and hastiest, that Vashti, unable to make her escape, had aroused Archelaus, and that Archelaus was unbarring the door for her on the pretence of hearing a knock. Even so, she would be caught as soon as she reached the shore. Still, occasion might be snatched to send Archelaus after her to warn her; she might hide for the night at the Castle under Mrs. Treacher's friendly wing. The instant need was to hold back the Lieutenant from discovering her in the passage, and to the Lieutenant's arm our Commandant clung.

"My good sir," expostulated Mr. Rogers, "it *must* be one of my men. Who else, at this hour?"

He fell back a step as the door opened.

"A person to see you, sir; from Saaron!" announced Archelaus. "Shall I show her in?"

Before either could answer, Vashti herself stood on the threshold.

Of the two men, the Lieutenant excusably showed the blankest astonishment. But the Commandant had to catch at the rail of a chair. Vashti had discarded her cloak of furs, and faced him now in such garb as is worn by the poorest in the Islands: a short gown of hodden gray, coarse-knitted stockings, and stout shoes. Across her shoulder, for a "turn-over," she wore a faded shawl of Tartan pattern. (The Commandant recognised it for a surplus one which Mrs. Treacher kept in the Barracks kitchen, to wear "against the draughts" on occasions when she helped Archelaus with the cooking.) But most wonderful of all was her hair. By some swift art the heavy coil had been drawn into two flat bands, brought low over the forehead, and carried back over the ears in a fashion almost slatternly. By no art could Vashti conceal that she was beautiful. She was also too wise to attempt it. But, for the rest, she had transformed herself.

"If you please, sir," she began timidly, with an Island curtsey, and paused as if uncertain, at sight of Mr. Rogers, whether to hold her ground or to flee: "If you please, sir, I be that frightened!"

Accent, intonation — both were perfect, of the true Island speech, that delicate incommunicable sing-song. The Commandant's eyes grew rounder yet with amazement, and Vashti — afraid, perhaps, of meeting them — flung a glance of mock terror behind her, as though she had caught the footfall of a pursuer.

"But — but who in the world — " stammered Mr. Rogers.

"If you please, gentlemen" — she turned, with another quick curtsey — "my name is Vazzy Cara, and I come from Saaron. I live there with my sister, Ruth, that is wife to Eli Tregarthen—"

Mr. Rogers gave a low whistle.

"It's true, sir — true as I stand here! The Governor knows me, and will bear me out — won't you, sir? . . . A terrible way from Saaron it is, and at this hour of night. . . . But ask the Governor, sir, and he'll tell you I am a respectable woman; sister to Mrs. Tregarthen, and lives with her to look after the children."

"Yes, yes," interrupted the Lieutenant, losing patience. "But the question is, how you came here, and why?"

Vashti stood panting. By the heave of her bosom it was plain to see that either her fears still possessed her or that she had been running for dear life, and must catch breath. Her hand went up to her bodice.

"I came, sir, to see the Governor — all the way across from Saaron. Eli — that's my sister's husband — is in terrible trouble over there, because the Lord Proprietor means to turn him off his farm. Yes, say!" — she drew a letter from her bodice, and went on with rising voice. "Turn us out he will, though the Tregarthens have lived on the Island ever since Saaron was Saaron. The Governor, here, in his time would never have done such wickedness, nor suffered it, being a just gentleman and merciful, as all the folk can bear witness. And so, thinks I, he may be able to help us yet; and if able he will be willing."

She held out the letter towards the Commandant, who took it and turned it over vaguely between his fingers, not opening it, nor daring to meet her eyes.

"And so," continued Mr. Rogers, "you took your brother-in-law's boat — without his knowledge—"

Vashti nodded. "Yes, sir; I took it unbeknowns. He's a very quiet man, is my sister's husband, and don't like it that other folks, 'specially women, should mix themselves up in his affairs."

"Then he's a sensible fellow as well as a quiet one."

"Yes, sir." Vashti took the correction meekly, with downcast look.

"And still less, I'll bet," Mr. Rogers continued, "would he be pleased to know that one of his woman-kind was straying across to St. Lide's at this hour of the night."

"Oh, sir," she caught him up, "but that's where I've been hindered! For, wishing to have word with the Governor, and no one the wiser, I brought the boat to shore down yonder, under the Keg of Butter, and there the coastguards have found it, and are waiting by it to catch me, and what answer to give them I can't think, nor how to account for myself. Seemin' to me they're everywhere, and all around me in the darkness!"

Mr. Rogers broke into a laugh. "It appears, Commandant, that I have found a mare's nest; always supposing that this tale is a true one. You'll excuse me, ma'am, but service is service."

The Commandant had turned to his writing-table, and was holding the letter under the lamplight.

"I can go bail for Miss Cara," he answered, but without looking up. "Undoubtedly she comes from Saaron, and is Mrs. Tregarthen's sister. Also this letter, though we cannot deal with it tonight, is addressed to Eli Tregarthen in the Lord Proprietor's handwriting. It gives him formal notice to quit and deliver up his farm. I can give no hope of help — no hope at all." Here his voice trembled slightly. "The most I can promise is to consider it."

"And the best we can do for the moment is to escort Miss Cara down to her boat and get one of my men to sail her back to her island."

"I incline to think," said the Commandant, after a pause, "that Miss Cara — from what I have seen of her skill — is competent to sail back alone. If not, I would suggest that you or I escort her, towing my boat across for the return journey. In any case, if we can get your men out of the way, it would be wiser, perhaps, for her sake."

"And for mine, begad!" agreed the Lieutenant! "Else I shall have every man of them grinning behind my back for a month of Sundays. 'Rogers' smuggling-chase' — I can hear the villains chuckling over it. . . . But I say, though" — he turned on Vashti admiringly — "you'll want an escort across, eh? You don't tell me you're man enough to handle that boat alone?"

"If you please, sir."

"The Channel's none too easy on a dark night."

Vashti smiled. "My father taught it to me, sir, before I was ten years old. I could sail it blindfold."

"And you have the nerve? . . . And yet just now, the dark frightened you, and you ran for your life!"

"No," said Vashti, demurely, "I just stood still."

"Well, come along! And when you get to the Battery, you'll have to stand still again, and wait until I report the coast clear. Commandant, will you give Miss Cara your arm, while I run ahead."

They stepped out together into the night. Vashti neither took the Commandant's arm nor spoke to him, even after Mr. Rogers had passed ahead out of earshot. Only when the pair had reached the dark battery, and were waiting there on the dark platform above the sea, she turned to him and asked —

"Shall you be busy tomorrow?"

"I am never busy."

"I have left my cloak and the guitar with Archelaus."

"I will bring them to Saaron tomorrow."

She turned away and leaned over the low parapet to the left. Some way below a footfall sounded, on the track leading to the watch-house — -the footfall of Beesley. A stone, dislodged by his tread, trickled and fell over the cliff into night.

*****

"Curious!" remarked Mr. Rogers, confidentially, to the Commandant, twenty minutes later, as they stood and peered into the darkness after Vashti's boat. "Here I am, stuck on these Islands (so to speak) with a telescope held to my eye. Of the folk upon 'em I see next to nothing. Now, I don't know if you took note of it, but that's a remarkable looking woman; a remarkably handsome woman; and I've spent these years here without guessing that such a woman existed hereabouts. Eh?" Mr. Rogers relapsed into mild facetiousness. "If you were a younger man, Commandant, I could hatch up a pretty story out of tonight's doings — and if I didn't mind a laugh against myself."

CHAPTER XXII

PIPER'S HOLE

Annet, Linnet, and Matthew Henry sat side by side on the granite roller by the gate and watched their friend Jan eat his mid-morning snack — or "mungey," as it is called in the Islands. It consisted, as a rule, of a crust of bread, but Jan had supplemented it today with a turnip, which he cut into slices with his pocket-knife. He had been pulling turnips since six o'clock. "And I reckon this'll be the last time of askin'," he commented, letting his eyes wander over the field as he seated himself on a shaft of the cart, which had been brought to await the loading.

The children knew that they would soon be quitting Saaron, and that the prospect distressed their father and mother. They had discussed it, and agreed together that it was a great shame to be turned out of their home, and that the Lord Proprietor must be a hard-hearted tyrant; but secretly they looked forward to the change with a good deal of excitement, not being of an age to fathom the troubles of grown-up folk. After all, Brefar lay close at hand and was familiar. Brefar was populous, and across there they would find many playmates. Brefar, too, held out great promise of adventure after sea-birds' eggs and expeditions of discovery; and if ever the home-sickness came upon them they would cross the sands at low-water and revisit the old haunts and the deserted house. All these consolations, however, they kept to themselves. It would never do to abandon the family grievance merely because it presented a bright side. They felt, as older folks have been known to feel, that a sense of injury carries with it a sense of importance.

"I wonder," said Linnet, severely, "that you can have the heart to talk about it, Jan."

"Jan has no feelings about leaving Saaron," said Annet, more in sorrow than in anger. "Why should he — coming from the mainland?"

"But Jan was born on the Islands," Matthew Henry objected; "and that will be a long time ago."

"Silly! As if you could belong to the Islands by being born here! Why, to belong to them, your father and mother must have been Islanders, and your grandfathers and grandmothers, and right back into the greats and great-greats. And then you never want to go away or live anywhere else in the world."

Matthew Henry pursed up his small mouth dubiously. He himself had sometimes wished to live in the wilds of America, or on a

South Sea Island; even to visit Australia and have a try at walking upside down. There must be a flaw in Annet's argument somewhere.

"But if Jan comes from the mainland — " he began.

"Cornwall," said Jan, tranquilly, his mouth full of raw turnip.

"Then you ought to want to go back to it."

"I mean to, one of these fine days."

"I shouldn't put it off too long, if I were you," advised Linnet, candidly. "You're getting up in years, and the next thing you'll be dead."

"But didn't your father ever want to go back?" asked Matthew Henry, sticking to his point.

"No fear."

"Why?"

"Because, if he'd showed his face back in Cornwall, they'd have hanged him; that's all."

"Oh!" exclaimed the three, almost simultaneously, and sat for a moment or two gazing on Jan in awed silence.

"But why should they want to hang your father?" asked Annet.

Jan sliced his bread with an air of noble indifference. "Eh? Why, indeed? He used to say 'twas for being too frolicsome. He never done no wrong — not what you might call wrong: or so he maintained, an' 'twasn't for me to disbelieve. Was it, now?"

"You'll tell us about it, Jan dear?" coaxed Annet.

"There's no particular story in it." (The children put this aside; it was Jan's formula for starting a tale.) "My father, in his young days, lived at a place in Cornwall called Luxulyan, and arned his wages as a tinner at a stream-work—"

"What is a stream-work?" asked Matthew Henry.

"A stream-work is a moor beside a river, where the mud is full of ore, washed down from the country above — sometimes from the old mines. The streamers dig this mud up and wash it through sieves, and so they get the tin. There was enough of it, my father said, in Luxulyan Couse to keep a captain and twelve men in good wages and pay for a feast once a year at the Rising Sun Public House. The supper took place some time in the week before Christmas, and they called it Pie-crust Night, though I can't tell you why. Well, one Pie-crust Night, after this yearly supper — the most enjoyable he had ever known — my father left the Rising Sun towards midnight, and started to walk to his home in Luxulyan Churchtown. He had a fair dollop of beer inside of him, but nothing (as he ever maintained), to excuse what followed, and he got so far as Tregarden Down without accident. Now, this Tregarden Down, as he always described it to me, is a lonesome place given over to brackenfern and strewn about with great granite boulders, and on one of these boulders my father sat down, because the night was clear and a fancy had come into his head to count the stars. He sat there staring up and counting till he reached twenty score, and with that he felt he was getting a crick in the back of his neck, and brought his eyes down to earth again. It seemed to him that, even in the dark, a change had come over the down since he'd been sittin' there, and the whole lie of the ground had a furrin look. Hows'ever, he hadn't much time to puzzle about this, for lo and behold! as he stared about him, what should he see under the lew of the next rock but a party of little people, none of 'em more than a thumb high, dancing in a ring upon the turf! They broke off and laughed as soon as my father caught sight of 'em; and, says one little whipper-snapper, stepping forward and pulling off his cap with a bow, 'Good evening, my man!' 'Sir to you!' says my father. 'There's a good liquor at the Rising Sun,' says the little man. 'None better,' says my father. 'I know by a deal better,' says the little man. 'Would you like to taste it?' 'Would I not?' says my father. 'Well, then,' says the little man, 'there's a shipfull of wine gone ashore early this night on Par Sands, and maybe the Par folk haven't had time yet to clear the cargo. What d'ee say to *Ho! and away for Par Beach!* Eh?' 'With all the pleasure in life,' says my father, thinkin' it a joke; so '*Ho! and away for Par Beach!*' he calls out, mimicking the little man. The words weren't scarcely out of his mouth before a wind seemed to catch him up, though gently, from his seat on the boulder, and in two twinklings he was standin' on Par Sands. There was a strong sea running, and out beyond the edge of the tide my father spied a ship breaking up. But if she broke up fast, her cargo was meltin' faster, for a whole crowd of folk had gathered on the sands, and were rolling the casks of wine up from the water and carting them away for dear life. My father and the little people couldn't much as ever lay hands on a solitary one, and, what was worse they hadn't but fairly broached it before a cry went up that the Preventive men were coming. Sure enough, my father, pricking up his ears, could hear horses gallopin' down along the road above the sands. 'Dear, dear!' says the little man, 'this is a most annoyin' thing to happen! But luckily I know a place where there's better liquor still, and no risk of bein' interrupted. So *Ho! and away for Squire Tremayne's cellar!*'

"'*Ho! and away for Squire Tremayne's cellar!*' called out my father; and the next thing he knew he found himself in the cellar of Squire Tremayne's great house at Heligan, knocking around with the small people among casks of wine and barrels of beer galore. To do him justice, he never pretended he didn't make use of the occasion. In fact, he fuddled himself so that when the little gentleman called out 'Ho! and away! for the next randivoo' (whatever that might ha' been), he missed to take up the catchword, bein' asleep belike. So there the piskies left him asleep, with his head in a waste saucer and his mouth under the drip of a spigot; and there the butler found him the next morning, knocking his shins among the butts and barrels in the darkness, and calling out to know what the dickens had taken Tregarden Down and the rocks o't, that they grew so pesky close together. The butler haled him upstairs to the Squire, and the Squire heard his story, and not only said he didn't believe a word o't, but (bein' a magistrate) packed him off to Bodmin Jail for burglary. I don't blame the man altogether," said Jan, reflectively; "for, come to think of it, my father's account of himself lay a bit off the ordinary run, and belike he wasn't in any condition to put it clearly.

"At any rate, to jail he went, and from jail he was delivered up to the Judges at Assize, and the Judges sentenced my poor father to death, which was the punishment for burglary in those times, and, for all I know, it may be the same on the mainland to this day.

"The morning came when he was to be put out of the world; and, as I needn't tell you, it gathered a great crowd together, to have a look at the last of a man that had so little sense of wickedness as to take liberties with a gentleman's wine and spirits. There my poor father stood under the gallows-tree with none to befriend 'en, when all of a sudden he heard a shouting up the street, and down along it, through the crowd, came a strange little lady, holding up her hand and a paper in it. The folk opened way respectful-like, seein' by the better-most air of her that she belonged to one of the gentry, and along she came to the scaffold. 'Good mornin', ma'am, and what can I do for you?' says the Sheriff, steppin' forward, with a lift of his hat. He held out a hand for the paper; but the little lady turns to my father, and pipes out in a little voice, very clear and sweet, 'Ho! and away for the Islands!' Glad enough was my father to hear the sound of it. 'Ho! and away for the Islands!' he answers, pat; and in two twinks he and the little lady were off in the sky like a puff of smoke, and the crowd left miles below. The next thing he knew he was sittin' on a rock, over yonder in Inniscaw, by the mouth of Piper's Hole, and starin' at the sea. So he picks himself together and walks up to North Inniscaw Farm (as 'twas called in those days), and there he took service and married and lived steady ever after. Least-ways—"

"Leastways," said a voice at the gate, "he gave over drinking except when his master ran a cargo of brandy, and he never gave his wife trouble but once, when he took home a mermaid and made the good soul jealous."

"Aunt Vazzy!" cried the children. "Why, how long have you been standin' there?"

"Long enough to hear the end of the story, and how Jan's father came to the Islands through Piper's Hole."

"But," Linnet objected, "Jan didn't say that his father came through Piper's Hole; only that he found himself on the rocks in front of it. They came through the air, he and the little lady, didn't they, Jan?"

Jan shook his head. "They started to come through the air," he answered cautiously.

"Everybody knows that the fairies always pass to and fro through Piper's Hole," said Annet, in a positive voice. "The mermaids, too. The cave there goes right through Inniscaw and under the sea, and comes up again in the mainland. Nobody living has ever gone that way; but Farmer Santo had an uncle once that owned a sheep-dog that wandered into Piper's Hole and was lost, and a month later it turned up on the mainland with all its hair off."

"It do go in a terrible long way, to be sure," Jan admitted; "for I made a trial of it myself, one time, at low water. First of all you come to a pool, and, then, about fifty yards further, to another pool, and into that I went plump, coming upon it sudden, in the darkness. I swallowed a bellyful of it, too, and the water — if you'll believe me — was quite fresh. I didn't try no further, because, in the first place, the tide was rising, and because, when I pulled myself out, I heard a sound on t'other side of the pool like as if some creature was breathin' hard there in the darkness. It properly raised my hair, and I turned tail."

"Fie, Jan! Ran away from a mermaid!" said Vashti, laughing. "You should have brought her home and married her."

"I don't want to marry no woman with a tail like a fish, nor no woman that makes thikky noise with her breathin'," maintained Jan. "That's to say, if merrymaid it were, which I doubts. But you're wrong about my father, Miss Vazzy. He see'd a merrymaid sure 'nough; but he never took her home. No, he was too much of a gentleman, besides bein' afeard o' my mother. If you want the story, he was down in Piper's Hole one day warping ashore some few kegs of brandy that had been sunk thereabouts by a Rosco trader. Mr. Pope's father, that was agent to th' old Duke, used to employ my father regular on this business, knowing him for a silent man, and one to be trusted; and my father had made a very pretty catchet some way back-along in the cave, big enough to hold two score of kegs, and well above reach of the sea-water. But, o' course, while he was at this kind of work, Mr. Pope had to wink an eye now and then if one o' the kegs leaked a bit. Well, my father had finished his job that day in a sweatin' hurry, the tide bein' nearabouts on the top of the flood, and at the end, all the kegs bein' stowed, he spiled one 'for the good of the house,' as he put it, and drew off a tot in a tin panikin he kept handy. With this and his pipe he settled himself down 'pon a dry ledge and waited for the tide to run back.

"Out beyond the mouth of the hole he could see a patch of blue sky, and the little waves under it glancin' in the sunshine; and belike the dazzle of it, or else the tot of brandy, made him feel drowsy-like. Anyhow, he woke up to see that the tide had run out a bravish lot, leavin' the sands high and dry. But, as you know, there's a pool o' water close inside the entrance, and what should my father see in the pool but a woman's head and shoulders!

"She had raised herself out of the water with her hands restin' on a slab of rock, and over the rock she stared at my father, like as if she wanted help, and again like as if she felt too timid to ask. And when I called her a woman I said wrong; for she was more like a child, and a frightened one, with terrible pretty eyes, and her long hair shed down over her shoulders, drippin' wet, and in colour between gold and sea-green. 'Hullo!' said my father, 'and who might you be, makin' so bold?' At the sound of his speech she gave a little scritch at first, and bobbed down face-under, so that her hair lay afloat and spread itself all over the water like sea-weed. My father walked up closer. 'Nonsense, my dear,' says he, in his coaxin' voice, 'there's nothin' to be afeard of. I'm a respectable married man, and old enough to be your father. So put up your face — come now! — and tell me all about it.' After a bit she lifted her face, very pitiful, and says she in a small voice, 'I was afeard you had been drinkin', sir.' 'A little — a very little,' answers my father; 'we'll say no more about it.' 'And I was afeard,' says she, 'you would want to carry me home and marry me against my will!' 'Lord,' says my father, 'trust a woman for putting notions into a man's head. No, no, my dear; I can get all the temperance talk I want without committin' bigamy for it.' 'An' you couldn' marry me,' says the merrymaid, with a kind o' sob, 'because I'm married already, an' the mother of two as pretty children as ever you wished to see. I can hear 'em callin' for me,' she said, 'down there, beyond the bar,' and she went on to tell him (but the tale was all mixed up with sobbin') how she and the children had been swimmin' along shore that afternoon, and liftin' their heads above water to glimpse the sea-pinks and catch a smell of the thyme on the cliffs; and how she had left 'em to play while she swam into the cave to sit for a while and comb out her pretty hair. But the tide had run back while she was busy, and she couldn't crawl back to the sea over the bar, because on dry sand all her strength left her. 'And if I wait for the flood,' she said, 'my husband'll half murder me; for he's jealous as fire.'

"My father listened, and, sure enough, he seemed to hear the children's voices callin' to her out beyond the water's edge. With that, bein' always a tender-hearted man, he knelt down and lifted her out o' the pool. Now, if he'd had more sense at the time he'd have struck a bargain with her; for the merrymaids, they say, can tell where gold is hidden, and charm a man against sickness, and make all his wishes come true. But in the tenderness of his heart he thought 'pon none o' these things. He just let her put her arms round his neck, and lifted her over the sands, and waded out with her, till he stood three feet deep in water in his sea-boots; and then she gave him a kiss and slid away with a flip of her tail. 'Twas only when he stood staring that it crossed his mind what a fool he had been and what a chance he had missed. Then he remembered that she had dropped her comb by the edge of the pool — he had heard it fall when he lifted her, and back he went to search for it: for the sayin' is that with a merrymaid's comb you can comb out your hair in handfuls of guineas. But all he found was a broken bit of shark's jaw, and though he combed for half-an-hour and wished for all kind o' good luck, not a farthin' could he fetch out."

"Is that all?" asked Matthew Henry, as Jan arose from the cart-shaft, dusting the crumbs of bread from his breeches.

"It's enough, I should think," said Linnet, the sceptical, "seeing that it's nothing but a story from beginning to end."

Vashti looked from one child to the other with a twinkle of fun. "We will pay Piper's Hole a visit one of these days," she promised, "and perhaps Linnet will see a real mermaid and be convinced."

"I don't care for mermaids," announced Matthew Henry. "It's the cave I want to explore, to see if it really does lead through to the mainland. And I won't be afraid, like Jan here, and run away from a little noise."

"You wait till you get there before you boast," advised Linnet.

But Vashti's eyes, resting on the boy, grew tender of a sudden. "The way through to the mainland?" she said, musingly. "Matthew Henry is right. It all depends on the heart that tries it; but there is nothing can do him harm if he keeps up his courage; and the end of the road is worth all the journey, for a man."

"Why, Aunt Vazzy, you talk as if you had been there!" cried Annet.

"And so I have, my dear; there and back again."

The three children stared at her. "Aunt Vazzy is joking," said Linnet, severely. Annet was not too sure, and her brow puckered with a frown as she searched for the meaning beneath her aunt's words. But Matthew Henry believed them literally.

"Then," he exclaimed joyfully, "it's all nonsense about Farmer Santo's uncle's sheep-dog. For Aunt Vazzy has beautiful hair!"

CHAPTER XXIII

THE LORD PROPRIETOR HEARS A SIREN SING

Sir, — In answer to your letter of the 19th ultimo, I am directed by the Secretary of State for War to say that a Commission, the composition of which is not finally determined, will shortly be visiting the Islands, with a view to reporting on the adaptability of their existing military works for Coast Defence. Notice of the probable date of this visit shall be sent to you, and the Commissioners will doubtless be glad to avail themselves of any information you may be good enough to put at their disposal. At the same time, there will be given an opportunity of inquiring into the allegations contained in your letter. The Commission will be presided over by Maj.-General Sir Ommaney Ward, K.C.B., R.E., H.M. Director of Fortifications. — I am, sir,

Your obedient servant,

J. Fleetwood Cunningham.

Thrice a week — on Tuesdays, Thursdays, and Saturdays — the steamer arrived at St. Lide's Quay, bringing the mainland mail, and the Lord Proprietor's post-bag usually reached him soon after luncheon. It carried, as a rule, a bulky correspondence, and since the steamer weighed anchor early next morning, the Lord Proprietor set aside the early part of these three afternoons to letter-writing.

The passage had been smooth today, and the bag had been delivered to him and opened as he took his solitary meal. Also the mail for the great house was a light one, and out of it the Lord Proprietor, catching sight of the official stamp on the envelope, had at once selected the letter quoted above. He perused it, and re-perused it, to the neglect of the rest of his correspondence, tilting it against a bowl of Michaelmas daisies in front of his plate.

It was satisfactory, he decided — that is to say, on the whole, and so far as it went. He foresaw that short shrift would be given to those idlers on Garrison Hill. On the other hand, he frowned at the prospect — call it the chance, rather — of seeing that establishment replaced by one more efficient. To be sure, if the necessities of Coast Defence demanded it. . . . Still, for his part, he would have preferred to be let alone. The Islands, with their many outlying reefs and poor anchorage could never afford room to such battleships as were built in these days; and to erect new fortifications to cover a roadstead that would seldom if ever be used appeared the plainest waste of public money. . . . He really thought that the War Office might have consulted him before coolly proposing to plant a new garrison above St. Lide's. He was not even sure they had a right, without his consent. . . . He would confer with Mr. Pope on this point. At the very least, it would have been courteous to start by asking his opinion; for, after all, he owned the Islands. He was responsible, too, for the general good conduct of the population; good conduct which the advent of a body of soldiery would certainly affect — nay, might entirely upset.

Nevertheless, he reflected that — however the Commissioners might decide (and he would take care to press his opinion energetically) — his letter to the Secretary of State for War had at least done no harm. The Commissioner's visit had obviously been projected before the receipt of it, and at the worst it would enable him to call quits with Vigoureux.

He reflected further that these roving Commissions to report were often no index of Government policy, but were simply appointed to shelve, while professing to consider a question which the Government found awkward.

So, luncheon over, he sat down and wrote a letter thanking the Secretary for his communication, and very politely offering to do all in his power to make the Commissioners' visit "to these out-of-the-world Islands" a pleasant one.

Having copied the letter and read it over with no little approval, the Lord Proprietor dealt briefly with the rest of his correspondence; consulted his pocket-diary, looked at his watch, and, finding that he had an hour to spare before granting an interview to Eli Tregarthen, stepped out upon the terrace, where Abe Jenkins was cutting back the geraniums that had well-nigh ceased to flower.

"But is it necessary?" asked the Lord Proprietor. "Here, in the very mouth of the Gulf Stream . . . and last winter we escaped with nothing worse than two degrees of frost."

"Last winter and this winter be two different things, sir," protested Abe, gently but firmly. "Last winter, sir — as you may have taken notice — we had next to no berries 'pon the holly; and no seals, nor yet no mermaids."

"Seals? Mermaids?" Sir Cæsar echoed.

"Which I've always heard it said, sir," Old Abe went on, with the air of one carefully, even elaborately, deferring to superior ignorance, "as how than seals you can have no surer sign of hard weather. Of mermaids I says nothing, except that with such-like creatures about you may count 'pon something out of the common."

"Since," said the Lord Proprietor, "there are no such things as mermaids, we will confine ourselves to seals. . . . I had no idea that seals — er — frequented our shores."

"No more they don't, unless summat extr'ord'ny has taken the weather. But I've heard tell of a season when, for weeks together, you could count up two or three score together baskin' on the beaches to the north of the Island here. Sam Leggo can tell you all about it" — Abe jerked a thumb in the direction of North Inniscaw Farm. "He and his father used to hunt them, one time, along with Phil Cara of St. Hugh's. You know where the old adit goes into the cliff under Carn Coppa? Well, they tell me that if you follow the adit for fifty yards you come to a kind of pit that breaks straight down and through the roof of a cave — Ogo Vean, they call it — to the west of Piper's Hole, and this cave fairly swarmed with seals. The three men would lower themselves by rope-ladders — I reckon old Leggo had learnt the trick of it in by-gone days when the Free-traders used the adit — and get down upon a strip of firm shingle at the inner end of the cave; and there Sam Leggo would hold the lantern while his father and Phil Cara blazed away. They never shot more than a brace at a time, because of the difficulty of getting the bodies up the ladder, for they had to be gone before high-water, and likewise there was always a danger that the seals might charge 'em in a herd, bein' angered by the loss of their mates. In this way they pretty well cleared out the cave — all but one great beauty that old Leggo had sworn to take alive. For, instead of bein' yellow or motley-brown like the rest, this fellow was white as milk all over, besides bein' powerful as any other two. He seemed to know from the first that the three men didn't mean to shoot him. The lanterns and the firing never hurried him a bit, and he never threw himself into a rage over the loss of his relations. He just kept out of reach, looking like as if he despised the whole business, and refused to quit. He was cautious, too; wouldn't trust the cave in weather when a boat could follow him and block up the entrance. On fine nights he had a favourite rock just outside Ogo Vean — you can see it from the top of the cliff — and there he'd lie asleep and dare 'em; out of reach, but plain enough to see, even in the dark, because of his white skin.

"Now, as you may have taken notice, sir, the tide runs out dry to this rock on the inshore side; but seaward it goes down, even at low springs, into more'n three fathoms of water, and my gentleman always took his forty winks on the seaward slope. Half-a-dozen times did Phil Cara, thinkin' to catch him—"

"I beg your pardon," interrupted Sir Cæsar, "'Cara,' did you say?"

"Yes, sir; Philip Cara, father to Eli Tregarthen's wife over to Saaron; and likewise, o' course, to Eli Tregarthen's wife's sister, that is lodging at Saaron Farm, having come home from service a while back."

"Eh? From service?" the Lord Proprietor echoed, with quick-ened interest. "What sort of service?"

"Why, as to that, sir, I can't say that I can tell you for certain; but it's somewheres on the mainland, and the young woman seems a very respectable young woman. But whether she means to bide wi' the family or has come to lodge while lookin' out for another place, I can't certainly say — the Tregarthens bein' a close-tongued lot, as you know."

"A lady's-maid?" hazarded the Lord Proprietor.

"May be. Well, as I was tellin' you, half-a-dozen times did Phil Cara, bidin' his time till the tide was low and the sand hard—"

"But it's impossible," said the Lord Proprietor, pursuing his own train of thought.

Abe regarded his master rather in sorrow than in anger. "To be sure, sir," said he, in a tone of delicate rebuke, "if you don't want to hear my story—"

"Eh? Yes, certainly, my wits were wool-gathering, Abe, and I beg your pardon. Let me see. . . . You were saying that Cara used to wait till the tide was low—"

"Yes, sir. He'd creep along the sand, he and the two Leggos, and th' old seal would lie there sleepin', innocent as a child, and let them come close under the rock, and even climb it. But soon as ever they made a pounce — c'lk! — he rolled off the slope and into deep water. Regular as clockwork it happened; quiet and easy as a door on a greased hinge; and every time it made the three look foolisher and foolisher.

"After half-a-dozen tries, Cara allowed that he couldn' go on bein' mocked by a dumb animal; so he set his brain to work, and thought out a new plan. The two Leggos were to take a boat and drop down wi' the tide close in the shadow of the rock 'pon the sea-ward side, while Cara himself crept, as usual, hands-an'-knees, across the beach. So they planned, an' so they did; and sure enough when Cara made a pounce for the seal, my gentleman rolled down the ledge and slap into the boat! 'Now you've got 'en!' yells Cara. 'Darn it all!' yells back old Leggo from the scuffle, 'Seems more like he's got WE!' For that seal, sir, fought like ten tom-cats; and before the Leggos got in a lucky stroke and knocked him silly with a stretcher he'd ripped one leg off th' old man's trousers and bitten the heel clean off Sam's right boot. They took him home and skinned him, and sold the skin that same year to a Dutch skipper for thirty shillin'. But Sam has told me more than twice that he don't mean to tempt Providence again by catchin' any more seals."

The Lord Proprietor looked at his watch. "I must get Leggo to show me that adit this very afternoon. I've an appointment at three-thirty to meet him and Tregarthen at the farm."

"Indeed, sir? Then you've brought Eli Tregarthen to his senses? — if I may make so bold."

The Lord Proprietor flushed, remembering that Abe had witnessed the interview in the walled garden. "I fancy the man has begun to see the red light," he answered, carelessly. "At any rate, he has consented to meet me and take a look over North Inniscaw."

"Well," said Abe, "you'll find him a good farmer; none better."

"And he'll find me a landlord, willing to let bygones be bygones. By the way," added Sir Cæsar, yet more carelessly, "I am curious to know if I met that sister-in-law of his the other day? — a decidedly handsome woman, and strikingly well dressed. In fact, I should say she bought her clothes in Paris."

Abe stared, as though his master had suddenly taken leave of his senses.

"I never been to Paris," he said, slowly. "When I seen her last she was nettin' sand-eels, with her legs bare to the knee."

*****

Sir Cæsar walked indoors to fetch his hat and his gun. Though he rarely used it, he invariably carried a gun under his arm in his walks about the Islands. It helped his sense of being monarch of all he surveyed.

That sense was strong in him as he took the path which led across the middle of the Island to North Inniscaw Farm. St. Lide's lay directly behind him, to the south, and thus no Garrison Hill obtruded upon his view to remind him of annoyances. The sea shone, the air was pure, the whole seascape flashed white upon blue — white gulls wheeling aloft, white breasts of puffins congregated on the smaller islets, white caps of tiny waves where the breeze met the tide-race, on North Island the white shaft of a lighthouse fronting the almost level sun. With a touch of imagination the scene had become a prospect of the Cyclades, the lighthouse a column to Aphrodite or the twin brothers of Helen. But the Lord Proprietor was a Briton. He halted on the hill-side to inhale the vigorous breeze, and his heart rejoiced that all he saw belonged to him.

The path descended a stony hillside, crossed a marshy green hollow, and mounted a second stony hill. Over the summit of it the low roofs of a line of farm-buildings hove into sight. This was North Inniscaw; and the Lord Proprietor, arriving punctually at three-thirty, found Eli Tregarthen at the gate in converse with Sam Leggo, the hind in temporary charge of the farm.

If Eli had begun to see reason, his face held out no promise of it. It was dark and gloomy; a trifle weary, too, as though he kept this appointment rather through politeness than with any care for its outcome. He saluted the Lord Proprietor respectfully, but at once bent his eyes to the ground.

"Good afternoon! Good afternoon, Tregarthen!" Sir Cæsar began, in his heartiest voice, to show that he bore no malice. "I like punctuality, and those who practise it. Punctuality, if I may say so, is not a wide-spread virtue in these Islands. Shall we go round and take stock?"

"If it will give you satisfaction, sir," assented Eli.

Sir Cæsar led the way, pausing at every gate to discuss the soil, the crop, the present price of oats, barley, roots of beef and mutton; drainage and top-dressing; aspect and shelter; a hundred odds and ends. He talked uncommonly good sense, too, as Eli confessed to himself. The Lord Proprietor had taken up with agriculture late in life, but he brought to it a trained and thoroughly practical mind. Once or twice he submitted a point to Sam Leggo, who had worked all his life on this very farm, and Eli was forced to admire the pertinence of his questions and cross-questions.

He talked with great good humour, too, although Eli gave it small encouragement. The shadow of leaving Saaron had hung over Eli's mind for more than two months; heavy, oppressive, but until this morning intangible as a cloud. Vashti had remarked that the days deadened him while they should have been nerving him to action; and Vashti, this very morning, had forced his eyes open by asking, in a business-like way, if he had ever thought of emigrating to the mainland. Were it not wiser, since the wrench must come, to make it complete? — to go where regret would not be kept aching by the daily sight of Saaron? The children would find better schools on the mainland, and it was high time to be thinking of Matthew Henry, who deserved a better education than the Islands could afford.

In arguing thus, Vashti was not entirely serious. She knew that Eli would never cut himself loose from the Islands; but she hoped, by forcing him to face the alternative, to shake him out of his torpor. In this she had partly succeeded. For the first time the man opened his eyes and saw hard facts — facts that in a few weeks' time he must grapple with, since neither grieving nor grumbling would remove them. But for the moment the discovery, instead of nerving him, inflamed his wrath.

A strong man, finding himself helpless, suffers horribly. Especially he suffers when, with a dim sense that in the last resort all power depends on strength, he finds himself tripped up and laid on his back by a man physically his inferior. Had the Lord Proprietor inherited the Islands from a line of ancestors — had his tyranny rested on any feudal tradition — Eli was Briton enough to have acquiesced or submitted. But this whipper-snapper had bought the Islands: money — dirty money alone — gave him power over men who were Islanders by birth and by long generations of breeding. While the Lord Proprietor talked, Eli felt an impulse almost uncontrollable to lay hands on him and wring his neck.

The three men had reached Coppa Parc, an enclosure of twelve acres bounded along the north by the cliffs' edge, and deriving its name from a mass of granite rock — Carn Coppa — that, rising in ledges from near the middle of the field, ran northward until it broke away precipitously, overhanging the sea. The slopes around the base of the Carn showed here and there an outcrop of granite, but with pockets of deep soil in which (or so the Lord Proprietor maintained) barley could be grown at a profit. He appealed to Eli.

"Come, what does Mr. Tregarthen say to it? A piece of ground like this — hey? — oughtn't to beat a man that has grown barley on Saaron?"

He said it intending no offence, but in a bluff, hearty way, which he meant to be genial. After a second or two, Eli not answering, he turned and saw to his amazement that the man was trembling from head to foot with wrath.

"What right have you? What right— " Eli stammered fiercely, and came to a full stop, clenching his fists.

The Lord Proprietor stared at him. "My good fellow, I hadn't the smallest wish to hurt your feelings. What ails you? An innocent remark, surely!"

"What ails me?" echoed Eli, and stopped again, panting. "Man, have done with this, and let me go — else I'll not promise to keep my hands off you!"

For a moment he stood threatening, his eyes — like the eyes of a dumb animal at bay — travelling from the Lord Proprietor to Sam Leggo. The blood ebbed from his face, and left it unnaturally white. But of a sudden he appeared to collect himself; thrust both hands in his pockets, and, turning his back, walked away resolutely down the slope.

"Well!" said Sam Leggo, after a pause. "Well!"

"The man has never been thwarted before," said the Lord Proprietor, as they gazed after him together. "That's what comes of living alone in a place like Saaron; and I'll take care his children don't learn the same folly. Feels the curb, as you might say. Have you ever seen a horse broken late in life?"

"You take it very quiet, sir, I must say," protested Sam, admiringly. "So disrespectful as he was, too — and to the likes of you! Well! I've known Eli Tregarthen forty year, and if any man had come and told me—"

"The worst is, we have wasted an afternoon," said Sir Cæsar, easily. "But since we are here, with half-an-hour to spare before sunset, what do you say to showing me the adit?"

"The adit, sir?"

"There's an old adit hereabouts — eh? — that leads down to a cave. . . . Come, come, my good man, you don't deceive me by putting on that stupid face! We don't allow smuggling on the Islands in these days, and I like to know the secrets of my own property. The cave is called Ogo Vean, or something like it; and if I must explain more precisely, it is where you and your father used to go hunting seals."

"Yes, yes, to be sure," Sam admitted; "an adit there is, or used to be. But," he went on more cheerfully, "you'll find it nothing to look at. I han't set foot inside it for years, and I doubt but the entrance is choked."

"Take me to it," said Sir Cæsar.

Sam, without further remonstrance, led the way. They scrambled out to the edge of the Carn, and there, where the last great boulder thrust itself forward over the sea, Sam scrambled off to the left, and lowered himself down upon a turfy ledge. Warning his master to leave his gun behind and beware of the slippery grass, he sidled out alongside the jutting slab, and suddenly ducked under it. The Lord Proprietor, following, crawled under the stone, and found himself staring into the mouth of the adit — a dark hole less than four feet in height, and overgrown with ivy. Sam had spoken the truth. The passage, whithersoever it led, had been disused for years.

"Cur'ous old place!" said Sam, reflectively, plucking at the ivy. "I've a mind to try the inside of it again, one of these days."

"I've a mind to explore it now," said the Lord Proprietor.

Sam stared at him. "You couldn't, sir; not without a lantern. You'd be breakin' your neck, to a certainty."

"Then fetch a lantern. Look sharp, man! Run back to the farm and fetch a lantern. I'll wait for you — no, not here: a few minutes on this ledge would turn my head giddy — but on the Carn above."

Without further words, he worked his body around carefully, and led the way back to the summit.

"You'd best hurry," he advised Sam, who showed no eagerness for the job. "In another twenty minutes the dusk will be closing down fast."

Sam slouched off at a fair pace across the field. Sir Cæsar watched his retreating figure until it reached the gate, and then, picking up his gun, disposed himself to wait.

Seals? They ought to give good sport — better sport, he should imagine, than deerstalking. A pity, too, to let it die out . . . if seals still frequented the Islands. . . . He must consult Sam about it, and pick up a few wrinkles. He peered over the edge of the Carn, scanning the water, a hundred feet below him, for the rock which Abe had described. He could see no such rock. Maybe, though, it would be covered by the tide, now close upon high-water.

Then he bethought him that the rock must lie a little to the west, towards Piper's Hole — that is to say, in the next small indentation of the shore. He strolled in that direction, following the cliff's edge, still with eyes upon the sea.

Of a sudden he stopped and straightened himself up with a gasp.

What sound was that? . . . Surely a voice — a woman's voice — singing up to him from the depth!

Was he awake or dreaming? . . . Beyond all doubt someone was singing, down there: a mournful, wordless song. He was no judge of music, but it seemed to him that, let alone the mystery of the singer, he had never heard a voice so wonderful. It rose and fell with the surge of the tide.

The Lord Proprietor laid down his gun. He had come to a shelving slope that descended like a funnel or the half of a broken crater, narrowing to a dark pit, in which the sea heaved gently, but with a sound as of a monster sobbing; but still above this sound rose the voice of the singer.

He flung himself on the verge beside his gun and craned forward. . . . Yes, there was the rock; yes, and there on the rock sat a figure — a woman — and combed her long hair while she sang.

CHAPTER XXIV

LINNET SEES A MERMAID

Annet, Linnet, and Matthew Henry sat together in a niche of the cliff to the west of Piper's Hole, and panted after their climb.

They had raced up the hill in the gathering twilight for this (their Aunt Vazzy had assured them) was the time, if ever, to hear the mermaids singing in Piper's Hole, and perhaps to catch a glimpse of them; this, and the hour of moonrise — which for them would be out of the question.

For some days they had been discussing the adventure — not, it scarcely needs to be said, in their parents' hearing. But they had once or twice consulted with Aunt Vazzy, who understood children, and had a sense (denied to most grown-ups) of what was really interesting; and today, at dinner-time, Aunt Vazzy had allowed that no time could well be more propitious than this evening, when the hours of twilight and of low water almost exactly coincided. But in private she warned Annet very earnestly to look well after the two younger ones, and see to it that they did not risk their necks — a caution seldom given to Island children, who grow up sure-footed as young goats.

Annet had promised. The main difficulty would be to give the slip to Jan, who usually pulled across from Saaron in good time to fetch them home, and smoked a pipe by the shore while waiting for school to be dismissed. It would take them a good forty minutes to reach Piper's Hole and return. If they gave Jan the slip and delayed him so long, he would undoubtedly lose his temper, and probably report them. After discussing this, they decided to take Jan into the plot. "Maybe," said Annet, "he'll come along, too. I almost think he will if we put it to him all of a sudden, for he's mighty curious about mermaids; but if we give him time to think it over he'll feel ashamed, and say it's all children's whiddles, and back out — I know Jan. So we must wait till school is over and then coax him to come."

Annet did not know that her father, having an appointment with the Lord Proprietor at North Inniscaw Farm, designed himself to call at the school on his way back, and row the children home. Had she guessed this it would have prevented the adventure, which, in fact, it furthered; for, coming out of school and hurrying down to the shore to catch Jan and wheedle him, she found the boat moored there empty. Jan, no doubt, had taken a stroll up to the Lord Proprietor's garden, to have a chat with Old Abe. They had caught him napping; and now, if they kept him waiting, he could not grumble.

So off the three children set for Piper's Hole; Annet and Linnet with long strides, Matthew Henry trotting to keep up with them. Arrived at the cliff's edge, they deployed with great caution — that no noise might scare the mermaids from coming forth — and searched for a nook where, themselves hidden, they could command a view of the cove at their feet.

Linnet, searching to the westward, found just such a spot; a rocky ledge, well grassed, close under the topmost cornice of the cliff, and quite easy of access. To be sure, a rock on their right cut off their view of the cove's inmost recess, where the funnel-shaped slope broke sheer over the mouth of the Hole. But the ledge looked full upon the Mermaid's Rock and the heave of black water surging past it to gurgitate between the narrowing walls of rock.

Even the matter-of-fact Linnet could not repress a shiver as, after panting a while, she raised herself on one elbow and looked down into the awesome pit. For not only was the water black, but the whole shadowed base of the cliff wall; black as though stained by the inky wave. Black, too, showed the hither side of the Mermaid's Rock against a gray sea, from which the last tint of sunset had faded. Now and then, between the sobbing of Piper's Hole, the children caught the murmur of the tide race, half-a-mile off shore, slackening its note as it neared the time of high-water and its turning point. Out there the sea was agitated; within the line of the race, sharply defined on the gray, it heaved and sank on an oily swell.

"My!" said Matthew Henry, gazing; and Annet turned on her sister and said, "There, now!" The words may seem inadequate, but Linnet understood them, and that they conveyed a question which she felt to be a poser. How could she doubt the existence of mermaids in such a spot as this? If a mermaid were to swim up to the surface under their very eyes, would she be more wonderful than the actual scene — the black rocks, the sobbing water?

"Folks," said Annet, incisively, "that laugh at stories about Piper's Hole, ought to come and see the place for themselves."

"Yes," Matthew Henry agreed; "and after that they can begin to talk."

"I didn't laugh," protested Linnet, flung upon her defence. "Besides," she went on weakly, "I don't see why it must be mermaids. If anything lives down there, why shouldn't it be a dragon —or a giant, perhaps—"

"Linnet's improving," put in Matthew Henry, with fine sarcasm.

"Well, it sounds to me more like the noise a dragon would make," Linnet persisted, finding as she went on that her argument was carrying her through very creditably; "or a giant snoring, as they always do after meals."

Annet scanned the black water pensively. "I've heard tell," she said, "of great cuttles that sit and squat under the water; and sometimes, when they are hungry, they fling up their suckers and pull you down off the rocks and eat you."

Matthew Henry drew back from the brink, visibly daunted.

"Look here," he began, "I don't mind mermaids. Mermaids, so far as they go—"

But here he came to a halt as a tinkling sound — the sound of a stringed instrument, gently thrummed, rose from out of the abyss.

It fell on their ears in a pause of the surging water. It came from the Mermaid's Rock, and thither all three children turned their eyes, to see, over the crest of it, from its hidden seaward side, a woman's head and shoulders emerge into view!

In the gathering dusk, even had she lifted her face to them, they could not have discerned her features. But as she climbed into view her loosened hair fell all about her; on the summit of the rock she turned and seated herself fronting the sea; and while the three children drew together, cowering, at her gaze, she began to sing.

And she sang marvellously. If her song had words, they were foreign words; but whether articulate or not it was beautiful beyond all human compass — or so at least it seemed to the children, whose experience rested, to be sure, on the congregational efforts of Brefar Church.

It rose and sank upon the swell of the tide. It held such sweetness in its mystery that, frightened though they were, the wonder of it drew tears to their eyes. It seemed to open pathways into that world of their desire, on the boundaries of which they were forever treading; yet forever vainly, because they had not the passwords, and in their ignorance could only guess that miracles lay beyond, sealed, unimaginable.

The children huddled together, lost their fear in wonder, as the voice of the mermaid, growing more and more confident, pierced new roads for them — roads upon which the twilight closed at once; rays into a glory they felt, and trembled to feel, but could not apprehend, because the vision was of mere beauty, and music divorced from words is the last of arts to convey form and meaning.

Yet though wholly indefinite, almost wholly meaningless, it spoke to something to which the children felt all their blood thrilling, responding. Listening, they forgot their fear altogether....

The singer laid down her instrument. The grey of the twilight ran over her bare shoulders as, with a turn of the arm, she swept her tresses back, and — still singing — drew out mirror and comb....

They craned to watch.

Suddenly from the height of the cliff, close on their right, rang out the report of a gun. The song ceased abruptly, lost in the echoes that beat from cliff to cliff, and amid these echoes the children heard a noise of falling stones, followed by a heavy splash.

Annet had sprung to her feet. Linnet and Matthew Henry, too, had picked themselves up, though more slowly. . . . A wisp of smoke drifted by the rock to their right. When they turned their eyes upon the Mermaid's Rock the singer had vanished.

Annet caught Matthew Henry by one hand; Matthew Henry stretched out another to Linnet. The three scrambled up to the cliff-top, and thence raced homeward, panic-stricken, across the darkening fields.

CHAPTER XXV

MISSING!

"Sir, — I am directed by the Secretary of State for War to acknowledge receipt of your letter of the 19th ultimo, the contents of which shall receive his attention.

"I am, sir,

"Your obedient servant,

"J. Fleetwood Cunningham."

The Commandant, from long disuse, had forgotten the formalities of official correspondence. His hand shook as he tore open the long envelope, expecting to read his fate, and in the revulsion, as his eyes fell on the few lines of acknowledgment, he caught at the table's edge and sank into his chair with a sudden feeling of faintness.

For a few hours, then — possibly for a few days — he was respited. He put the letter aside and walked out, to take his afternoon stroll around the fortifications and steady his nerves.

By the Keg of Butter Battery he halted for a long look across the Sound and towards Saaron. Unconsciously for a week past, he had fallen into a habit of halting just here and letting his eyes travel towards Saaron. It was just here that Vashti had seated herself the first morning, and had asked him the fatal question, "For what, then, do they pay you?" He remembered the words, the inflection of scorn in her tone. Here at his feet on a cushion of wild thyme lay the stone she had prised out absently, while she spoke, with the point of her sunshade. Just here, too, she had taken leave of him on the night of her escapade, the night when (it was bliss to remember) she had recanted her scorn, had asked his forgiveness.

For a whole week he had not seen her. Was she careless, then, of the answer? — of what resulted from the train she had fired? . . . But, after all (the Commandant told himself), she had no need to concern herself about it. She had but set him in the way of doing his duty; for the rest, a man must accept his own responsibility, stand by his own actions, abide his own fate.

Yet he would have given a great deal, just now, for speech with her, to tell her that, unimportant though it was, some word from the War Office had reached him.

Throughout his stroll his mind kept harking back to this letter, seeking behind the few and formal words for meanings they did not cover; and again that evening, after his frugal supper, he drew the envelope from its pigeon-hole, spread the paper on the table before him, and sat studying it.

He lifted his head, at a sound in the passage. The outer door had been burst open violently, as though by a gust of wind, and a moment later Archelaus came running in with a face of panic.

"The Lord behear us!" gasped Archelaus. "Oh, sir, here's awful, awful news! The Lord Proprietor's been murdered, and his body flung over the cliff, and Sam Leggo and Abe the gardener be running through the streets wi' the news of it!"

"Murdered! The Lord Proprietor!" echoed the Commandant, laying down his glasses and rising to his feet in blankest amaze.

"Yes, sir; shot with his own gun, and, they say, by Eli Tregarthen! The two men have pulled across from Inniscaw for help, and to fetch the constable. . . . I had the news from Sam Leggo hisself, as he raced off to knock up Mr. Pope."

The Commandant sank back in his chair. Dreadful though the news was, he saw in a flash that it was not incredible. Eli Tregarthen owed the Lord Proprietor a grudge, and a bitter one. Eli Tregarthen was a man capable of brooding over his wrongs and exacting wild justice for them. The Commandant's thoughts flew to Vashti.

But even as he passed a hand over his eyes, another footstep invaded the outer passage, and Mr. Pope himself rushed in, mopping his brow.

"My dear friend — " Not in his life before had Mr. Pope addressed the Commandant as "my dear friend." He glanced from one scared face to the other. "You have heard? Oh, but it is terrible! . . . And what on earth are we to do?"

"I beg your pardon," answered the Commandant, recovering his presence of mind. " 'We,' did you say?"

"Naturally I came first to you. . . . You being a magistrate, and — if this dreadful news be true — the chief magistrate left on the Islands."

"True," said the Commandant, yet more quietly. He had regained his self-possession. "I had forgotten. To be sure, I had renounced the office — as I supposed — at the Lord Proprietor's own wish; but doubtless it reverts to me, and, in any case, this is no time to discuss proprieties. Will you tell me what has happened and what has already been done?"

"Done? I have done nothing except send for the constable, with word that he was to follow me here to the Barracks and take your orders."

"But where is the body?"

"The body?" Mr. Pope shivered. "God knows. That, my dear Commandant, is the cruellest part of the mystery — at least, according to Sam Leggo. It appears that Sir Cæsar, Leggo and Eli

Tregarthen were at North Inniscaw this afternoon, taking stock of the farm, which Sir Cæsar was persuading Tregarthen to rent. Tregarthen was sullen — you may have heard that he resents being given notice to quit his holding on Saaron. In the end, on some chance word of Sir Cæsar's he blazed up, completely lost control of himself, and used threats of personal violence. Leggo will swear to this; but it is immaterial, for I myself have heard him indulge in similar threats, and so has Abe, the gardener. Well, Tregarthen swung off in a huff, took his way down across Pare Coppa — it was there, just under the Cam, that the outbreak occurred — apparently for the landing-quay by the school, where his boat lay. He left Sir Cæsar and Sam Leggo standing there."

"At what time?"

"The time, according to Leggo, was close upon sunset. Sir Cæsar — as his habit is — carried a gun under his arm; but whether or not the gun was loaded Leggo is unable to say. After expressing surprise at Tregarthen's display of temper, Sir Cæsar turned the conversation upon an old adit which lies under the seaward face of the Cam, and leads (I am assured) down to Ogo Vean. Its existence is known to very few — and Leggo was surprised to hear him mention it; but it now appears that he had learnt of it this very afternoon, in casual talk with old Abe. He desired then and there to explore it, and — having examined the entrance — either because the adit itself is dark, or as a precaution in the gathering dusk, he sent Leggo back to the farmhouse to fetch a lantern. Leggo declares that it took him less than fifteen minutes to reach the farm, find the lantern, and return with it to the lower gate of Parc Coppa; also that he used his best speed because the dusk was gathering. As he reached the gate he heard a shot from somewhere on the edge of the cliffs. This did not perturb him, for he supposed that the Lord Proprietor was potting at a stray rabbit. As he climbed the field, however, towards the Carn, on the summit of which he had left Sir Cæsar seated, he saw three small children running along the cliffs to his left, making for the slope towards the landing-quay, and recognised them for Tregarthen's three children. He called to them to stop, for they seemed to be running in a panic. If they heard, they did not obey, but ran down the hill out of sight. By this — and because he could not see Sir Cæsar on the summit of the Carn — he began to grow alarmed, lit the candle within his lantern (for it was now nearly dark), and shouted. He received no answer. He ran to the edge of the Carn, climbed down thence to the mouth of the adit, and — finding no trace of his master — began to hunt, still shouting, along the cliffs to the left, in the direction where he had first spied the children. To cut his story short," resumed Mr. Pope, after taking breath, "his search led him to the edge of the cliffs over Piper's Hole, and there, in a tangle of brambles, his lantern shone on something bright, which proved, when at no small risk he climbed down to it, to be the barrel of Sir Cæsar's gun. Below the brambles (he says) the ground breaks away very precipitately to a sheer fall of rock over the entrance of Piper's Hole. He could not trust himself here, but declares that the earth below the brambles — so much his lantern showed him — had evidently been disturbed, and quite recently; as also that the slide was bare and smooth, with no trace of a body between it and the last ledge over which a falling body would plunge into the water; and the tide, as he says — and as, indeed, we know — was almost at full flood. Having satisfied himself of this, he ran back, down the hill and past the school to carry the alarm to the house; and from the quay beside the school he saw Tregarthen's boat crossing to Saaron, and Tregarthen in it with his three children. Sam called to him, and his call brought out the schoolmistress, who no sooner heard the story than she fell to screaming. Tregarthen, though he must have heard the noise they made, did not respond, but continued pulling calmly towards Saaron.

"Leggo could not say precisely, but admits that the boat was already nearing Saaron, and that the man, if he heard, possibly did not understand — that is, if one can suppose him innocent."

"We will suppose him innocent," said the Commandant, "until we have better evidence that he is guilty. What was Leggo's next step?"

"He ran on smoking-hot to the house, the schoolmistress after him; up through the gardens to the terrace, where they met old Abe returning home from work. The schoolmistress went on to alarm the servants, while the two men made for the private landing, unmoored the Lord Proprietor's boat, and pulled across for Garland Town to break the news to me. But on the quay and along the streets they told it to a score of people, and it is spreading through the town like wildfire."

"Naturally." The Commandant had fetched and slipped on his great-coat, and stood buttoning it. He glanced at his watch. "If the constable does not turn up in a minute or so, we must start without him. Archelaus, run you down and call up Mr. Rogers. Ask him, with my compliments, to call out the coastguard—"

"Pardon me," Mr. Pope interrupted, "but that is unnecessary. Mr. Rogers has already started for Inniscaw in the jolly-boat, taking Leggo with him. They are to search the shore around Piper's Hole."

"Thank you," said the Commandant. "That was obviously the first step to take, and I am obliged to you for having thought of it so promptly."

Mr. Pope coughed apologetically. He had grown of a sudden very red in the face. "In point of fact," he confessed, "Mr. Rogers was at my house when the news came. We were — er — indulging in a quiet rubber."

The Commandant understood. Had the occasion been less serious, he might have smiled. Not since the night which brought Vashti to the Islands had he received an invitation to Mrs. Pope's parties.

"Ah, to be sure!" said he, quietly, reaching for his forage-cap; "I had forgotten that this was your whist-evening."

Mr. Pope coughed again awkwardly, and was about to make matters worse by further apology, but a rat-tat on the door prevented this, and Archelaus, hurrying out, admitted Dr. Bonaday, the physician of Garland Town, followed by John Ward, the constable, and old Abe.

Of these three old men you would have found it difficult at first sight to decide which was the eldest: and you have not made Dr. Bonaday's acquaintance until now; because it was unnecessary. As the saying went in the Islands, "the old doctor troubled about nobody, and nobody troubled about he" — that is, unless an Islander needed to be helped into the world or out of it. He was a bachelor, a recluse, and (albeit his neighbours were ignorant of this) a European authority on lichens and mosses. A small private income allowed him to indulge a habit of forgetting to charge for his professional services; and, on the strength of it, the Islanders forgave one who never remembered a face, and who, when summoned to a sick-bed, had to be guided thither by a messenger, lest he should knock at half a dozen doors in error by the way. There was a tradition in St. Hugh's that once, running from his surgery with a hot poultice, he had clapped it on the harbour-master, who was politely intercepting him to point out that another two strides would take him over the quay's edge into deep water. In person, Dr. Bonaday was remarkable for a completely bald head, a hooked nose, and a pair of vague, impercipient eyes, as of an owl astray and blinking in the sunlight.

If Dr. Bonaday was an authority on lichens and mosses, Constable Ward was an authority on nothing at all, even in his own house, where his youngest grand-daughter attended to his wants. Amid a population which seldom broke the law and never resisted it, he had sunk of late years into a peaceful decay of all his faculties. He carried his emblem of office, a small mace, attached to his wrist by a string, and his hand shook pitiably as he fumbled for it, but less with excitement than from shock at having been aroused and dragged from his bed into the night air.

"I see no reason for taking the constable with us," the Commandant decided, after a compassionate glance at the old man.

"In case of an arrest — " began Mr. Pope.

"First let us be certain that a crime has been committed."

"To my thinking, all the circumstances point to murder, and to nothing else."

"And, if they do, we can accuse no one until we have found the body. . . . Constable, you can go back to bed."

"I thank you, sir." Constable Ward, for the instant plainly relieved, checked himself, and stood trembling, irresolute. "You mustn't think, gentlemen, that I'd shirk doing my duty."

"No, no, Ward: I quite understand," the Commandant assured him.

"The Governor," said Mr. Pope, slipping back to the old form of address, disused for years — "The Governor rather doubts that you are equal to it."

"For God's sake, gentlemen, don't put it in that way! This affair'll get into the newspapers, over on the main, and if 'tis said that Constable Ward was too old for his duty, whatever'll become of me?"

Mr. Pope turned away with a sniff of disgust. "People of a certain class," said he half-audibly, "can see nothing but as it affects themselves. Of his duty this old dotard thinks nothing at all, nor of the scandal of his continuing to draw public pay: yet, mark you, how keenly he scents a danger of losing it!"

The Commandant winced, and shot a glance at the aged, unheroic figure. "And there," thought he, "but for God's grace and a woman's word, stands Narcisse Vigoureux! Even so, a few days since, did I consent to be incompetent and dread only to be detected."

Aloud he said: "Mr. Pope is too hasty, Ward, in suggesting that I don't mean to use you. Tomorrow, after a night's rest, there may be work enough for you. Come, we are to pass your door, and will see you home. You, Doctor, will accompany us, I hope? We may need you."

They set forth down the dark road towards the quay, Abe and Archelaus walking ahead with lanterns, and guiding. Having restored Constable Ward to his youngest grand-daughter, they pushed forward more briskly, hailing the boat which (according to Mr. Pope) would be standing by for them on Mr. Rogers' instructions. Sure enough, voices answered their hail, and under the shadow of the quay steps they found the six-oared Service gig, with her crew seated ready at their oars: also on the quay itself the whole town gathered, canvassing the dreadful news.

At their approach the confused voices dropped to silence. In silence the town watched its men of authority as they stepped down to the boat and took their seats. And, amid silence, the coxswain called his order, "Give way!"

CHAPTER XXVI

THE SEARCH

Ahead of them, across the Roads, and up the narrow length of Cromwell's Sound, many lights twinkled: for already two-score boats had put out from St. Lide's Quay and were hurrying to the search, with lanterns and hurricane lamps. The windows of the Great House on Inniscaw fairly blazed with light. The upland farm-steads, too, were awake, here and in Brefar, and the cottages around Inniscaw schoolhouse and Brefar Church. Only Saaron, as they passed it, showed no sign of life, no glimmering ray from the windows of Eli Tregarthen's house, dark upon the dark hillside. Mr. Pope called the Commandant's attention to this.

"Patience," said the Commandant. "We will land and question him on our way home."

"You will admit that it looks suspicious."

The Commandant did not answer.

"If Leggo's story be true," said Dr. Bonaday, addressing the cox-swain abruptly, as though awakened of a sudden from a brown study, "the accident must have happened just upon high-water; in which case Mr. Rogers will do best to start searching to westward along the north shore of Brefar, following the set of the ebb."

"I reckon he'll take that line, sir, if he finds nothing at Piper's Hole," the coxswain answered. "But his plan, as he told it to me, was to land Leggo, with two of our men, by the schoolhouse, and send them up the hill with ropes and lanterns, while he pulled round and searched Piper's Hole from seaward."

The Doctor appeared to digest this plan for a full minute. "Pope," he said, abruptly as before, "do you happen to know if the Lord Proprietor had made his will?"

"Good Lord!" answered Mr. Pope, testily, "I am not his lawyer."

"He has relatives?"

"Some distant cousins, I believe; none nearer. Why do you ask?"

"Because," answered the Doctor, imperturably, "it occurred to me as a natural question under the circumstances. Then it would appear, my friend, that Sir Cæsar's decease (if we suppose it) is a very serious affair indeed for you?"

"Man alive!" snapped Mr. Pope. "Of what else do you suppose I have been thinking, ever since I heard this news?"

Dr. Bonaday did not reply in words; but the Commandant — who happened to be gazing just then towards North Island, where the great sea-light seemed to search the outer tides with its monstrous eye — heard, or fancied that he heard, a sound as of a quiet chuckle. Suddenly he remembered Mr. Pope's scornful criticism of old Constable Ward: remembered it, and glanced at the Doctor. But the Doctor was an uncanny fellow, and inscrutable.

Though the coastguardsmen, pulling with a will, overtook and passed at least a dozen boats on their way, it cost them close upon an hour to reach the upper end of Cromwell's Sound and open the coast along the north side of Inniscaw. They had no need to search for Mr. Rogers and the jolly-boat. Flares were burning and torches waving in and around the entrance to Piper's Hole, and as the gig drew closer the Commandant discerned the figures of half-a-dozen searchers, roped and moving cautiously with lanterns from ledge to ledge of the dizzy cliff. The jolly-boat lay beached on a bank of fine shingle left by the receding tide at the entrance of the cave, and beside it stood Mr. Rogers shouting orders.

He hailed the newcomers as soon as he caught sight of them. Leggo and his two men had found Sir Cæsar's gun, and recovered it from the bushes overhanging the cave. But of Sir Cæsar himself no trace could be found. It was clear to his mind that the body had rolled down the cliff into deep water, and had been carried out to sea. His fellows up yonder had examined every foot of the descent, and were risking their necks to no purpose. He would give them another ten minutes to make a clean job of the search, and would then call them off and seek along shore to the westward.

Had the cave itself been searched? This was the Commandant's first question as he stepped out upon the shingle.

Yes; they had begun by searching the cave. They had followed it for fifty yards, and come to a ridge of rock, heaped with ore-weed, beyond which (it was certain) no ordinary tide ever penetrated. The floor of the cave shelved pretty steeply up to this ridge, and beyond it lay a pool of fresh water, about twenty yards long. It was impossible that a human body could have been swept over the ridge into this pool. Nevertheless they had explored it. But would the Commandant care to satisfy himself?

Mr. Rogers, without waiting for an answer, picked up a lantern and led the way under the great arch. The Commandant followed, his feet at every step sinking ankle-deep in the fine shingle. He found himself in a passage nine or ten feet wide, the walls of which rose about twenty feet above him, and vaulted themselves in darkness. At first this passage appeared to him to end, some fifteen paces from the entrance, in a barrier of solid rock, but Mr. Rogers, stepping forward with the lantern, revealed a low archway to the left and a second passage, partially choked with ore-weed. Through this they squeezed themselves, crouching and stooping their heads — for the roof in places was less than five feet high — and after a couple of zig-zags drew breath at the entrance of the second chamber, at least as lofty as the first and a full twenty feet wide. Across the entrance the floor sloped up to the rocky ridge, of which Mr. Rogers had spoken; and beyond the ridge lay the pool.

"Taste it," said Mr. Rogers, and the Commandant, kneeling by the edge of the pool, scooped up a palmful of water to his lips. It was fresh water, undoubtedly; very cold, and not in the least brackish.

"Look down," said Mr. Rogers, holding his lantern so that the Commandant could peer into the depths. "You can see every stone at the bottom, and my men have searched it all." He lifted the light above his head and gazed into the mysterious darkness beyond the pool. "I must explore this place to the end, one of these days. The chief boatman waded through, and reported yet another passage beyond; but of course I wouldn't let my men waste time in exploring it. What a place for seals, hey?"

"Seals?" queried the Commandant.

"Leggo gave me a sort of description of the place on our way here. He tells me that this cave and the next are a favourite haunt of the seals when they visit the Islands. In fact, he used to hunt them here with his father. But of late years, for some reason, they have given the Islands the go-by."

"You think it possible," suggested the Commandant, "Sir Cæsar may have seen one, and taken a shot at it?"

"That's not likely; and anyway it doesn't help us. It won't account for his gun being found in the bushes, halfway down the cliff, nor for his disappearing. Among a deal that's mysterious, this much is clear: Leggo left him on the cliff above us; within twenty minutes Sir Cæsar's gun went off, whether fired by himself or by someone else; and whether wounded or not, he slid down the cliff and over the ledge above the cave. His body is not in the cave; therefore, presumably, it was sucked out to sea by the tide, and presumably has been carried somewhere to the westward. Shall we turn back?"

The Commandant nodded. "You will have plenty of folk to help your search," said he, "to judge from the number of boats we passed on our way. By spreading your forces, in less than two hours you can have the whole shore examined, from here to the west of Brefar. By the way, who has possession of Sir Cæsar's gun?"

"It was passed up to Sam Leggo, on the cliff. But if you wish to take charge of it—"

"It will probably be wanted for evidence."

"Come, then." Mr. Rogers led the way back to the entrance, and called up an order to have the gun lowered by a shore-line; which was done, the coast guardsmen on the cliffs fending the line clear of the bushes, and so passing it from one to another until it dangled over the ledge within grasp. The Commandant, as the taller, reached up for the gun, took it, and examined it by the light of the lantern which Mr. Rogers held for him.

The gun was undoubtedly the Lord Proprietor's; a breechloader of curiously fine workmanship, bearing the name of a famous St. James' Street maker. Of the hammers, one was down, the other at half-cock; and, pulling open the breech, the Commandant drew forth two cartridges, the one empty, the other unused. He pocketed these and examined the barrels. Clearly, one shot — and one only — had been fired since the gun was last cleaned.

He invited Mr. Rogers to verify these simple observations; and then, turning the gun over, was aware of a trace of earth on the trigger-guard and another on the point of the butt. These were easily accounted for. The weapon, no doubt, had slid for some distance down the cliff — probably from the very top — before lodging in the bushes where Leggo had found it.

Half an hour's exploration of the cave, the cove, the cliff-face, had yielded no further clue. Mr. Rogers drew off his men, and, embarking them, started to search the shore to the westward.

By this time some thirty boats had gathered, and through the long night, in every creek and cranny of the shore, from the extreme east of Inniscaw to the extreme west of Brefar, the search went on. The wind, chopping to the north-west, rose to a stiff breeze, and not only blew bitterly cold, with squalls of rain and sleet, but raised a sea that made it dangerous to explore the rocks closely. Nevertheless, not a single boat put back, and not a few took incredible risks.

Day broke — a dull smurr of gray in an interval between two sleet-laden squalls. In the cheerless light of it the Commandant, who, albeit numb with cold, had had not yet found time to feel fatigue, caught sight of Dr. Bonaday's face, and was smitten with sudden compunction. The old Doctor had sat through six distressful hours like the stoic he was; but his face showed like that of a corpse, and the usually plump and florid cheeks of Mr. Pope hung flaccid, blue with the pinch of the cold and yellow for lack of sleep. The Commandant spoke to the coxswain, and, running up the gig alongside the jolly-boat, suggested to the indomitable Mr. Rogers that the men were almost dead-beat, to which, indeed, the faces of all bore witness in the broadening daylight.

"We must not exhaust ourselves utterly," suggested Mr. Pope. "It is already day, and the Council of Twelve ought to meet before noon."

"Indeed? Why?" asked the Commandant, absently.

"Why, to advertise the Lord Proprietor's disappearance, with a printed description of him!"

"Is that necessary? Surely by this time everyone in the Islands has heard the news; and, as for describing him—"

"It is the proper course to pursue," insisted Mr. Pope, who was something of a formalist; "in such — er — crises one should proceed regularly. Doubtless the Council, when called, will proclaim a reward."

"For what?" asked Doctor Bonaday.

Mr. Pope turned on him impatiently; but the Doctor's eyes, like the simpleton's in Scripture, were fixed on the ends of the earth. "Why, for the discovery of the body," said Mr. Pope.

"You might offer twenty rewards," said the Commandant. "You cannot make men work harder than they have worked tonight. Still, if you desire to summon the Council—"

"I am suggesting that you should do so."

"But I am no longer a member."

"On the contrary, as Governor, you are now its President."

The Commandant reflected for a moment. "True," he murmured, "I keep forgetting." Pulling himself together, with a shake of the shoulders, he turned again to Mr. Rogers.

"Mr. Rogers," said he, "you know better than I of how much fatigue your men are capable. For my part, I am returning to summon the Council of the Islands to meet me in the Court House at twelve o'clock noon, to summon volunteers and organize a general search. Your presence and advice will be of the greatest service to us; and as I see some fresh boats coming up the Sound, I submit that you leave them your instructions and draw off your tired crews to take what rest they need"

Mr. Rogers looked up sharply, surprised by the new ring of authority in the Commandant's voice. "Very well, sir," he answered, after a pause. "I shall be happy to attend the Council and concert measures with you. It occurs to me that the body may just possibly have been carried towards North Island on a back eddy, and with your leave I will tell the new-coming boats to seek in that direction."

"I thank you," said the Commandant, and at once gave the word to his own crew to pull for home. "And on our way," he added, "you shall land me for ten minutes at the East Porth, under Saaron Farm."

At the East Porth, where they found Eli Tregarthen's boat at her moorings off the grass-grown landing-quay, the Commandant stepped ashore. Mr. Pope offered to accompany him, but he declined, and went up the hill alone.

At the yard-gate he caught sight of Jan Nanjulian, faring forth with his pails to milk the cows; and, hailing him, demanded where he might find the farmer. Jan directed him to a line of furze-stacks at the back of the byres, and, turning the corner of these, he came face to face with Eli Tregarthen, who had loaded himself with a couple of faggots for the kitchen fire.

"Good morning!" said the Commandant.

"Ah? Good morning to you, sir," answered Tregarthen, clearly surprised, but showing no sign of guilt or confusion.

"You have heard the news?"

"No, sir."

"The Lord Proprietor is missing."

"Missing?" Tregarthen set down his faggots and stared at the Commandant.

"He has been missing since yesterday at dusk. I understand that you were in his company shortly before then, on Carn Coppa?"

"That is so, sir. I left him and Sam Leggo standing together there at the top of the field."

"A few minutes later he sent Leggo to the farmhouse to fetch a lantern. Leggo declares that on his way back he heard a gun fired."

Tregarthen nodded. "That's right. I heard the shot, too, and reckoned that the man had let fly at a rabbit. He carried a gun."

"You don't speak too respectfully of the Lord Proprietor, my friend."

"I speak as I think," answered Tregarthen, his brow darkening. "He was no friend to me or mine."

"I advise you very strongly to keep that sort of talk to yourself, at any rate for the present. To begin with, Sir Cæsar is missing, and we have grave fear he will not be found again alive: so that it is not seemly. But, further, I must caution you that you parted from him using threats, and your threats have been reported."

"Turn me out of Saaron, he would — " began Tregarthen, but checked himself at the moment when passion seemed on the point of over-mastering him. "Well, sir, I didn't shoot him, if that's what they are telling," he added, quietly.

"I should be sorry, indeed, to suspect any such thing. But let me tell you the rest. Hearing the shot, Leggo made good speed back to Carn Coppa. His master had disappeared; but away to the left, near the edge of the cliffs, he saw three children running down the hill, and he declares that those children were yours."

Tregarthen put up a hand and rubbed the side of his head.

"*My* children?" he repeated. "I can't make this out at all, sir. What could my children be doing anywhere near Carn Coppa?"

"You had best ask them."

"No," said Tregarthen, picking up his faggots, "I never brought them up to be afraid of the truth. Come with me to the house, sir, and they shall tell what they know."

He led the way, and the Commandant followed him indoors to the kitchen, where they found Ruth stooping over the great hearth, already busy with the morning fire. Across the planching overhead sounded the patter of the children's bare feet.

In a couple of minutes they came running down together, laughing on their way, and the Commandant had to wonder again — as he had wondered before, on the afternoon when he had sailed them home from Merryman's Head — at their beautiful manners. They were neither shy, nor embarrassed. Indeed, it was the Commandant who felt embarrassment (and showed it) as he asked them to tell what had taken them to Piper's Hole, and what they had seen there.

"We saw a mermaid," answered Annet. "She was sitting on the rock outside the cove; and first she was singing to a kind of harp, and afterwards she sang as she combed her hair. And then someone fired a gun at her from the cliffs, and she disappeared, and we were frightened and ran away. We did not see who fired the gun, nor if she was wounded. It was not brave of us to run away so quickly, and we have been sorry ever since."

"What nonsense is this?" growled their father. "Annet, my child, we tell the truth — all of us — here on Saaron."

"It may have been a seal," hazarded the Commandant. "I am told that Piper's Hole used to be a famous spot for seals."

But Annet lifted her chin and answered, her eyes steadily raised to her father's face. "No, it was not a seal; it was a mermaid. She sang and combed her hair just as I told you. It was beginning to grow dark, but we could see her quite plainly." She turned for confirmation to Linnet and Matthew Henry, and they both nodded.

Their father growled again that this was nonsense; but the Commandant, lifting a hand, asked what had taken them to the cliffs above Piper's Hole. It could not (he suggested) have been that they expected to catch sight of a mermaid.

"Yes," answered Annet again; "that was just the reason." She was speaking frankly, as a child can speak; but children have their own code of honour, and it forbids them to give away a friend. "Jan was telling us, only the other day," she explained with careful lucidity, "how his father had once caught a mermaid in a pool there. We wanted very much to see one, and so we planned to go. But afterwards, when father rowed us home, we did not like to tell him about it. We were afraid he would laugh at us; and we were frightened, too; afraid that the mermaid had been hurt; and — and we were upset because father had brought the boat for us instead of Jan Nanjulian—"

"But most of all," put in Linnet, "I was upset because I had been saying that there were no such things."

"You silly children, of course there are no such things," said their mother.

But Matthew Henry, ignoring her, and more in pity than in anger, turned on the Commandant. "Are you come," he asked, "because she is hurt?"

"She? Who?"

"The mermaid. We didn't mean to bring ill-luck to her. Jan said there was no good luck ever in spying on a mermaid, but Aunt Vazzy said that was nonsense, and of course we believed Aunt Vazzy—"

But here the child came to a full stop, startled by a swift change in the Commandant's look, and by a sudden sharp exclamation.

"Your Aunt Vazzy?" The Commandant's hand went up to his forehead. It seemed that, under the shadow of it his face grew pale and gray as he gazed from Matthew Henry to the two girls, and from them again to their mother.

"Ma'am," said he, in a shaking voice, "is your sister in the house?"

With his question, it seemed that in turn he had passed on his pallor to Ruth, who, however, drew herself up and answered him with spirit. "Sir," said Ruth Tregarthen, "you are asking too much. Must we be accountable to you for my sister's doings?"

"For God's sake," cried the Commandant, "let us waste no time in misunderstandings! Can you not see that your children are telling only the truth? — that she — your sister — was the mermaid? And if she did not venture home last night—"

"She took her own boat," quavered poor Ruth. "She started yesterday afternoon soon after the children had left for school — and she told me not to worry if she came home late. . . . My sister, sir, has queer ways of her own. . . . Maybe she heard the news on her way back, and has been searching all night with the others."

The Commandant had fallen to pacing the room. "She was not among the searchers," he said, impatiently. "And, moreover, she has not returned: her boat is not at the landing-quay."

"A moment, sir!" interposed Tregarthen. "I see what you fear, and it is terrible. But one thing is not plain to me at all. Vashti took her own boat, we hear. Now, suppose that the shot wounded her, or worse, still we have the boat to account for: and the boat, you say, is not to be found."

"Was ever a more hopeless mystery!" cried the Commandant, flinging out his hands.

But Eli Tregarthen turned to his wife, who had dropped into a chair by the fire and lay back, gripping the arms of it.

"Courage, wife!" said he, laying a strong palm over one of her trembling hands. "And you, sir, take my thanks; go you home, and leave the search to me."

CHAPTER XXVII

ENTER THE COMMISSIONER

It was noon, and in the Court House all the Councillors rose as the Commandant entered and took his seat.

In the fewest possible words he opened the business, and leaned back in his chair of state, waiting for the talk to begin. He scarcely knew what he had said, and yet he had spoken well. With his restored authority had come back the old easy habit of it.

At such a moment the Councillors would not have allowed, even to themselves, that they breathed more easily and fell to business almost with a sigh of relief, under the presidency of their old chairman. Yet so it was. The Lord Proprietor had been autocratic in council, impatient of opinions that crossed his own, apt to treat discussion as a tedious preliminary to enforcing his will.

After five years, then, the Councillors enjoyed, without confessing it, a sense of liberty regained; and it was the more to the Commandant's credit that in spite of it he kept a firm rein on the debate, cutting short all prolixities of speculation, and briefly ruling Mr. Pope's theory of foul play to be, for the present, out of order. They were met, he reminded them, for two practical purposes; in the first place, to organise a thorough search for the Lord Proprietor, and, secondly, to determine, as briefly as possible, how the government of the Islands should be continued and carried on during his absence. He would take these two questions only.

Mr. Rogers attended, and was cross-examined at length. With a chart before him, and with the help of Reuben Hicks, the St. Ann's pilot, he traced and described the currents to the northward of Inniscaw, the Chairman meanwhile, with pencil and paper, assigning the search-parties to the various rocks and groups of islets in or around which it was deemed possible for a floating body to be carried — so many boats to North Island, so many to seek along Brefar to W. and S. W. of Merryman's Head, so many to explore the difficult passage between the Outer Dogs. A sheet of foolscap had been pinned on the outside of the Court House door inviting volunteers; and while the Councillors deliberated they could hear the murmur of the crowd surrounding the notice and the scratching of pencils as one man after another painfully wrote his name. At intervals — time being precious — Constable Ward would step out, unpin the paper, replace it with a new one, and bring it indoors to the Commandant who was thus enabled to form his crews with despatch.

It was during one of these intervals (the Court House door being open for a moment) that Councillor Tregaskis, happening to glance out at the crowd from his raised chair, and over the heads of the crowd at the line of distant blue water sparkling in the afternoon sunshine, jumped up from his seat with an exclamation:

"A yacht, by Gorm!"

"Eh? What?" Fully half the Councillors turned towards him, and craned their necks for a view through the doorway. "A yacht?" The Commandant laid down his pen and stood up, raising himself a-tip-toe on his dais in the endeavour to gain a glimpse of the horizon from the window high on his right.

"A steam yacht!"

The Councillors stared one at another, wondering if this new arrival could have any possible connection with the Lord Proprietor's disappearance.

"What's her flag?" demanded Mr. Rogers.

"She carries no ensign," reported Mr. Tregaskis; "but a reddish-coloured square flag — a house-flag, belike. And yet, seemin' to me, she don't look like a private-owned craft."

"She's the Admiralty yacht from Plymouth," announced Mr. Rogers, confidently. He had set a chair close to the window and climbed upon it. "Yes, yes — the old *Circe*; I could tell her in a thousand. . . . She's slowing down to anchor; and see, there's the gold anchor on her flag! Listen, now . . . there goes! . . ." Through the open doorway, across the clear water, their ears caught the splash of a dropped anchor, and the music of its chain running through the hawse-pipe.

The Commandant rapped the table.

"Gentlemen," said he, "oblige me by returning to your places and resuming our business. We shall not advance it just now by catching at hopes which may be baseless, though I admit the temptation. That these visitors bring us any news of the Lord Proprietor or any that bears, even remotely, upon his disappearance is — to say the least of it — highly improbable. On the other hand, it is certain that by detaining Mr. Rogers here we hinder him in the discharge of those courtesies which, as Inspecting Commander, he will be eager to pay to the newcomers. I suggest, then, that we briefly conclude the inquiry, in which he has given us so much help, and allow him to put off to the yacht, while we, restraining our curiosity, take further counsel for the interim government of the Islands. If" — he turned to Mr. Rogers — "if, sir, our visitors can throw any light on the mystery, I may trust you to bring them to us with all despatch."

Accordingly Mr. Rogers, having briefly completed his evidence, was allowed to depart, and the councillors fell again to the business of distributing the crews of the searchboats.

Meanwhile, in the Court House, it was agreed that supreme control of the executive reverted naturally to the Commandant, subject only to such power of criticism or restraint as the Council claimed over the action of the Lord Proprietor himself. The twelve shouted "Aye" to this with one voice.

The Commandant, however, reminded them that he had not yet put the resolution, and that it was doubtful — he spoke as one who, some years ago, had made a study of these constitutional niceties — "if the Council of Twelve had really any say in the matter. They could, of course, elect their own President—"

But at this point a noise of women's voices on the quay, followed by a knocking on the door of the Council Chamber, put a period to the impatience of his auditors.

The door was opened, and Mr. Rogers appeared on the threshold with a tall officer, gaunt and white-haired, in military undress — at first glance indisputably a person of distinction — standing close behind his shoulder.

"I beg your pardon, Mr. President, if we interrupt the Council," began Mr. Rogers; "but I have brought a visitor here, Sir Ommaney Ward, who has business with you so soon as the sitting is over."

" — But who has no desire at all to interrupt it," added Sir Ommaney courteously, stepping forward and bowing to the Council. "Good afternoon, gentlemen! Good afternoon, sir!" He stepped forward to the dais holding out his hand. "Hey? my old friend Vigoureux, have you quite forgotten me, in all these years?"

"Ward!" exclaimed the Commandant, his face brightening with sudden recognition. A moment later, even more suddenly, it grew gray and haggard, almost (you might say) with terror. But the visitor did not perceive this.

"My dear fellow, why not give me the name as it rose to your lips? 'Tubby' Ward it used to be in the trenches, eh? Gentlemen" — Sir Ommaney turned to the Council — "your President and I have interrupted each other's work before now — as gunner and sapper — under Sebastopol. But I have no desire to interrupt yours, knowing how serious it is. Mr. Rogers brought off the news — this disquieting, not to say dumbfounding, news — to the yacht just now; and I hardly need to tell you that it puts my own errand into the background. Sir," — he turned to the Commandant again — "I allowed Mr. Rogers to bring me here only on his surmise that your business would be over. If you will give me, having announced myself, your leave to withdraw—"

"We shall have done in a very few minutes," answered the Commandant. His lips were dry, and he marvelled at the careless sound of his own voice. He had not a doubt of the true meaning of Sir Ommaney's visit. Nay, the very swiftness with which it followed upon his letter of confession proved how serious a view the War Office must take of his case. He pulled himself together desperately. "If you will take a chair, sir, here on my right, I promise that twenty minutes will see us at an end."

So the business of the Council was resumed, and the Commandant, still wondering at his own coolness, took up the thread of his discourse.

It was, on the whole, an admirable discourse. He had the constitutional system of the Islands at his fingers' ends, and today, with despair in his heart, but thinking nothing of them nor recking at all, he expounded them lucidly. His words, too, had a real effect upon his hearers; an emotional effect which Sir Ommaney, sitting and listening seriously, could not but note.

At the conclusion, Mr. Pope rose again, and proposed, and Mr. Fossell again seconded, that the supreme government of the islands reverted naturally, for the time being, to the Commandant: so that, for practical purposes, it may be contended he had spoken superfluously. But, to one who looked beneath the surface, this did not matter.

The Court rose, with its ancient formalities. "Reginæ et insulis ejus sit Deus propitius," said the President, closing the Bible, which at all meetings of the Council lay open on the table before him. "Ita et laboribus nostris, Amen," duly responded the twelve Councillors, standing in their places while he walked with his guest to the door. On the threshold he faced about, and made them a bow, which they as ceremoniously returned.

Out of doors the afternoon sun shone with a brightness almost dazzling after the shade of the Court House; but the tonic northwest wind, blowing across the Roads from Cromwell's Sound, held an autumnal chill, and the Commandant shivered as he halted a moment to con the *Circe* in the offing.

"I travel in state," said Sir Ommaney, with a laugh, as he followed this glance; "and with the cabins of half-a-dozen Sea Lords to choose between. In point of fact, our department has no boat at Plymouth capable of performing the passage comfortably: so, my business being partly theirs, I applied to the Admiralty, and the Admiralty placed their yacht at my disposal."

The Commandant did not understand; or perhaps he had not been listening intently. By tacit consent, the pair bent their steps towards the slope of Garrison Hill.

"Also," Sir Ommaney resumed, "the Admiral at Plymouth added a word of advice, to take advantage of this spell of weather and make the passage at once. No doubt he had a professional distrust of a soldier's stomach. Still, he meant it kindly. And that accounts for my arriving some days ahead of scheduled time, and dropping into the midst of this disquieting business. What's the meaning of it, think you?"

"The meaning of it?" echoed the Commandant.

"You don't doubt the man fell over the cliffs and killed himself?"

The Commandant shook his head. "I don't doubt his having met with an accident," he answered. "But I have some hope of finding him yet, and of finding him alive."

"To me, that doesn't seem likely. . . . But I want to tell you at once that my business can wait. I repeat, I am ahead of time. I can employ myself on board, or get out the steam-launch and explore the Islands; or again (if you will use me), I will gladly make one of a search party."

The Commandant thanked him. "But I have no particular business, at any rate for an hour or two. The boats have gone, and I leave it to Mr. Rogers to direct the search, now that we have laid down the plan of it. On these occasions, one captain is always better than two." Sir Ommaney might talk easily of postponing this or that; but the Commandant, poor man, craved to get the worst over and learn his fate.

"By the bye, Vigoureux — if you'll not mind my saying so — you handled that Council of yours admirably."

The Commandant flushed. "They are old friends of mine, Sir Ommaney."

"Why, and so am I an old friend; at least, as I supposed. Cannot you manage to drop the prefix? . . . Very well. . . . And now, if you have nothing better to do, take me over the old fortifications."

They climbed the hill together to the Garrison gate, and thence, bearing away to the left, started to make the round of the batteries. He flinched as they came to the first — the King George's Battery — and stood by the deserted platform. The bitter humiliation to be here, master of a fortress without one single gun! Almost he dreaded to hear his guest break forth with a contemptuous laugh.

Sir Ommaney, however, surveyed the ruin in silence, and when he spoke it was only to ask a question concerning the trajectory of the guns which had once furnished it. The Commandant walked by his side, a man torn by many emotions. For the first time in fifteen years he, an enthusiast in gunnery, had an opportunity to talk with one who really cared for gunnery and understood it. On the other hand, and eagerly as he jumped at every question, he could not help perceiving that these batteries — of which he had been so proud —

of which in recollection he was yet so proud — were to Sir Ommaney but obsolete toys. This visitor of his, this friend of his gallant youth, had moved with the times, and the times had carried him to an infinite distance, beyond all understanding. Thus, as he moved on from battery to battery, at times our Commandant talked earnestly, wistfully, and at times fell to a despondent silence; and still between his eagerness and his despondency the personal question awoke — "He is kind, but he is here to pass judgment on me. What can the sentence be but disgrace?" Arrived at the Keg of Butter Battery, Sir Ommaney seated himself on the low wall, hard by the spot where Vashti had dug at the stones with her sunshade.

"My dear Vigoureux," said Sir Ommaney, after a long look seaward, "I haven't a doubt you regret your guns, obsolete though you know that they were. For that matter, your batteries — their build and their very positions — are quite as hopelessly out of date."

"Man," exclaimed the Commandant, with a sudden rush of blood to the face, "do you suppose I cannot guess why you are here? Oh, for God's sake let me hear the worst! If for five years I have been an enforced idler here, do me at least the justice to believe that I know the range of modern artillery and something of what a modern battleship can do. Fifteen years ago when I came to take over the command of the Islands, the old *Black Prince* was the last word in ships and gunnery. Think of it! Yet, the basis of defence, the simple principle, lies here, and has always lain here. If you had come to discuss this—"

Sir Ommaney lifted a hand. "But that is partly — even chiefly — what I am come to consider."

"Ah!"

"And I have seen a letter about you, addressed to the War Office by the Lord Proprietor: an unfriendly letter, I may say."

The Commandant's cheeks were already warm with excitement, but at this their colour deepened.

"I beg you to believe," said he, heartily, "that if Sir Cæsar has written about me, my letter was sent without knowledge of it, and in no desire to anticipate—"

"My dear fellow," Sir Ommaney interrupted; "I have some little sense left in my head, I hope. But will you put constraint upon yourself for a moment to forget these letters, to dismiss the personal question, and simply to resume our talk."

"I will try," agreed the Commandant, after a painful pause. "But it will be hard; harder perhaps than you can understand. Honours have come to you — deservedly, I admit—"

"And too late," Sir Ommaney again took him up. "My dear Vigoureux, when we knew one another in the old days, honours seemed to both of us the most desirable thing in the world. Believe me, they always come too late."

The Commandant looked at him for a moment. "Yes," said he at length, "we have talked enough of ourselves. And what do we matter, after all?"

They walked back to the Barracks together, side by side, discussing, as one soldier with another, the problem which the one had opened, on which the other had brooded in silence for years.

Arrived at his quarters, the Commandant applied the poker to his fire, motioned Sir Ommaney to the worn armchair, excused himself, and hurried off to seek Archelaus and discuss the chances of a cup of tea.

Sir Ommaney, left to himself, took a glance round the poverty-stricken room, and stretched out his long legs to the blaze. The evening air without had been chilly. The sea-coal in the grate, stirred by the Commandant's poker, woke to a warm glow with a small dancing flame on top. Sir Ommaney stared into the glow, lost in thought. . . . A tapping on the pane awoke him out of his brown study. He sat upright, but almost with the same motion he sprang to his feet as a hand pushed open the window behind him.

There was no light in the room save that afforded by the dancing, uncertain flame. It wavered, as he turned about, upon the figure of a woman entering confidently across the sill, and upon a face at sight of which he drew back almost in terror.

"Pass, friend, and all's well!" said Vashti, with a light laugh, as she effected her entrance. Then, catching sight of the man confronting her, she caught at the curtain, and said, simply, "O-oh!"

"Lord, bless my soul!" exclaimed Sir Ommaney, in a low voice, but fervently.

"I — I thought you were the Commandant," stammered Vashti, for once in this history taken thoroughly aback.

"Mademoiselle Cara! . . . You? And here, of all places in the world!"

But upon this they both turned, as the door opened and the Commandant stood on the threshold.

"Miss Vashti!" The Commandant stared from one to the other.

Vashti broke the silence with her ready laugh.

"Sir Ommaney Ward and I have met before. He does not know that this is my native home; but" — she dropped them both a curtsey — "the point is that you are both to come with me, and at once."

CHAPTER XXVIII

THE FINDING

The two men followed her out into the darkness and across the turfed slope towards the Keg of Butter. The Commandant, amid much that was bewildering, guessed that her boat lay moored there, and that she meant them to accompany her, either to Saaron or to Inniscaw. There was no danger of meeting anyone by the way, either on the hill or down by the shore; for the search had drawn off all the coastguard. Nevertheless, though he carried a lantern, he did not light it.

The moon would not be up for an hour yet, but the nor'-westerly breeze had blown the sky clear of clouds. The stars — bright as always when the wind sets over the Islands from that quarter — lent a pale radiance by which Sir Ommaney managed to steer his way, and at a fair pace, beside his more expert companion, and the Commandant, when they reached the cliff-path, lent him a hand.

"But you don't tell me you have come over from Saaron in that cockleshell of yours?" asked the Commandant, peering down into the darkness for a glimpse of the boat.

Vashti, who was leading the way down the track, turned with a laugh. "No, and for a very good reason. I could not take you two back in her, for she would not carry you, and I could not borrow yours and leave her here for the coastguard to discover; and again the wind, though it has fallen, is against us — we shall have to pull, and there would be no sense in towing a boat, even a little one, for we are in a hurry. So I sailed across in Eli's. But please do not deride my poor cockleshell, as you call it; for without her I had never such news as I bring you."

"When are we to hear it?"

She laughed again as she stooped and found the shore-line of Tregarthen's boat. "Not yet. No, and you need not light the lantern. We shall want it just before our journey's end; not until then."

The Commandant helped her to draw in the boat, and they clambered on board.

"But surely you don't expect me to steer!" protested Sir Ommaney, gazing blankly around at the darkness, as Vashti directed him to take his seat in the stern sheets.

"No, I have unshipped the rudder, and you will have nothing to do but sit still and wonder." She snugged away the sail. "Now, will you take bow oar or stroke?" she asked the Commandant. "Better perhaps leave me the bow oar and the steering."

"Might one ask whither?"

"For Inniscaw, and for the landing beneath the Great House. It will give us the farther to walk, but towards the north of the Island we shall find ourselves in a press of boats. To be sure, no one is likely to suspect us; it will be supposed that we are joining the search. Still, I would rather run no risks, and the southern landing is almost certainly deserted."

She shipped her oar; and as the Commandant set the stroke she took it up with a will. At the fifth or sixth stroke she began to sing — not a set song, but little trills and snatches of melody, as though health, happiness, the joy of living, the delight of swinging to the oar in the cool night air — these together or something compounded of them all — filled her being and bubbled over.

"You are silent, you two." She said it almost reproachfully, pausing to throw a glance over her shoulder and direct the steering.

"And with excuse." Sir Ommaney answered. "Who is not mute when Mademoiselle Cara sings? And who, an hour ago, could have promised me that I should hear her sing, in this place, beneath the stars?"

"Few will hear her any more," said Vashti, lightly. "She is tired of the stage and thinks of marrying."

"Indeed, mademoiselle? And whom are we to congratulate? Who is it that selfishly appropriates what was meant for mankind?"

"Faith, sir, I cannot tell you," she answered again, still in the same light tone. "But I came, just now, to kidnap the Commandant!"

Without giving a chance of reply, she broke into singing again; the air, *Ah, fors é lui*. It gushed from her lips like a very fountain of happiness, irrepressible, springing towards the stars in jets and spurts of melody, falling with a ripple in which the music of the stars themselves seemed to echo; almost in the moment of its fall rising again, as though it panted with joy — not with weariness, for the spirit of it called impetuously to life. The two men listened, marvelling. Nor when the song ended was the spell broken; for still, as she pulled towards the looming shadow of Inniscaw, sinking her voice almost to a murmur, she took up the melody as though in echo, caressing, repeating it, loth to let it go.

They came to the dark landing-quay. Sir Ommaney, stepping ashore, stretched out a hand; but she disregarded it, as she disregarded the Commandant's, held out to take the painter and make fast.

"Thank you" — she stooped, apparently groping among the bottom-boards. "I will moor the boat myself. But wait: I have something for each of you to carry."

In the darkness she passed up a double tackle and a coil of rope. "I fetched these from Saaron on my way to you," she explained. "We shall need them. Have you fairly strong heads for a climb? Very well, then" — she sprang ashore with the painter in her hand, made it fast to a ring above the quay steps, and picked up the lantern. "Now forward! And no talking, please, until we are well past the house and out of hearing!"

Sir Ommaney picked up the tackle, the Commandant the coil of rope, and the pair followed her one behind the other. In Indian file they stole up through the plantations, almost to the foot of the glimmering terrace; thence, bearing to the left, along dim paths through the mazes of the gardens, thence again through the north-west plantation, and out upon the path which the Lord Proprietor had taken, on his way to North Inniscaw. Here, on the uplands, the breeze met them, and at his feet Sir Ommaney, for the first time, saw spread the wonderful circle of the great sea lights. Smaller lights twinkled like a thread of gems along the north and north-eastern horizon. They belonged to the boats still prosecuting the search.

From the first Vashti had led the way without faltering or appearing to hesitate for a moment. Even when clear of the woods her companions observed the prohibition she had laid upon them at the start, and exchanged scarcely a word.

"You have followed well," said Vashti, as they reached the foot of Pare Coppa. She pointed to the mass of shadow ahead, and the granite blocks on the summit faintly touched by the starlight. "I know now what it feels like to command soldiers, and it feels good. There, by that high rock to the left, our march ends."

They breasted the slope and arrived at the rock panting, after seven or eight minutes' climb. It was the same on which Sam Leggo had last seen the Lord Proprietor sitting with his gun across his knees. But why she had brought them to this spot the two men were as far as ever from guessing; for almost straight beneath them lay the sea.

After a minute's rest Vashti lowered herself over the western edge of the rock, at the same time warning them to follow with extreme caution; and so all three came to the ledge of the adit. But their business did not lie here. Indeed, in the darkness neither Sir Ommaney nor the Commandant observed the opening, and Vashti had no leisure to call their attention to it. Clambering, still to the left, across a boulder which fairly overhung the sea, she struck a match, lit the candle in her lantern, and held it up before a dark hole — a second adit — pierced in the cliff-side and running west, as the other ran south-by-east.

"Be careful, now!" she warned them again, and ducked her head as she entered the tunnel, which was scarcely more than five feet high. They stooped and followed down the slope of it for about thirty yards, and halted behind her as she waved the lantern over what appeared at first to be a terrific chasm, opening at her feet.

"Eli, ahoy! Ahoy, there!" she called.

"Ahoy!" the voice came up from the depths. "Ahoy, there, Vashti!"

"I have brought the Commandant, with a friend — and the tackle. Shall I fix it here?"

"That's no work for you, my dear," called up Eli. "Let them come down if they've heads for it, and afterwards I can climb up and fix it. Or, stay! Let the one come down, and the other bide aloft, to help me."

"Do you dare?" Vashti asked the Commandant, pointing down to the pit, and then with a wave of her lantern indicating the stairway by which he must descend. It was a ladder of rope, suspended from an iron bar driven into the solid rock about a foot above the floor-level on which they stood. It dangled down into darkness, and the Commandant perceived to his horror that its iron rungs lay close against the cliff.

"Surely you are never going down that way?" he asked.

But Vashti was already stooping to slip off her shoes.

"You need not follow unless you choose."

"Where you go, I go. Let me lead the way."

But while he unlaced and kicked off his boots she had already grasped the iron bar and swung herself out over the abyss, feeling with her toes for a rung and a good foothold.

"For my part," said Sir Ommaney, controlling with some difficulty the tremor of his voice as he saw her anchored safely for the moment, "I am content to smoke a pipe here and wait. For God's sake be careful you two!" he added, as the Commandant also gripped the bar, then a rung, and began to lower himself.

Far below the Commandant could see a light glimmering, drawing faint twinkles from the wet rock around him. Just beneath him he could hear Vashti's hands rhythmically catching at the rungs — down, down. . . . Once his feet slipped from the staves, and he hung for a moment by his hand-grip only. Twice Vashti spoke up to him, warning him to press a knee against the rock, and so make room for his toes to catch the rungs. . . . At length they reached a point where the ladder hung clear of the cliff; but here a hand from below caught it and held it steady.

"Nervous work, sir!" said Eli Tregarthen, as the Commandant, with a gasp of relief, felt his feet touch solid rock.

"But where are we?" demanded the Commandant; for close at hand sounded the boom of heavy waves.

"In Piper's Hole."

The Commandant stared aloft. Slowly the explanation dawned on him. The adit, piercing its way from the cliff top, broke through the wall of the cave, high up, close to the roof. He turned, and his eyes followed Vashti, who had caught up Eli's lantern, and was picking her way across the rocky floor. Presently she bent to a kneeling posture, as the rays fell on what at first appeared to be a long bundle. He hurried after her, but stopped short with a cry.

"Sir Cæsar!"

"Even so, my friend. Alive, thanks to our friends here; and, but for a shaking and a twisted ankle, sound as well as safe. Yes, and the ankle is mending, thanks to Miss Cara's skill and a plenty of salt-water bandages."

The Lord Proprietor's face was pale as he leaned on his elbow and stared at the Commandant across the lantern. It was scratched, too, and scarred; but it was the face of a sound man.

"But how in the world— ?"

"Easily enough. I was leaning over the cliff above here, with my gun beside me, when a piece of earth gave way under my head. I went down the slope head foremost, as I guess, and my coat must have caught in the gun's trigger-guard. At any rate, it went off, and by the mercy of Heaven without wounding me; but either the noise of it stunned me or the fall must have knocked me foolish, for tumbling among the bushes that grow in the hollow above the cave's entrance, I had not the sense to catch hold, but slid through them, and clean over the edge into the sea."

"Eh? But pardon me, how can you possibly remember this?" stammered the Commandant.

"I saw it," said Vashti, quietly.

"Oh!" The Commandant stared at her, and began to understand. "So you *were* the mermaid!"

She nodded. "I happened to be on the rock, outside the entrance, with my small boat lying in a low spot under its eastern shelter, and so I put off to him at once. There was a strong run of water into the cave; the depth was not above three feet when the waves ran back. So I clutched hold of him — though making sure he was dead — and drew him into the cave, above high-water mark. It was hard work, though not so hard as dragging the boat after us."

"Why should you want to drag the boat so far? . . . You don't mean to tell me that you have been hiding here, on purpose, while the search has been going on all around you!"

Vashti laughed. "Why, of course we have! I heard you and Mr. Rogers last night. You were standing together on the very spot over which I had hauled the boat: only I had taken the precaution to smooth the sand over the track of her keel. From the ridge of rock there I launched her on the freshwater pool, and paddled her across with the Lord Proprietor safe on board. I was dreadfully afraid, while I listened to your voices, that you would cross the pool and discover her.

"It lies close?"

"About thirty yards from where we stand."

"To confess the truth," put in the Lord Proprietor, "my fall seems to have knocked some daylight into me, or else Miss Vashti is a witch. While she bound up my hurts we had some conversation together—"

"It was I who did the talking," interposed Vashti.

"And that, perhaps, explains why in so short a while I learnt so much. I learnt enough, sir, at any rate, of you and of Eli Tregarthen to make me suspect that I had done you both some injustice. I was willing to hear more; to prolong the adventure which" — he bowed after a fashion towards Vashti, and not ungallantly — "had its — er — romantic side. I decided that if Miss Cara spoke with knowledge, it would do me good to see myself for a brief while as others in the Islands see me, even to hear what they said of me by way of obituary criticism."

He paused at a sound on the far side of the cave. It came from the ladder; the sound of Eli's hobnailed boots, rung upon rung, as he climbed aloft towards the adit, to fasten the tackle there.

"It seems a monstrous height to be swung in air, helpless as a babe. But Tregarthen says it can be done, and I am willing to trust him. If at the top you can rig up some kind of litter for me, and convey me home without noise . . . . I have a fancy, and it is also Miss Cara's, that we keep the main part of this mystery to ourselves. But who is the helper aloft there?"

"Sir Ommaney Ward."

"Hey?"

"Sir Ommaney Ward."

"The devil! And I sent for him! Forgive me, Commandant—"

"And excuse me, Sir Cæsar, but I prefer to believe he is here because my letter brought him."

The Lord Proprietor held out his hand.

"Will you take it, Commandant? Miss Cara has told me of that letter. You are a good man, and I have wronged you."

CHAPTER XXIX

CONCLUSION

Three years and a few months have passed. The date is Easter Monday (Easter falls early this year), and from the Keg of Butter Battery the Commandant, as he stands looking seaward, hears the school-bell ringing in the town at the foot of Garrison Hill, though the school has been closed a week since for the Easter holidays.

He hears it, but for a while pays no attention to it, though it keeps ding-dinging insistently. His eyes are bent on the sea; yet not in the direction of Saaron, where, if they sought carefully, they might detect a trace of smoke coiling up from the fold of the hills which hides Eli Tregarthen's farm; but westward, towards the main, whence the steamer will arrive before nightfall. She is not due for hours, yet the Commandant's gaze searches the horizon.

The Keg of Butter Battery mounts no guns as yet It is no longer the ruined platform above which Vashti sat on the crumbling wall and poked at the wild thyme with her sunshade. The Government contractor has transformed it: the wall has disappeared, and a smooth glacis slopes from the Commandant's feet over hidden chambers, constructed to house those quick-firing guns. The chambers are ready: the guns will arrive within a week. It is not for them, however, that the Commandant scans the horizon so intently.

Although it is holiday-time, the bells in the town below are ringing to the school-house; but the school-house is filled with flowers. Two years ago the Lord Proprietor called his Islanders together, and explained how he hoped to bring back prosperity to the Islands by means of daffodil culture. For an experiment, he offered to present a thousand Dutch bulbs to every cottager who would give them soil and cultivation, and today the Islanders celebrate their first daffodil show.

In years to come, as the trade increases, the market will keep them too happily busy to waste time on exhibitions. We see them, and we part with them, on the eve of prosperity. So much, at any rate, has grown of the few bulbs carried by Archelaus for a peace-offering.

*****

The Commandant takes out his watch, discovers that it is close upon time for the opening ceremony, and descends the hill in a hurry. At the school-house door he meets the Lord Proprietor, and they shake hands as they enter the building together. But after going the round of the stalls, the Lord Proprietor looks up.

"She is coming this afternoon, is she not?"

"She is coming," says the Commandant, and looks forth from the open window over the sea.

THE END

www.ingramcontent.com/pod-product-compliance
Lightning Source LLC
Chambersburg PA
CBHW020320260626
47156CB00004B/1301